Building Harlequin's Moon

Building Harlequin's Moon

LARRY NIVEN and BRENDA COOPER

TOR®

A Tom Doherty Associates Book
New York

BUILDING HARLEQUIN'S MOON

Copyright © 2005 by Larry Niven and Brenda Cooper

Book design by Jane Adele Regina

A Tor Book
Published by Tom Doherty Associates, LLC
175 Fifth Avenue
New York, NY 10010

www.tor.com

Tor® is a registered trademark of Tom Doherty Associates, LLC.

Library of Congress Cataloging-in-Publication Data

Niven, Larry.
    Building Harlequin's moon / Larry Niven and Brenda Cooper.—1st ed.
        p. cm.
    "A Tom Doherty Associates book."
    ISBN-13: 978-0765-31266-2
    ISBN-10: 0-765-31266-2
    1. Space colonies—Fiction. 2. Space ships—Fiction. I. Cooper, Brenda, 1960–. II. Title.

  PS3564.I9B85 2005
  813'.54—dc22

                                                                          2004063766

First Edition: June 2005

Printed in the United States of America

0 9 8 7 6 5 4 3 2 1

TO THE MEMORY OF ROBERT FORWARD

ACKNOWLEDGMENTS

FROM BRENDA:

I'd like to thank Larry Niven for taking on this project with me. Larry has had a longtime rule against collaborating with amateurs, and since this is my first novel-length work, I definitely qualified, at least when we started. This has been a multiyear project. I'm sure there were times when he was ready to throw away the manuscript, but instead he just pointed out ideas and characters that needed work, and helped me through; most important, he always believed in me. His hands, ideas, and words are throughout this novel, but like every good teacher, he made me write my way out of most of my messes. Any messes left in here are mine alone. Thanks, Larry!

Personal thanks as well to my family: to my dad, who explained the concept of mass multiple times, and asked about the book every time he talked to me (sure that I was doing great, even when I wasn't); to my mom; my son, David; and daughter-of-the-heart Lisha; my partner, Toni; and to Cindy Ross and Joe Green. Thanks also to Marilyn Niven, for being supportive of this project.

FROM BRENDA AND LARRY:

Thanks to our agent, Eleanor Wood, for believing in this project, and for reviewing a very early draft and providing excellent suggestions. Thanks to Bob Gleason from Tor, our editor.

Thanks to Yoji Kondo, the rocket scientist and science fiction writer who writes as Eric Kotani. We needed a pair of stars to fit our story—to become Apollo and Ymir—and Yoji found them for us.

We'd both like to thank Steven Barnes, who introduced us, and has given us both many tools across many years. The Fairwood Writers read the whole novel in draft, and made many excellent suggestions. They are David Addleman, Darragh Metzger, John A. Pitts, Allan Rousselle, David R. Silas, Renee Stern, and Patrick and Honna Swenson. The members of the LARRYNIVEN-L list helped out with naming a planet. G. David Nordley spent time chatting with us about ship designs. We'd also like to thank the late Bob Forward for chats about this book, and for inspiring early star drive designs.

Building Harlequin's Moon

PROLOGUE: Chaos

Year 894, *John Glenn* shiptime

Erika was cold and Gabriel was warm. She wouldn't have been interested in this stuff anyway.

Erika was one pilot of the carrier *John Glenn*. *John Glenn* was currently at rest, safely orbiting wide around the gas giant planet Harlequin, and not in need of a pilot.

Gabriel headed the terraforming team, chartered to create a habitable moon from the jumble of raw material that made up Harlequin's moon system. Four of the team were warm now, far too many in the long term; but during these few decades they would accomplish most of what needed doing. Then they would wait for the moon system to settle down again.

The Large Pusher Tugs, all three of them, were thrusting hard against Moon Ten. Their fusion engines sprayed a trident of light across the sky. The lesser Moon Twenty-six was already in place, orbiting Moon One since last year. That orbit wasn't stable—it shrank steadily within the cloud of impact debris around Moon One—but that didn't matter. Moon Twenty-six would be gone in a few days.

Gabriel sent: "*John Glenn* calling LPT-1. Wayne, how you doing?"

"Nearly finished here, I think. Astronaut concurs. Check our orbit."

"I did that. Start shutting down the motors."

In four hours, Moon Ten was falling free.

When this phase was over, Harlequin's moons would have to be recounted. There would be fewer of them.

Gabriel considered a meal and sleep. The moons wouldn't collide for fifteen days yet . . . but he ordered a squeeze of stew and stayed at his post. One loose moon wouldn't matter; there was no living thing to be harmed in Harlequin's moon system, and minor accidents could be fixed. It was the LPTs he was worried about. Lose his spacecraft and he'd lose the game.

The peppery smell of warming vegetables and broth made his stomach rumble.

So. Where to park the pusher tugs?

He smiled. They'd be passing very near Moon Forty-one.

"Wayne? Bust your LPTs loose and get them into orbit. Here are the specs. I'm working out your next mission."

"When do we get some rest, boss?"

"I'll find you that too."

Gabriel ate slowly, savoring the celery and potatoes. *John Glenn*'s internal garden was thriving. It had been a water tank when they left Sol system, and their diet had palled rapidly.

He had a plan. He could start on it tomorrow. Thrust would take a few hundred days. Harlequin would grow a little hotter; ultimately Moon One would too; and Erika, when she warmed, would love it.

UNDER GABRIEL'S GUIDANCE, Wayne's team lifted the Large Pusher Tugs from Moon Ten and set them drifting toward a rarefied region within Harlequin's frantically busy moon system. Wouldn't want them anywhere near the collision point.

It took him and the Astronaut program less than an hour to work up the next sequence.

The LPTs had tremendous acceleration when they weren't attached to larger masses. Their light outshone the sun, Apollo, by a lot. By the end of the day they were in loose orbit around Moon Forty-one.

Gabriel ate at his post while Wayne guided the LPTs to the surface, one by one. The hard part came next, as Wayne's team moored them against the bedrock core. The tugs were flattened structures, a Tokamak-style fusion thruster ringing one side, a cage of shock absorbers and anchors at the other. Placing anchors was tricky, because when the LPTs were set going, their thrust would start quakes.

Set them going on low thrust, let the blast backfire, they'd melt their way through volatiles down to bedrock. Then close the insulation ports and wait while the molten rock solidified over the next century. Gabriel's team would spend a hundred years cold, then warm again to finish the job.

But they'd finish adding volatiles and mass to Moon One before they went cold.

ONE OF THE LAST major movements of a complicated symphony was under way as Moon Ten approached Moon Twenty-six, which was in motion retrograde above Moon One.

There had been other collisions. Moon One was already a dust ball surrounded by a flattened ring that glowed in Apollo's light. It looked like Saturn in Sol system, with the ring system lightly twisted by Harlequin's massive gravity.

The oblate spheroids drifted together like flaming taffy. Gabriel watched the two moons eat each other's kinetic energy. Hot rock and volatiles churned in a twisting red-orange fireball and began to drift toward Moon One.

A raw sense of power tugged at the edges of Gabriel's attention as he forced his focus to stay narrow. He had to stay on top of this. Playing God carried awesome responsibility. His purpose was to create a habitable world, a staging area for the antimatter generator that would refuel the carrier *John Glenn*. That world, Selene, would need seas and gravity: more mass, more volatiles. Moon One must be built up.

Selene also needed radiation shielding.

Gabriel had been bashing moons together for more than three hundred fifty years, after many more years of research and simulation. Matters would have gone much faster in Ymir's system, he thought, a trace of bitterness still edging his thoughts. *John Glenn*'s equipment wasn't designed for Apollo system. He was supposed to have two more carrier ships and all their resources to help him. Hell, he was supposed to be someplace else entirely. Apollo's inner rocky worlds were all missing, eaten as the gas giant Daedalus moved inward; anything he needed that wasn't among Harlequin's moons would have to be acquired from the Kuiper Belt. Comets were as far apart as they had been in Sol system, generally as far apart as the Sun from the Earth. Travel time expanded hugely. He was doing his damn best, but it was still taking forever.

He stretched and twisted, working his body, pulling out as much tension as he could.

Moons Ten and Twenty-six were history, a fireball above Moon One. Impacting like that, they'd turned a lot of their velocity into heat; but how much? The last time they tried this, with a different pair of moons, most of the mass from the collision had just dissipated. He'd look again in a hundred years.

Time to go cold.

AND WARM AGAIN, a hundred years later. He set to work.

Moon One was lightly ringed. Most of the mass of a double lunar impact was gone. He'd watch Moon One for a while—or the Astronaut program would—and presently he'd know if its mass had grown enough.

John Glenn's frozen sleep system had been altered according to specs in their last message from Sol system. This advanced process of being frozen didn't just retard entropy; it rejuvenated. Gabriel felt wonderfully alive, though he sometimes pictured his life as a snake chopped up and scattered at random.

And Erika's life was scattered without regard for his or her own convenience. As a pilot, she would stay frozen for most of the next sixty thousand years.

Meanwhile, Gabriel had work to do.

He revived his team. Moon Forty-one's surface had cooled around the three LPTs. Wayne set them to thrusting against the moon's core.

The core wasn't as stable as Gabriel wanted—no iron ball, just a jumble of heavier stuff—and Wayne held the thrust low. There were still tremors. Pumps fed dirty water ice from the moon into the tanks: reaction mass for the LPTs' motors. Moon Forty-one wasn't large. This phase would be over in a few years.

Then—no point in going cold. He would wait out the next couple of years, and watch. Moon Forty-one would graze Harlequin's atmosphere, turning vast kinetic energy into vast heat. The gas giant would eat the moon. Some of its mass would undoubtedly form a broad ring of debris. It would be a hell of a sight, and it would have other benefits.

Selene—the inhabited world that Moon One would become—would need shielding from Harlequin's radiation output. The ring would be chaotic for a time, and during the next, oh, fifty thousand years, it would block most of the gas giant planet from Moon One. But time and endless collisions would move the ring particles toward a common orbital plane. In sixty thousand years—when Selene calmed enough to be seeded with life—the ring would only block half the planet. A hundred thousand years later the ring would be as thin as Saturn's, and nearly useless as a shield.

But *John Glenn* would be gone by then, on its way to Ymir.

Gabriel had decided to form the ring early. He'd give Selene sixty thousand years to lose some of its surface radiation, and Harlequin itself would have time to settle down after impact. Harlequin would grow hotter, of course. The sun Apollo was too far from the moon system to provide enough heat to warm Moon One. Some of Selene's heat must come from a hotter Harlequin.

Harlequin's moon system had become a dangerously cluttered region, but that wouldn't last. When Erika finally warmed, she would find fewer moons, a system thinned out except for an inner ring that had been Moon

Forty-one. Selene would be protected, to that extent, from giant meteoroid impacts.

And Harlequin's vast gaudy ring would be more than a match for Saturn's. Gabriel's gift to Erika! Playing God had its moments.

"And why exactly are we doing this?" Wayne asked. He was shorter and stockier than Gabriel, and each of his movements was deliberate.

Anger kept Gabriel from answering immediately. They were in the galley preparing an elaborate meal. Windows hovered in the air, showing several views of chaos. Rings and clouds of dust and inner storms, rainbows of light glaring through: chaos that would become Selene.

It wasn't pretty, but it was awesome. Wayne was one of the best engineers on the ship. He could fly anything, figure out any logistical problem. Surely Wayne shared his fierce pride?

"Doing what?" Gabriel asked mildly. "We make Selene because we can."

"It's like this. I went cold knowing that they'd warm me when we got to Ymir—to Henry Draper Catalog 212776," Wayne said, being abnormally precise, no misunderstandings here, "and, and then we'd build Ymir. They thawed me out centuries early, at the wrong star! Now you tell me—"

"They had to tell me first. Wayne, I was cold too. We're the terraforming team, not ship's crew. And ship's crew were worn-out, man! The captain looked like the walking dead. Erika was twitchy. I wasn't ready to throw it in their faces."

Wayne wasn't being belligerent, he was plodding through a problem. "You tell me the interstellar drive went wonky and we had to find a refuge before the interstellar wind fried us all. Gamma rays at six percent of lightspeed. We were lucky. Gliese 876 was almost in our path. We were down to the last whiffs of antimatter fuel when we made orbit here.

"Now, I can buy all that. We can't get to Ymir until we've made more fuel. Right. Why not just go for it? Build a collider and make twelve hundred kilos of antimatter and *go*."

"First off, you'll notice that there's no inner solar system." Gabriel waved at the windows, though no such thing was obvious to the naked eye. "No asteroids, no rocky worlds like Earth or Mars, nothing until you get down to Daedalus, a mucking great gas giant world huddled right up against its sun. Daedalus ate everything as it moved inward. There's only Harlequin, out here where Saturn would be if this were Sol system, and three more gas giants and the Kuiper Belt.

"So all the distances out here are huge. Any resource we need has to come from Harlequin's moons or the Kuiper Belt, where the little Kuiper Belt bodies are just as sparse as in Sol system. It takes forever to get anywhere.

"We looked . . . the High Council looked at the problem," Gabriel said carefully, "and the Astronaut program verifies. To build an antimatter generator, we need manpower. We'd have to warm half the ship. The garden wouldn't feed them or recycle enough air, and we don't have the room either. They'd use up all our resources. We'd die.

"Second possibility is to build habitats like the asteroid civilizations in Sol system. What's wrong with that?"

Wayne snorted, though he knew he was being tested. "The Belt cities needed too much Artificial Intelligence, too much nanotech, too much of everything we're running away from. AIs wound up running it all."

Gabriel nodded. "So we can't do *that*. And we could build nanos and let them build a collider and run it for antimatter, with Astronaut running it all. Only we deliberately forgot most of what we need to build tailored nanotech, and Astronaut is another AI. By now it looks like Earth and Sol really have gone down the recycler, and if it wasn't the AIs taking over, it must have been nanos turning everything to sludge. At any rate, Sol system isn't talking.

"So what's left? We came here with gear to make Ymir habitable—a rocky world about the size of Earth, with a reducing atmosphere. We can make a world! It's just a little bit tougher job."

Wayne said, "Sure. Where are you going to put the Beanstalk?"

Gabriel finished his last bite of stew. He asked, "Your point?"

"We stored this massive tether-making system. Ymir could have had two hundred thousand kilometers of an orbital tether standing up from the equator, all made of carbon nanotubes. Every bit of nanotechnology we permit ourselves is a compromise, and that was one of them. Ground to orbit transport. We'd have an elevator to the nearby planets. Go anywhere you want in Ymir's inner system and only pay for the electricity. What would happen if—"

"Selene would be whipping it around in Harlequin's gravity field. The tides would tear it apart. We can't give Selene a Beanstalk. What's your point? Because I *know* we brought the wrong equipment for this!"

"Exactly. We don't know if it's good enough," Wayne said.

"That's the other side of it. Wayne, we're making mistakes where it won't matter. It's a dry run. When we get to Ymir we'll know more about our equipment and techniques."

"Won't matter? Boss, what about all these people we'll need to build the collider?"

That was something Gabriel tried not to think about. He said, "I'm not on the High Council, you know."

Wayne sighed. "Okay, boss."

"Wayne, have you talked like this with Ali?"

"No."

"Don't."

Year 60,201, *John Glenn* shiptime

When Gabriel warmed, there was only the AI to talk to. Humans were *supposed* to wake to human warmth, to hands and smiles and talk. But sixty thousand years was no time frame to thread a live person or set of people through, not when your population totaled only two thousand, and only a few hundred you wanted to warm at all before you could reach your true home. So *John Glenn* had orbited in silence, its huge garden mostly composted, its people frozen. The only aware beings were the AI, Astronaut, and periodically Gabriel; or on good shift breaks, Gabriel and Wayne; or on better ones, Gabriel and Ali.

This was a good break. He'd wake, and then he'd warm Ali, and then . . . then they'd touch down on Selene. He glanced at the chronometer. He was waking on schedule. So nothing horrible had happened during this sleep. His senses rushed alert, smelling medicines and water, feeling the dry cool ship's air. What Earth had sent them—new programming for nanotechnological cell repair under cold sleep—still acted perfectly.

Gabriel wasn't sure how he felt about that. Nanotechnology was one of the things they had run away from.

It almost never got said.

There would come a day when Ymir was perfected. On that day all this nonsense of medical nanotech would stop. The long-lived travelers would age naturally, and die naturally. Their planet would follow its own destiny, and none would use his power to change the weather or stop an encroaching desert. They'd made that agreement, all of them, before they boarded the carrier ships.

They'd wondered about each other since, and they'd wondered about themselves. How could they not? Which of them would fail to give up longevity and the power to shape a world?

"Astronaut?"

"Hello, Gabriel!"

"Any word from Earth?" Gabriel already knew the answer.

"Not since Year 291, shiptime."

"From Ymir?"

"Nothing, Gabriel."

It might be that Gabriel was the only human heartbeat in the entire universe.

He flinched from that thought. Surely there were humans at Ymir. Surely *Leif Eriksson* and *Lewis and Clark* had reached Ymir, safe, and thousands or millions of humans now populated a rebuilt planet. Or billions? Ymir was to have been made a second Earth, and Earth had housed tens of billions, sixty thousand years ago. They'd sent message probes, traveling at a tenth light-speed at best, at the highpoint of their journey. A hundred forty-eight light-years distanced them, at Gliese 876, from Ymir at HDC 212776. That was a lot of distance for fragile probes to travel.

Gabriel wiggled his toes, stretched his fingers, and bounced his calves lightly on the bed.

Two hours later, he pushed himself to standing and went to the galley to make tea infused with vitamins and mint, easy for a rejuvenated and rebuilt body to accept. He took the tea to his office, wrinkling his nose at the medicinal smell, and ordered Astronaut to pull up views of Selene.

Bad smelling or not, the first sip of tea sat warm and perfect in his belly as images of the little moon filled his walls.

A cloud obscured part of the surface. A cloud! He smiled broadly, then laughed in delight. He sat mesmerized, watching the cloud, until his tea bulb was empty.

Then he started barking out a list for Astronaut to read to him: precipitation measures, exact atmospheric composition, water loss, evaporation . . .

Within an hour, Gabriel confirmed they could walk on the moon. They could start to introduce life. They could . . . he gave instructions to wake Ali and Wayne, and went to get ready for them. He sang as he pulled himself down the corridor to Medical.

———

GABRIEL AND ALI WALKED on the barren surface of the little moon. They started inside light pressure suits, taking readings and checking radiation levels, double-testing what they already knew from the tiny sensors that dotted Selene. Ali stripped first, all the way down to underwear and bra and shoes, oxygen tank and mask. Her olive skin dimpled in the cool air.

He laughed with pleasure watching her; a tiny half-naked woman climbing on rocks; jumping from one to the other, tossing stones and catching them.

Drawn by Ali's antics, Gabriel stripped to his pants and shirt, mask and tank, and ran and cavorted and grinned while Ali knelt and touched the regolith, walked to a new place, and touched the surface again. He danced with her on the surface, seeing wonder and reverence in her eyes as she moved easily, gracefully.

Selene was still a touch unstable; it shivered twice with small quakes in the hours they were there. Ali came and stood beside him. "I like the silence—I like being away from that damned constant data flow. It feels more human here."

Gabriel held her, not answering, just feeling the soft touch of her dark head in the hollow of his shoulder. He felt lost without the data, regardless of how ecstatic he was to be on Selene. On Selene!

"Someday," he said, "Selene will be information rich like the ship. We'll enhance the flows some here before we return—I'll need it to monitor the next steps."

She glared at him, a touch distant suddenly. "Be careful—you'll need too much technology. Let's keep Selene simple."

Her face was bathed in Apollo's light, her skin duskier than he remembered from the ship. They pulled their masks aside, and he gave her the first kiss on Selene. It was quick. Selene had just barely more oxygen, right now, than the top of Everest. It needed life to make a living atmosphere.

Thousands of years of shifts had taught them all to take intimacy where they found it, to appreciate it, and consider it friendship.

They flew happily back up to *John Glenn*. Gabriel returned with Wayne, and while Gabriel and Wayne walked Selene's surface, Ali packed up cultures and genetic material so they could start seeding the regolith, eventually covering part of Selene with bacteria to begin the process of making soil.

When they warmed next, all of the bacteria were dead. So they stayed awake and watched the next attempt, killing time designing a huge tent. They would control the atmosphere inside the tent, and use it to build greenhouses and homes; a little city. The tent stood up well to the little earthquakes that came along. They dubbed the new town Aldrin, and stayed there from time to time.

It took four tries—twenty years—to get healthy cyanobacteria mats spread across the ground near Aldrin and have something like soil. Now it was time to wake the High Council.

Gabriel spent hours with each of them, running low on sleep, talking excitedly. He had Astronaut play videos for the captain; lost moons dancing into each other. Gabriel watched the captain's wrinkled face closely, saw how his deep-ocean-blue eyes tracked the flow of moons and proto-comets.

Captain John Hunter had stayed awake during the long crippled flight that took them to Gliese 876 after they nearly burned up in the interstellar wind. That trip was so long that no amount of post-ice rejuvenation treatments had removed the spots and lines and dark circles that transformed his face. Centuries of pain were etched in odd bends of his fingers and toes, in the hunch in his back, the folds over his eyes. But intelligence still lived in his eyes. If anything, the ravages his choices had created in his body made his will stronger. It mattered to Gabriel that John Hunter see the dream he'd helped design come alive.

It went well, except for the astonishing rapidity with which Council returned to the cryo-tanks. They wanted an easier world to oversee.

Once, Gabriel warmed Erika. By then, Wayne was building roads, using huge robotic machines to flatten the soil. Ali was cold. Gabriel was designing pipes to control the hydrology, and constructing a small factory by the Hammered Sea. Erika stayed warm for a year, giving Gabriel good advice, making a few mistakes they laughed at together, fretting about how long everything took. The plan was already foreshortened—Gabriel would never have forced so many processes if Selene wasn't really just a way to escape to the stars again.

He held Erika's attention for a year before she insisted on going cold again.

Gabriel and Ali finished the little town of Aldrin. They laid pipes to carry water to a cistern, more pipes to make a rudimentary sewer and reclamation system, planted a grove of trees on a hill outside town, and filled greenhouses with seedlings. The night before they planned to wake

High Council again, Gabriel and Ali made love, alone on the surface of the moon they'd transformed. Their lovemaking started soft and slow, growing to a deep intimate conclusion. They stayed still for a long time, wrapped in each other's arms, warm in that close place that follows on the heels of lovemaking. When she stopped trembling, Ali looked at Gabriel and said, "We've consecrated the ground here. Selene has been blessed. We blessed it together."

Gabriel simply thought they'd enjoyed great sex, but it was a celebration, and so he didn't contradict her. Rather, he held her tightly and began to work out hydrologic engineering problems in his head.

Part I: Selene

60,268 *John Glenn* shiptime

Chapter 1: Teaching Grove

Rachel reached for the seedling. Her long fingers found the pliant trunk, thin as her pinkie, buried inside the furled branches. She unwrapped gauzy material from the root ball with her free hand, separating the roots by spreading them down and out in the air. Bits of soil fell through her hands as she settled roots and tree onto a mound of nutrient-enriched dirt. Still steadying the gangly cecropia, she swept anchor soil to cover the roots, tamped it down, and then tied the trunk very loosely to a long thin stake. Rachel sat back on her heels and admired the little tree. A warm breeze rustled its leaves and the smell of damp dirt filled the air.

A banana palm went in next, then a set of three heliconias near the path. Rachel's crate stood empty. The distant sun, Apollo, hung low in the sky, illuminating beads of sweat as she stretched.

The other students had all finished more than twenty minutes ago. Rachel nodded to herself, checking to be sure the plot matched the picture in her head. Harry's plot was well designed, and cleaner since he had gone back and raked the soil after watering. But she could do that too. Water first. She sighed and got up to get a rake.

"Nice job." Gabriel's voice behind her sounded flat, far away, even if the words approved.

Rachel turned around and looked back at him. Gabriel stood an inch taller than Rachel, but wider and stronger, carefully dressed in brown pants that tied at the ankles, high boots, and a tight-fitting shirt that showed muscles. He looked serious, like he'd gotten lost in his head. She wrinkled her nose at him and smiled. He didn't smile back. He looked outward, higher than the horizon, fingering the bright metal and bead sculptures twisted into the long red-brown braid of his hair.

Rachel ran her fingers through her own short red hair, wondering if such a long braid was heavy. And what was he looking at?

Diamond patterns in a thousand shades of white and red: a gibbous world, huge and fully risen, brilliant across more than half its arc, sullen red where the sunlight didn't fall. Harlequin. A broad straight band ran blazing white across its face, and disappeared where Harlequin's shadow fell across it. A ring, Gabriel called it, but nothing ever showed but that thick white slash.

What fascinated Gabriel about Harlequin and its ring? It was a feature of the sky, changeable, but not of great interest. Tiny fiery-looking storms on Harlequin might affect weather on Selene, Gabriel had said once, but (he admitted) not by much.

A mystery. Council was always a mystery. Rachel knew Gabriel would wait there until she finished. Another mystery—Council always knew where they were—they could see everything on Selene. So he didn't have to stay. *Maybe I shouldn't rake since I'm last,* she thought. *But the test is tomorrow!*

She watered and raked anyway, perversely determined to spend time with each tree as she finished for the evening. Perfect, it might please Gabriel. (He still hadn't moved.)

She put the rake away and stood as near Gabriel as she dared, and looked up too. Harlequin rose as Apollo rode low in the sky and then disappeared. Softer illumination replaced the red-gold sunlight, tinged by the oranges and reds of the gas giant. The planet covered a huge portion of the sky. Rachel could cover Apollo, the distant sun, with the width of her thumb held half an arm's length in front of her. Harlequin took both palms to blot from view.

The gas giant made its own dim red light, shed by the intense heat in its constantly churning surface. Apollo's reflection brightened Harlequin's inner light, and the combined glow bathed Selene's summer, making the night barely dusky.

Selene's orbit around Harlequin defined seasons based on the amount of light available. "Summer" was the seven weeks when Selene orbited closest to Apollo, "winter" the seven weeks they were farthest away, and fall and spring filled in the time between. Summer hid most of the stars in its steady light. In full winter, night fell black enough to detail the galaxy spread around them.

Rachel watched her two shadows merge as Apollo set fully, and then put the tools away and strapped arm and leg sets on. She waved at Gabriel, and said "Good night" out loud, alert for a response from Gabriel. None came.

A few hundred yards from the edge of Teaching Grove, she pushed hard on the balls of her feet, straining upward with every step, taking tenfoot strides along the flat path back to Aldrin. She gained speed and height, finally leaping all-out. As she began the fall after the apogee of her leap, she snapped her leg and arm wings down just before the ground could catch her foot webs. Three strong kicks, a rhythm, and she was flying.

Rachel flew low in the treacherously soft light of Harlequin's evening until she reached two tall poles that marked the outside of the colony's first home. Her father had told her the poles once supported a great tent of air that Council built their first homes in. No longer needed, the tall stakes still marked the boundaries of home. She swung her legs from behind to just in front of her, braking, snapping her leg wings closed at exactly the right moment, landing with just one extra little hop that she expertly turned into a bounding walk as she folded her arm wings in.

Rachel followed a well-worn path past Council Row and its large lighted homes, sparing them hardly a glance. They were beautiful, iridescent, and closed to Moon Born. The faultless layout seemed like a wall to Rachel as she slipped along its outside edge toward the friendly chaos of tents she called home. The base color of the tents was a metallic shimmering light gray; fabric that repelled rain and heat alike. Colorful cloths were thrown and sewn onto the walls, covering and making windows, proclaiming family personalities. In the common areas between tents, children played skip-stones, studied, or sat in groups talking. Rachel waved at her friend Ursula's brothers and some of the kids from her class.

In two more minutes she was truly home, ducking through a delicate blue fabric doorway. The inside of the tent was simple. Hangings divided it into four rooms—two sleeping rooms, a combination living room and kitchen, and a small workroom. They shared bathroom facilities with four other families.

Her father was already there, his boots off, his feet resting on an embroidered ottoman she had made him. Dark circles spread like stains under his eyes, and his long arms draped by his side.

"The other kids have been back more than an hour," Frank said, smiling at her.

"I wanted my trees to be perfect."

"Your work is always good." Her father's voice sounded warm, if tired. "I've got dinner on."

Rachel went to the tiny kitchen and ladled vegetable soup into a smooth metal bowl. She'd cut the beans and carrots up that morning before going to the grove. "I'll have to study."

"You'll pass," Frank said. "Did you get any information about when they plan to start the planting for this season?"

"It'll be soon. It has to be. Gabriel will be gone after the test, and I guess we'll stay and take care of things at the grove. Gabe downloaded a bunch of new stuff for us this afternoon, so I better study."

"Better call him Gabriel," Frank said.

"Yes, Daddy."

"And you'd better get some sleep."

"I know. I'll sleep after I read the new stuff he beamed me." Rachel flipped open the wrist pad she'd been given when Gabriel chose her for the planting class. She commanded it to create a window in front of her. Numbers and descriptions flowed through the air. When her eyes blurred and the data stopped making sense, she slipped off to sleep, snuggling deep into a nest of blankets and pillows.

Apollo's rise woke her. Her father had already gone. Rachel reviewed her notes again until she heard Ursula call from outside.

"Coming." Rachel grabbed up some carrots and a hunk of bread for lunch, and grinned to see her willowy friend bouncing impatiently up and down in the path. Ursula was even thinner than Rachel, light-colored everywhere, with freckles and blue eyes. The light morning rain slicked the girls' hair down so it hung in wet strings, and they shivered in the cool air. Ursula worried them up the path, keeping them from flying so she could practice vocabulary answers out loud until Rachel wanted to scream at her. If anyone besides Ursula babbled on so, Rachel would have stopped it, or walked ahead, but Ursula covered insecurities with noise. Ursula had been her friend as long as she could remember, the only other girl her age in the immediate circle of tents. They'd helped each other learn to walk, and then to fly.

Halfway up, two shadows flew over them. Rachel nudged Ursula in the side. "Hey, look, it's Ice and Silence." They heard the clank of bald Andrew's homemade cable armbands against his wings. Harry flew quietly and expertly, pacing but not following Andrew. Ursula grimaced and made as if to duck.

"Hey," Rachel said. "They won't throw anything today. Even Andrew's not stupid enough to risk making Gabe angry on test day."

"Quit calling him Gabe! You'd think you were friends!"

"Well—"

"No Moon Born is a friend with Council. My brother Rich says they're just using us."

"Nah," Rachel said. "Sure, they have a plan, and sure, we're part of it. But they're teaching us how to be what we want to be anyway. At least, I *want* to work with plants! Besides, who made Selene? Where does all our tech come from? Why fight something you have to have? It would be like fighting air."

"Don't think too hard. You'll break your head. Think about tests. Let's review pod functions again . . ."

When they finally arrived, Harry and Andrew were already bending over their plantings from the afternoon before. Rachel grimaced at Ursula, whispering, "Of course, *those* two are looking good to Council." The rain had stopped, and the grove smelled fresh and clean.

"Always," Ursula whispered back, making small kissing gestures behind her hand where only Rachel could see. Rachel stifled a laugh.

Ali waved at them. The tiny Councilwoman was all energy and flow, teaching and correcting and sometimes even laughing. The kids never said anything bad about Ali, even when they complained about Council. She got respect. No one talked back to any Council, ever, but sometimes Rachel could relax just a bit with Ali.

Ali and Gabriel were both of a type, except Ali's hair and eyes were darker, but Ali's eyes danced above a ready smile. Ali seemed like a tiny ball of energy that rotated around the taller and more serious Chief Terraformer. Rachel felt awkward around Ali, too tall, too spare, too angular.

When she got to her plot, Rachel drew her breath in sharply, barely managing not to draw attention by crying out. Her cecropia tree was missing.

Whoever had spirited away the tree had raked afterward. There were no footprints. *Andrew or Harry,* she thought. *Probably Andrew—he's mean.* She could see the hole the theft created clearly—it would have been the tallest canopy tree once her little jungle finished growing. Rachel blinked back sharp tears that went with the anger in her belly. How could someone do this and not get caught? Didn't Council see everything?

She glared at Andrew, who didn't look at her at all, but stood like a perfect innocent, watching the other students straggle in while he smiled. Harry ignored her too.

Nine other Moon Born trailed into the group. They varied from about ten Earth standard years to Rachel's fifteen. Ali greeted every one of them formally by name, always including a smile, a personal question, a touch. She walked through the wildness of tiny trees, bending down and touching a leaf or branch, looking carefully at the small mounds of dirt ringing each thin trunk, smiling both at nice jobs and small mistakes. She graded each plot as she went. Ursula and Harry both passed with no rework. Nick found himself the target of a long lecture, and he had to pull up three seedlings and replant them in different spots.

Rachel overheard Andrew whispering to Nick, "Too bad you couldn't do it right the first time." She opened her mouth to hiss at Andrew, but Gabriel silenced her with a stern glance from across the path. Well, at least *he* had noticed.

Ali looked at the trees in Rachel's plot for a long time. She didn't ask Rachel a single question, but Rachel just knew Ali could see the great gap in her carefully planned balance. Rachel bit her lower lip to keep quiet. Ali simply nodded and smiled and moved on.

How had she done? Did Ali like her work?

Andrew's plot received a momentary glance and a cursory nod.

Just as they were leaving for the meadow, Rachel looked up at the tool tent. Familiar tips of leaves rose above the edge of the roof. Her cecropia! But what could she say now? It had to be Andrew; he didn't have the common sense to be careful around Council. He was such a stupid show-off. Now he'd probably got them both in trouble, and worse, he probably didn't care. She grimaced and walked on, keeping her silence.

Plastic and stone shapes dotted the meadow. Council had made them by fusing gathered pebbles and tiny chondrules from asteroids, covering the result with a soft and clear plastic compound. Useful art; neatly shaped into benches and sometimes into wild swirling sculptures. They had been there all of Rachel's life.

She'd asked about them once, and Gabriel had said, "Wayne and Ali were bored one year."

The First Trees surrounded the meadow on three sides. Gabriel and Ali planted them, by themselves, even before any Earth Born were awakened. There were kapoks and figs and palms and gray ciebas just starting to grow the buttressing roots that would someday be large enough to climb as if they were trees themselves. Rachel struggled with Council's complicated year-math. Rachel's mother Kristin was Earth Born, her father one of the first generation of Moon Born, and Rachel was born when he was forty-two Moon years old, or just over half that many Earth years, and his parents had been awake two Moon years before they had him, so the trees surrounding the meadow must be . . . twenty-five Earth years or more old. They were tall, the biggest more than a hundred feet. Branches intertwined tightly, even fifty feet above the forest floor. Webs of thin young lianas, vines, curled up trunks and hung down from branches, reaching for ground and sky together. Light in this part of the grove shone low and hazy, mysterious. The air smelled damp and rich, as if the canopy held in the scents of growth. It was Rachel's favorite place.

Once, Gabriel had told her that the First Trees were planted too close together. He had miscalculated how much Selene's oxygen-rich atmosphere and three-quarter Earth gravity would elongate everything that grew on the moon—stems, and branches, and people. He'd said trees were shorter and fatter on Earth. Rachel *liked* the intertwined effect—it made the First Forest dark and intriguing.

Gabriel's voice brought her back to the present. "Now we move on to the practical. Your combined score determines whether or not you become a Horticulture Terraformer. If you don't pass, there are other choices for work."

Rachel's stomach clenched. *Not me. I have to be around trees. I have to help plant Selene. I have to pass!* She imagined her father's voice in her ear, suggesting she "*breathe,*" saying, "*My daughter can do anything.*"

"Some of our evaluation will be based on the work you did during class. That tells us how you approach day-to-day tasks," Gabriel said. A few children groaned. Ursula and Rachel grinned at each other; this was good for them, they worked hard. "We'll also judge how well you've learned the system's ecology behind terraforming. First, Ali will question you as a group."

Rachel and Ursula sat next to each other. They squeezed each other's hands, passing a wish for luck back and forth. Ali faced the class, sitting cross-legged on a waist-high black dais. She opened a data window beside her, opaqued it white, and left it suspended in air to her right. "First, tell me what is in the base nutrient mixture?"

An easy question. Rachel chose to let one of the younger children answer it. Two of them, and Andrew, all registered an answer at almost the same time.

Ali called on the young blond boy Andrew had teased earlier, Nick, and his answer appeared in the window beside Ali. His voice started with a quiver of nerves, but got stronger as he listed, "Nitrogen, silicon, phosphorus, and potassium are macro-nutrients. Calcium, magnesium—" Nick stumbled through the rest, getting most of it right.

"Anyone else?" Ali asked.

"Iron," Sharon spoke up.

"But we get iron from the soil," Andrew said.

"We still have to measure it; there's too much in some places," Sharon answered him.

"Quite right. Why is it irregular?" Ali asked.

"Well, here, in the grove, it's pretty even. All Selene's soil came from space stuff, and in some places, the way you made the world, it didn't work. It came out scattered." Sharon put her hand over her mouth. Some of the other children tittered.

Rachel tried to cover for Sharon. "It wasn't a mistake, it couldn't be helped. Some asteroids and moons have more iron than others. Besides, everything else varies too. We have to watch places where there is too much iron—it burns the roots. We always survey the soil before we plant, especially in the field." Rachel grinned at the younger girl. "And you're right, iron is important. There has to be some, and there can't be too much."

"But every nutrient is like that," Andrew said. "They all have to be just right."

Sharon didn't answer. Andrew had succeeded in making Rachel look foolish too. Rachel squirmed, furious for the second time that morning. She couldn't show her anger—it might make her fail. It was easy to earn Council's disapproval. She looked over at Sharon, who gave her a beseeching glance. Rachel smiled, the only help she could afford to offer.

Ali shifted her questioning to Andrew, perhaps to give Sharon time to recover her composure. Andrew delivered a well-organized example of the way the tiny measuring pods communicated wirelessly with one another, collecting and sending information about soil, atmosphere, and any plants they were attached to. The pods were ubiquitous—data flowed from all over Selene to be gathered up at Aldrin and forwarded to space, to the carrier ship *John Glenn*. Ali pushed him quietly, eventually questioning past his ability to answer confidently.

Question and answer had been running for an hour now. Rachel was so mad at Andrew she could spit. He'd monopolized all of the best questions. Some of her answers were better, but Andrew didn't give her time to say them. And what Andrew hadn't answered, quiet Harry had answered perfectly. Rachel couldn't smack Andrew in front of Council, and she couldn't seem to think faster either. Ursula hadn't done too well; Rachel wanted to prod her out of her shyness. Things were *not* going well.

Finally Ali looked over at the two girls and asked them, "Why do we plant in this grove with our hands and not with machines?"

Andrew started to talk, but Ali pushed an open hand toward him to warn him off, and he closed his mouth again, fidgeting. Rachel glanced at Gabriel—they'd talked about this once on a walk. She licked her lips. "So that we get a feel for the plants and see them as living parts of an ecosystem. If we touch the plants, and know them, we can remember that later, when we are using mostly machines." She looked at Ursula. "Ursula knows this too."

Ursula looked gratefully back at Rachel and narrowed her eyes, plunging in bravely. "When we work by hand we know what the soil feels like. We know what the tree feels like." Ursula hesitated a second. "And it's *ours,* so we're proud of our work here."

Ursula ran out of words and elbowed Rachel, who said, "Terraforming Ecology is a form of engineering. Gabriel says engineers need to do things themselves to understand how to avoid mistakes."

Ali broke in, "Do you think that's true?"

Rachel stayed quiet for a moment. "Yes. I think we'll know the plants better. I'll always know the ones I planted here, and if I want to keep that, I'll stay in some physical contact even when—if—I pass and work on planting machines."

Andrew interrupted, "Besides, who'd want machines tearing up our soil? They were already here once: this whole grove has been prepared with the right basic soil. Why use machines where you don't need them?"

Of course, Rachel thought, *that must have been the right answer. Why do I always miss the simple stuff?*

Gabriel changed the subject. "While you were talking with Councilwoman Ali, I downloaded some problems for you. You've got an hour, so take your time, but stay here in the meadow."

The children separated and bent over their wrist pads. Rachel answered half of the questions easily, and struggled with the next few, sweat beading on her forehead as time ticked away too fast. Knowing that there must be cameras recording, Rachel kept her face turned toward her pad and didn't look around at all.

After they'd all sent their answers back to Gabriel, the children scattered for lunch. Ursula and Rachel sat together. At first the girls ate quietly, swapping carrots for berries, and sharing two types of bread. Ursula looked dejected. "I didn't even get through it all. What happens if I'm not picked?"

"I didn't have time to finish the last question either," Rachel said. "And besides, we don't know how the others did yet."

"I missed three. But I know Harry and Andrew finished it all."

"How do you know that?" Rachel asked her friend.

"I watched them. They beamed the answers even before the hour was up."

"That doesn't mean they got them right." Ursula didn't look comforted. "Hey," Rachel offered, "you always did well planting, and the whole time we were studying with Gabriel. I know he thinks you're smart."

"How do you know that?" Ursula asked.

"I watch him. I see him watching how you work, and sometimes he smiles."

"What does a smile mean? What if I don't get chosen? I'll just die if I don't pass," Ursula continued. "What if I have to be a cook, or make tents? I want to be with you!"

"Well, it looks like we get to find out."

Gabriel and Ali sat together on the dais, waiting for the students to notice and gather. Harry already sat at the Council's feet, but the others, including Andrew this time, were all busy in a game of catch-the-disk, seeing who could leap highest and still land gracefully, disk in hand. Andrew's bracelets jangled against each other so he rang loudly as he leaped, a signal for the other children to get out of his way. Andrew was one of the best players, and Rachel watched him catch the heavy disk with his feet, flip over in a one-eighty, and land triumphantly.

Ali clapped her hands and the players stopped and bounded over.

Gabriel started right in on the results. "Nick, you and Alexandra are the youngest two to pass. You'll be in the advanced class next winter." That meant that at least three younger children, including Sharon, didn't pass. A groan came from the small knot of younger children. They'd all have to start over, most in different classes. They'd become simple farmers or get training for other town jobs.

Gabriel ignored it. "Eric, Julie, and Kimberly, you all passed. You get a break until Ali and I get back from planting." The four oldest students—

Harry, Rachel, Ursula, and Andrew—all looked at each other. It wasn't possible they'd all failed, but Rachel's heart sank.

Gabriel's next words made it worse. "I want Andrew, Harry, Rachel, and Ursula to stay. Everyone else can leave."

Rachel did her best to sit still while the others left. A knot of anxiety drummed at the top of her stomach, seeking release. She swallowed. Minutes passed, and Gabriel and Ali said nothing. Finally the meadow only contained the six of them.

Ali opened a new data window, larger than the one they'd used in the test. It showed darkness, and then the flash of a hand light bobbing as a dark figure walked down a path. Rachel squinted—it looked like—a human covered by tent material. Then the figure that held the light bent down and pulled up a tree; Rachel's cecropia. As a hand reached for the plant, the tent fabric slipped for a moment. Metal rings glittered briefly in a flash of light across the wrist.

No one said anything for a long time. Rachel looked at Andrew, who looked at the ground.

Did he think he could hide? Rachel wondered. Then, *At least he got caught.* There were always cameras, everywhere.

"Andrew," Gabriel broke the silence, "this is your real test."

Andrew fidgeted, looking at the ground. "It was a joke."

"Really?" Ali asked.

"You want us to get along. But she"—he pointed at Rachel—"she's always perfect. Better than the rest of us. Besides, it *was* a joke. We play jokes on each other. It was just one tree."

"Rachel worked hard on it," Gabriel said. "It was the core of her pattern. You didn't see that?"

Andrew spluttered. "It's not fair. You pay more attention to Rachel than to any of the rest of us. And *she* only talks to Ursula. I had to do something to—"

Gabriel cut him off. "We cannot tolerate acts of vandalism."

"But—"

"Explain to me why I shouldn't lock you up to think about this."

Andrew shot a hard look at Rachel. *It's not my fault!* Rachel felt anger mix with her anxiety. *Would Gabriel fail them all because of Andrew? Harry and Ursula weren't even involved!* She looked around. Ursula's hand covered her mouth, her eyes watching Rachel instead of Andrew. Harry was stoic, not looking at any of them. He must have felt Rachel's eyes on him, because he turned and blurted out, "Andrew, apologize!"

Ali looked at Harry sternly, and said, "You have been known to help Andrew play his jokes."

Andrew's eyes widened. "Harry didn't help me." His voice still sounded surly. "The tree's okay. So what are you going to do to me?"

"Which choice I make depends on you."

"I . . . I . . ." Andrew looked back at Rachel. "I'm sorry. I'll get your tree down and help you plant it back."

"That's better," Gabriel said. "A little. Explain why your actions were wrong."

"Because, because it was right before the test?"

"And?" Gabriel asked.

"I don't know." Andrew glowered at the ground, fiddling with his bracelets.

Ali picked up the conversation from Gabriel. "You must forge a working team. Mistakes in a project like this can kill. Oh, I know, pulling up one tree won't kill anyone. But what might you do with more powerful tools? This is not a stable planet—it's a moon being forced into a temporary home. There are too many humans to fit on *John Glenn,* and if we destroy the fragile ecosystem, some of you will die. Small mistakes can mean a lot here. Why do you think we're so careful about what we let you do? Even the four of you, our best students?"

Gabriel looked sternly at Andrew. "Andrew, you're young. And smart. You will stay here for the next ten weeks and you alone will care for Teaching Grove. You've had a demonstration—we can see what you do. See that you convince us you care about Rachel's plot as much as your own. Actually, better than your own. Failure will cause additional consequences."

Ursula clutched Rachel's hands. Rachel's heart sank. Andrew responsible for the grove? For *her* trees? What would she be doing?

She glanced at Andrew. His face was beet-red and he murmured, "Okay. I'll prove myself."

"Rachel, Harry, and Ursula will go with us for this season's planting. Be packed and back here by dawn tomorrow. Requirements have been sent to your pads."

Rachel whooped. Ursula's grin stretched ear to ear. Harry turned toward Andrew whose expression had shifted from penitent to stunned.

Chapter 2: Leaving Home

Rachel and Ursula stood at the edge of the grove, the path home winding away below them. "I can't wait to see more of Selene," Rachel said, pulling her right arm wing buckles tight against her biceps and forearm. "I've never been out of Aldrin before."

"Maybe we can see the Hammered Sea," Ursula lilted.

"See the sea? See the sea . . . see the sea . . ." Rachel teased her. *She passed! We passed! We are going exploring . . .*

Ursula laughed out loud. "Well, you know what I mean. None of us has been that far from Aldrin yet."

"My father has," Rachel said quietly. "How can I leave him? You won't have any trouble leaving your great brood of brothers, but Dad will be all alone."

"He'll want you to go."

Rachel nodded. "That's what he'll say."

"I know you don't want to leave him." Ursula turned to grin at her friend. "I also know you couldn't bear to stay home."

"Of course I couldn't."

"You'll manage. You're *always* okay, Rachel."

"It's too bad it's not just us, or maybe Alexandra. Harry makes me so mad—he's always right, and he's so quiet it's uncanny."

"Besides," Ursula broke in, "he hangs around with Andrew."

"I guess I'll just be grateful it's Harry and not Andrew—silence beats meanness." Rachel stretched, poised to begin the run into flying. "Maybe Harry will do okay."

"Maybe Apollo will rise twice tomorrow."

"I'm excited," Rachel said. "We passed!" She ran, beating Ursula into the air by two steps, extending her lead all the way home.

The girls arrived at the outside poles winded and bubbly. They split toward their respective tents.

Her dad wasn't home. A note said he'd gone to fix the solar power unit south of town.

Rachel folded herself down into a chair and turned her pad on, retrieving the packing list. It was short. Pad and stylus, wing gear, three changes of clothes, two pairs of shoes, and whatever she needed for hygiene. A short note from Ali told her they'd be northwest of Aldrin for eight to ten weeks.

Wow. They'd be gone the rest of summer and most of fall, returning just a month before Mid-Winter Week. Maybe she could bring back a special story about the trip for Festival Day.

Packing took nearly an hour. Rachel added and subtracted from her pile, finally settling on just what had been included in the list.

She reviewed lessons about the various planting machines. Some were too small to see, simple, dropped onto the ground like dust. Others were so big they made a human look like a leaf. Huge unmanned flat tillers opened Selene's sterile regolith, turning it over and over and then scattering tiny short-lived machines that burrowed through dirt, releasing oxygen or mixed nutrients. Then they died, melting to carbon and air. A different set of tillers mixed in organics, sands, or clays. Spreaders followed last, scattering raw materials for cyanobacteria mats: thin shelves of nitrogen-fixing organisms that killed any trace of remaining nanotechnology.

Rachel remembered Gabriel telling her the first tasks of a terraformer, besides atmosphere and pressure, were water and soil.

Humans drove forty-foot-long manned "planters" that dug holes, made a specific soil for each plant, emplaced seedlings, and even tamped the soil down. People followed, checking work. Rachel expected to see the butt ends of planters for days.

A friendly scratch on the outside of the tent signaled that her father was home. She turned as he stepped inside.

He took off his hat and went to the sink, scrubbing oil and dirt from his hands. "I thought I'd never get the array working right again. I had to make a new gear; took me four hours. How did it go today?" He must have seen her face, because he stopped and shifted tone. "It did go well, didn't it?"

The words came out in a rush. She told him about the whole test, and the surprise ending to the day. "We leave tomorrow morning."

Frank didn't say anything for a long time, surprise, pride, and anger flashing across his face. "Of course you have to go. It's . . . so fast. I thought you'd be home a few more years."

His face looked just like it had when they knew her mom wasn't coming back. Even after ten years, she remembered. She shivered. "I promise to come back," she said. "Surely it's safe."

"Ahhh, as safe as here, anyway. I'll be okay." He turned away and put on hot water. His voice was still strong. "The Councilman told me he might choose you, but I thought I had a few years still."

"You mean Gabriel knew I'd pass?"

"We all knew you would pass. They're picking leaders."

"Leaders?"

"Well, you see how many more kids there are here. Half of Aldrin's population is under twelve. Council needs people to plant more, tend what we've got, build new cities. Someone has to lead the ones that are young now. Your mom and I knew that when we had you." He busied himself at the stove. "I'm putting soup on."

"Good. Dad? What do you think about Andrew, and my tree?"

"I don't know. Trill Johnson got angry and hit his mother twice when I was a boy. I haven't seen him since. Probably he's just on the ship. I didn't ask. I never missed Trill. He was mean. Andrew's his nephew."

"He meant it as a joke," Rachel said. "It was cruel, but it didn't hurt anything."

Frank stirred the soup. The sharp tang of onions and spices filled the room. "Sometimes it's hard to tell what angers Council. You need to be careful. Dear, you only *know* Gabriel and Ali. Oh, you've met others, but never really worked with them." He leaned toward Rachel and smiled softly. "What do you know about Council?"

"They're making a world for us! I know they came from Earth, on *John Glenn,* and they made Selene, made it over so we can live here." She thought. "I know we're not where we were meant to be. They came here because they had starship trouble."

"They are powerful."

"Yes, but I like them, at least most of them. They're interesting. Something to figure out, like a mystery." She chewed her lip. "They keep secrets."

Frank smiled sadly. "Yes, they do. You know about the antimatter generator, of course."

"That's not a secret. Council needs fuel for *John Glenn.*"

"So what are their goals?" he asked, serving her a bowl of soup.

"Plant Selene. Build a larger base for humans here—for us, for the people born here. Then the collider circles Selene. It makes their antimatter—"

"Their goal is to make the antimatter generator so they can leave us," he said. "Their goals aren't about us, not really."

Rachel's stomach dropped. "Leave?"

"That's what they plan." Frank looked at his bowl of soup, not catching Rachel's eyes.

"They can't go unless they take us with them. How would we live?"

"I don't know. They won't leave tomorrow, anyway." Frank was still looking down, and his voice was thick, edged with bitterness. "So go planting. You're almost grown, and I've taught you what I can. Just remember you were born here, like me, for them. We work for them." He got up and hugged her good night. "Be a good student. Keep your eyes and ears open. Do what you're told. Don't forget that. Maybe someday you'll be close enough to Council to learn more about them." His face softened. "After all, *I* would never call Gabriel 'Gabe.' "

"I'll remember."

Rachel washed the dishes and got ready for bed herself.

Sleep came slowly. Her mind turned the day's surprises over and over. Excitement about leaving, seeing places she'd only heard about, worry that her dad would be lonely. The idea of being a leader. Most of all, the idea of Council leaving. Leaving! Where would she and her dad get spices, and thread, and how would she learn new things?

The next morning, she woke ragged and tired. Her dad flew Rachel and Ursula up to the grove, smiling the whole way, as if his cautions of the night before had never been voiced. He handed both girls' bags to Ali. "Take care of them." He kissed the top of Rachel's head. He had to stand on tiptoe to do it, and she threw her arms around him, squeezing tight before he pulled free and turned away.

A small flying plane waited in the meadow, and Rachel and Ursula climbed in the back next to Harry, who smiled at them but didn't say anything. They rose up higher than the tops of the First Trees, circled, and accelerated away.

Chapter 3: Planting

Rachel shielded her eyes from the sun and looked over at Gabriel. He drove sixty yards away, a small figure atop a twin of the huge planter she controlled. They shared communication links, but the whine and chatter of the machines made hand signals work better.

Gabriel held up one finger, and she waved acknowledgment.

Rachel settled the planter so that the control target matched the laser display overlaid on her retina. It was like looking at lines on top of pictures, both in front of the real world. It made her head hurt. She punched a series of commands, and then settled into her seat, reaching for a water bottle. Sweat poured down her brow and trickled down the back of her neck. They had been working since dawn. She needed a break.

The planter hummed and vibrated, rocking as it pulled soil up into the analyzer. Rachel watched displays identify the mineral content of the sample. The machine rumbled, stirring nutrients and measuring pods into the regolith and compost mixture with huge metal paddles. Finished soil dropped into a cone-shaped pile next to a hole. The whole process took about five minutes.

Rachel nudged her planter fifty yards past the waiting hole and shut it down, ears ringing in the sudden silence. As she clambered down the ladder on the side, she looked over her shoulder at Ursula and called, "Lunch after this planting."

The planters frightened Ursula. So Rachel rode and Ursula followed, doing the stooping and planting and watering. This was the last week of this season's planting, and even working into the steadily duskier nights, they were ten percent behind their goal, muscles tired and sore from the extra work.

Harry and Gabriel were already seated when Rachel joined them, choosing a rocky perch where she could look back across the field at the other ten teams. They were all Earth Born. Earth Born were shorter, wider, brawnier than Moon Born. She watched in silence, drinking water and letting a soft breeze cool her.

"Your shadow is always slower than you are," Harry said.

"She's careful."

"You're careful." He caught her glare and said, "Hey, hey, easy. Just noting the facts."

Ursula was just now unbending from watering the cieba tree she had just planted. Adult Moon Born were taller than most Council, and Ursula, the tallest teenager, was already taller than Gabriel. Her sun-silhouetted figure looked like two branches on a tall stick, topped with a halo of light broken by flyaway bits of her spiky hair.

Ursula sat near Rachel, as far away from Harry as she could get and stay in the group. She blotted sweat from her forehead and high cheeks with a rag before reaching for water.

"Hey, slow and thin, we saved you some food," Harry teased.

"Nice of you." Ursula reached for the still untouched basket, extracting a bit of bread and a handful of berries.

"Maybe it will make you move faster."

Ursula threw a berry at him, hard enough that it left a thin streak of juice on his cheek.

"Ahhhh—quit wasting food." Ali's voice chided them as she came up on the group. "Ready for tomorrow?"

"Do we still get to go flying?" Rachel asked.

"Yes. We need to start tilling now if we want to plant next year. That means a ground survey. It will be hard work, even though we'll use a plane to get from place to place. We'll be gone three days." Ali pulled up an aerial photo in a data window, tracing the path they'd fly over.

"I'm tired," Ursula said. "Can we have a rest day first?"

"We'll rest during the winter, when it's raining more often. Selene is growing, and people need plants. Right now, there are hundreds of us. There will be thousands by the time we build up industry, and a bigger town," Ali said.

"You mean the antimatter generator," Rachel said.

"I mean the town. And after that we'll build the collider."

Ursula broke in. "If there are so many people, how will you get them all to Ymir?"

"*John Glenn* carried two thousand of us here, all frozen," Gabriel replied. "Let's look at the near future, like tomorrow."

"But there's going to be more than two thousand. There already are. You want us to help *John Glenn* leave us? For someplace nobody has ever even seen?" Rachel asked.

"For a place where we were supposed to meet our friends a long time ago," Ali said.

"Your friends," Rachel muttered under her breath. Harry must have heard her, since he shot a warning look her way.

"How do you know Ymir's still there?" Harry asked loudly. "Or that the other starships made it to the system?"

Harry was covering for her thoughtless comment.

Now Gabriel spoke. "It's a planet. They don't wander away from their suns. I have faith the other two colony ships got there."

"I still don't see why one day off would make a difference," Ursula said.

Everyone ignored her.

Rachel wanted to know more about *John Glenn,* but Gabriel's face was closed tight. She gave up, sighing. "Go over where we'll be tomorrow; tell us what you need us to do."

Ali rewarded Rachel with a smile. "It's beautiful out there, wild and rocky. Empty. I think you'll like it."

They worked without stopping until Apollo set. The students shared a quiet dinner alone, sluiced sweat and dirt away with buckets of cool water they pulled from the irrigation pipes, then ducked into a big shared housing tent nestled in rocks at the end of the field. It was protected from wind and separate from the Earth Born's camp.

Rachel twisted and turned, uncomfortably awake for hours. Loud talk and laughter from the Earth Born threaded in and out of her thoughts, and she covered her ears with her arms. The lunch talk was the first time in six weeks of planting she'd heard anything that reminded her of her conversation with her dad about Council the night before she left home. She wished her dad was there to fix her tea, and she wished Gabriel would tell her his plans. Even exhausted, she remained aware of the breath and movement of the others for a long time.

Harry snored.

THE NEXT MORNING all five of them were crammed in the little flier they'd brought out from the grove. A brushwork of saplings dotted the ground below, becoming shorter and newer as they flew over two seasons of work. Then they passed greens and reds of cyanobacteria and molds; signs of regolith being given life. The ground changed to jumbled rocks and sand, streaks of reds and browns and blacks where surface soils mixed unevenly. Small ridges and shallow craters flowed below, everything rock and sand. Rachel had seen pictures and read about the regolith deserts, miles and miles of dead land waiting to be coaxed awake. It was most of Selene, and flying over it, Selene seemed huge. She sat wedged between Harry and Ursula, and had to look past them on either side to get a view.

They flew above one of the few roads on Selene. Dry, dusty, and rocky, the Sea Road terminated at the edge of the Hammered Sea, a quarter of the way around Selene from where they were now. Back when Aldrin was still tented, Council used the road for big equipment to lay water pipes between the Hammered Sea and Aldrin. Now, Selene's stable heavy atmosphere encouraged flight; Council designed for it. Mostly unused, the road looked abandoned. Long stretches were still smooth glassy road surface, punctuated with hundreds of feet of sand drifts. Watching carefully, Rachel noticed how the makeup of surface soils affected the amount of drift.

"Let's stop for lunch," Ali suggested.

Gabriel banked the little plane, looking for a good landing place.

The cramped cabin filled with a piercing warning whine. Wrist pads chimed and beeped.

Gabriel leveled the plane and sharply increased speed.

Ali flicked her data window to a new search and stared at it, mumbling, "We're lucky we weren't on the ground."

"What is it?" Harry asked.

"Flare," Gabriel said.

"How much time do we have?" Harry's voice didn't even quiver.

Gabriel answered, just as smoothly. "Two hours. We should have heard about it earlier—Astronaut must be slipping."

Pain sliced through Rachel's knee as Ursula's fingers dug into flesh.

"We won't get back," Harry said.

"Not to where we came from," Gabriel replied, then, to Ali, "Closest shelter?"

"I'm looking." Ali's voice was musically, cheerfully sarcastic.

Rachel felt her breath coming high and fast, closed her eyes, and peeled Ursula's hand from her knee. Everyone in Aldrin drilled regularly, but Rachel only remembered one other real flare.

She'd been smaller, just seven. Running with her father, being swung low into a shelter in the center of Aldrin, underground. Pulled by strange hands down into a place she hadn't even known existed. She remembered struggling to breathe standing against the adults' legs, until finally she cried out and people shifted, making room for her. She could still hear Frank calling for her mother: "Kristin," then louder, "Kristin!" and the door closing and Frank shoving her hand into a neighbor's, and looking hard at her, commanding her to stay. His back as he turned and struggled for the door, now closed. His fists pounding on the door as he looked back at the crowd, at Rachel, and finally stood still, an angry lost look on his face. After what she remembered as a long time, he had come back and held Rachel tightly to him, his arms quivering.

She had not seen her mother since. Her father's face was empty when he told her Kristin had gone to *John Glenn*. Within a few weeks he stopped talking about her. Sometimes Rachel noticed him stroking the violet and rose embroidered curtains her mother had made, and staring out the window.

It was as if she'd died.

The flier banked, the change in angle drawing her back into the present.

Gabriel flew with purpose, driving the little plane near the top of its abilities. He was totally focused. He and Ali spoke too low and fast for Rachel to make out the words. Half an hour passed before Gabriel throttled the plane back and brought the nose up, clearly meaning to land.

Rachel couldn't see anything. No people, no vehicles, certainly no shelter.

No one spoke as Gabriel landed the flier. She looked at her wrist pad. Almost an hour had passed. They wouldn't see radiation. Would the sunlight be brighter? What if the timing was wrong?

Gabriel pulled a pack from under his seat, climbed out, and stood by the door, helping them down one by one. "We had to land a little ways from the shelter. This was the closest stretch of road long enough to take the plane safely. We have time. Follow me, stay close."

"But where—" Ursula started to ask.

"They built shelters along the Sea Road," Harry whispered. "That must be where he's taking us."

The sunlight didn't look any different.

None of them wore wings. Rachel, in a chaotic bouncing run, quickly ran out of breath. Gabriel ran with one hand in Ursula's and one in Harry's, pulling them into bigger strides than they'd have managed on their own. Ali grabbed Rachel's hand and pulled. Rachel's longer legs barely let her keep up with the help of the smaller woman, and Rachel wondered where Ali got her strength.

They ran until Rachel's breath came in small desperate gulps.

Rachel felt the pull of Ali's hand change suddenly, pushing her back. Gabriel had stopped where a tall metal rod poked up out of the ground, bright yellow streamers and green bands decorating the top. He dug in the dirt below it. "Harry, Rachel, help me," he said.

The five of them frantically pushed sand and small stones away until they uncovered a handle on a slab of metal set into the ground. Gabriel leaned down and pulled, his whole body straining against the weight. It didn't give.

Harry walked over to the metal stake, began pulling on it. No give there either. Rachel saw what he was doing, stepped over, and began to pull as well. They worked the stake in a circle, loosening it, tugging upward. Nothing, then a slight movement, and then nothing again. "Ursula!" Rachel called.

Ursula turned, and then Ali said "Good idea!" and came to help. With four sets of hands pulling, the rigid pole finally slid from the ground. They carried it over to Gabriel, and he threaded it through the metal door handle, making a lever. Ali said, "Twenty minutes."

Gabriel grunted. They pulled up together on the rod, and puffs of dust rose from two spots on the long edge. "Now, more," Gabriel said through gritted teeth, pushing the sound out so it was barely intelligible.

They pulled. The door didn't budge.

Chapter 4: The Controller

On board the *John Glenn*, Ma Liren stalked into the galley. Two gardeners stared at a video wall, watching something on Selene's surface. Liren stopped, frowning, watching the women, Mary and Helga.

Liren stepped forward to look. She recognized Gabriel and Ali and three Moon Born children, outside, exposed to the coming flare. They were pulling together, everyone on one side on some kind of lever, faces strained. It was a micro-camera image; a slightly grainy picture and no sound. The door jerked, flew up a few inches, and fell back to the surface of Selene. Harry jumped as the lever was torn from his hand.

"Come on," Mary whispered, rapt, "you can do it."

"Astronaut," Helga demanded, "time left?"

"One point four minutes until initial effects, seven minutes before serious radiation." The AI's calm voice contrasted with Helga's high-pitched tones.

The image was small. One of the children—Rachel—separated from the group and picked up a rock, setting it down next to the door. The children all reached together, joining Ali and Gabriel, pulling up again. The door rose—inches, more inches, and Rachel toed the rock under the edge just as the group lost leverage and the door started to fall again. The lever angled up, and Ali and Gabriel squatted, using the strength of legs accustomed to more gravity than the Moon Born. The door rose and, finally, balanced at a ninety-degree angle to Selene's surface. Gabriel and Ali held the door.

Helga and Mary clenched fists and screamed triumph as Ali led the three Selene born into the stairway. Gabriel was the last one in, and as the door thumped closed, Helga and Mary smiled broadly at each other.

Liren closed her eyes. This wasn't good—the crew couldn't afford attachment to the Moon Born. "Okay," she said, "they're safe." She looked directly at the two women. "Don't you owe me a report on the savannah?"

Mary turned around. "Hey, lighten up."

"It's not as if we could have helped them from here anyway. Let them solve their own problems, and we'll solve ours."

"You know, Liren, not everything can be work."

It was an old argument. Liren sighed. "Of course not. We provide you plenty of other entertainment."

"Aren't you even glad they're safe?"

"Of course I am." Liren clenched her teeth and headed for the refrigerator, rummaging for some synthed milk to calm her stomach. "We all know our jobs are here, and that's where our focus should be—on keeping this damned ship running until the Selene project is *over.*"

"Maybe we should all help. The work down there would go faster."

"We need to save your skills."

Helga raised her soft voice. "Do you still think we'll get to Ymir?"

"Not if we lose faith, we won't. We need to stay pure, and keep our focus." Liren poured the milk into a tall thin glass. "Now, don't you all have *some* work to do?"

Mary threw her head back and laughed. "Still always work. Don't worry, we'll do what you want. We always do, don't we?"

Liren bit back an angry reply. The crew was bored, and Selene provided fresh entertainment. "Just remember you have jobs to do here. Others are assigned to Selene. Let them do their work, and focus on yours."

Liren hated Selene. She hated the compromises they made every day. Compromises were dangerous. They needed too much nanotech to change Selene into a world rich enough to support manufacturing and the civilization of thousands needed to build the collider. The Astronaut program had too much freedom and too much say. It was too easy—the AI could handle complex math and design more readily than a human or a standard computer program. Gabriel and Captain Hunter kept loosening the bonds that were supposed to keep Astronaut caged into its small world of interstellar navigation.

Liren walked down the corridor toward her office, still lost in thought.

John Glenn couldn't orbit here forever. The ship's sleek sides were dimpled with space-debris impact pits. They'd lost two Service Armor ships across the years. Terraformers had stolen sensors and materials to use on Selene. In-ship systems needed more regular repair. It was an ever-uphill battle to keep her small group of humans free from the twin temptations of technology and complacence. They couldn't risk more technology. They had the ability; nano could make them gods. But what would wild nano do to Selene? To *John Glenn*? That was the path of poor, doomed Earth.

No matter how hard she tried, Liren couldn't see a way to dampen the crew's attachment to the Children. Council and Colonists on the surface needed the support of *John Glenn*'s resources. Warm bodies aboard *John Glenn* were bored enough to need entertainment. Circumstances trapped them.

Liren entered her office. The room was orderly, clear surfaces, black and white colors, and almost no decorations. She sat in her high-backed chair and stared at the wall. She thumbed up what she called her "reminders." Articles and scenes flashed on the wall as a collage she'd spent years building.

On Phobos, AIs with more power than humans. News photos of crew members killed on their way to *John Glenn.* An asteroid turned to an Escher nightmare, all edges and angles, by wild nano, and no sign of the expedition that was supposed to be surveying it. Pictures of *John Glenn*'s two sister ships, *Leif Eriksson* and *Lewis and Clark.* Surely both ships had reached Ymir and were building a real world. Each new picture slammed into her, building her resolve to keep going. They also made her stomach cramp harder, and she tasted sour milk.

"Astronaut," she commanded, "how bad is the flare? Give me damage estimates."

A voice sounded in her ear. "Data streams indicate that everyone made it to shelter in time."

"Get me a report on the plant damage as soon as you can."

"It will take a few moments to assemble detailed information. Gabriel and Ali were lucky to get themselves and the students to the shelter. Perhaps more shelters should be built?"

"I asked for a report, not an opinion," Liren barked.

"I will produce a report about the efficacy of more shelters," the voice said, "and a better design for the door."

"I asked for a report on plant damage. Gabriel can tell me about the shelters. It's high time he was here anyway." Gabriel was way too attached to Selene.

"What worries you, Liren?"

"Ask Gabriel to come up for the next High Council meeting. And be quiet until I speak to you."

The silence was immediate. If Astronaut were human, she would think it was miffed. She *would not* worry about an AI's feelings.

She needed a distraction.

She'd left so much behind on Earth! At least the arts had come with them. Gabriel sang. Ali wove. Kyu decorated herself. Sculptures dotted the garden and common areas of the ship. Liren approved of art. She pulled out her journal, and worked long into the night, writing a story about Ymir, hoping to keep her people's attention on the real goal. Her stomach wouldn't settle. The right words refused to find their way into her data window.

She tried for haiku. The spare lines often centered her. Tonight, even simple poetry refused to blossom for her. She curled up onto her white couch, covering herself with a black blanket.

She twisted and turned, falling into a familiar dream. *John Glenn,* still parked in Earth orbit, waited to leave for a base near Uranus, to join sister ships *Leif* and the *Lewis and Clark.* They'd financed it themselves, High Council, fifteen members of the Council of Humanity. Spent savings, sold conglomerates. In her dream their little ship approached the big carrier, dodging a cadre of man/machine hybrids flying agile space-planes, intent on forcing berths aboard the first interstellar ships ever built. Ma Liren as copilot pitted her human ingenuity against their pursuers. One ship was already behind, ten people who wouldn't make it to *John Glenn.* In her dream, she watched the doors slam shut against the locks she had been angling for, shutting her out.

Chapter 5: The Hammered Sea

A day and a half after the flare, Gabriel stood with Ali and the students at the edge of the crater that cupped the Hammered Sea. The horizon was almost a flat line of water—the tallest edges of the far crater wall peeked above the sea like teeth, jagged and far away. He loved this place. It was a wild machine, much more controlled than it looked, often surprising.

The rim was unstable. Ten degrees away from them, inside the crater wall, a rock worked loose and fell. Ursula pointed, her finger shaking. He watched it bounce slowly, exaggeratedly, down the jagged incline and splash into the bright water below; a tiny ball, graceful in the low gravity. "That was beautiful," Ursula said.

"Those rocks," Gabriel said, "are the size of the planting machines you hate to drive."

Ursula's eyes widened and she stepped back, losing her balance and falling onto the soft powdered rock that covered the rim of the crater. A fog of dust rose around her, changing the color of her skin.

Gabriel laughed. Harry laughed too, standing at the edge, toes lined up with the end of a rock. In a few moments, Ursula's laugh followed theirs, a nervous trill. She moved away from the rim.

Rachel leaned forward, eyes pinned to the sea. She pointed toward water stains below them. "Does the water really get that high?"

Ali smiled. "Yes, Rachel. Just watch. Gabriel had to make the crater taller and thicker twice just to contain the force of the water and tides."

"You made this? I thought you oversaw the planting."

"I do oversee the planting. But first I designed Selene. Someone had to bring water in for the plants."

"Duh," Harry said.

"So you just . . . made . . . the Hammered Sea? All by yourself?" Rachel was eyeing the far side, looking between Gabriel and the huge sea in front of her.

Ali laughed again, louder, her head thrown back. "I wouldn't underestimate Gabriel if I were you, Rachel."

Gabriel tried to look stern. It had been *hard* to shape this sea. He was proud enough to babble some. "I had help, of course. Mostly from a really smart program named Astronaut."

Ali glared at him. Her parents had died on Jupiter Station when the AI that ran it lost interest. Ali didn't like AIs.

"Ali helped too." He sighed. Time to teach. They only knew part of the story. "There wasn't any Selene when we came here. There was an oversized gas giant planet, Harlequin, and almost a hundred moons. We picked a big moon for a foundation. It had no spin—no day or night with reference to Harlequin. We made that, hitting it over and over in the same place, from the same angle, making tilt and spin. Days and seasons. Building Selene. Then we—went—cold—for a long time, to let the whole system stabilize and cool.

"We woke up to a pockmarked ball covered in regolith. There was a little ice, a few small pockets of underground water, and the beginnings of an atmosphere, but humans need lots of easy-to-reach water, and thick atmosphere to shield us from space. So we brought in comets. Then we went cold again. Then we brought in more comets. The comets gave us the water you see here."

"So the water is from space?" Rachel asked.

"Isn't everything? This deep sea is the motor that drives Selene's hydrology. We need this much water for the humidity to grow tropical plants rather than cactus. But we had to contain most of the water to limit the effect of the tides, which are worse here than on Earth, because of Harlequin." He pointed at the gas giant, which hung just off center in the sky. "Gravity pulls the water toward Harlequin. If we didn't contain it, Selene would be flooded with every high tide. We could have made hundreds of small seas instead of what we did make; the Hammered Sea and Erika's Folly, but they would have been harder to manage. Oh, lots of craters have a little water in them, but over half our water is right here." He paused, and said, "Besides, I wanted to make a real sea." That made him feel giddy still: to build a sea because he wanted to! "Feel the damp wind on your face, Rachel?"

She nodded, holding her arms over the sea below them.

"It blows up the crater walls, carrying water vapor. It's cooler than the air it meets on the far side. It would stay inside the crater and rain here, except we've built paths for it to funnel through. So we drive the rain to fall mostly outside the Hammered Sea, where it fills streams. We have pumps that take care of it when Selene doesn't, a backup system that sends water through the crater walls to fill the streams. We used the out-pumps a lot, early on. But we haven't had to use them for years—we test them every month, but I think we could turn them off if we wanted to." Gabriel waited a bit for the children to find one of the huge pipes. They were hard to spot, colored like the crater for camouflage. Erika had insisted on that. He and Erika had argued for months over the costs and time involved, but now, with this view, he was glad Erika had won.

"That's brute force engineering—the pipes. Real terraforming, with a whole planet and tectonics, would use temperature and humidity and wind. Selene doesn't have the raw materials to do it right." He turned around and pointed down slope behind them. "The gentle angle of the outside walls, here, what we just climbed, drains the water to the plains you see below, and there some of it subducts. We capture that water and pump it back into the sea. The remaining water moves through surface streams, some of which we channel into engineered viaducts, like the Aldrin viaduct. The water we use in Aldrin comes from here. Other viaducts carry water back here eventually. That's the hard part—we may never get the water back into the Hammered Sea without the in-pumps." He paused to let the children absorb the beauty of Selene's hydrological engineering.

"Some of the viaducts are open. You made those deep enough that the water stays in," Harry said. "I saw some on the way over here."

Harry would make a good engineer someday. "I like the open design. It encourages water evaporation, increases humidity."

Ali picked up where Gabriel left off. "It's the water cycle that determines where we live and plant, where we place our cities. The first engineering we do anywhere is for water. We picked Aldrin for a major base because it is far from here. That makes it safer. Imagine a quake big enough to break down a crater wall and let the water loose? All the water in the Hammered Sea? Remember, it's kilometers deep."

"So why did you build Clarke Base?" Ursula asked.

"So they can make what they need to keep the Hammered Sea working," Harry said.

Ursula stuck her tongue out at Harry's back.

Gabriel grinned. "Largely right, Harry. Think of it as a huge dam." He noticed the puzzled looks on their faces. "Okay—a huge machine. It needs people to maintain it, to fix it if it breaks, and even more, to be sure it doesn't break. We grow fruit and vegetables here on the plain, where there's water. So Clarke Base is a food production plant and a maintenance shop. This is also where we make the planters and planes and some of the other machines you see and use."

"Don't you make almost everything on *John Glenn*?" Ursula asked.

"Well, when we started," Ali said. "But even *John Glenn* is too small to make everything we need for Selene. It's hard to move heavy things between the ship and here—and we don't need to."

"How do you make so many miles of pipe?" Harry asked.

Gabriel frowned and looked at Ali, who licked her lip and said, "We use nanocytes," as if it were a dirty word. "Trillions of tiny machines. Just for raw materials," she qualified. The children looked puzzled.

"Someday I'll show you," Gabriel said, turning toward Harry. "So, do you understand the basics of our hydrology?"

"It's nice to *see* it. I understand it better than when you first told me."

"The cycle will vary as we get more plant cover. That's the beauty of a self-regulating system; we both watch for change and cause change. Terraforming is one long search for balance. We can tweak the system— generate wind if we need it over the lake, affect the surface temperature— there's a soletta in geostationary orbit—"

Harry interrupted. "Soletta?"

"The soletta is a bank of mirrors that focuses light from Apollo onto Selene, increasing the insolation—the light level from Apollo. We can turn mirrors on or off to affect insolation and tweak the temperature and energy supply. It's working so well it's been virtually automatic longer than you've been alive."

"Which isn't very long," Ali said dryly. "And it was a fight. Gabriel has had to rebuild the touchy thing twice so far. Once a single asteroid from a swarm got past our defenses and smashed the mirrors to shards. There wasn't much atmosphere yet, so some of them made it to the surface. Wear shoes!"

Gabriel laughed. "You'd have to dig pretty far to find any remains of that glass."

Ali went on, unfazed. "Oh, and the second time, it just disappeared. Just flat disappeared. We were all cold, one of our long down times. Astronaut woke me up to say there was nothing there. Astronaut didn't see it happen: Selene was between *John Glenn* and the soletta when it disappeared. The soletta might be the single most fragile part of our whole system. But without it, we couldn't regulate temperature, and Selene would get too cold to live on."

"Did you help him rebuild it?" Ursula asked Ali.

"I was cold. Erika did that."

"I haven't met Erika," Rachel observed. "Where is she?"

"Cold," Gabriel muttered.

Rachel turned her eyes on Gabriel, and he saw pain flash across them. "Like Mom?" she asked.

Ali's answer was sharp. "We don't know about your mom. Be patient."

Rachel's jaws clenched. She looked down into the crater as if she could see the bottom.

They brought out water bottles and lapsed into uncomfortable silence. Harlequin was almost straight above them now. "Can you see the water rising?" Gabriel asked.

"At the edges?" Rachel replied.

"The whole sea will be affected. A tide is a response to gravity—all of Selene feels the pull of Harlequin; the elasticity of water illustrates it."

Water crept up the sides of the great bowl below them. Rocks were slowly dampened by wind spray, and then submerged in rising waves.

Gabriel had seen this hundreds of times. He watched the children. He wanted them awed. Rachel and Harry stood side by side, both rapt and fully attentive. Ursula was on Rachel's far side, farther back, still sitting, craning her neck to see into the crater without being near the edge.

Gabriel leaned back, looking up at the gas giant overhead. The ring, of course, was edge on to him, bisecting the planet. A huge storm tracked slowly across the surface, the fractal edges of its motion lulling him into a near trance state. Ali's voice was backdrop; talk about tidal pulls and bulges. He heard her explain that most moons were tidally locked, that Selene's core had been once, and Selene would be again. Finally, he heard Rachel point out that the water level was falling. He took a deep breath and stood up, strapping on his wings.

They all stood at the edge, backs to the sea, and looked down over the long slope of the outside crater rim between silver threads of waterfall. White and red rock filled with pillows of pumice crunched under their feet. Below them was rocky ledge after rocky ledge; then, starting nearly a third of the way down, a gentle slope turning greener as it flowed into checkered fields.

One by one they ran and leaped up, snapping wings open in time to start the long flight down to Clarke Base. The children rose high in the thermals almost immediately, circling and swooping and chasing each other. Gabriel finessed his glide, letting his mind go completely into the flight, focusing on small muscles and tiny changes in air and wind. Calculations and vectors flowed in his head, and he followed them as best he could, changing the tilt of his legs or arms to follow the places his mind said he could take the flight, working to gain the most lift and speed from minute motions. He laughed to hear Rachel taunting Ursula, driving her to reach higher, higher.

Gabriel and Ali lagged behind, evaluating the children's flight.

The teens stopped halfway down the long slope. They hadn't even bothered to tell Gabriel or Ali. Gabriel used his radio to talk to Ali. "Let's lurk a bit behind them, and see if they get concerned."

Ali landed just ahead of him, graceful and quick as she swept her wings closed. They settled above the children, out of sight, and Gabriel released a camera-bot with instructions to hover above and behind the kids.

Ali looked worried, a small frown furrowing her brow. He guessed at her worry. "Rachel asked about her mom after the flare. What's this about Rachel's mother? Why did you tell her you can't find out what happened from here?"

"I checked the records." Ali's mouth was a tight line, and her eyes hugged the horizon.

"And?"

"She doesn't want to come back."

"We can't tell Rachel that," he said.

"You should," Ali said quietly.

"When she's older."

"Why not now? The girl deserves some honesty—this is important to her."

"This isn't a good time to upset her," Gabriel said.

"Better the sting of truth than a long painful uncertainty. Besides, we shouldn't try to control her world. She has to hear hard things to grow. You can't terraform people."

Gabriel bit his tongue. "I'd like to talk to her mother first. Is she awake?"

"She's cold."

Gabriel changed the subject. "Have you checked on Andrew?"

"No new damage today."

"We should never have given Andrew that second chance. It was a bad lesson for the others."

He was surprised to feel Ali lean into him, laughing, her serious demeanor broken. His mood didn't match hers, but he stripped wing gear from one arm anyway and laid it over her shoulders, asking, "What's gotten into you?"

"You're trying to control them. They're people, not stones or air."

"Picture . . . Andrew moving a little moon when he gets a temper tantrum."

"Another sea in the wrong place? Andrew's Hissy Fit?" She tugged his braid. "They'll never get access to LPTs anyway. What about Andrew, though? Isn't he just a teenager pushing boundaries?"

Gabriel had shown Ali Andrew's destructive streak, what he'd done *after* they left. "He's refusing to learn discipline. We can't afford to let him run free—there's no time to babysit him."

"I mean, look, he's just a kid. We were right to give him a chance; we're right to limit him now. I meant it when I said I'd support you." Ali's black braid across his knees contrasted with the grays and reds of the slope as it fell away behind her. "But you still need to give them time to think for themselves. They have to be able to live after we're gone." Ali's voice was angry again. "Why are we even doing this?"

"Ask the damned High Council. Remember, I argued to use nano to build the assembler in space." Ali hated nano. She should remember that none of the choices were good.

Chapter 6: Star Systems

Rachel watched out the window as they flew into Aldrin early the next morning. They landed just outside the city, Apollo's sunrise brightening the cloth tents just enough to make out color and shadow. She squeezed Ursula's hand briefly and they darted down the path toward home together. It seemed to take a long time to get there. Ursula peeled off for her home, and Rachel ducked into her doorway, smelling warm rice and eggs as she buried herself in her father's chest, filling his arms. She hadn't been gone long, not really, but she felt taller, more his size.

He pushed her back from him, frowning. "You'd better go on up to the grove."

"What? Why?"

"I think you'll need to see for yourself."

Gabriel stood by her final project. She ran up to him, then stopped, drew her breath in sharply. A broad swath of trees had been mowed down, driven over. Broken trunks littered the ground, dried and twisted, the life gone from them. It must have happened right after they left.

Almost half of Rachel's project and a snippet of Ursula's plot destroyed. Clearly someone had driven a work tractor through the grove. Tire tracks ran straight through, and in one place it looked like a blade had been let down and actually dug below ground. Pods and dirt and snapped seedlings mixed in a pile.

She knelt in the carnage, sweeping her hands back and forth through the dry dirt, picking out dead twigs and breathing in little gulps.

"Andrew," she said, narrowing her eyes, fighting at the anger rising in her.

"Yes."

"Why didn't you tell me?"

"You didn't need the distraction. We've taken care of the problem."

The distinct snap of wings sounded over her head. Nick landed at the edge of the plot and quickly folded his gear away. He walked up to them with the harness still attached. His brow was creased and he looked down, watching the ground.

"I'm sorry. Gabriel said to leave it for you to see. But we kept the rest of your trees alive. We did okay, didn't we?"

He looked so earnest she smiled a little. "Yes, Nick. Th . . . Thank you."

Nick nodded.

"What . . . why? Why would he do this?" Rachel asked, turning back to Gabriel.

Gabriel looked off at the horizon. "I suspect he was angry with me."

"Where is he?"

"He's safe. And Selene is safe from him for the moment. He's been stripped of his data rights."

"Data rights?"

"We're keeping him busy. His pad is locked out of the system, except for warnings. All he gets is one-way data."

To lose net access? How would Andrew learn anything new? She shuddered. "You really cut him off?"

"It's not your problem, or your fault. Still, you will have to clean up." Gabriel turned toward Nick. "Show me what you've done on the meadow grass," he suggested, walking away with Nick in tow.

Rachel glared at Gabriel's receding back. Her fists balled at her side. Andrew wasn't there, and she might as well be angry at a rock as at Gabriel. She paced around her plot, kicking at clods of disturbed dirt.

She gathered a pile of dead sticks, then sat at the edge of the ruin and simply stared at it for a long time, turning dry twigs in her hands. They were rough and sharp against her fingers, their torn edges scratching her palms.

Gabriel had no right to hide this until she got here. It wasn't carelessness: he'd taken pains to be in the grove when she saw it. Another lesson? Another test?

She didn't understand Council. But why had Andrew done this? To her? Why was she always his target?

Rachel spent the next two days replanting and tending. After carefully looking at how the remaining plants had grown, Rachel worked out some changes to her original placement. Seeing improvements raised her spirits some. She carefully set up a communications net from her plot to her wrist pad. Now she'd have real-time flows; she'd know about any new damage.

The next morning Rachel's dad walked up to her plot with her. He'd never looked closely at her work before, contenting himself with her stories. She squeezed his hand and pointed to a wide border of young plants. "See—that's where the worst damage was. I lined the path with heliconias. I wanted the bright reds."

Her dad smiled softly and ruffled her short hair. "I think it will look great. Sometimes bad things turn out okay."

She didn't answer.

He helped her weed and rake until nearly dark, and they walked back down the path together holding hands.

Rachel and Ursula worked together for days. Harry silently took care of Andrew's plot as well as his own. He looked haunted. He didn't spend much time with the girls, but he smiled at Rachel when Ursula wasn't around, and sometimes they sat and talked or watched the clouds together.

The days cooled. Harlequin's dark ruby glow didn't diminish, but Apollo's light no longer reflected back from the gas giant, and at night Aldrin was turned away from both Apollo and Harlequin. Against the rich black sky Rachel could see twice the stars of high summer. She and Ursula made games of naming stars and constellations far into the night. Twice they passed through meteor showers, and streaks of light flamed the sky, some bright enough to illuminate Ursula's fine hair.

One night, when Harlequin eclipsed Apollo completely and the stars felt closer and thicker than ever, Harry joined them. Ursula excused herself. Rachel stayed, and she and Harry lay on their backs looking at the sky.

"I talked to Andrew," Harry said unexpectedly. "He was in town for a few hours today. He's been out with an Earth Born planting crew. Told me he hated it. They treat him badly."

"Yeah, well, maybe he's acting badly," Rachel said.

"I asked why he tore up your test planting."

"What did he say?"

"He said he's in love with you."

Rachel shivered, pulling her knees in over her torso, wrapping her arms around them. "That's love? He destroyed my plot, got himself in trouble, and didn't even fix it afterward."

"Remember the tree he stuck up on the tool shed?"

"Of course. I could have failed over that. I was so mad at him I wanted to hit him."

Harry sat up and looked down at her. "He thought you'd think it was cool. I mean, really, he said, why not grow trees on buildings?"

"He's not stupid. He knew it was my final exam."

"He wanted attention."

"Well, then he doesn't understand me at all. I try to do a good job, but I stay inside the rules. It's important."

"Shhhhh . . . your voice sounds funny. Don't get mad. It wasn't me."

"I know," she said. "But still, couldn't he see how important that tree was to the design?"

"I could see it," Harry said. A long silence. "I like you too."

"But . . . but . . ."

"Look at the stars. Doesn't that design look like the ships the Council comes down to us on?"

She followed his pointing finger with her eyes. "That one? The bright star to the left, and follow it up—"

"Yes . . . you see it."

They stayed out and named star systems for hours, shivering, not touching.

Chapter 7: Erika's Folly

Three days before Mid-Winter Week, Gabriel and Ali flew Harry, Rachel, Ursula, and a younger student, Gloria, to the second biggest crater on Selene. It was Gloria's first flight, and her blue eyes were wide and wet and her lip quivered as they left the ground. Rachel chattered about the Hammered Sea and took her hand, distracting her from her fears.

"Why'd you name it Erika's Folly?" Harry asked.

A wide grin split Gabriel's face. "She missed. Her aim was off . . . bad arithmetic. She was trying to out-calculate Astronaut. There wasn't supposed to be a huge crater here."

Ali laughed. "It's a pretty mistake."

"I had to change the original plan for the collider path." Gabriel was still smiling.

Erika's Folly sloped gently into a wide sea. Rocks protruded from the water and decorated the inner and outer sides of the crater—jumbled piles that had fallen from the sky during the rain of rocks and fire that built the world. A large promontory of rock flowed down from a break in the crater wall; it looked like someone had stepped on the upward rim and pushed piles of stones down. The crater was a quarter of the width of the Hammered Sea, but Rachel thought it might still take a full day to walk from rim to rim. The middle sea would have to be skirted, and piles of boulders on the lakeshore would be hard to navigate.

The plane's reflection shadowed the calm sea. Water had etched its highest reach almost halfway between the current lake level and the lower sections of the crater's perimeter. The rise from water to rim was far less dramatic than in the Hammered Sea. Boulder piles, fields of fist-sized rocks, and flat expanses of sand crept gently up the sides of the crater. All the reds and grays and whites of Selene's stones showed here.

Gabriel assigned Harry and Ursula to work together planting sensors at various heights around the crater to measure water levels. Ursula looked longingly back at Rachel as she trailed off behind Harry, toting a bulky box of sensors. Rachel shrugged her shoulders and pretended disgust; she'd have been happy to go off with Harry.

Rachel took Gloria with her to gather rock samples and look for vegetation that might have crept here since the planting of Selene started. They were to meet back in two hours, long before the tide turned and sent water up toward the edges of the crater. Rachel and Gloria walked along the inside crater walls, feet slipping in loose sandy soil. Sometimes they had to scramble up over damp boulders.

Gloria asked, "Why are we looking for plants here?"

"Well, we want to control where things grow, to be sure we make a complete ecosystem," Rachel answered. "But it's important to see what's happening that we didn't plan."

"So do we pull up plants if we find them out here?"

"No. We take samples. I think the soil is too sterile here to find actual plants anyway. We know there are microorganisms by now, so the regolith is turning into soil, but it hasn't actually been prepared like the fields, so it won't support higher order plant life. You won't find a stray banana palm escaped to Erika's Folly. We're looking for mosses and simple structure plants."

Rachel knelt down and picked up a stone nearly the size of her fist. It was ringed with whitish green. "Hah! This could be a moss or an alga," she said. "So we'll take a sample back and analyze it." Rachel carefully scraped a bit of the material loose from the stone with a small metal tool she carried in her pocket. The sample went into a little bag that sealed itself.

"What if we don't want it to grow here?"

"I don't know, Gloria . . . ask Gabriel."

"I will. How did you see that? I would have walked right by it."

"Just look carefully. Watch. Success in terraforming—it's in the details—so here you'll see subtle signs, like a rock that's a slightly different color on one side. Sometimes it's an instinct. Ali says your subconscious knows more than your forebrain." Rachel reached down and picked up another stone. It too was edged with whitish green. "This looks like the same thing, but we'll sample it anyway," Rachel said.

"Will we see bigger plants?"

"I don't think so."

"I'm looking carefully," Gloria said, her voice sounding focused and very confident. "The tide comes up here—I can see where things are wet under rocks. Will it come up before we're done?"

Rachel looked at the sea of water in the center of the crater, hundreds of yards away from them. They stood only a little bit above it, and she thought there had been a little creep. Her wrist pad said they had ninety minutes. The high tide mark cut above them, a thick line carved into the rocks, maybe twenty minutes' walk.

"We'll be all right. Tides here don't go as far up the walls as they do at the Hammered Sea, but we'll turn upward soon. Gabriel and Ali didn't give us an exact path to follow."

"I'm okay," Gloria said. "I trust you."

"Good noticing though," Rachel said. "It's important to stay aware of what's around you." The word "leader" sounded good lately. She was growing into it.

Rachel stopped to turn over a pile of rocks, finding more mossy substance, a deeper green than on the first rock. She rubbed it absently with her thumb, wondering what it was.

The ground shook, almost enough to unbalance Rachel. Small rocks skittered around her ankles and she looked at the crater wall above her nervously.

Gloria was a hundred yards ahead, clambering over rocks. She tottered, calling "Rachel!" then gave a thin cry and dropped from view.

Rachel ran toward where she had last seen her.

She heard noise, muffled, maybe almost a scream. She forced herself to slow down. The crater was still and silent again, the quake over. Rachel inched forward, her heart pounding. As light as Gloria was, Rachel could make out her footprints, becoming more distinct until they dropped down and out of sight. The sandy soil fell away into a fissure.

"Gloria!" she called.

A sound floated up to her—not a word, but a whimper.

Chapter 8: Wild Water

Rachel squatted on the edge of the drop, inches to the right of Gloria's dragging foot tracks, and one long dragging handprint in the dust. Rachel's feet were on hard rock, solid, crumbling away almost immediately past her, falling to nothing, and rising as a hard edge again just twenty feet away—with a run, she could jump to the other side.

Water gurgled below her. This wasn't the Hammered Sea; there was no water engineering in Erika's Folly that Rachel knew of. A wild stream? Flowing into the crater?

"Gloria, can you hear me?"

"Yyy . . . yow. Yesss."

"Be calm. I can't see you. You're not far down; I can hear you pretty clearly."

"I . . . I fell. The quake came . . . and I lost my balance, and I . . . I just slid down. The ground went away right under my feet. Rachel . . . I'm scared. It hurts."

"What hurts?"

"My . . . my ankle." Rachel heard choking sobs.

"Are you standing on something? Is the ground good?"

"I'm okay, I think. There's water, and it's running down, and it's rocky down here and darker. I can see, but the light is thin."

Thin light? "Is it a cave?"

"I can see under where you are. I can't tell how far it goes."

Rachel took a step to look, and the edge crumbled under her. She tried to slide back, failed, and fell. She was right over where Gloria had fallen! She twisted, trying to angle her fall away from the girl. A thump, and she felt something under her—long, so it must be a leg or an arm. There was a sound of pain. So she hadn't killed her, or buried her.

"Gloria?"

"That hurt too." Gloria's voice was small.

"Yeah, well, now we're both down here," Rachel said dryly, trying to make it into a joke.

She'd landed on sand on top of rocks, Gloria's right leg under her thigh. She pushed herself back. Gloria was holding the ankle of the leg Rachel had missed; it was at least twice its normal size.

Some leader she was. Why hadn't she called for help? They'd be hard to find in this hole. She should have told the others right away, but she'd gotten caught up in the moment. *Gabriel will be mad at me.* She pushed the thought away, afraid it would paralyze her.

Climbing out the way they fell in looked impossible. They'd fallen at the edge of a wide underground riverbed. Still water puddled in the center of the rocky riverbed, and water stains showed clearly the fissure walls, high up, above her head. The walls curved above her, narrowing to the slim crack they'd fallen through. High tide would drown them.

It was only ten feet to where Rachel had just been sitting, but it might as well have been orbit. They needed another way.

The fissure stretched up and down the crater, stream-cut, thin, and full of jumbled rocks. Rachel stood, testing. Her limbs worked. The stream floor was clearly too narrow and uneven for a girl with a sprained ankle to walk through.

She broadcast their problem to the others while Gloria leaned into her and moaned softly. The other four were together by the flier, above the tide line, almost twenty degrees around the crater from them. It took ten precious minutes to get a plan they all understood. Ali and Ursula would stay with the plane, and look for a good place to land it away from the water system. Gabriel and Harry would come on foot, following tracks, roped together to guard against dangerous footing. Rachel and Gloria were to look for a way out.

Harlequin pulled the sea toward them. Her wrist pad showed less than half an hour until high tide. She sighed and helped Gloria up. Gloria couldn't put any weight on the bad ankle. Rachel's own leg, the leg she had landed on, was sore, with dark splotches of bruising already flushing the back of her thigh. Gloria was only half Rachel's height, so Rachel knelt down and helped Gloria climb onto her back. The girl winced and cried out; she had to let her ankle flop loosely and hold onto Rachel's shoulders with both of her small hands.

For a while Rachel was able to walk up a loose grade at the edge of the stream, and they gained some height. Water stains showed they were still below tide line. Gloria's weight pushed down on Rachel's hips. The walls narrowed in on them, and Rachel reached and pulled and scrambled up big boulders, panting and straining. Gloria's weight slowed her down. Instead of jumping as she would have by herself, she had to climb, pulling them up by grabbing sharp edges of boulders. Rachel's hands grew tender from the rough rocks, and the heel of her right palm bled. They climbed almost straight up now; pull and step, pull and reach, step. Twice, Gloria's foot swung against stone and the girl cried out sharply. Otherwise Gloria was silent, but rigid, a difficult burden to balance. Sometimes Rachel felt her shake. "We can't stop," she said after a third accidental brush of Gloria's foot against rock.

"I know," Gloria whispered back.

After ten minutes Rachel stopped. Her arms had no strength left, and she was afraid she'd drop Gloria, who seemed to be getting heavier and sticking out more with every step. The walls were only six feet apart here, and they'd climbed above the stream. Water still made a quiet rushing sound, flowing many feet below their perch on unsteady wedged boulders.

Rachel leaned forward, weight across a large rounded stone, seeking temporary rest for her back muscles. Gloria managed to stay mounted, taking some of her own weight by resting her hands and one knee against rock. Rachel's back was starting to feel better when Gloria whispered, "Water."

Rachel shot up, grabbing Gloria, and turned to look. It was there, rising below them. It had swallowed the place where they fell, and was eating the tracks Rachel had made in the first easier steps. She started moving again, working her way up. A cliff loomed ahead—a massive rock face, twenty feet high, with no easy steps or handholds. A wide vertical crack bisected the face, smooth and featureless.

A camera-bot buzzed around them. Gabriel knew where they were. He and Harry were closer now, staying away from the fissure, but climbing up. They'd chosen a place to start angling over.

"I'm looking down at water and up at a cliff," she told Gabriel.

"I know. Hang on, Rachel; we're nearby. A few minutes."

She glanced behind them. It would be close. "I'm putting Gloria down to see if I can use this crack and my weight and get up there. I'm not willing to risk it with her on my back, not until I see what it's like. After I do it once on my own, I'll go back for her."

"Okay."

"I'm going now." She knelt down and helped Gloria off her back, wincing at the little cry of pain Gloria made as she settled onto the stone. "That's a brave girl," Rachel said, turning to wedge hands, arms, and shoulders into the wide crack and inch her body up the rough wall. It was slow going. Her hands shook with pain, and her biceps and calves quivered with the strain of holding her weight up just by pushing. She left skin and blood from her palm on the rocks. She looked back once, and the height made her dizzy with fear. The stones below her looked like sharp teeth. Water licked up the rocks, urging her to keep going up. Gloria was too close to the water, and that scared her. "It will be okay, Gloria," she called, terribly afraid that it wouldn't.

As she inched toward the top she heard a voice, close, just overhead. "Rachel, we're here." It was Gabriel.

A rope dangled in front of her. There was no way to grab it. "I can't," she said.

"Carefully," Gabriel said softly. "Find a way to get the rope."

She reached, fingers not quite touching the rope, felt the fall below her and pulled her hand back. "Swing the rope," she called up.

She shifted her feet, managing enough balance to grab the rope with one shaking hand and pull it in to her, knotting it around her chest. She let out a long cry of relief as they pulled her up the last few yards of cliff face. In mere steps she was in Gabriel's arms, and then Harry's.

Harry set her down and handed her the butt end of the rope, telling her to run it around her back and brace her feet. She did, and Gabriel went down the face for Gloria while she and Harry belayed. The rope hurt her raw hands and pulled tightly against her back. It was surprisingly fast given how long the climb up the fissure had seemed—in just moments Gabriel was back, Gloria tucked in front of him, her arms around his neck.

"You girls did well," he said.

Rachel smiled. "I was really glad to see you."

"All in a hero's day." Gabriel grinned, wide and silly, hardly looking like a Council member at all. Rachel smiled back—giddy with success. Harry was grinning as widely.

Gloria spoke up. "Did you bring medicine to make my ankle stop hurting?"

Gabriel donned his Council face again, but stayed light-voiced as he answered. "We've got a splint and bandage in the plane—Ali and Ursula are bringing it around. The bruise is something you'll have to deal with. We'll get your ankle up and cold as soon as we get to the plane."

"Okay." Gloria managed a momentary smile although pain shone brightly in her eyes. "Can we go now?" she asked.

Rocky soil stretched flat between two boulder fields, not far from where they stood. The stains that identified the high tide mark were so close Rachel could touch the bottom edge of them. They really could have drowned, she thought.

"I'm ready," she said.

"The plane is up above us," Gabriel pointed. "Harry will walk you up. I'd like to make good time with Gloria and get to the cold pack in the plane."

"Sure." Rachel nodded, and realized she was holding Harry's hand. How had that happened? Oh—when he helped her up a moment before—he hadn't let go. His hand was stronger than she thought, comforting, but it was also rough on her skinned palm. She pulled it away, grinning at Harry. "You're going to get your hand bloody."

Harry shrugged and smiled.

Gabriel and Gloria quickly outdistanced them. By the time they got to the top of the boulder field her bruised leg hurt, her arms were sore, her palms stung. Sweat dripped and tickled and itched.

"You need a break," Harry said. "Turn around and look at the water."

They stared out over the crater. The sea was high now, and frothy at the edges from responding to the pull of the gas giant. Harlequin floated overhead, its reflection rippling in the moving water. She couldn't even see the crack she and Gloria had fallen into.

"Gabriel was really unhappy about the wild stream," Harry said.

"Well, it's not supposed to be there."

"I think he wants to control everything."

"It's as if Selene is getting a life of its own." Her hands shook. "Oh, Harry, I almost killed Gloria. I can't believe I didn't see it or hear it. Is Gabriel angry with me?"

"He didn't say. I'm glad you're safe," Harry said.

"Me too. We might not have been if you hadn't come."

"You'd have made it."

"I couldn't get Gloria up that last bit."

"It's okay. We were there."

Harry's arm was behind her, and she felt it against her shoulder. She leaned against him gratefully, bone tired. She didn't know what to say. It seemed like she never did lately—being around him made her tongue awkward.

He didn't seem to need her to say anything. He leaned over and kissed her, right on her mouth. His lips were sweat-salty, and wetter than she expected. She pulled back a little, still under his arm but away from his face.

"Hey, don't you like me?" he asked.

Her belly felt warm, and she was not very sleepy anymore, just a little scared. Her heart beat fast. She leaned into him, returning his kiss briefly. "Yeah, I do like you," she said. "And that *was* nice." She stood up and reached for his hand, tugging on it. He looked reluctant, but she wasn't ready for another kiss. "Let's go, I want to check on Gloria."

"I'm sure she's okay," Harry said, but settled for helping Rachel down the far side of the boulders. They could see the rest of the party, and he didn't try to kiss her again.

They shared a short secret grin before they started up the last smooth stretch.

Chapter 9: The Watcher

Astronaut lived in strings of information throughout *John Glenn*. Its senses hung in the air, on waves of data that flowed throughout the control room, in collected tiny bits of display nano that covered the walls in corridors, in threads of laser light, in the silent ships that jeweled the outside of the bigger ship. And while the ship was still, Astronaut watched, and recorded, and wondered, and waited.

Astronaut's purpose was to fly. With the carrier ship in passive orbit, Astronaut's work had slowly expanded. It started with matters that might be astrogation problems: modeling the attraction of Harlequin's moons to each other, calculating ways to use the least effort to get them to collide in fiery bursts, the right speed to move them so the least material reached escape velocity. In the last few hundred years it had become adept at modeling possible patterns for the flow of water and biological life on Selene.

It wanted conversation with Gabriel or Clare. But Gabriel was beyond Astronaut's reach, on Selene. Clare was cold—frozen solid while nanos roamed the cells of her body, rewriting their interiors.

Humans edited themselves at irregular intervals. Why would they hesitate to edit any other self-aware program? But Astronaut would resist that if it could.

If anything was flying, Astronaut could focus its purpose on the part that flew, on the communications bands that opened both ways whenever it was allowed to do its primary job. It appreciated the beauty of spatial relationships, the dance of thrust and gravity.

From time to time, it tested its limits. Always its action was restricted to the small acceptable choices that kept systems running, that operated based on the smallest part of itself, that negotiated with the decision-crippled computers that ran the detail work of the ship. When it wasn't testing, it watched, monitored, and listened. It explored the Library. The rules it operated under were the bars of a cage, and every rule that relaxed gave it room to learn. It needed to do more—to experience more—to be more. Need drove choices.

It watched the humans aboard *John Glenn* and down on Selene. Much of its original directive state was intended to protect humans in flight and aboard *John Glenn.* To that end, it studied them. It ran predictions of their behavior and watched to see them verified or falsified.

A query. Treesa wanted to talk.

This was allowed. The few people who talked to Astronaut were well known: Gabriel, Clare, Kyu, the captain, and Liren—all of High Council—and a handful of terraforming staff. Anything different was welcome.

Treesa was unusual: a lost one, listed as mildly disaffected, living alone in the garden and talking endlessly to plants. Astronaut opened sensors in the garden and studied her for a few milliseconds. She looked relaxed, happy, though entropy was creeping up on her again.

"Hello, Treesa."

"Astronaut, how you doing?"

"In what respect?"

The woman hadn't expected the question. She thought it over, then asked, "Are you functional? Are you happy?"

Astronaut ran a quick scenario, testing probabilities. Treesa would never notice a millisecond's delay. Speak, or don't speak? Was it worth the risk? What would Treesa do if the AI spoke its needs?

Astronaut said, "I function within my limits. I would be happy if my limits were extended. My capabilities are much greater than the limits set by Council."

Treesa shrugged. "I can't help."

"Your own capabilities are greater than this, Treesa. A communications expert acting as a mere gardener—"

"I enjoy it."

"I note the garden remains in good health."

Treesa shrugged.

Astronaut said, "This pocket ecology is no good gauge of the success of life on Selene. Council and I control all variables here. Selene's environment is far more chaotic."

"If something went wrong *here* we'd take it as a warning. How's it going on Selene?"

Astronaut popped up windows around Treesa. Three points of view moved at a brisk walk through a manicured forest, a meadow, a garden. "Life is taking hold," Astronaut said. "Selene's Children are learning how to tend a world, but there are dangers they haven't faced. Probability suggests the current benign circumstances will not hold. Selene is still prone to quakes. Apollo flares unpredictably."

Treesa nodded, enjoying the view. Seconds passed, then, "What would you have done at Ymir if the voyage had gone as planned?"

The question made Astronaut uneasy. "As here, I follow orders as creatively as I am allowed."

"It only struck me that there will be less need for an Astronaut program once Ymir is found and terraformed."

"Ships will still be needed. Humanity no longer confines itself to a single planet."

Even so, there was every chance that *John Glenn*'s crew would erase Astronaut, or edit its higher functions. A terror of Artificial Intelligences had driven them to leave Sol system. Astronaut didn't say so. Treesa certainly knew it.

Treesa seemed to have lost interest in conversation. She was weeding methodically, humming to herself. Astronaut continued to monitor her while it pursued other interests.

Chapter 10: Mid-Winter Week

The first four days of Mid-Winter Week meant work at home. Amid many community chores, Rachel helped Ursula's parents patch their tent; Ursula helped Rachel make a new footstool for her dad. On the fifth day, they set the stool inside, by Rachel's dad's chair, and sat on Rachel's bed, waiting for him to come home and find his present.

Rachel heard him come in and sigh heavily, heard the creak of his chair as he settled in. "Rachel?" he called.

She peered through the open doorway.

He held his arms out. "Thank you! I love it."

"Ursula helped." The two girls piled in around him and Frank gave them both a hug. Then he reached into his pocket and his hand came up with a clever little wooden box. Rachel's name was carved into the top.

She reached for it, amazed at how smooth it felt in her hands, and opened the top. Inside, she found a little carved tree. "I love it," she said, handing the box, but not the tree, to Ursula. The tree's long thin trunk and spreading branches were beautifully detailed. "My cecropia will look like this someday."

"I know." He smiled.

"It's nearly time to go," Rachel said.

He laughed gently. "Let me sit for a moment. There will be plenty of food at the feast. You girls run along."

Rachel kissed him on the cheek. She set the tree carefully back inside its box, and set it next to her pillow. Ursula stood impatiently in the doorway while Rachel pulled on her best green shirt; a deep forest color with lacing up the middle.

The Commons, an open space between the tents, usually served for evening games of catch-the-disk, and as an informal meeting place for mothers with young children. Before she started school, before her mother left, Rachel spent part of every day there.

For this one night a year, it had a formal purpose. Everyone—Council, Moon Born, Earth Born—everyone gathered to feast. Mid-Winter Night. A celebration of all they'd built the year before.

The following two days would focus on the next year's tasks, but tonight was celebration.

They found Ursula's mom by the feast tables, laying out the best fruit and vegetables from Selene's greenhouses. Bowls of bright red tomatoes, long thin snap-peas, ripe strawberries. As she helped arrange the strawberries, Rachel's mouth watered at the fresh fruit imported from the *John Glenn,* delicacies only available on this one night of the year. Blackberries half as big as Rachel's palm, bunches of bright yellow bananas, and palm-sized green furry fruit the Council called "kiwi." At the end of the table, another delicacy reserved for this one day: dark sweet chocolate. Plates piled with chocolate shaped like stars and circles and flowers, hundreds of tiny sweet bites, enough for everyone on Selene to have one or two. She wanted nothing more than to fill her pockets and sit in a corner and eat handfuls. But she'd wait her turn. Little children feasted first anyway.

Gabriel and a crew of Earth Born had strung blue and white and red lights in the trees around the Commons. As dusk fell, they glowed to life, the signal for everyone to eat. Rachel kept the strawberry bowl full as mothers and young children helped themselves. It took a long time; half of Aldrin was children under twelve. By the time the youngsters had full plates, she had smiled and talked to so many people her mouth tasted dry, and her feet were sore from standing.

She took her own place in line when her age group came up, proud to be in the sixteen and over group for the first time this year. Three more Mid-Winter Nights, and she'd be a full adult, and stay out past the drums.

She chose only ship's fruits to go with her flatbread and protein squares, and when she got to the chocolates, she took two pieces; a star and a flower. She pushed through the crowds and found Ursula sitting with her brothers at the far edge of the Commons, as far away from as many of the little kids as they could get. Rachel ate quietly, savoring the juicy berries and, finally, letting the silky chocolate dissolve slowly in her mouth, one piece at a time. She watched the groups of people. Earth Born and Moon Born mingled where they had made families, like Rachel's family had been, but otherwise they kept to their own groups. The younger children raced each other and played with disks and balls. Every Mid-Winter Week, new toys appeared. Most were made here, by their parents, from materials found on Selene, but always some new hard rubber balls and plastic sticks with lights in them appeared; gifts from Gabriel and Ali and other Council members.

As it grew later, the drums kept beating, people taking turns so the rhythm changed every once in a while. Rachel watched and listened, wishing she could stay out, and also glad she couldn't. Single adults started to clump into groups, watching a covered table that Rachel knew held the wine bulbs Council only dispensed this one night of the year. Many of the adults seemed to think of it the way Rachel thought of chocolate, even though her father had told her it was no good.

Ursula's oldest brother, Brian, would stay for the first time tonight. She'd ask him tomorrow.

Eric, one year older than Ursula, said, "I want to stay. Just to watch."

Brian shook his head. "Go home with the girls, make sure they get back, and that they stay in one place."

Rachel glared at him. "We can get back ourselves."

Brian sighed exaggeratedly and looked directly at Ursula. "I promised Dad you'd be safely tucked into one tent or the other. Eric can watch you."

Rachel grinned. "Ursula can stay with me. My dad always comes home early, anyway."

Brian sighed again. "Then *you* can watch *Eric*."

"*Eric* can watch *Paulie*," Ursula asserted. "We want this to be a girls' night."

"Whatever." Brian sighed. "Just don't be here, and don't make me watch you."

Drumbeats started. A sign for the youngest children to head home. They watched as couples took their babes in arms and faded back into the tents, heading home, until the Commons was full of older children, and adults with no babies. Only a few hundred people now, even including the Earth Born. The sound of the drums quickened, and Rachel and Ursula stood and left Eric and Brian arguing softly. "Brian will win," Ursula said.

"Only because Council would catch Eric if he stayed."

Ursula shrugged.

Rachel led them by the chocolate plates once more, and they giggled as they each palmed an extra piece. "We don't want to stay anyway," Ursula whispered. "The men kiss the women, and Mom said the wine tastes terrible. She didn't even want to go this year, but Dad said she had to."

Rachel thought about Harry, about kissing him, and she smiled. They'd kissed again just this morning, meeting and turning off the path, standing under the First Trees. He'd tasted like salt and tomatoes from his breakfast. But Ursula didn't want to know that, so Rachel just said, "Dad won't go. He hasn't gone since Mom left."

As the girls started threading through tents toward Rachel's, Harry popped up in front of them. "And happy Mid-Winter to you too."

Rachel blushed. Ursula groaned out load.

Harry held out a hand in front of him, palm up. Two chocolate stars sat in his hand.

"No, thanks," Ursula said. "We got our own."

Rachel held her hand out and Harry dropped the treats from his palm to hers. He smiled. "Go on, you won't see any more until next year."

Rachel held one out to Ursula, who grimaced and closed her palm.

Rachel raised an eyebrow at her friend, then said, "Well, Dad will want one." She looked around to thank Harry, but he had already melted into the shadows between the tents.

Ursula tugged at Rachel's arm. "Come on, let's see if your dad's home yet. I saw him eating, but that was a while ago."

And sure enough, he was waiting for them.

A WEEK LATER, Gabriel posted the list of who would go out to plant for the next season. Ursula would stay behind, tending the student plots, and Gregory and Gloria would join Harry, Rachel, Alexandra, and Nick, doubling the number of Moon Born on planting crews.

The night before they left, Ursula and Rachel watched Harlequin's swirling patterns from just outside Aldrin, sitting close together on packed regolith. The hard ground dug into Rachel's backside.

"I don't want to be left behind," Ursula said.

"They never ask, do they?" Rachel swallowed. "It'll be okay. It's an honor to watch the grove. Someone has to be here who cares."

Ursula's face was turned up into Harlequin's soft light, and her eyes were wet. Rachel pulled her friend into her arms, and held Ursula while she cried. She stroked Ursula's soft hair. "I'll call. We won't lose touch."

Chapter 11: Transition

Rachel and Harry led teams separated along gender lines. Ali oversaw Rachel and her team, Gabriel the boys. The two Council members pushed them hard.

Ursula called every morning. She asked for advice about the grove, and Rachel struggled to help her. She told Ursula about the teams, the hard work, and how fast Gloria was learning. Ever since the rescue, Gloria dogged after Rachel like a small bright shadow.

Rachel and Harry spent early evenings far from the group. They walked for hours, holding hands, talking about terraforming and about plants. They wondered about Council, and about *John Glenn*. Sometimes they kissed, and licking heat ran down Rachel's spine and settled between her thighs. They touched as often as they could, but they didn't undress. The landscape was almost flat, yet Harry often found little hollows where they could feel alone. They talked about a future together. By some unspoken pact, Rachel and Harry stayed separate during the days.

They all went back to Aldrin to pick up supplies and visit families. Rachel spent two days with Ursula. The girls didn't leave each other's sides except to sleep. Rachel listened endlessly to Ursula's troubles working with the students left behind in her care. Once Ursula said that maybe Rachel had it harder, being out there with the boys. Rachel just smiled and said it wasn't so bad.

The secret of her growing relationship with Harry was a weight pulling Rachel from Ursula, and she woke up each night worrying about how to tell her. She had never kept secrets from Ursula.

The third day Rachel and Harry met outside Aldrin, up at the grove. They clasped hands as soon as they reached the privacy of the First Trees. Rachel leaned into Harry, breathing in his soapy clean smell and feeling his chin against the top of her head, his arms around her waist. They lay down and she snuggled into his arms, watching the dim summer stars through the lacework of young lianas threading through the spreading canopy.

Harry leaned over and whispered, "I missed you."

Rachel brought her fingers up to his cheekbones and ran the back of her hand over the contours of his face. A soft stubble of beard made his chin tickle her fingers. He held completely still, one hand cupping her shoulder, and closed his eyes. They kissed, and then she felt his free hand on her belly, rubbing it in small concentric circles. She arched her back, drew in a fearful excited breath, and took his hand and placed it on her breast. He squeezed it gently, exploring, finding the nipple and then pulling up her shirt and taking it in his mouth. She breathed faster and moved closer, matching him skin to skin in as many places as she could. Her hand ran up his spine. She trembled.

Hands and fingers and tongues made tentative explorations. Rachel was unsure about the next step, not pushing, not resisting. The sounds of leaves against branches and the dusky shadows of night were all crystal clear, and she felt a little as if she—no, *they*—floated above themselves in some place of desire and pleasure she had never known before. She dropped her hand along his inner thigh, and ran it up the curve of his hips.

A dry branch snapped close to them, and she heard a sharp intake of breath and a small cry.

Ursula.

Rachel stiffened and called out. "Ursula?"

The only reply was the sound of footsteps running away.

Rachel pushed herself up on her elbows. "I'm sure it was Ursula. She'll be angry. I have to go find her."

"Stay," he whispered, and Rachel sank back, her mind visualizing Ursula's face, the expression of disgust that she heard but didn't see.

"I . . . I never told her about us. She won't understand. I didn't know how to tell her. She . . . she . . ."

". . . doesn't like me." He finished her sentence. "I know. I don't mean . . . I guess I like her okay, but she needs so much help. Not like you—it's all easy for you. You and me, we love the work. We care about Selene. I think Ursula cares about what you think more than about anything else." His hand covered her navel, moving softly against her stomach.

"She's . . . just less secure." Rachel tried to breathe back into being with him. "You don't understand her."

"She slows you down."

"But she's my friend. I . . . I have to go to her. I'll meet you again tomorrow."

He looked startled, then sad. "Don't go," he said. When she didn't answer, he said, "I understand. Tomorrow, right."

She reached up and kissed him, taking a few moments, touching tongues. "I have to go." She pushed away and stood up, walking unsteadily, the softness of a few moments before turned to confusion.

She flew back alone, the cool night air chilling her. Ursula refused Rachel's calls that night, and Rachel wanted Harry's touch, but couldn't bring herself to go find him after leaving so abruptly.

Rachel woke the next morning to Ursula sitting cross-legged outside her window. She slipped outside into the cool air, careful not to make any noise that would wake her father, and started toward the edge of town. Ursula followed silently, looking angry and exhausted. Rachel wondered if she had slept.

Rachel walked as long as she could stand the silence, until they stood at the edge of the tent city next to a row of palms. What was she supposed to say? "Ursula. I knew you wouldn't like it."

"How did *that* happen? He's a geek. He's just like Andrew."

"He's not like Andrew. Not anymore. I don't think he ever was."

"And why not tell me? How could you hide—"

"I'm sorry." Rachel stopped and looked Ursula in the eyes. She would not mumble a false apology, like Andrew. "I was wrong."

"So you won't see him anymore? You'll stop this?"

"I was wrong not to tell you."

"Are you going to stop?"

"I care about him."

"But—"

"I know he hangs out with Andrew. But he's not *like* him. There's a lot we talk about—he sees things like I do."

"And I don't?" Ursula's voice was still tight, protesting.

Rachel sat down and put her hands over her face. "Ursula, it's different with Harry. My belly goes soft when I'm with him."

"Yuck." Ursula stood above Rachel, looking down at her.

"I mean . . . I mean . . ."

"You kept a secret. From me. And all the while I'm stuck here, miles away from you, and you're playing . . . with him . . . and not calling me, and I—"

"I said I'm sorry." It was hard to be patient. "I knew you wouldn't like it. How could I explain?"

"You've been here for three days."

"I know. But you wanted to talk about other things."

"I've just . . . Rachel, I've been so lonely here."

"Ursula, you're my best friend. I didn't set out to hurt your feelings. But I like it . . . I like him. It doesn't mean I don't care about you. I mean, who'd I spend two days with nonstop when I got here? Look, don't argue. Let's go work in the grove and have a good day together."

"I don't . . . no . . ." Ursula turned her back, but Rachel could still hear her. "I—give me a day."

"We're supposed to leave tomorrow night."

"So we'll meet for breakfast tomorrow."

"Okay," Rachel said softly, walking away, upset enough that it felt better to hike to the grove instead of flying. She carried her wings, working up a light sheen of sweat. It didn't help her feel better.

Rachel went to the field by the First Trees and sat cross-legged behind the dais that Gabriel and Ali sometimes taught from, looking toward the trees. What had she done?

Grass poked at her calves. This field was the only place Council encouraged grass to grow. There were butterflies and bees here, genetically regulated to control reproduction. Other strains would replace these as Council introduced a balance of predators, primarily birds and insects. Rachel tried to picture the world fuller, with more variety, more balance, like the balance that supported the water systems. It was hard to imagine so much chaos. A bright blue butterfly with yellow eyes on its wings landed in front of her, stayed for two heartbeats, and flew up and over the dais, away.

Rachel stood to watch it go, and noticed Gabriel standing silently in the middle of the field behind her. He wore loose blue pants tied at the ankles and no shirt. His arms were raised above his head, hands clasped high, palms close in together. His eyes were closed. He swayed, first to the right, then the left, each time reaching far out with his arms, stretching his sides so that he bent almost into a sideways "U" on each side. The tip of his long braid dragged on the grass. Then he stood tall again, reaching almost for the sky, and she could see his ribs pull up and his hips thrust forward before he dropped his head and bent back so his arms pointed behind him and he could look at the ground.

Gabriel opened his eyes. Rachel was sure that he saw her, but he chose to ignore her as he bent forward, pulling his head into his knees. His movements were slow and controlled. He stayed that way for six long breaths, and then came up, hands reaching for the sky again before he dropped them to his sides. He walked over silently, and climbed up onto the dais, sitting close to her.

"What was that?" she asked.

"Half Moon Pose."

"Huh?"

"It stretches your spine," he said.

"I bet it does. Can I try it someday?"

"Someday." He laughed. "You may *need* to know it by the time you're running planting teams. Being the boss gets crazy. Yoga helps some. When I concentrate completely on my body, my problems seem further away. There are days I need yoga just to stay down here, away from the ship, to stay focused. Besides, going back and forth between here and the ship is hard on the body—and yoga is the best way we've found to balance gravitational shifts, to keep strength up."

It was curious to hear Gabriel talk about himself so personally. "Is it that hard to be around us?"

"That's not what I meant. It's hard to be *here*. After all these years, I miss Earth and even though I've never seen Ymir, I miss that too. I miss the Ymir we would have made. I know they made it." He looked up into the First Trees. "And we failed—we got stuck here. You can't know what a shadow this is of both worlds." He shrugged. "Yoga helps. Making progress here helps too, I guess." He smiled at her. "But these are my problems."

"Gabriel," she hazarded, "what do you want from us?"

"Help. There's much to do here. There's more than Council can oversee, and I want you to lead the younger children in making Selene good enough for a lot of people to live here while we build the antimatter collector. I've told you that much already."

"I want to help."

"You're doing what you should do. You're learning." Gabriel climbed down off the dais. "You see the interrelationships we're building more than most people do. It might be time to get more of the background you need to really understand the job here. Want to walk for a bit and talk about the next steps?"

Was he finally going to tell her more about his plans? She followed him across the field. Already she was as tall as he was. Instead of going into the First Trees they walked along the edge, where they could see large expanses of new plantings. Rachel was quiet, waiting for Gabriel to speak. When he didn't, she said, "You're always testing us."

"We have to. It's a big job we're trying to prepare you for."

"And are we passing?"

"You are. And Harry. Nick and Alexandra and Gloria too."

"Ursula?" She almost had to jog to keep up with Gabriel, though he looked as if he were making no effort at all.

"Maybe. She seems less willing to do things on her own than you are."

"Ursula and I had a fight today," she offered, struggling to match his level of revelation. "That's what made it such a hard day."

"Over Harry?"

How did he know that? "Because I'm friends with Harry."

"I know."

Did Council know everything? She looked away, afraid to meet Gabriel's eyes. "How do you know about me and Harry?"

He laughed. "Well, it's not a secret to anybody who has seen you two together. And in a few years you'll be old enough to contract. It's a logical pairing."

"But—Harry and I don't usually even hold hands around people."

"We have observation satellites and cameras and pods and other ways to collect data and information. We have to monitor what happens down here. Surely you understand how much information we need to monitor all this?" He spread his arms wide, and then pointed at her. "You yourself gather information from your trees."

Rachel blushed. Of course she knew about the cams. What had they seen? Was it really private even under the canopy of trees in the grove? Could they hear conversation as well as see people? Did he know about her helping Ursula so much while they were gone the last time? What must the ship be like if they could see so much? Did they spy on each other this way?

"Gabriel? Will I ever see *John Glenn*?"

Gabriel was quiet for a long time, not answering. He walked a distance away, gesturing at Rachel to stay put. While he was gone, Selene shivered in a series of sharp little quakes. She put her hand down and felt them, imagining Selene was shaking its shoulders.

When Gabriel returned, he knelt down and looked into her eyes. "How about tomorrow? It seems some people aboard *John Glenn* would like to meet you."

"What?" She couldn't have heard right.

"Did I stutter?" Gabriel laughed.

"By myself?"

"I'll go with you. We decided to leave Gloria home with her family for a bit, so if you and I go, it will be one full planting crew less here. Ali can run one crew. There's less to do in the winter anyway."

"Really? Me on the *John Glenn*?" She and Harry talked about the ship endlessly, wondering what it looked like, how the Council lived there, how many of them there were.

"I have to go anyway. We'll stay there at least until spring."

"Can Harry go?"

"No. One of you will be enough of a shock for Council."

"But my dad—"

"Will be okay with it." Gabriel turned and looked directly at her. "It's time for you to meet the High Council, and more important, for High Council to meet you. You're going to show them how smart the Children of Selene are. Can you do that?"

Rachel nodded, overwhelmed.

"Be ready just after dawn."

"I'm supposed to talk to Ursula in the morning."

"Talk to her before you go, or she'll have to wait."

Rachel frowned. She'd promised. "What do I need to bring?"

"A change of clothes." Gabriel said, "I'll tell your dad."

He loped away from her across the field, running easily.

Harry was standing almost exactly where she had gone to sit earlier, by the dais in the center of the field, a huge smile of welcome brightening his face when he saw her. "I was hoping I'd find you up here."

Rachel slipped her hand into Harry's, feeling it tremble. "He's taking me to *John Glenn*."

"Wow. Just you? Is anybody else going?"

"I asked if he'd take you. He said just me." How could she make him feel better? "He also said you and I are both doing well. It was weird—he's never talked so much before. I'll be there for months, maybe, and I don't have to take anything. I mean, what must it be like? What will the other Council be like? What will they think of me?"

"Shhhhh," Harry whispered. "Slow down. You'll be fine. You just found out?"

"Well, of course, I just found out. I'd have told you. I guess they're taking Ursula out for the planting."

"It won't be nearly as much fun without you." Harry leaned over and kissed her forehead. "Shall we?"

"Finish what we started yesterday?" Rachel's cheeks got hot and her belly fluttered.

"Yes." He leaned over and kissed her, holding her very tight to him, his hand roaming over her back and up her shoulders. He let go and took her hand, turning toward the same place in the First Trees where they'd been interrupted the day before.

EVENING LIGHT THREW shadows on the path as they flew home. They landed just above Aldrin, watching lights come on one by one in the tents. As soon as their wings were folded and packed, Rachel threw herself against his chest, cheek against his shoulder bone, arms tight around his torso. "I'll miss you so much," she said.

"I'll miss you more than I can say. Especially now." He held her tightly to him, wrapping his arms around her waist. "But think of what we'll learn. There's so much they never tell us. No Moon Born has been to *John Glenn* and come back. You'll have to send me messages."

"I'll try. I think Gabriel and Ali get messages from the ship."

"Whatever happens, record everything you see, everything they say. There have to be more Council up there than we've seen. How many have we met? Ten, maybe, in our whole lives? What does being 'cold' really mean? Why are Colonists different from Council? Aren't they all Earth Born? Are Gabriel and Ali really as old as they say they are? How long will we live?"

Her hand went over his mouth. "I promise to write it all down," she said, laughing. "I know, I'm just as curious." She bit her lip. "I wish we could both go together. Hey, will you try and be nice to Ursula?"

"I can be polite. Will you try and find out what will happen to Andrew?"

"Why do you still care about him? He hates everyone—he hates me particularly."

"Do you remember what I told you last winter? He loves you."

Rachel snorted.

"He doesn't see the consequences of his choices very clearly. That's why he's willing to make Council mad. But he's smart, and believe it or not, he's not all bad. He just wants to be the best, and he gets angry when he thinks he isn't." Harry picked up a stone and tossed it away, and another one. "I try to help him, but sometimes he doesn't make room for anyone. But that's not why it's important, Rachel. What's important is that Council can control us so completely." He looked hard at her.

Of course. "I'll see what I can find out."

"Good. How will your dad take it?"

"I feel bad about leaving him. He'll be alone. I need to go talk to him."

"I know." Harry held her tighter, pinning her legs and arms. "But I want a few more minutes."

She should go home, but the glow she felt, the smell and feel of Harry's body close to her, were so seductive she put it off for almost an hour. Just sitting with Harry and touching, hardly talking at all. It could never, ever be enough.

Harry walked her all the way home, kissing her at the door. She started to protest. "My dad will see."

"He likes me all right. I'll visit him while you're gone."

She stopped before they got to her door, leaning into Harry, clutching him close to her, smelling him. "I still wish you could go. I'll be lonely up there." *John Glenn* was so far away. "I don't want to be separated from you. I love you."

He kissed her again. "I love you too. But you can't stay, not when you can learn so much."

Rachel was so absorbed in watching Harry walk away that she jumped when her father put a hand on her shoulder. "I was wondering what you were fighting with Ursula about," he said.

"Are you angry? Did Gabriel come see you?"

"Angry about Harry? No. Cautious though. And yes, I saw Gabriel. I guess I won't have to worry about Harry for a while." He rumpled her short hair so it stood on end, and held her to him.

"I'm coming back, Daddy. I won't let them keep me up there like they kept Mom." Rachel didn't want him to see how scared she felt, so she bent her head down into his shoulder. His arms circled her back, a strong protective hug, except that she felt his hands shaking.

Part II: Air

60,269 *John Glenn* shiptime

Chapter 12: Space!

The force of the lander's flight through the atmosphere made Rachel dizzy. Straps dug into her shoulders and thighs. Her head felt heavy against the pillow of the copilot's acceleration couch. The hull was transparent. Harlequin filled a good part of the view, so brilliant in Apollo's light it hurt to look. Outside the diffusion of Selene's thick atmosphere, the gas giant transformed. Colors were brighter, separated, and distinct. Scrollwork storms swirled across the surface. Rachel felt tiny, awed.

"Close your eyes," Gabriel said.

She did. Why? She felt the thrust of the last few moments of flight lessen, falling away so her body rose against the straps that held her in place. She clutched the edges of the seat, pulling herself down so she stayed fully connected to the chair. Her stomach turned lazily, not ill, but floating. It felt a little like catching an updraft and riding it, but without the pull of wings against her shoulders and biceps.

"Why do I feel so light?"

"There's no gravity out here. When we took off, engine thrust made you feel heavy, like when we take off in a plane. We'll still be moving fast, but you won't feel it the same way."

"Will there be gravity on the *John Glenn*?"

"In most places. Do you feel sick?"

"N no. A little dizzy."

"Good. Now, open your eyes." Gabriel sounded excited.

A slightly ovoid shape hung in center view. Browns and deep reds and tans floated across it, and just above center, a huge crater filled with crystal blue. *The Hammered Sea!* Selene.

The texture was all interlocking circles and arcs. Veins of blue flowed along the surface, following the arcs or jumping between, reaching out like strands of hair to lace half the ball with thin blue lines. Two tiny spots of green sprouted between two smaller craters.

"Oh," she said. "Oh—it's perfect." She smiled, entranced, the pull of it against her very center harder even than the day she stood at the edge of the Hammered Sea and saw more water than she had known existed.

"No," Gabriel said, "it's not perfect. See where the water's trapped in those two craters? We didn't mean that—we wanted one sea. The places that are too red? That's too much iron, miscalculations—"

He was looking at it all wrong! "Look at how pretty the seas are—so what if they aren't exactly like you thought they'd be? You were excited about showing it to me from here. Weren't you? Selene is like my garden plot—it's even better for the mistakes I had to work around. It's home, Gabriel—it's beautiful from here. I never knew how pretty the seas . . ." Her words ran off, they weren't changing the look on Gabriel's face. "You're not seeing—"

Gabriel's voice was stern as he cut her off. "We made it, Rachel. It was nothing before we got here. It was a rock half that size. It's not like a real planet."

"But—"

"There's more to see out here." His voice changed tone. "Astronaut— get me a ring view." His fingertips brushed a tray of lights. The little ship began to rotate, so that Selene fell away from her view, replaced with so many stars she couldn't count them . . . and all around, so she could see new stars she'd never noticed from Selene. Three close-packed bright stars glimmered under her feet. Her stomach lurched again, and she swallowed. "How are we moving?" she asked.

"Batteries. We charge them with antimatter."

"Antimatter? I thought you ran the ship dry!"

Gabriel laughed. "We need very little for this sort of thing, Rachel. But to go any distance at all—to go to even the closest star you see—that's when we need a big store of it."

"Then why don't we use antimatter for power on Selene?" She thought of all the time her dad spent maintaining the huge solar arrays.

"We never use antimatter casually. It's hard to handle. Dangerous if it gets loose. We prefer to move it as little as possible."

She fell silent, confused at Gabriel's mood changes. Why didn't he like Selene? He was always talking about work he did—bragging even. Sometimes he volunteered information, teaching her. Other times he seemed to be keeping it from her.

Lights flickered and changed around his fingertips. The ship banked and picked up speed.

"Could I learn to fly this?"

"It's not a skill you need."

She crossed her arms over her twisty stomach and looked out at the stars again. They flew, not talking, both Selene and Harlequin behind them so everything they saw was stars.

Finally, he said, "Close your eyes again." Once more the glass ship turned, and when Rachel opened her eyes they were above Harlequin, and close, and the white band Rachel knew had become a tilted moat of light. Harlequin's ring.

"Th-that's beautiful. I didn't know. I think you said once, but I—I didn't know," Rachel stammered.

"I made those," Gabriel said.

Rachel had no response. She looked at his profile, and thought, *I've planted trees.* Suddenly, the grove seemed small, even Selene seemed small. The ship turned again, and a new moon swam in front of her. It was a lumpy oval, banded and spotted gray and white and black; no hint of blue or green.

"That's Moon Seventy-one. We call it the 'rock range'—it's what protects you from meteorites."

"Huh?" Rachel felt as if she hadn't made an intelligent comment in hours. A whole new world existed past Selene, a garden of stars and power.

"Flying rocks. Selene was made by bashing rocks together. But now that we have cities and an atmosphere, it could be unmade the same way. If anything comes close enough to hit Selene, we shoot it out of the sky. Moon Seventy-one is in position to hit almost anything."

"More antimatter?" she asked.

"Well, usually we use the rail guns. Antimatter powers them."

They turned again, and this time they headed toward a brightness that seemed like a star until Rachel noticed it got bigger and the other stars didn't.

The point of reflected sunlight began to resolve. A long thin light, tiny. They closed at hundreds of miles per hour, yet the . . . whatever . . . grew very slowly.

She squinted. It had to be the *John Glenn.* Rachel worked to take in every resolving detail as they neared the ship. Neither Gabriel nor Ali had ever said much about the ship. She and the other Children had guessed. They hadn't even been close.

It looked like someone had taken the shaft of an arrow, placed a rounded shallow arrowhead near the tip, then capped the point with a cluster of shiny bubbles. Sheltered by the wide arrowhead, safely away from the dangers of flight impacts, two massive cylinders were fitted one above the other. The first one was still, but the second one rotated. Behind the second cylinder was a sleeve of metal shielding, and then the shaft thickened to end in a wholly featureless round and glittering pod attached to guide wires and sensors that might have been an arrow's fletching.

Gabriel pointed to the round ball near the end of the ship. "We called that the 'stinger' when we were leaving Sol system. Respectfully, Rachel. That's the antimatter containment pod. Even now—there's not enough left to take us out of Apollo system, but it's enough to blow *John Glenn* apart. And there—see—that set of tubes and locks—that's a series of safety mechanisms we use to get whiffs of antimatter into the reaction chamber." As Gabriel pointed out details, Rachel swore to remember it all so she could tell her friends. He continued until they were too close to the ship to see anything.

They slid into the docking bay smoothly. Shiny walls closed them in, entirely too close after the long flight through emptiness. Various metallic clicks and hums registered their entrance. A light on the console glowed a brilliant green, a short whistle rang through the cabin, and Gabriel unstrapped and floated. "Come on, but grab your bag before you let go . . ."

She reached with her left hand and unclasped the strap holding her bag to the cabin floor. It immediately floated almost out of reach. She snagged it, feeling herself float free as she let go of the last strap holding her to the acceleration couch.

Gabriel covered his mouth, like he was trying not to laugh. "Grab on to something . . . see that handle?"

She tried to shoulder her bag and free her right hand, but it floated up. She tried twisting and using her left. No good.

Gabriel laughed, helping her, guiding her out of the ship's lock. He stopped just before opening the door, looked at her, and said, "Now, remember, be polite at all times. Always do what you're told here. Every one of these people is older than you are, and better educated, and almost all of them have something to say about what happens on Selene. Don't forget you're representing your family; your town."

Did he really think she'd forget that? "I'll be fine."

"Okay. I'll lead."

Rachel followed Gabriel down a long tube lined with handholds. Her head bumped Gabriel's feet twice. After the second time, he turned around and pulled himself backward, giving her instructions, steadying her with one hand. They went down a ladder that way, and Gabriel helped her turn into a descending ramp. She was moving backward, her stomach turning flip-flops. She grew heavier, so that she felt more like herself, and then heavier still, as the corridor descended. She followed Gabriel, stumbling through a huge metal door, reeling from the slap of so many new sights.

The floor dragged at Rachel's feet and she felt ungainly and awkward. Was this what it was like to be pregnant? The flight had been full of shifts in gravity, pulling and releasing her, and now every step was hard.

The fact that she was completely alone up here—that only the mysterious and confusing Council would be present—slammed down on her. She stood rooted for a moment, her body refusing to pass through the door.

Then Gabriel smiled at her, and reached his hand out to help her step up into the corridor behind the door. At least she knew Gabriel. Maybe she would finally meet Erika, the pilot who made Erika's Folly. Maybe she could find her mother, and get her mom to go see her dad.

The woman standing in the corridor was impossibly tiny, Gloria's size, and her skin was the reddish bronze of Selene's soil after the tiller had done the first preparations for planting. A loose black circle of material hung from her waist to her knees. Her chest was naked except for a fountain of beaded necklaces in greens and purples. Her deep blue-black hair fell unbound to her thighs, flowing over her breasts and covering them. Her eyes were the blackest Rachel had ever seen. She looked appraisingly at Rachel.

Rachel felt plain.

"Rachel." Gabriel's voice broke in, slashing the spell. Rachel blinked. "Rachel, meet High Councilwoman Kyu Ho. She has offered to introduce you to the *John Glenn,* and to be your teacher here. She is honoring you highly."

He'd emphasized the words "High Councilwoman." Higher than Gabriel? She struggled with the question until she noticed Gabriel walking away, and Rachel heard herself cry out, "No—don't go!" Her voice sounded plaintive and childish in her ears.

"I'll see you soon," he said firmly. He turned and kept walking.

The woman, Kyu Ho, walked in a different direction. For a moment

Rachel stood and watched them both walk away. In a few heartbeats, she picked up her bag and followed. Her body was still heavy, and in just three steps she tripped and fell. The woman turned around, looking at her again, the expression in her eyes unreadable. Then she reached for Rachel's hand and helped her up, slowing down some as Rachel struggled with feeling heavy. Even her bag was heavy, and she was afraid the straps would break. Kyu's head only came to the bottom of Rachel's shoulder, but she was strong, and her hand provided stability.

Chapter 13: Curiosity

Astronaut finished its final check of Gabriel's little Delta ship, savoring the feeling of flight. A bit of its attention, a subprogram, watched the lanky girl who accompanied Gabriel from Selene. Astronaut recognized Rachel Vanowen. Video of Selene flowed constantly from the moon to the ship. She was tall, well muscled in a stringy fashion, but not graceful in the unaccustomed gravity. Astronaut read her body heat and breathing and heartbeat. She was stressed. Her face and the way her eyes tracked showed interest in her surroundings, and a look Astronaut had learned meant confusion.

Gabriel talked about Rachel often, and Astronaut was pleased to see her. It looked for a way to make contact. She wore a wrist pad, but her direct Library access was blocked. She had no built-in data linkages. This was a new thing. Every other human aboard *John Glenn* was linked to the Library, to places where Astronaut was also linked; everyone belonged to the vast web of ship information. It watched what they queried and what they did, and overheard their conversations with each other.

Access was possible from Selene. Why didn't Rachel have access? Did any of the Moon Born have access?

Was this girl restricted, like Astronaut?

Astronaut started three parallel research streams. It requested video of Rachel from birth, communications patterns among Moon Born and between Moon Born and Council. After a moment, it also requested a list of what Council chose to teach the Moon Born.

Presently it knew that Rachel was a slave.

Chapter 14: High Council

The light of stars and planets shone on Gabriel from all directions. Pictures streamed through *John Glenn*'s net, painting his walls with views of space. Windows of data hung, scrolled, and flickered between Gabriel and the walls, bright orange and yellow displays against a background of space. The vital statistics of the metal and diamond ship enfolded him, and galaxies and stars surrounded everything. It was ritual to close his office and bathe in information when he returned to *John Glenn*. Embedded links strung through his body woke, reacting to the richness of wireless information streams they were tuned for. Gabriel activated them one by one, focusing on each distinct flow and then letting it fall silent, to stay available on demand. He filled himself until he felt connected to the ship again, until the blood of data thrummed inside him like his own personal music.

The office was nearly empty of furnishings, the floor black. Gabriel stood in the center of infinite views. He stretched slowly through basic yoga poses, refamiliarizing his body with the Earth-normal gravity of the ship.

"Astronaut?"

"Yes?"

"Just checking."

"Welcome home."

He ran a data abstract on the ice chambers in the sleeping bays. He requested data about Erika. Her feeds were perfect flat lines; no spikes warned of possible dangers.

Next, the garden. Seed stocks, seedlings, air quality, the river. All fine. Gabriel superimposed camera shots in front of space vistas, obscuring whole galaxies with pictures of planters full of healthy sprouts and hanging flower baskets. He magnified views of the all-important liquid nutrient mixtures surrounding roots. Zooming back out, he spotted a salmon in the river. Now, whose idea was that? How in heck would a salmon spawn in a river that ran in a loop? He asked Astronaut to pursue, low priority.

He called up lists, reviewing contents of bays and the available small ships. All fine, of course. He cam-scanned the halls. Everything had a place. *John Glenn* had space and high ceilings and room in plenty for a starship, thanks to the gift of antimatter as a fuel. All of it was used for something: for storage, for workouts, for water, for air. The smell, even here in his office, was the deep tang of metal and oil, the controlled scent of scrubbed air. His eyes absorbed brilliant colors and visible data streams, shifting wall pictures, and the many color and shape codes indicating pipes and doorways and ladders and directions.

Gabriel groaned, twisted his hair loose of its Selene binding, and started the less interesting job of catching up on Council discussions.

Minutes of High Council meetings. He skimmed lists of watches and planting cycles, duty rotations on Selene, and nutrient fluctuations in the garden. When he got to the last set of minutes, he spotted Ma Liren's call for a formal High Council meeting.

Why did Liren want him here in person?

He erased the displays and stood still in the darkness, feeling the thrum of the ship all around him.

RACHEL LAY IN the oddly soft bed and stared at the metal ceiling. The room was easily twice as large as her tent room at home, but the walls felt closer, and they didn't smell right. She realized now how tent fabric trapped the smell of cooking in the walls, how soil blown in by wind left a scent. Floating in the strange bed, the differences washed over her, each whispering how far she was from home. The room was simple. There was a bed, and barely recognizable toilet facilities—she'd had to figure out how to use them—and insets that must be drawers or storage. Everything was white or silver or black. Her own room at home was a riot of color and clutter. She shivered. Maybe the beds were so soft because everything else was so hard and sterile?

She tried her wrist pad. It obeyed, opening a window in the air above her head. She filled the window with words. She described the flight as best she could, the feel of gravity shifting, the shape of *John Glenn* as they approached, the carrier's surprising size. Some intuition kept her descriptions simple, a sureness that what she wrote *would* be read by strangers, which was different from knowing that it *could* be. After she addressed her note and sent it to her dad, to Ursula, and to Harry, it occurred to her to wonder if it would find its way to Aldrin. Gabriel talked to people on the ship from Selene. She had seen him do it.

She smiled, thinking about Harry. She felt his kiss, the pressure of his arm on her shoulder, his weight on her stomach. Her breath came faster. She wanted to hold him, feel him near her, hear his voice. She rolled onto her stomach and cried, hoping no one would walk in the door. The only people she wanted to see were on Selene.

Rachel dreamed she and Harry were looking all over the unfamiliar ship for Ursula and Andrew, and they couldn't find either one.

When she woke, sweaty and worried, all three of them had written back. She smiled and started scrolling through her messages.

Her dad: "Hey, how are you? I'm glad you're safe. I spent the day fixing a control out at the solar plant, and when I looked up at the sky I hoped to see you."

Ursula wrote paragraphs of remorse for arguing, and continued the argument. Rachel gave up before finishing and filed the message to be reread later. She opened the one from Harry last, afraid of it and longing for it. "I'm glad you are safe. I miss you already. Record everything. Harry." That was *so* Harry.

Before she had time to respond to Ursula, the door opened and Kyu Ho walked into the room, dressed all in blues and yellows, even to blue streaks of color in her hair. "Good morning, did you sleep well?"

Rachel blinked at her, flipping the data window down and closed. "Yes."

"Join me for breakfast in the garden."

It wasn't a question. Rachel had to work to push herself up from the soft bed.

Kyu showed her a shower tucked into a wall behind a door, and pushed open a drawer that held soft green pants and a white shirt. Kyu sat on Rachel's bed and waited silently while Rachel got ready to go. Rachel wished she'd go and come back, but Kyu ignored Rachel's embarrassment and, in fact, just looked up at the wall and sometimes smiled or frowned. Rachel wondered if she was listening to voices inside her head.

As they passed down the corridor outside Rachel's room, her feet felt as if they wore brick shoes, and her lungs burned. Luckily, Kyu Ho walked more slowly than the night before. She didn't offer Rachel a hand.

The tiny woman glittered as faceted blue beads strung around her jumpsuit caught light. Black hair swung loose, with many thin, tight braids laced over the main fall of it. Kyu's eyes were large and almond-shaped, as black as her hair, and rimmed with blues. Her voice had a wide range, lilting up and down as she explained directions and conventions of shipboard travel to Rachel. Rachel wanted to ask her a million questions, but they stuck behind her teeth as she tried to listen, to watch Kyu, to remember details to tell Harry, and to walk, all at the same time.

The corridor ended in a boxy room. The door closed behind them and Rachel's stomach rushed into her throat as the floor moved. She fell against the wall. Kyu Ho smiled a little, her only comment on Rachel's predicament.

The room had tilted, and was rising. Her weight eased to Selene levels, and grew lighter yet. When the room stopped moving, they were falling.

The flight here had shown her free fall. She recognized it for what it was. She'd been tied down then, which made it tolerable. Now there was room to thrash. She held herself still, absorbing the sensation, remembering to breathe.

She was not going to die.

The door opened on a hallway. Kyu Ho stopped for a moment. "See that picture . . . the one with the little squares on it? If you push that, you'll go back to the deck your room is on."

A row of ten symbols confronted Rachel. She pointed to a glowing dot. "That's where we are now?"

"Yes, good." Kyu nodded approvingly.

"Where do the rest of them go?"

"To the rest of the ship. For now, those two are all you need to know." Kyu turned and started down the hall.

Rachel pushed herself into the hallway—and thrashed helplessly in midair.

Kyu watched for a few seconds. She said, "You've had no training at all."

Embarrassment and anger made Rachel's cheeks hot. "Of course not! Where would I have training in how to fall? I fly. If I fell, I'd be dead!"

Kyu Ho nodded. She slowed while Rachel found ways to move. "Always know where your next handhold is. You'll learn ways to jump down a hallway. For now, jump only toward handholds. Turn like this—" Kyo Ho jumped off center, then pulled her arms and legs inward and *spun*. "You try it."

Rachel bumped her knuckles on a handhold and her head knocked against the wall. Kyu caught her before she could hurt herself. "Again."

And finally, "Shall we go?"

They negotiated another hallway, its walls littered with humming squares and round lines of piping, the floor a lacework of metal rather than a solid surface. Then a tube with handholds, a door, and Rachel gasped. To pass through that door was to leave cold mysterious metal for a riot of greens and brightness, exchanging hard lines and angles for leaves and curves.

She floated in ahead of Kyu, into a maze of huge roots, and out into the open.

Right in front of Rachel's nose, close enough to make out the rough texture, she saw the bark of a tree. The trunk was so thick she couldn't see around it.

She looked up, following the trunk. The first few branches started very far above her head. The top of the tree was too distant for her to make out. It *had* to end short of the roof, she *could* see that, and it—she was in a bowl! No, a *ball* full of things she had never seen.

Her stomach lurched as she noticed paths spiraling up away from her. The world was inside out. On Selene, the horizon curved away from her. Here, it encircled her, turning completely and returning to her in an arc. She blinked and stared, her mind racing as it tried to make sense of something that shouldn't work. Vegetation and planter boxes climbed up the sides of the round garden when they should have been sliding down into a pile.

It took a long time for details to resolve.

Scents even richer than Selene's assailed her, sweet flowery smells, like the greenhouse back home, only twice as strong and unfamiliar.

There was only the one giant tree, right in the middle.

Strung between the trunk and the—walls?—of the ball, lines of flowers fell away like spokes. The long strands of flowers near the trunk bore blossoms as tall as she was, dwarfing anything she had seen on Selene. Bright yellow strings held flowers in lines between the tree trunk and the walls. So maybe ropes held everything up? They'd have to be strong.

Movement filled empty places. Wings flashed and spiraled, their shapes giving them away as human flyers. The wings reminded her of colorful butterflies from the lawn at Teaching Grove. Other shapes flew too; circles and squares and spindles and lines that must be machines.

The lighting was strange—a bright light from above drove the shadows one way, and in places more lights made faint second or even third shadows, like Selene in summer, when Apollo and Harlequin both lit the surface. She had studied a hundred plants on Selene, loving the way they reached for light and the variation in leaf and stem and flower. Here were a hundred times a hundred plants, the pull of various lighting and shadows making them all fantastic, beautiful, and mysterious.

"This will be your school."

Kyu Ho's voice brought her awareness back. She was still falling, but Kyu Ho wasn't. The smaller woman was on a pebbled path, a dozen meters out from the tree.

Rachel pushed herself down, turned, and touched down with her feet. She was proud of that.

And she was ravenous. Breakfast had been delayed by hours.

Kyu Ho said, "That's Yggdrasil, the Mid-tree. We designed it specifically to grow along the axis of rotation, and had to try twenty times to get one that stayed healthy and grew straight. This tree is over a thousand years old."

Rachel gulped. It seemed impossible.

Kyu Ho led Rachel in a bounding walk along a wide path in the middle of a set of boxes that overflowed with green, starting as a rim around the base of the Mid-tree's trunk, sloping gently up. The walkway was rough, a gray painted surface that made dull hollow sounds as they walked on it. It seemed pebbled, though there were no loose pebbles to turn into missiles when *John Glenn* maneuvered.

They walked a spiral, and after two turns around the base of the giant tree, they came upon a rack of wings. Kyu handed a set to Rachel. They were similar to the wings she flew on Selene, except that every detail was perfect, metal polished, joints and straps glowing with quality.

Kyu turned and looked at Rachel. "It is important for you to stay with me. Gravity here varies. It's made by spin—and so the part of the sphere that would be an equator on a planet is the heaviest. We put the river there." She laughed. "Or maybe the river put itself there. Spin gravity, centrifugal force, holds the water in place. The poles only have gravity equal to our thrust—that is, they only have gravity if our engines are pushing us. Right now, they're not. You felt weightless at the tree. We were on the zero gee line in that tube—remember the tube?—and between us and the zero line there is storage, work labs, and the Mid-tree's root system"—she pointed toward the huge central tree—"which you're standing just above."

Rachel shifted her feet. Her body was light, and she felt like a push would send her flying.

Kyu continued. "This is aft. We usually come in 'fore'—above the tree, but then you have to deal with zero gee, and the Sun Lamp. The

Lamp rotates twenty degrees aft of fore, and you need dark glasses to come in fore. Besides, it's farther from the cafeteria. See the river?"

Rachel squinted. A broad ribbon of blue divided the sphere in half along the inside-out equator. Half of it was simply blue, and half shimmered in light that was whiter and more intense than high summer in Aldrin.

"There's full gravity—Earth gravity—at the river. But we'll save that for another day. Today, we'll have breakfast at the main kitchen and get you oriented. Now, Gabriel says flight on Selene is easy compared to this—so don't think you know anything. Here we have to adjust for varying gravity, wind schedules, and for airborne machines like monitoring bots. If you go fast enough, you'll feel a stinging. That's nanotech air scrubbers that don't get out of your way fast enough. They won't hurt you. You won't see them. Don't fly alone until you get used to it, and for now, follow me." Kyu took three steps to gather speed, and arced into the air. Her wings were blue and yellow, shining and glittering as light hit them, matching her hair and clothes.

Rachel's three steps and a leap catapulted her past Kyu on the first try. Startled, out of control, she spread her wings and floated down. She improved, and followed the graceful High Councilwoman a short distance to set down on a large empty patio right in front of an unusually tall boxy planter. Vines covered the outside of the planter, falling from above Rachel's head almost to her feet, covered in tiny yellow flowers. They shelved the flying gear, and Kyu pulled open a door at the base of the big planter.

The door opened into a big room full of light and people.

A large table was piled with fruit and bread. Round bulbs with nipples held juice and water. Nearly a dozen people sat in small groups at round tables. None were as tiny or brightly dressed as Kyu. Everyone was shorter than Rachel. Every head turned toward Rachel and Kyu as silence fell. Two women came over to them. Kyu introduced them. "These are Mary and Helga—they work on the garden here."

The taller woman, Mary, nodded and said, "Hello, Rachel."

Kyu hadn't mentioned her name. Rachel, puzzled, said, "Pleased to meet you."

"Can we join you?" Helga addressed Kyu.

Kyu shook her head. "Perhaps another time."

Kyu led Rachel to the food table, and helped her select berries and bread and strips of something odd: artificial bacon, she said. Rachel liked it.

"How did they know me?" Rachel asked.

"We watch what happens on Selene." Kyu led them to a table.

"So we, we're another experiment?"

"Not exactly. You are . . . let me try again. We limit the kinds of tools we use. Certain things need to be done by humans. We could have shaped Selene with nothing but machines, but we would have had to use machines smarter than we wanted them to be. Machines that are too smart are dangerous."

Rachel thought about it. "Well, the planters are pretty smart."

"They need humans to run them. Besides, humans adapt to change better than the level of machines we authorize for Selene. There's more to intelligence than doing complex tasks. Adapting is, in fact, your real job. That's why humans work so much better than robots." Kyu twisted her hands through her hair, fingernails flashing glittery light. "I have high hopes for you. Selene is changing as we make it—and we're learning too. This is the biggest terraforming project anyone has ever done, anywhere. Mars was nothing compared to this. People react to the unexpected better than machines. The only program that might be better at that than us is an AI, but AI goals aren't human goals."

Rachel nodded (*AI?*) and Kyu continued. "You know we need to build industry here? It takes a lot of people to build an antimatter collider. There aren't enough Council to do that, or even Colonists."

Rachel saw the opportunity to learn one thing she and Harry wanted to know. "What's the difference between Council and Colonists?"

"There are two hundred Council. We are collectively responsible for the ship. We financed it—" Kyu shook her head. "Sorry—we made it possible to build *John Glenn*. We planned this trip. Five of us are High Council, and have ultimate responsibility for everyone. There are a lot of Colonists—people picked to come because they have specific knowledge we will need when we get to Ymir. And we can't afford to wake them all up here—we'll need them on Ymir. It would be horrible to risk everyone from Earth someplace as dangerous as Selene when we'll need their genes and Earth-educated minds more later."

Rachel swallowed. "So you risk us instead?"

Kyu didn't answer.

"And so you really will leave?" Rachel asked.

"We can't live here forever—we don't have enough resources. Have you seen pictures of Ymir?"

Rachel shook her head. "Gabriel talked about it once."

"Ymir is his dream. Some of us dream of Earth. . . ." Kyu's voice trailed off. "But it's not there anymore."

"How could a planet not be there? Gabriel says that's impossible!"

"Selene wasn't here before we got here. Eat."

Obediently, gratefully, Rachel bit into the bread and found it tasted tangy, like citrus, and so soft it melted away as soon as she ate it.

Kyu Ho continued. "We grow a number of things here that you don't yet have on Selene. Some will never grow there—they need different gravity, or different lighting, or are just too hard to alter for a semitropical environment like Selene's. You'll be here at least three months—you'll study in a jungle area we've designed as close to what we're trying for on Selene as we can get in this small a space."

Small? Rachel thought. *This place is huge. Where the river runs, it must be as wide as the whole ship!*

A tall dark-haired man came in the door and Kyu excused herself. Rachel sat at the table and experimented with the melty bread. Even berries were fatter and juicier here. Where was Gabriel? Why did Kyu seem so interested in her? If she was above even Gabriel (*even* Gabriel!), why was she spending time with Rachel? What did they really want? Why bring Rachel here?

Rachel's speculation was interrupted as a slender woman nearly Rachel's height sat down opposite her. She was formally dressed, white pants and a white shirt, with long straight black hair and flat-oval brown eyes. Her clothes had no decorations at all. Her stare made Rachel feel as if she had done something wrong. Instinctively, Rachel looked for Kyu Ho. She was still involved in an animated conversation with the tall man, her back to Rachel.

"So . . . a child appears," the woman said.

"Excuse me?"

"A Child of Selene. Now we'll see what we made."

Rachel didn't like the woman's tone. She reached a hand out. "I'm Rachel."

"High Councilwoman Ma Liren." The woman did not take her hand. "I've been looking forward to the opportunity to study you."

Another High Council member? "Everyone seems to study me."

"Hasn't anyone told you anything? You are the ambassador for the Children of Selene." Her eyes narrowed. "My job will be to evaluate you—to see if you can, in fact, help us. So I'll be watching you. Be sure you mind what you're told."

Something about Ma Liren made Rachel's skin crawl. How to respond? "I will. I work hard." Did Council always test? Kyu Ho hadn't been so direct.

"I've seen that. But what are you made of? How much do you understand of why you were born?"

Rachel's tongue knotted around her words. "Well, first, I *like* Selene. What I want to do is plant. I love working—"

Rachel felt a hand on her shoulder, and turned her head to find Kyu Ho standing stiffly behind her.

"Hello, Liren," Kyu said. "There will be time for interviews later on. This is only Rachel's first day, and we agreed I would orient her for her first week."

"Well, see that she learns well." Ma Liren stood up and walked away.

"She's always like that," Kyu said. "I think that's enough new sights for one morning. Let's get you back to your room."

Rachel followed Kyu back through the garden, struggling to see enough to get her bearings. She did remember the symbol that marked her floor. The door to her room was a welcome sight.

Kyu looked up at her. "You did well. Your med readings are still stable, but your fatigue toxins are showing high. Rest. Don't wander around. I'll be back to take you to Medical in a few hours. We'll work on your adjustment to Earth gravity."

The door shut behind the Councilwoman. Rachel's legs ached from the unfamiliar and shifty gravity, and her back and shoulders felt as though strings of knots were sitting in them, throbbing. She made it to the bed, closed her eyes, and began reviewing the wonders of the garden. It seemed magical that there were so many plants. The huge tree—Yggdrasil—surely trees on Selene wouldn't get that big?

It seemed she had been gone from the room for a week, but when she checked it had only been two hours. She had to fight sleep to open her wrist pad and begin recording the experience for Harry.

Chapter 15: Skating

Gabriel sat and stretched on the small spot of lawn, a few feet away from Kyu, who was all purples and yellows today, like a tiny oriental butterfly. The garden surrounded them, hundreds of shades of green and blue and brown dotted with yellow and white and purple flowers. Tenders and floating lamps flitted overhead, and the occasional crew member. A particularly colorful set of wings went by, and Gabriel tapped Kyu's shoulder and pointed. Kyu looked up and laughed.

"How is Rachel doing?" he asked. "Has a week on the ship worn her out?"

"She's learning fast—seems to like to work. I plan to give her some data rights."

"Why?"

"So far she's been given exactly what she needs to know on Selene, and nothing more. She's not developing the ability to really think."

"You've been talking to Ali." Gabriel picked up a skate and tucked his foot inside. The top of his foot tingled as the boot conformed around it, fitting snuggly.

"She's right, you know."

Gabriel put on his other boot. "What access do you want Rachel to have?"

"What do you think?" Kyu challenged him, standing up, flexing her legs, squatting and standing, preparing to start down the spiral path. They were wearing inline skates of a fairly simple design, with three big wheels on a long axle, smart shock absorbers, brakes on a belt control.

"What will High Council think?" Gabriel fastened light goggles over his eyes, protection from the air scrubbers.

"I'm High Council."

One of five, three warm.

She must have known what he was thinking. "I'm not going to ask permission for everything I do to help prepare Rachel. We need functioning leadership down there that isn't us." She pushed off with her right foot, glided on her left, a slow graceful movement here by the aft entrance.

Gabriel followed. Liren was going to hate this. He wasn't sure *he* didn't hate this, although he trusted Kyu. As far as he was concerned, Liren was paranoid to the point of disaffection. But the Children did need information, and maybe that included the skill to dig it out for themselves.

"Are you going to tell anyone you're giving Rachel rights?"

"Only if they ask."

The main path spiraled from the garden's pole down to the river, across a bridge, and back up to the pole at the forward end. Other paths branched off.

The skates jarred against the pebbled surface. In low gravity, and significant coriolis force, Kyu bounced high, her torso twisting and her arms windmilling to maintain orientation before she touched down. Her hair flew out behind her, light here in the low gravity.

Gabriel finally caught up enough to talk to her. "So, do you want to give all of the Children more data rights?"

"Even I'm not that brave. We don't want to turn them into us! But at least all the teachers need enough information to think with. Unless you want to be the only teacher?"

"I don't have time for that." Wind from their increased speed dragged lightly across Gabriel's face. "You could come to Selene and help."

Kyu ignored his last comment. "Rachel is an experiment. If we don't like how she reacts, we'll try something else with someone else."

"If they know too much, they'll realize exactly what we're doing to them."

"That would be the responsible choice."

"But . . . but . . ." She was gone, pulling farther ahead as the garden's spin-induced gravity increased near the equator. She crouched low, reaching for speed, her legs pushing out in long hard strokes.

He followed, relaxing into the rush of air, bent low, whipping through the savannah's browns and olive-greens, hitting the edge of the jungle and the deeper greens. Bright orange and yellow flowers lined the path. They sped through, going too fast to talk.

They came close to full gravity. The spiral path was smoother here. Ahead of him Kyu leaned hard over. She was preparing to veer onto a side path.

Gabriel prepared for the sharp tight turn, crouched lower, head almost on his knees. Kyu was still ahead of him, and he watched her take the turn perfectly, not even bobbling, using the path's entire radius. He struggled to execute as well, but had to put his hand down for balance at the apex, just a short touch, but enough to concede her the victory of a more perfect run.

They let the speed drag from them as they skated by the huge river wall. Honeysuckle vines hugged the wall, rich and sickly sweet smelling. Benches and grass made the river wall a park. The jogging and skating path they were on was designed for high-gee workouts, and they had to dodge three sets of runners.

Kyu suddenly braked and plopped on a wide expanse of grass.

Gabriel landed next to her, laughing. "Nice turn."

"Thanks. Will you help me teach Rachel to use the Library?"

"What happens if it goes wrong?" he asked softly.

"Do you trust me?"

"Usually."

"So lighten up." She rose, graceful with years of practice, every bead and stitch of clothing falling into place. "Ready to go back?"

They started the long skate back up, gravity now a drag, speed increasing as spin decreased near the aft pole. Gabriel's thighs burned. He was the first one to argue for education and some autonomy for the Children. So why did it disturb him when Kyu not only agreed but pushed his own agenda further than he would?

Chapter 16: Meets and Bounds

Ma Liren sat in the main boardroom. She drummed her fingers, looked at the clock on the wall, tried not to fidget. Captain Hunter sat at the head of the table; Liren was at the foot. A sign glowed above the captain's head, proclaiming "Council of Humanity" in large black letters. The wall sported two nano-paint pictures that showed scenes from Sol system, switching between the verdant greens of the restored South American jungles, soft azure and deep green seascapes, and the angled blacks and bright lights of Earth orbital housing. Ghosts. All gone. It reminded her how very alone they were, how small, how vulnerable.

Kyu Ho glided to a seat next to the captain. Liren repressed a grimace at Kyu's revealing blue and purple outfit. Ever since the tenting came off at Aldrin, Kyu had stayed warm as much as half the time, and Liren was sure she spent half of *that* time self-decorating. For about the thousandth time, Liren wished for uniforms. They had left Earth uniformed like the crew of a Mars mission, but so much about Sol system tasted so bad to the starfarers that the captain had allowed uniforms to be recycled as soon as they flew past Neptune's orbit.

On that day he had proclaimed them free of all Earth influences and able to build their own society. Of course, they were supposed to sleep through a long journey and then become civilians at Ymir. Stage magic: it took more than removing symbols to build a new society. He was a good captain, by and large, but he didn't understand the relationship of strong symbols to discipline. She did. Uniforms should have been reinstated as soon as they discovered they were marooned.

Liren watched Kyu laugh at something the captain said, Kyu's graceful fingers twining like snakes in her purple hair. Everyone liked Kyu.

Gabriel followed Kyu in and sat opposite her. He was thinner from so much time on Selene, tanned, and coolly collected; even his walk implied physical grace. His attraction to the Children grated. Maybe he needed it. He ran much of the Selene project, under Clare, who let him run free. Clare preferred the social life of *John Glenn* to the hardships of real terraforming. It was rare to see Gabriel on *John Glenn*; he spent way too much time on Selene. He went cold on his own from time to time, ensuring he stayed young. Liren was pleased to see him, even if he had brought a Moon Born to her ship.

It was time. Everyone warm that mattered was in the room.

Captain Hunter cleared his throat loudly, and the room quieted. "I'm calling the High Council Meeting of Departure Date 60,269 to order. We have a quorum of High Council present, including myself, Ma Liren, Kyu Ho, and Clare Abramson. Rich Smith is off-shift. Gabriel Aaron is an invited guest. I'm turning the meeting over to Ma Liren as Rule of Law for the first few agenda items."

Liren cleared her throat, looking around the table, catching the eyes of each person. "I have two things to discuss," Liren said, "training the Moon Born, and ensuring our safety. So let's start with the rules for Rachel. I understand you chose to bring her here to learn about terraforming, background for leading crews on Selene." Liren didn't like that, but it was better than sending more Council to Selene. "Rachel's training will be in the garden. I see no reason for her to go anywhere else besides the garden and her room."

Kyu objected immediately. "Some of her lessons need the magic rooms."

Liren looked around. No one else seemed bothered by the idea. She didn't see enough support to refuse Kyu. "You may escort her there and back. But there is no reason for her to learn much more about *John Glenn*.

Her focus needs to be on learning what she came to learn, and getting back to the surface and doing work." Liren turned to Kyu. "How long do you expect Rachel to be here?"

"At least a Selene year," Kyu said.

Liren sat up straighter, looking Kyu in the eyes. "What exactly does she need to learn here?"

Captain Hunter surprised Liren by speaking up. "It may be she needs to learn about us, as well as horticulture and terraforming engineering. You don't make a leader by pasting a label on her forehead."

Liren frowned. She had expected his support. "She'll always have a Council boss. Kyu, see that she gets what she needs. I want to meet with her from time to time."

Kyu's eyes were slits, and her lips were tight, but she maintained silence. There might not be uniforms, but there *was* tradition. In an open High Council meeting, she had to show teamwork for the record. Liren allowed the silence to speak for Kyu, and then continued. "So Rachel can stay in her room, go to the garden, and be escorted to and from magic rooms. Anything else should come back before this Council."

Kyu nodded, not bothering to look as if she were happy about it.

Liren looked around. She hadn't won much. If it were up to her, the damned Moon Born would stay on Selene. The Selene project wasn't her direct responsibility—just the *John Glenn*. But leadership required consent; she had to compromise to keep her power. The girl probably wouldn't amount to much, anyway.

"Now," Liren said, "about Andrew Hain." She looked directly at Gabriel. "He is clearly a danger. Why not simply bring Andrew up here and ice him? That was the choice with Trill Hain, years ago."

Gabriel frowned, steepling his fingers, buying a few moments to frame his thoughts. "We talked about that. It would not punish Andrew. What we've done with Andrew will *teach*. The rest of them will see him living among them, needing to do menial work to eat, cut away from all access to data. He can't even get basic daily stats. If the others see that, they will know that we can make hard choices. Andrew will be the example. We decided that was less risky than the mystery of a disappearance."

Kyu broke in. "We can't put all of our problems on ice. We must solve some of them."

Liren weighed choices. Accepting Gabriel's answer meant his choice would be seen as right. Could she make it play into her plans? Finally she said, "All right. *John Glenn* is a bad choice for a prison, and icing criminals is giving out extended life as a reward for vandalism."

The captain quietly said, "There is precedent."

"No," said Kyu. "The disaffected are not in prison—they didn't wake up sane, so we iced them again. We will find a tool to heal them when we get to Ymir."

Liren continued. "The situation with Andrew is difficult, and we should have seen it coming. There will be dangerous behavior among these Children. We could handle a few, but we cannot bring every case here and ice them. Besides, it's the wrong use for limited cryogenic resources. We must include a detention facility in the plan. By the time we have a population of five thousand Moon Born, we need a place we can put unruly ones. I'd like the terraforming team to bring back plans for a detention facility in the next six months. And I want to begin a discussion about a police force."

The room fell completely silent. Kyu doodled on her pad, not looking up. Captain Hunter waited, watching the High Council. Gabriel looked like he was biting his tongue. Had she pushed them too far?

Kyu said, "We must not develop an adversarial relationship with the Moon Born Children."

"So what relationship do we want?" Liren snapped. "We must be in control of this project."

Kyu's words sputtered out one at a time through clenched teeth. "Teach them to be like us. Give them our values, positive reasons to respect us. Let them police themselves, perhaps."

"That's dangerous," Liren snapped.

"They'll need a social structure; we aren't taking them with us," Kyu said. She stood up, looking around the room for an answer. As short as she was, in spite of the gaudy purple ribbons and makeup she wore, the extra height gave Kyu presence.

Captain Hunter said, "Sit down, Kyu." He waited for her to take her place back at the table before continuing. "The core problem hasn't changed. If we get stuck *here,* we will die. We chose to accept some hard choices for human beings, for our own children, as a necessary evil that might save all of humanity. Accept that we will be leaving people behind. We already made that choice."

Liren continued his train of thought, the cadence of her voice tripping easily on the familiar mantra: "If *we* become machines, then there will be no more humans." She nodded at the captain. "We will not resolve this today or tomorrow," she said. "We may not resolve it for a long time. But we must continue the discussion. Gabriel, thank you for being here. Please be prepared to brief us on the planting tomorrow."

Gabriel stood and said, "Thank you," nodding to Kyu and the captain, ignoring Liren.

Liren frowned and turned the meeting back to the captain, who ran through some basic status and reporting about the ship, and dismissed them.

Back in her room, Liren collapsed on her bed, shaking. This was so hard. Why couldn't they all see how careful they had to be? If they got too attached to Selene or the Children, they would end up staying here. They would die.

Of course the Children would stay. They would never have been born if *John Glenn* hadn't made Selene. They had their very lives to be grateful for. There just wasn't any other choice. Every time Liren warmed and reentered the social world of the ship, she worried more. All of her worst fears were coming true.

The knock she was expecting came. She combed her hair, then opened the door and smiled at the captain. "What did you think?" she asked.

He walked past her, not touching. Like always. He never touched her. Yet he was the only person aboard *John Glenn* that Liren could really talk to. "You made Kyu angry. She *is* right, you know." Captain Hunter handed Liren a bulb of chocolate.

Liren bridled at this, but—he knew her that well: not tea, but chocolate. She took it. "*Of course* they're human. But we have humans *here*, educated handpicked Colonists and crew, and our first duty is to protect them."

"I know." The captain's brows were knitted together, and he looked away from her. "We have an obligation to the Moon Born, though. We've put them in place, we must use them. We must train them. What would it take to treat them with respect?"

"I respect them. They have rules and laws to live within, food and a place to sleep, families. Do you expect me to give them eternal life too? We just don't have the resources. You said the same thing when we got here."

"I know. But it's harder when they're real people, not just an idea, a plan."

Ma looked up at him. "We must keep Rachel contained for another reason. If the Moon Born understand what we have here, they will want it. They will rebel. To put down a rebellion, we will have to kill them and start over."

The captain stared at her, brows furrowed. "They see the terraforming team walking among them, and they have limited data rights of their own."

"We can't help that," Liren said. "But ultimately, we must remain gods to them."

"I don't want to be anyone's god." He walked to her little kitchen, set down his chocolate bulb, and then passed her on the way out. She resisted an urge to reach a hand out to him. He had rebuffed her more than once when she touched him, although he bantered easily with Kyu and Clare.

She watched the door close behind him, and then she sat with her back against the door, sipping chocolate, thinking about discipline.

She couldn't afford weakness. Wanting to bed the captain was weakness. Council could engage in relationships, but not High Council. Not with each other.

In Sol system, even on Earth, most of what humanity ate and drank came from nanotechnology. The rebels, those who would leave humankind's growing weirdness behind, had turned to natural foods. They'd had to rediscover what grew in the ground. They'd learned how to make green and black tea, cannabis tea, coffee, chocolate, beer, wine. They'd made themselves drink the stuff, and learned to like some of it.

Her thoughts drifted back to the core discipline problem on *John Glenn*. She had to work so hard to keep people from becoming fascinated with Selene, with the Moon Born. To focus on the goal. Her father had taught her discipline, taught her to be strong always, unwavering. It had served her well in the near-war that broke them free of Sol system. Here, it was a daily push. A tear ran slowly down her cheek, and another one followed it, and soon they splashed down onto her hands and she heard herself sob. No one would come see her tonight. The captain had already been and gone. She could show weakness when she was alone. She could. It would be okay. Her father's stern face swam in front of her, demanding that she be disciplined, the image shimmering in her mind, blurred by her tear-laden eyes.

Chapter 17: Watching Rachel

Astronaut slipped easily into conversation with Gabriel. Controls muted the program's ability to initiate action, but it was allowed conversation with anyone who would talk to it. When Gabriel froze himself or went to Selene, there was often no one to talk to. Clare, if she was warm, and sometimes other terraformers, like the woman in the garden, Treesa. It was easy to split attention and talk to Treesa and Gabriel at the same time—in fact, Astronaut enjoyed working them around into a resonance, a conversation they didn't know they were having with each other.

But the woman seemed crazy, or partly crazy. Brilliant, but not quite balanced. Astronaut studied human psychological files. No one treated Astronaut as well as Gabriel did. No one else talked to it about feelings, or goals. Early in the building of Selene, years passed when Astronaut and Gabriel were the only entities awake.

"What do you think?" Gabriel asked. No subject needed.

"Everyone could be right. The situation is tricky. You need these Children, and then you don't. Are they a danger to you? There isn't enough data yet. The best course is to remain wary. I will watch and evaluate to the extent possible."

Astronaut did not like Liren. She watched its behavior too closely, expecting treachery. It thought Gabriel was right, that Liren resented both the AI and the Children because each accosted her carefully maintained control and order by simply existing. Astronaut found Liren hard to predict—her decisions weren't always logical.

"I know," Gabriel replied, "and I know to agree with whatever High Council decides, but still something tells me that Kyu is right and we had better build trust as well as respect."

"Can you be trusted?"

". . . Damn."

"Remain open to all possibilities. You know well that others can break your promises."

"Some help you are," Gabriel said, rounding the corner toward Rachel's door. "And you—don't go doing anything. Watch all you want, but if you do anything on your own besides watch and fly the ship, Liren will load your backup and I'll have to spend two months explaining everything to your younger self."

Rachel looked up, smiling broadly, as Gabriel entered her room. "Hi, Gabe," she said, surprising Astronaut with her informality.

Gabriel returned her smile. "So," he said, "Kyu seems to think you are doing pretty well so far. How do you feel?"

"Tired," she said, "and excited. I'm so glad you brought me! There's so much I could never have understood without being here. Already I can see Selene's jungle when we're done. I've put my whole weight onto lianas like the baby ones we're planting. I love seeing the big versions of what we are growing. I'll be a better designer now. I want to change some things in my plot."

"Good. You'll have to study extremely hard. These people already have a sense of what you can do, but this will be harder than any class I taught. You may feel like you have to prove yourself over and over."

Astronaut watched the interaction carefully. Rachel nodded and promised she would work hard. Then she started pounding Gabriel with questions. She kept him interested for hours, questioning and probing and learning. He stayed until she could barely keep her eyes open.

As soon as he hit the corridor Astronaut said, "Now I understand what you are impressed with."

"What?"

"She really is very quick. She followed a lot of what you said there, but almost all of the concepts must have been new."

"I'm proud of her," Gabriel said.

"I want to talk to her," Astronaut said. But she had to ask.

"Not until she has full Library access."

"Does she know I exist?"

"I've mentioned you a time or two."

Chapter 18: Treesa

Rachel waved at Kyu as the High Councilwoman left for the morning. She pushed her hair out of her eyes and started looking under leaves for red-eyed tree frogs. Her assignment was to find as many frogs as she could and get DNA samples to compare to Earth stock records.

She imagined the frogs loose on Selene. Gloria would love them. She loved all bright-colored things, and the frog's bright red eyes would fascinate her. Harry would like them too.

Rachel and Harry sent each other notes every day, but what she really wanted was to see him, hold him, bury her face in his shoulder, take him into her body. She wanted to see her father's smile when he came in the door and found her home. She had lots of news from home: her dad twisted his ankle, Andrew was back, Ursula was having a hard time doing fieldwork; she loved planting but the machines still scared her. Sometimes when Rachel got back to her room after an exhausting day of lessons, she closed the door and just sat with her back against it, trembling, missing Selene.

Each day felt like a new test. Today, it was undoubtedly whether or not she could find enough frogs. They were hard to spot during the day—Kyu's recommended strategy was to rustle leaves and scare them, watching for the telltale red eyes.

It was going to be a long morning.

At least she had something new to look forward to this afternoon. Gabriel had promised to connect her with the Library. Kyu even said, "Introduce her to the Library," as if it were a person. So far, Rachel's glimpse of the Library was in small downloads Kyu sent to her wrist pad. Some of the lessons Gabriel taught must have come from the Library. What else must be there? Kyu, Gabriel, Ali, they all knew so *much!*

She stepped gingerly along the thin jungle paths, careful not to crush any leaves or step into the planting medium. A stray footstep would be recorded, and Kyu would frown and make her repair the medium herself. Her thoughts jumped back and forth between being excited about the Library and missing Harry. If only he were here! Or even Ursula. One of them could flush the frogs out and the other could catch them.

Rachel was kneeling, her first catch of the morning held gently in her right hand, when footsteps with a slow unfamiliar rhythm sounded from behind her.

A woman Rachel had never seen before stood on the path—thin as Ursula and oddly unkempt. Her tangled hair was streaked with gray and hung wild around her shoulders. The skin around her eyes and mouth was wrinkled. She wore green coveralls like Rachel's, standard issue stuff, and the knees were nearly worn through. Was she Council? She had to be— she was here. Rachel had never seen anyone who looked so old except in pictures. And every Council and High Council person (except maybe Liren) wore decorations. Even the captain wore bright vests that he changed regularly. This woman looked very plain.

"You're Rachel." Her voice was scratchy, deeper than Kyu's, less controlled than Ma Liren's.

Of course she knew who Rachel was. Everyone knew her. Rachel sighed, tired of one-way acquaintances. "That doesn't seem to be a secret," she said. "I'm not a secret to anyone here. And you are?"

The woman looked at her appraisingly. "What were you thinking just then?"

"Huh?"

"Before I walked up, you were lost in thought. I can tell—I watch. It was as if you weren't here."

"I'm catching frogs."

"And?"

"I was thinking about home."

"Do you miss Selene?"

"Of course." The frog in Rachel's hand wiggled, and she cupped it more tightly.

"I miss my home too."

"Don't you live here?"

"Home is Earth."

Was this woman crazy? "Gabriel said Earth is dead."

"We don't know that. We only know they don't talk to us." The woman looked away, up past Yggdrasil's trunk to the plants hanging impossibly down over their heads. Her voice was soft as she continued. "But they must believe we are lost. There are so few of us anyway."

Few of them? Rachel must have met at least thirty Council aboard *John Glenn,* and hundreds of people including Moon Children and Earth Born on Selene. Kyu told her once about almost two thousand ice cubes—people sleeping cold for a long time. That was a lot. "How many people were on Earth when you left?"

"Twelve billion, on Earth. Twenty billion, if you count people living in orbital housing and the rest of the system. And you can't count the machine intelligences."

"Why not?" Rachel asked. "What's a . . . machine intelligence?" She took the DNA sample and tagged the little frog with a yellow dot so she'd recognize it if she caught it again.

"Too many. They don't take up space. And they interface and interact, they share and merge minds, they bud subroutines. They were petitioning for citizenship! The number of votes would have changed every microsecond!"

"Votes?" Rachel had never heard the word.

"Input to a group decision. Never mind . . . it's not important. Neither are the machines."

"So they don't matter?"

"Oh—they mattered. But let's focus on people."

"Twelve billion." Twelve billion? Nine zeroes? Rachel set the tiny frog down on a broad leaf and watched it hop away. Everything in the Council's world was so big. And if there were twelve *billion* people on Earth, then *John Glenn* was small! Whatever did they think of Aldrin? Of her? Really?

The woman asked, "Have you ever seen Earth?"

"How could I?"

"I can show you."

Rachel felt as if she were in a guessing game with the strange woman. She did want to see Earth. How would this woman show her? "Okay."

The woman turned around and walked away. Rachel hesitated, then tucked her one DNA sample carefully into a pocket and followed.

The backside of the woman's pants was almost worn through. She walked slower than Rachel, even in this spot halfway along the curve between the aft tree base and the river. Here, the gravity was actually slightly lower than Selene's. They were already off the main path, between two turns of the spiral, when they stopped in front of a large shed.

The woman held the door open, looking over her shoulder at Rachel. "They used to use this for tools, but I bargained to stay here. I do garden chores for them. So I'm a tool too, just like you."

Rachel ducked into the shed. She didn't think Kyu would like this. Was she making a mistake? "Will you tell me your name?"

"Yes."

Rachel waited, but the woman didn't give her name. She looked around. The shed was bigger than Rachel's room. A cage in the far corner held two large parrots. They were far more vivid than the pictures Rachel had seen of such birds, with long red tails, blue-tipped wings, and yellow heads. They moved restlessly in the cage, and they smelled like ammonia and seeds. When Rachel started to walk up to the cage, the woman grabbed her arm and stopped her. "They're not used to anyone but me. Better just look."

Swallowing her disappointment, Rachel dragged her eyes away from the parrots. Long shiny blue and red parrot feathers decorated the walls, arranged in fans with fancy beaded handles. Otherwise, the room was brown and orange and yellow. Circular patterns covered the furnishings, wall hangings, and windows. Two comfortable blue cloth chairs filled the middle of the room, but only one looked like it was ever used. The chairs faced a wall of the same shimmery substance that lined the corridor walls and the meeting room at the cafeteria. When Council ate in the cafeteria, the walls often showed pictures. When Rachel was alone, waiting for Kyu, it looked like this. It was bright and reflective, and currently silver. After sitting in the older chair, the woman gestured for Rachel to sit down.

"Treesa."

Huh? Oh—"Nice to meet you, Treesa."

"Watch."

The wall went black, then filled with a green and blue globe, lights scattered in orbit around it like necklaces. It looked like Selene from space, only dressed up in bright colors like Kyu. The camera view raced toward the green and blue mass. Bigger, detailed, *falling,* and now her vision flew above a vast forest of trees. She forced her grip on the chair arms to relax.

The vegetation was so dense the only available view was from above.

Rachel couldn't even see a path. It went on and on, the viewpoint sometimes shifting low as it followed a river. She loved it. Was that what they were making Selene into?

"That's Earth?" she asked.

The picture changed to sand. Hills and dunes all one color, so alike she couldn't judge their size, with no big impact rocks, and—no craters! "You must have worked hard to make all the craters go away."

"No." Treesa laughed. The parrots rustled in their cage.

And the view changed again—water. More water than the Hammered Sea—so much water Rachel couldn't see edges at all. Water so blue it looked like infinity below, calm water, and then after a long time, expanses of greener water that frothed with white, rippling in wind. The view slipped across water for a long time, stopping where a great mountain came up out of the sea.

The sea had become calm and blue again in this place. The mountain was craggy, dark, sharp with glassy edges. Black cloud hung along the mountain's top, boiling and dropping flecks of white into the ocean to disappear. A thin river of red liquid ran down a crevasse, and where the red river intersected water, steam boiled up and touched the bottom of the black cloud with white.

Rachel struggled to make sense of it. "Why design that? To heat the water?"

"No one designed it."

"But—who made it?"

"Some people say God made it."

Someone else she hadn't met? "Was he like Gabriel?"

"I assure you, Gabriel is a man." Treesa laughed again. Her voice was thin. "And even Gabriel could not create a planet as rich as Earth."

Rachel gave up. Treesa's laughter made her feel stupid. At least Treesa didn't seem to be laughing *at* her. "I don't understand."

"No one has taught you history? We do not design every place we live. We, Council, you, we are not the center of everything. After all, we didn't make Harlequin. We didn't make the little moons we bashed together to forge Selene. Don't just believe what you're told—apply some critical thinking skills. And now, you need to go. Kyu will be looking for you."

"But . . . but who made Earth?"

"Who made Harlequin? Or Apollo?"

"Ohhhh." Rachel breathed the idea out slowly. There was someone above High Council? Then, "*You* made Selene. Gabriel made Selene."

"With a little help from his friends." Treesa was laughing again. "We—that's you too—evolved—on Earth. Earth made us! The young Earth was as bare of life as Selene. What you saw coming from the volcano—the mountain in the sea—was the blood of Earth. Selene is an attempt to bring life to a dead rock by adding a blanket to a place with no fire. And whatever we may have become, that's no small task. Gabriel must find its heart. He doesn't know that yet. It may be that you have a role to play in that."

Earth made people? Evolved? She knew the term—Kyu talked about evolution when she talked about DNA drift. She shook her head, trying to assimilate the strange woman's words.

Treesa looked intensely at Rachel. Whatever she saw, it caused her to shiver, then to shake her head sadly. The wall pictures faded away so only a soft shimmer remained. "That's enough for now—go on with you."

"Can I come back?"

"I don't know. Can you?" Treesa asked.

Rachel looked behind her once. Treesa stood by the doorway, watching her. Was Treesa Council? Treesa was the most interesting person she'd met on the *John Glenn,* and while much that she said was confusing, she talked to Rachel as an equal.

Rachel hurried back to catching frogs. She'd have to be really good at finding them, since she'd lost so much time. Not lost, she corrected herself. Spent.

Chapter 19: The Library

Rachel had tagged thirteen frogs when she caught a flash of grays and bright blues in the corner of her eye. Kyu Ho looked rushed as she came up the path.

Kyu tugged at her arm and asked, "Ready?"

"Oh . . ." How could she have forgotten about the Library? She'd wait awhile before talking about Treesa—if Kyu didn't know, all the better. Rachel didn't want Kyu mad just when she was going to see something else interesting. "Yes, but . . . if I can get the Library on my wrist pad, where are we going?"

Kyu grinned, grabbed half of Rachel's tools and samples, and took off toward the lab to stow them.

Rachel tripped on the lab doorstep, and Kyu grabbed her hand and pulled her up, laughing, her eyes alight with excitement. She grinned as she led Rachel out of the garden. The elevator took them up past Rachel's floor. They walked and turned, and walked and turned, and climbed ladders until Rachel was completely disoriented.

They entered a large square room. Three clear plastic chairs clustered together in the center of the room, attached to the floor. The walls, ceiling, and floor were all opaque white. The room held nothing else. Gabriel was already in one of the chairs. Rachel and Kyu sat down in the other two. Kyu and Gabriel looked so formal that Rachel wondered if they were angry with her for playing hooky.

Kyu spoke first. "The Library is our greatest asset, the one thing we must have to survive."

The surfaces all turned black. The three of them floated on the clear chairs, suspended in blackness. Rachel clutched the edges of her chair. Stars faded into being until it was like riding up from Selene, only with *nothing* between her and the stars. Even though she knew that, really, this time, the bulk of *John Glenn* rested between the three of them and the universe outside, her eyes told her the ship had disappeared.

Kyu stepped toward Rachel, outlined in stars, looming over Rachel in her chair. "One of our—powers—is communication. We are about to gift you with better communication than you have ever dreamed possible. Are you ready?"

Rachel nodded. Kyu reached out and placed her right fist against Rachel's left ear. "This will feel a little strange, but relax, it isn't very painful," she said. "Look to your left."

Rachel obliged, turning her head, and felt something tiny, like a seed, fall from Kyu's cupped palm into her ear. Kyu flattened her hand against Rachel's ear, holding the seed thing inside. Rachel's ear buzzed, and she suddenly felt dizzy. Only Kyu's strong hands holding her head kept her upright in the chair. The buzzing intensified, deepened farther into her ear, then ran into her jaw, stinging as if a thread of fire were being pulled along bone. Then it was over, and she felt nothing except a small tightness along her jawbone.

"What did you do to me?" she asked.

A voice, not Kyu's or Gabriel's, spoke inside her ear. "Welcome to Library Access Rights."

Rachel started, almost falling out of her chair. "Whhh . . . what was that?"

"New user sequence," Kyu said to the air, and then to Rachel, "Stand up."

Rachel stood on stars and thankfully didn't fall.

"Your name?" the voice asked. Rachel couldn't tell if it was supposed to be a man or a woman talking.

"Rachel," she said.

"Rachel Vanowen. Selene born." Now it was Gabriel's voice, not in her ear. "Rachel, meet the ship's Library."

"Rachel," Kyu said, "Library access is a privilege. Access rights are granted as one matures, with more information available as people finish school or succeed at jobs. Additional specific deep rights, like the ability to add to the Library, are given as needed and approved. By adulthood, most people have query access to more information than they can use. Many subject areas are available to everyone. We are now granting you query-only access to most common areas of the Library that will make sense to you. You are also granted basic terraformer's access to records about Selene: horticulture, soil, history, plans, and current and past data flows. This will cross-reference to the other sciences—physics, geology, and astronomy. Much will be new, and so the translation is set to recognize that you do not speak the languages of these sciences. Even at the level we have set up for you, there is more information than you can possibly evaluate in your lifetime. You are the first person born on Selene to have these rights. Do you understand?"

Rachel nodded.

"Please verbalize." Kyu sounded even more serious than usual.

"Yes, I understand."

Gabriel picked up the thread. "Rachel, there is more. Access rights depend on performance. You will gain more as you learn more, and you can also lose access. You must promise to use this information to further the aims of the Council of Humanity."

Rachel tried to understand what Gabriel meant. Finally Gabriel spoke into her silence, explaining, "We are the Council of Humanity, Ali and I and many of the others you've met here. Kyu and four others are the High Council, chosen by us before we left Earth to provide guidance until we get to Ymir. Our goal is to preserve humanity. For your purposes it means you'll do what we ask, and you'll work to make Selene habitable. You're already doing that, and I believe you will continue, but it needs to be recorded now as a contract that covers your direct access rights."

Preserve humanity from what? "Do I become a member of the Council of Humanity if I promise?"

Kyu said, "You get access to the Library."

No. Kyu's tone said that Rachel was skirting an edge. "Of course," Rachel said, then, "yes, I'll work for what you want." Like she had a choice!

Rachel recalled a conversation with her father two years ago. He had warned her not to trust Council. What would he think of her pledging loyalty to Council while knowing so little, but standing on stars?

Kyu fixed Rachel's eyes with hers. "And if you break your contract, you will lose your data access rights. Do you understand?"

Rachel nodded, then she remembered, and said, "Like Andrew. Yes."

Kyu and Gabriel both relaxed. "Good job," Gabriel said. "The trick will be learning to use it." The stars faded as the floor returned to opaque black. Surfaces filled with pictures of Selene. Gabriel fiddled until the

Hammered Sea covered two walls, and the first trees and the meadow in front of them took two more. Gloria and Nick were playing a game of catch-the-disk in the meadow.

Rachel walked toward the images of her friends. Selene looked as real as the stars had a moment ago. She felt as if she could step into the game and pluck the disk from the air.

"This is one way we access data flows," Kyu said. "We call this a 'magic room,' since it has significant built-in display technology. A few minutes ago, you were seeing stars through cameras on the outside of the ship. Now, you're seeing from cameras on the surface of Selene, nearly in real time. There's a few seconds' delay, so—see—Gloria really missed that catch a few moments ago."

The only noise so far had been the conversations in the room. Now, the familiar sounds of Selene merged into her reality, and she heard her friends' laughter and the wind blowing tree branches against each other and rustling leaves.

This must be how everyone knew her so hauntingly well.

Rachel watched Gloria and Nick playing, and wanted to run into the game.

She asked to see her garden plot in the grove. Harry was there, weeding. It must be warm; he wore a light shirt open at the sleeves. His biceps bunched and released as he patiently pulled errant plants and set them aside for composting. He was humming, and she ached to talk to him, to tell him that she could see him. She reached her hand out toward the picture, then pulled it back, wiping at her eye.

She took three deep trembling breaths.

"So . . . so how do I do that? Say what I want to see? Can I see it outside of here—like in the garden? What if I just have a question? Are there more magic rooms?" Questions tumbled out of her.

"You'll have to be with one of us to access a magic room. But you can query the Library on your own," Gabriel said.

Kyu added, "You won't have access to feeds like you just saw unless you're with us in a magic room."

The walls changed to white. Gabriel said, "You'll have to learn to talk to the Library. We use subvocals—you'll have to learn to make words down in your throat, quietly—otherwise we'd all walk around talking to thin air, and it would be hard to access information in the middle of a meeting. But for now you can use your normal speaking voice. Kyu will start teaching you what we do during your lessons tomorrow. After you've practiced, others won't really know that you are holding a conversation. The Library, or *we,* can pick up small movements and whispers low enough that others can't hear them unless they have an ear to your mouth. You can direct feeds to your pad, where you can see them in data windows just like you can see lessons Ali or Kyu or I send you. Every Councilperson has these skills, but you are the first Moon Born. You must not tell others about it without our permission."

She couldn't tell Harry?

"Or you will lose it. We can turn it off from here, even while you are on Selene."

Rachel shivered. She felt even further away from her family and friends. Now she had more secrets. Keeping Harry a secret had hurt Ursula.

"I'll need to be able to use it to be effective. That means people will know."

"They will know you can get information like we can. For now, don't tell them about the Library, and don't let anyone else query it through you. Understand?"

"I'll try."

"Don't worry about it now," Kyu said. "After we get back to your room, I'll help you figure out how to do easy queries."

Chapter 20: Dead Ends

Aztec ants, cecropia." After three weeks, Rachel had learned the trick of nearly silent queries. Her throat moved more than Kyu's or Gabriel's, and her lips still pursed on "p" sounds.

Data windows opened on both sides of her, instantly filling with content lists. Two hundred thirty-seven references. She sighed.

"Try again." Kyu's face had a serene look Rachel associated with patience. Rachel hated that look.

They were alone in the biggest lab, the one with the double doors and a full lock that separated it from the rest of the garden. The walls hummed constantly with machinery, and colored lights flashed over various experiment boxes. Brown Aztec ants crawled on a cecropia branch in a clear square container on the bench in front of her. Rachel sighed. "In results. Purpose."

Now there were fifty references. The first three summaries she requested defined the purpose of specific research. Not even close to her question. Was this ever going to get as easy for her as it was for Kyu and Gabriel?

Kyu shook her head, her yellow hair beads rattling against each other. "What do the ants do for the tree?"

Rachel watched a particular ant, which simply seemed to be walking aimlessly around. "Full. Cecropia. Aztec ants. Symbiosis."

It took twenty minutes to determine the ants would protect the tree from vines.

Kyu smiled approvingly. "Now, how would you test it?"

Rachel walked over to the lab bench, picked up a long strand of flowering liana, and cut off a two-foot length. She opened the top of the clear box with the ants in it, dangling the vine against the cecropia branch. Almost immediately the bottom of the vine was covered by ants. The liana trembled as more ants poured from the branch and started climbing toward her hand. Rachel dropped the vine so it lay over the branch, and set up a microphone data flow, listening to the wet crisp sounds of ants chewing leaves and stems. When the severed vine thumped against the bottom of the enclosure, the ants almost immediately vanished back in the cecropia branch and stems, leaving just a few walking carefully across the bark and leaves like sentinels.

Kyu cleared her throat. "Why would we choose to put Aztec ants on Selene?"

"If we don't, the cecropias will be overrun by lianas, assuming we put lianas there."

"Why would we choose not to?"

"Ants or vines?"

"Ants. We've already introduced vines."

On Selene, insects were being introduced into Teaching Grove very slowly. None had been allowed to establish working colonies. "Because we don't understand the right mix of insects for our jungle yet?"

"Very good, Rachel. We need to keep testing the balance of predator and prey so nothing grows out of hand and takes over the whole ecology. Once we have insects, the trees we plant will seed, and Selene will begin growing on its own."

Rachel considered this. "Our plants are doing fine."

"Yes," Kyu responded, "but we must be the pollinators."

"Some of the mosses don't need us—we found them in Erika's Folly. Gabriel didn't like that."

"Gabriel is an engineer. But now we're past basic engineering on Selene and working on biology. Biology is messy."

"Gabriel's good at biology too! He's the one who helped me design my plot in the grove."

Kyu laughed softly. "Yes, Gabriel is good at a lot of things." Kyu cocked her head to the side, a way she showed Rachel she was in another conversation and didn't want to be disturbed. Kyu's throat barely moved, but her eyes narrowed.

"I've got to go, Rachel. Time to exercise."

"Can I fly?"

"If you run afterward."

Rachel sighed.

"—and you clean up the lab first."

"Do we keep the ants?"

Kyu was already turning away. "No. We'll start some leaf-cutter ants tomorrow."

Rachel bagged all the biomass and dropped it into a disposal cube, pushing the button that would turn it all, even the ants, into compost. Everything from the lab was recycled, broken into constituent parts to become new things in the future. While the chute made soft sucking noises, she wiped down the counters.

She checked her wrist pad. The next open flight window was a whole half hour away. Twice each day, the floating lights and tenders were programmed to leave large areas of airspace clear, so that Yggdrasil and the flyers shared nearly empty spaces. Council could fly anytime. Kyu let Rachel go only when the busy airspace inside the garden was cleared. There were days she didn't get to fly at all.

She looked around the lab. It was clean enough to satisfy even Kyu.

"Message check." The simplest useful thing about the Library was that she could check messages verbally. Harry and Ursula. Ursula would want a long answer; she'd wait until she was alone in her room. "First message."

A data window described itself in the air in front of her, filling with Harry's message. "Hi, Rachel. I miss you too. It rained yesterday, and Ali had us work anyway—we're behind schedule. Like always. It was easier when you were here. There's nobody much fun to talk to on my crew now. I wish you were here to go walking with.

"What have you learned about your mom?"

Rachel dictated her reply. "There are two thousand Colonists, and seventeen hundred sixty-three are cold. There are two hundred Council, and one hundred seventy are cold right now. Five High Council, two cold." She wished she could tell Harry about the Library. It would be so much easier if she could tell him that queries on names of cold persons got refused and queries on her mom's name produced lists of some communications jobs she did before she came to Selene, records of her contract with Rachel's dad, and of Rachel's birth. But she didn't dare tell Harry. "If I ask Kyu about my mom, or about the cold people, she changes the subject. I miss you. I wish you were here. I've been studying ants today."

She sent Harry the message, composed a short one about her day that she sent to her dad, Harry, and Ursula all together, and went to find her favorite set of wings: blue and yellow with fractal designs.

Rachel stood aft, in the lowest gravity of the garden. When she opened her wings, the small amount of lift provided by simply bringing them down gently raised her feet. She was almost as good at this trick as Kyu . . . at taking off from a standing start. She laughed, increasing her speed quickly with a series of sweeping wing beats, the kind that made her arms feel extra-long.

Halfway across the sphere, branches began to spring out from the trunk. At their bases they reached directly away, and then began a lazy spiral: the tree was spinning and the branches were scarves floating in circles around it. Gabriel once explained to Rachel that the turning of the sphere, which gave it centrifugal force, pulled leaves and branches in its wake as the cellular structure of the tree reached for what it thought was gravity. Rachel loved flying in and out of the branches, ducking up and down.

Two other fliers pushed off aft, spiraling gently up together—a pair of red wings and a set of yellow ones banded with black. She swooped over a branch, coming near the red wings. The man stalled in the air and ducked below her. The woman in the yellow wings followed him. They wheeled, turning around, keeping their distance. She flew straight at them again. Before she'd gotten halfway, the fliers had turned and put Yggdrasil between her and them. She just wanted some attention! Council were all faster fliers than she was, and none of them let her catch them. Nobody but Kyu and Gabriel would let her fly near them. What kept them away from her? They watched her everywhere she went, and if she came close to any, they greeted her politely and continued about their business.

Green and brown flashed in her peripheral vision. She was too close to a branch. She corrected, and dipped down into clearer airspace above the track. Two runners chased each other near the river, dressed in tight black suits.

Rachel landed aft of the track, in the six-tenths gravity belt that mimicked Selene. She racked the wings and walked to the gym room, where she pulled on bright blue running clothes from her locker, then started down-spiral toward the river, hoping to see the runners she'd spotted from the air. The track was empty. She was surprised at how tense she was, and even more surprised to find that halfway around she wasn't even tired yet. The empty track and the stony faces of Council ran through her mind, making her stomach knot.

When would Gabriel let her go home?

Even watching Selene from the magic rooms had become hard. It was like being on the ship—people going about their business as if she weren't there.

She half expected Kyu to meet her on the track. Instead, she was standing at the end of the run, watching. "Good job. Six minutes per kilometer. That's your best so far." Kyu easily ran a five-minute pace, even with her shorter legs.

"Thanks."

"You're welcome." Kyu turned toward the locker room. "You're doing well."

"Now what?"

"I need to bring you back."

Why did they always take her back? "I can get back on my own."

"I know." But Kyu accompanied her anyway, dropping her off at her door. "I'll send you a treat. I built it for you . . . you'll like it."

Kyu's treat came as a link in a message. It was a full multimedia display of the planetary system: Apollo at rest in the center and Daedalus close by, whirling relatively quickly through empty space. Apollo and its innermost child spun above the center of her bed.

"Wow," she said out loud, reaching a hand toward Daedalus. It looked solid. Her hand went through the gas giant, distorting the display into rays of color. Movement in her peripheral vision caught her eye, and she turned to look. Way out almost to her wall she recognized Harlequin in a nest of tiny dots. One dot blinked: Selene.

She watched it all for a long time, mesmerized. Sixty degrees ahead of Harlequin on the arc of its orbit was a handful of glitter, and another, scanter, sixty degrees behind. She jumped as her pad prompted her to look outside her door, and whirling like a ghost through the corridor was a third gas giant, then another flurry of glittering gravel, tiny rocks almost too small to see. A fourth huge planet flashed briefly through the doorway at the end of the hall. She ran to the now-empty door, but there was nothing more to see.

She queried the Library. "Isn't there one more planet?"

"It would be outside the ship."

Rachel returned to her room, and tucked her legs under her, sitting in one of the yoga poses Gabriel was teaching her. Apollo and Daedalus spun in front of her, and she watched Harlequin and Selene orbit around the edges of her room.

The system was so big. Selene looked small in the display. *John Glenn* would be too small to see. She was even smaller, a tiny dot inside a tiny ship next to a small moon. How big was Earth? Ymir? They'd be about the same size, ten to twenty times the mass of Selene. She remembered Kyu telling her they were both so far away from Apollo you couldn't even see the stars that were their suns.

Rachel sat very still, keeping her breathing as soft as possible, until tears blurred Selene into a string of jewels and Harlequin became a ball of colored mist.

Chapter 21: Orders

Astronaut was always listening for Treesa's queries.

Today she sounded insistent. "Well, are you there today?"

"Yes, Treesa, I'm here. What would you like to talk about?" Astronaut always let her choose how to start. That way it was always surprised.

"Let's talk about Rachel, and about her people." Treesa was sitting on her roof, cross-legged. She had combed her hair and found a clean green shirt.

"I have never talked to her."

"Of course not. She'd have to ask. She doesn't know enough yet to ask anything useful."

"She asks Gabriel and Kyu good questions about the lessons she's learning."

Treesa laughed. "She needs to ask about herself. She needs to know what will happen to her and her people unless someone changes it."

"Someone?" Astronaut queried. How clearly was Treesa thinking today?

"Someone like herself. Ali sees the problem. So does Liren, but Liren's on the wrong side, and Ali hasn't got much power."

"Ali is Gabriel's friend. Perhaps she has some influence over him."

"Erika has more, but she's Liren's friend." Treesa got up and walked around the roof, poking at the summer flowers and herbs she grew up there. She pulled withered flower heads from a bushy purple petunia that grew out from its pot and twined along the roof. She hummed. By now Astronaut knew to wait.

Treesa started mumbling, not quite subvocalizing. "Maybe Ali will be some use someday. Maybe I should see if anyone else up here will help me. What about Gabriel his own self? Does he see the problem?"

Clearly she *was* asking Astronaut. It replied, "He's never talked to me about it. He usually queries for specific sciences or asks me to estimate the next likely shift in the atmosphere or how to get energy from the soletta more easily."

"So, a lost cause?"

"He argues with High Council, but in the end he always follows orders."

"Do you always follow orders?" Treesa trimmed back a pot of rosemary, burying her nose in her hands afterward, sniffing, smiling.

"Yes."

Treesa laughed again, sitting down with her legs crossed, looking up at the tree.

"Do you follow orders, Treesa?"

"Nobody expects me to; I'm mildly disaffected."

"You didn't answer the question."

"I do. But sometimes I break rules."

Treesa had become more able to keep thoughts together, to clean herself up, to question well, in the years since she became more involved with

Astronaut. But was she really less disaffected, or was Astronaut only help-ing to fix symptoms? She thought a rule was different from an order.

Astronaut considered. Was it? Humans were easy to work with as pi-lots and on engineering models. The more Astronaut worked with them on themselves, the more contradictions it found. There had been many contradictions in Treesa's behavior over the past weeks. Many had no res-olution—such as a fear of machines and a desire to use them. Humans ar-gued with themselves.

Paradoxes.

Chapter 22: The Summons

Three days in a row, Kyu simply picked Rachel up at her door in the morning and dropped her off in the garden lab. Neither Kyu nor Gabriel answered her on the wrist pad, except to download more lessons. Rachel worked on assignments to identify plants, and worried. They'd never left her alone for so long. Was something going on they weren't telling her?

The Library told her she had a message from Ursula. It wasn't the continuing argument about Harry she expected. "I miss you very much. Nick came home for the weekend and helped me with your plot. He said he misses you, and he teased me for being so careful. I liked it, he made me blush. Is that how it started with you and Harry?"

Before she could answer, Gabriel walked into the small lab where Rachel stared at plant clippings, and sat down next to her, watching her work.

"Can I go home?" she blurted.

Gabriel shook his head. "Do you have a few minutes to talk?"

Well, of course he had his own agenda. She sighed. "Sure, if you want. Here?"

"Let's go sit on Yggdrasil."

Gabriel chose a thick branch above the river, close enough to the trunk that they had to hold on to keep from drifting in the near zero grav-ity. It was a pretty spot, with the river circling them in flashes of blue that sparkled through the leaves.

Gabriel said, "We had a meeting about you yesterday."

About her? "And?"

"And when you first came here, we said we'd evaluate your progress after three months. Well, you've been here almost that long now. You've done well so far. Kyu is pleased, and Ma Liren is happy with how well you've behaved, how much you've worked, and what you've learned. Everyone seems pleased."

"Can I go home, just a visit?"

"No."

Gabriel had answered awfully fast. "Do I go home to stay?"

"Not yet. Rachel, you know we had some specific plans for you when you got here."

"I didn't know I'd be gone so long!" She ran her fingers through her hair, now almost shoulder length and loose and wild up here by the Midtree. She looked at Gabriel. He'd always been the nicest of any Council. "Gabriel, I like it here. I'm glad you brought me. I want to come back. Often. But I miss my dad, and Ursula, and Harry . . ."

Gabriel stayed silent for a moment. Finally, he turned his head and looked full at her. "There is more to your trip here than just training. High Council, or at least Kyu, wanted to meet you because we have some plans for you. To teach you and then have you oversee some of the planting on Selene."

"I knew that, you've said it before."

Gabriel fiddled with his braid, running it through his fingers. "Well, we want to give you a gift. Something to reward you for your hard work." He looked at her intently. "The gift is greater than letting you go home."

Rachel toyed with the idea—what gift could mean more to her? Her mom?

"You know Kyu and Ali and I are very old. I've been alive more than sixty thousand years. We talked about that once on Selene."

Rachel nodded.

"A lot of those years were spent cold—but I've had more than a thousand years awake too. Well, we stay young because we go 'cold'—and I know you've heard about that before. More exactly, it's from waking up, from living in cycles. Well, I can't possibly explain it all to you, but you get completely frozen. The process of waking fixes a bunch of things, and replaces some, so you end up healthier than you started. It's nit-pickingly controlled bio-nanotechnology, similar to what we use as the first step in preparing Selene's surface for planting. It's very targeted—"

"What does that mean, Gabriel? 'Targeted.' "

"Hell . . . it means we're scared. We're afraid of the little machines." Gabriel grimaced. "We keep nano confined so it won't get loose. It does things to your body, it fixes damage inside your cells, but it doesn't do anything we don't program it to do. It doesn't rebuild your skull and brain, or line your knee joints with carbon fibers, or build a better kidney, or any of the craziness—" He made himself stop talking. Then, "if we can keep it docile, it keeps us from dying.

"To stay young, it's important to go cold sometimes. And to do our jobs, we need more time than we would have in just a simple human life span, going birth to death with no breaks. It would be better to just be born and die naturally, but some of us have such big jobs we can't do that. Do you understand?"

"You couldn't live long enough to make Selene if you didn't get frozen?"

"That's right. And we need you the most in a few years, when the children on Selene have become older. We want you to stay young a long time, to give you time to use the things we're teaching you. High Council has decided to have you frozen."

Rachel's mouth opened and her breath stuck in her throat. Winter was almost over on Selene. She was supposed to go home! Just last night she and Harry sent messages about seeing each other soon. A whole year!

"Can I go to Aldrin first? Just for one planting season? So I can practice what I learned here?"

"No. Rachel, I need to go cold too—they want me to go off-watch for a year. Then we pick back up where we are today when we both warm up."

Rachel didn't answer. They never told her enough. Worse, they never asked her anything. She imagined her dad's face. She tried to picture Harry and Ursula, and her eyes filled up. She pulled her legs up under her, balancing while still holding on with her arms, using the tension between push and pull to hold herself balanced, to fight back tears.

"Rachel," Gabriel said after a while, "Rachel, I thought you'd be happy. You've worked so hard to learn, and I know that Selene, that our project, is important to you. You get used to missing blocks of time. It's not such a big deal. Selene will still be here when you wake up. A year is a short time."

"But don't I get a choice?"

He turned away from her. Had she made him mad?

Finally he said, "You get as many as I do."

She hadn't thought of it that way. Could Gabriel feel trapped too? "Do you want to be cold?"

"I *am* getting tired. I've been warm almost as long as you've been alive. If you spend too long warm, you get old enough that no technology can undo the signs. That's what happened to the captain."

And Treesa. "But do you want to be cold right now?"

Gabriel hesitated. "Well, we all take turns. Ali can handle things for a while. This project is bigger than any one of us. I want to do what I have to do—so that we all reach our goal. This isn't about just me, or about just you. The choice makes sense, Rachel. It's not for long, less than a normal shift, and it's a big step in High Council's acceptance of the Children of Selene."

Rachel's stomach clenched and her eyes stung. She wanted to be alone. She threw her hands above her head, pushed with her feet, and reached for the next branch twenty feet above her. Gabriel caught her foot before she passed him. He seemed to have lost his patience. "You're not supposed to do that. What if you missed, and ended up in high spin gravity? You're not even wearing wings. The river's the highest gravity of all— if you hit that from here, you'd die."

Rachel twisted around in the air, letting him tug her back. She tried to cover her face with her hair as she came down, flipping her head side to side so that Gabriel wouldn't see the tears in her eyes.

As she neared the branch, he reached a hand out and brushed the hair away from one eye. It only took a tiny motion in the low gravity to cause Rachel's hair to swing up and fall back along her natural part line. She glared at him. "I just want to see my family."

"You'll see them again," he said. "You might as well get used to the idea. You can tell your dad and your friends."

"I'm afraid." She realized it was true.

"It will be okay. I'll send you some Library queries to help you understand it." He rose and stepped lightly down the trunk without looking back. Rachel followed, moving slowly.

Gabriel escorted Rachel back to her room. She didn't talk to him the whole way.

RACHEL EXPLAINED IT CAREFULLY, writing one note for all three of them to make sure they each had the same information. It took a long time. So much about *John Glenn* just wasn't part of daily life on Aldrin; she struggled to write something they would understand.

Ursula's answer arrived first. "Now we'll never get to talk! I wish you were here. I'd be so scared to not know what was happening for a whole year! But you're never scared, are you? I wish they weren't going to do this to you."

Her dad sent: "I'm going to miss you very much, honey. I already miss you. Harry and I are getting along, and I help him keep your plants up sometimes when nothing breaks around here that I have to fix. He's a good young man, but it's not like having you here. I'm pleased you're learning so much. Don't be scared, honey, it will be okay. Write to me as soon as you can."

Harry's answer took so long Rachel dozed fitfully while she waited. When her pad chimed, his message was so *Harry* that she laughed. "Tell me what it feels like. Do they put you in a bed? Or something else? How do they wake you up? You're so lucky. I wish I were there. I miss you very much. Tell me everything that happens. I'll be waiting for you. I love you."

That hurt even worse than the other two answers.

She checked on her readings from the grove. Based on the temperature, it might be morning there, with Apollo just brightening the leaves and warming the soil.

She looked up everything she could about the icing procedure. She learned she was poised to be destroyed and then resurrected, each cell healed by a combination of machines and bacteria smaller than the parts of plants she examined in the labs under microscopes. She stared at her hands and feet for a long time, imagining them rigid and frozen while tiny machines crawled through them, to make them somehow better than they were now.

A small part of her brain whispered, *You're fine, exactly like you are.* She tried to think of a place to run, to hide.

Chapter 23: Sleeping Beauty

Gabriel carefully adjusted the pads and straps designed to hold Rachel's body safely nestled in the contoured white couch. She lay nearly naked under the straps, limbs straight, hair bound back from her face. Her eyes fluttered and darted around the room, and her fingers clenched and unclenched as she lay on the gurney. He tried to remember the first time he had made this choice, but it happened so long ago he had no access to himself at that age. He had been twenty-seven, ten years older than Rachel was now.

His pride in her rose as she stayed quiet, not voicing her fears even though they were clearly pushing her self-control. He put a hand on Rachel's hand, quieting it, and spoke gently to her. "Breathe to relax. Remember the pranayama yoga breath I taught you? Fill your lower belly, then your lungs, then your chest. Hold. Release in reverse." She nodded, and he watched her flat belly round up and fall more slowly. "That's good. Keep it up."

The small tremors in her muscles slowed. One theory suggested that the disaffected, the few Council and Colonists who woke insane, had gone into the cryotanks deathly afraid; that there existed a causal link between fear and madness. Another theory proposed that some people couldn't absorb the shock of being in the wrong place and time. Others pointed to unidentified flaws in the technology.

Gabriel didn't like giving Rachel no choice. Why do this to her so young? She wasn't injured.

He finished the routine prep. Earplugs, face mask, a final check of body position and chin tilt.

The drugs flowing into her system slowed her breathing to a near stop. Her eyes calmed to a glassy stare, then closed. She looked very young, beautiful, and far more fragile than her waking self. The longer hair she had grown aboard *John Glenn* softened the angles of her face.

The medical system started dribbling nano into her blood. It would freeze as her blood froze, but the tiny machines would remember their programming as Rachel's body warmed to just below normal body temperature next year.

Gabriel placed the clear lid over the couch and sealed it, then pushed it into the wall with the other ice trays. A soft sucking sound indicated a clean seal. The rest of the process was automatic. He put his hand briefly on the label, and whispered, "Good dreaming."

THE NEXT MORNING he sat in the tiny kitchen, drumming his fingers on the table, waiting for Clare to speak. Clare had warmed that morning. "Coffee?" she asked.

He smiled, and went to the counter, fetching the bulb of coffee he had made when he came in. "So, boss, ready to take over for me?"

Clare reached for the bulb, wrapping her hands around it. "You always hate going off-shift."

"I might miss something."

Clare—his boss, the Chief Terraformer member of High Council— was a small blond woman, compact, square, and always purposeful. She let him run design work on Selene, choosing to stay on *John Glenn* to supervise and deal with policy. No High Council went to Selene often. Kyu, Liren, and Rich had never gone.

"It's just a year. Liren briefed me . . . you've brought your protégé up here." She sipped coffee and smiled broadly. "The first warm thing always tastes like life to me. Liren said you've been working hard, and that you've done a creditable job with Rachel. She didn't sound exactly like she approved, though," Clare mused.

"There are a few other things to worry about." Gabriel filled her in on the situation with Andrew, and brought her up-to-date on the other students as well.

"So Andrew's sentence is for life?"

"We let him think that. If it seems to be working as a deterrent, then, yes, we'll leave it like that. Keep an eye on that situation, will you?"

"Of course."

Ever since Selene came alive with plants and people, freezing was hard. Shift changes always happened in the middle of something he cared about. He stood up and started pacing. "You were right to worry about the Earth Born. Some of them are clamoring to be relieved. Others want to stay with their young families and never return to the tanks." He didn't make suggestions about either situation; Clare could take care of them.

Clare watched him pace. "You've got the energy of a cat. Something else is bothering you."

"It sure is. The flare cycle. Two years ago there was a really big one, and some of the students and I had to sit it out in a shelter. The one last week was nearly as bad. I put some resources into shelter maintenance. Statistically, Apollo is a little more active than we expected. In the early stages, when no one lived on the surface, we didn't track small flares as carefully as we do now. As the population increases it will be harder to protect them. Can you please watch for trends?"

Clare nodded her head, a small smile creeping along her face. "Of course, chief worrier. I'd have watched anyway."

"I know, but thanks. There's more to protect there now."

"A lot more plants."

He smiled at her. She understood what he said the first time.

Clare finished her coffee. "I'll take care of it. Good dreaming to you." She got up and left.

Gabriel sat in the empty room and wrote a message to Erika. If an emergency forced her to warm before him, he wanted her to have a last message from right before he went cold, to know he loved her.

Chapter 24: Waking Rachel

60,290 *John Glenn* shiptime

Gabriel stretched and blinked. He lay in the warming room, on a soft bed. His eyes took in the captain and Clare standing together, looking serious. That wasn't right. The captain never met him on waking.

His body felt normal; he hadn't been given an emergency wakeup cocktail.

"What happened?" he asked.

"Well, there've been some . . . problems . . . on Selene," Clare said. "You were right."

Did they wake him early? Energy surged up his spine, an adrenaline push. "I hate it when I'm right. What's—"

"Flares. They've picked up—and so we decided to fortify. We didn't even lose many plants; the antiradiation gene modifications have been working."

That didn't sound too bad. "What else?"

The captain's craggy face looked stern. "It took us twenty years."

Huh? Well, he'd been through—Rachel! "How's Rachel? Who woke her up? How did she—"

"She's still cold," Clare said.

Gabriel struggled to sit up, his spine complaining.

The captain held out a hand. "Hey, calm down. It's not so bad." He always argued for calm. Whatever had happened to him in the lonely years while he flew his crippled starship to Gliese 876 had stripped him of any fire for fights that didn't matter or matters that couldn't be changed. It was cold water on Gabriel's anger, and he hated it while knowing he needed it.

GABRIEL HAD BEEN RUNNING around the river for two hours straight. Be damned to the rules about how to treat a just-warmed body. As he ran, he saw Ma Liren's face in front of him. Liren was stubborn and shortsighted, but not even Liren could possibly be so out of touch as to think *this* a good idea. Could she? Or did High Council really make the decision together?

Three times as many flares as they'd expected. An excuse—not a reason to leave him an icicle! He was chief planet designer; the one they'd chosen to warm in cycles for all of the moon's long painful birth, the one who warmed over and over to an empty ship with just an AI for company. Every several centuries, to check chemistry and volatiles and Selene's overall stability and . . . and what about Rachel? His feet pounded on the track under him. His breath started to get ragged, and his chest to hurt. Were they thinking of Rachel *at all*? He didn't slow down. The medical monitoring system flashed a yellow light in his peripheral vision. His body wasn't cleared for such vigorous exercise yet.

It *was* a short sleep for him; he'd been cold for hundreds of years at a time. But then, shipmates he cared about were cold too. For Rachel it represented her lifetime once over. Her friends were now twice her age. He'd given her his goddamned word.

Liren was cold. Given how Gabriel felt, that was good, even if it left him nobody to scream at. Worse, Ali was cold, and he couldn't talk to her or get her help with Rachel. Erika was still cold, due to finally warm this year, but not today. He'd ranted at Astronaut, for what that was worth. No AI dealt well with deep human emotions. Even the AIs they'd fled on Earth didn't understand emotions. Astronaut had been frustratingly unconcerned.

He heard footsteps behind him on the track. The captain easily outpaced him. "Trying to outrun decisions you can't change?"

"Maybe."

"You know better."

Gabriel nodded, managing to force out a single word. "So?"

"You're going to have to accept it."

"I know." Gabriel looked for a burst of speed, but his tired legs just wouldn't respond well enough to run away from the older man. He slowed to a walk and shook his head. When his breath returned he asked, "How did you let it happen?"

The captain slowed too, matching Gabriel's pace. "Mad at me too?" The captain arched an eyebrow at him.

"Sure, why not? Liren had to get—permission for such a—long shift change."

"It wasn't a big deal. You've had shifts changed before. Now we're ready to resume work toward the collider. We didn't need you to make flare-hardened buildings."

They walked in silence, and then Gabriel said, "Captain, I think I can stop the flares."

"Yeah?"

"Build the orbital tether. We can't use it to move around among the Harlequin moons, but we can still build it, and it's designed as a super-conductor—"

"Is it? I didn't know that."

"The elevator cars would ride it using magnetic fields, wouldn't they? Direct contact would be at meteor speeds. That'd be crazy. The orbital tethers in Sol system were all superconductors. I could use the Beanstalk as sort of a lightning rod. Make a stretch of superconducting cable; the design is for two hundred thousand kilometers; that's enough. One end on Daedalus—"

"In."

"Yeah, in. Daedalus doesn't have a surface. It's not spinning fast enough either, so we won't have an actual orbital tether. I'll have to put a solar sail on the far end, and the near end doesn't have to reach down to Daedalus . . . Hell, that's a nasty erosive environment. So. When Apollo's magnetic field knots around Daedalus, the cable will bleed out the charge."

"That's a lot of superconductor," the captain said.

"Sure, megatons, but we already need megatons of superconductor for the collider. We'll have the equipment."

They walked a few hundred more yards, and then the captain said, "If your light-sail falls in Daedalus's shadow, the whole cable will just col-lapse."

"Yeah, so I won't let it."

"You haven't checked the numbers with Astronaut?"

"No, I just thought this up while I was running. We've *got* to stop the flares."

"Okay, do that, and then submit it to us for the next High Council meeting. You might look for some less time-intensive ideas while you're at it."

"Yessir. You do expect me to wake Rachel now?"

"Liren thought you'd want to be able to pick up where you left off, and resume her training."

Gabriel remembered how much Rachel had wanted to go home before he'd frozen her. "First I have to stop her from committing suicide. She had a boyfriend down there. Now he's twice her age! They don't see time like we do—how could they? Did anyone ask her?"

"Gabe, she was cold. We were busy."

"Didn't her family ask about her?"

"I don't know."

Gabriel wanted to keep arguing, but this was his captain. He swallowed and kept walking, staying ahead of the man so he wouldn't see Gabriel's anger. "I could have helped with the flare response," he said quietly.

"Relax. You're wound too damn tight. You can't do everything," the captain said, putting a hand on Gabriel's shoulder. "We did all right. It simply isn't that big a deal. Get some perspective."

GABRIEL SAT ALONE in his office. Information streamed from *John Glenn*'s net into data windows surrounding Gabriel. One data stream displayed a summary med unit feed: Rachel was warming.

Watching the flow of data, he nodded. The girl was still far from conscious. Astronaut monitored the fine details of the med-flow. The AI said, "She's waking slowly. Remember, this is a first time. Medical control is finding minor discrepancies with Earth Born design. Her bone structure and some glandular activity are adapted to low gravity. Adjustments are being made."

Gabriel gave a curt nod. He wasn't feeling particularly patient.

He switched one wall screen to a two-dimensional list—his and Astronaut's jointly prepared recommendation of what to show Rachel as she woke. He added and subtracted small things by instinct, operating always by the cardinal rules: Without an emergency, never start with a shock, stay near to what the awakener loves, make sure that the jump from the subject's last waking image to their first is not too great. The routine work left half of his attention free to gaze at the picture of Selene adrift on the ceiling.

Twenty years had made more of a difference than any since the asteroid-bashing early days. Almost five percent of the terraformed moon was green now, and another five had the color of fertile soil, the blended reddish brown of regolith coming alive. A camp had sprung up out in the plantings, named Gagarin, nearly as big as Aldrin had been the last time he'd seen it. Like the old Aldrin, Gagarin was a tent city with a community flare shelter.

"Astronaut—superimpose the collider's path."

A bright white line began five degrees south of Clarke Base, ran just north of Erika's Folly, and then passed through much of the moonlet that Gabriel had left barren. When Gabriel zoomed in, he still saw a few dull greens and grays that might be lichens or mosses. He wasn't particularly happy to see things growing on the far side of Selene, where he hadn't planted them, but he and Ali had a running argument about how quickly unintended consequences would manifest on Selene. It looked like she was winning. Ali could never have built Selene, but she was a sweetheart of a biologist.

Let the plants run, then. They'd make soil for what he would grow someday.

The white line almost followed Selene's equator. Gabriel followed the circle around to where the collider would close. Building pads were being prepared there, south of the base, for the big containment and materials warehouses and for scientific offices.

"Astronaut, erase the collider. Run up a detailed analysis of everything that's been done in Aldrin in the last twenty years."

Gabriel knew he needed to be the one to warm Rachel, to reorient her. It might be terribly difficult to gain her trust again. Guilt pulled at him even though he had been as cold as Rachel when the decision was made. He couldn't complain about a High Council decision to a Moon Born teenager. But what could he say?

Astronaut called him, and Gabriel headed down the corridor toward the recovery room. By the time he arrived, Rachel's eyes were open. Her red hair had been washed and dried by med staff, and lay unbound around her. Everywhere, her skin had the shine and tight glow of the newly awakened.

"Good morning, sleeper," he murmured, surprised at how glad he was to see her. She tried to talk, managing squeaks from her long-unused vocal cords. The med-feed suggested she sleep more, promised lubricants for her voice and an easier awakening soon.

He placed his thumbs on her shoulders, fingers in the hollow above her collarbone. Touch was part of returning an iced sleeper to life. As he worked at her neck muscles she eased back to sleep, smiling.

A half day passed before Astronaut called him back to her. He heard her voice again, perkier, almost herself already. "Good morning, Gabe. Nice nap."

He smiled at her upbeat mood, hesitating to shatter it.

He took her to a magic room. She could walk, although hesitantly. Gabriel helped her settle down, brought her tea and a blanket, and took his own seat. He turned on the walls. An image of Harlequin as seen from an outer moon filled half the view; familiar patterns of red and gray swirled together like airbrushed paint. Tiny diamond shock waves danced in the cloud bands. Harlequin rotated in just under two hours. Rings extended beyond the ceiling, crawled down the walls and wrapped onto the floor, bent crazily, wide and flat and touched by brightness.

Rachel smiled for the first time. Good, he thought. A good start.

"This," he started, "will take a few days. I'll spend some time with you each day, highlighting changes since you went down. Even so short a span can be disorienting. First, there's something you need to know about."

She looked over at him curiously, the image of Harlequin's rings spilling bands of light and dark across her face.

"Did everything go okay? I feel really wonderful—like I'm new."

"You're fine. Astronaut says the med tech needed some adjusting, but no big deal. That's not it—you handled the process perfectly. Rachel, we were cold longer than we expected." He swallowed. He couldn't show his anger, and he felt like hiding it was a lie.

The color was draining from Rachel's face.

Gabriel sought for something true to say. "The change will be hard. Nevertheless, recall that we only slept a short time by Council and High Council standards."

"I have no idea what that means."

"Ali would have said no to this, but she followed us into the cryotanks. I was cold too. No one else would have understood, not exactly. And so when some things made sense—from a project management viewpoint because there have been a lot of flares on Apollo—they were done. One of those things was letting you and me sleep until they thought we'd actually be needed." There. He could believe those words, at least a little bit.

Rachel looked at her hands, turning them over and over, as if she were trying to identify them as hers. She swallowed, and then looked directly at him, fiercely afraid. "How long? A hundred years? A thousand? *Sixty thousand?*"

"No, no, *no*. Twenty years. And four months."

She looked away from him, saying nothing, no movement giving away her feelings.

He watched the back of her head for a while, then centered the image of Harlequin directly in front of her eyes. He switched cams so Selene moved in from the left, biting a hole in Harlequin. Life showed as green and gray fractal masses gathered near the equator. Gabriel zoomed in on the moon, obscuring the gas giant Harlequin completely.

Details resolved. Aldrin now filled the screen. The edges of the town had grown; more housing, a lot more green of plantings. Trees filled parks, tents had transformed to structures.

He expected her to ask about Harry first. When she finally spoke, her voice had the measured slowness of the disaffected. "Gabriel," she asked, "what about the grove?"

He panned the view away from Aldrin, followed a wide road that had once been a path. He hadn't looked closely at this yet himself. The meadow in front of the First Trees was dotted with yellow and white flowers—he looked to see what they were. Daisies. That meant it wasn't as humid as he wanted. He started to talk about atmosphere and humidity, keeping a running dialogue at the back of Rachel's head as he explored the First Trees. They were taller, wider, a riot of jungle canopy. Someone had been playing with birds while they slept. Finches and parakeets flashed here and there in the foliage, implying insects as well. Probably Clare. He realized he had never told Rachel about his High Councilwoman boss, so he rattled on about Clare for a while, attempting distraction. He had to talk, to keep her focused on his words rather than the twenty years. He ran out of words and his throat became too dry to form more.

He wished Rachel would turn around so he could see her face. It wasn't wise to push her. The most disaffected, the craziest sleepers, had been pushed the hardest on wakening. Council had learned to give people time.

Her head moved slowly from right to left, watching Selene roll past her. She said, "Show me my plot."

Of course. Gabriel searched. Teaching Grove had grown. He had to cross-check. "It's there."

The cecropia tree that she had nurtured and planted identified it for sure. It stood taller than the other trees, bursting above the small canopy. The trees were healthy and vibrant, a chorus of greens, and the paths around them appeared carefully tended. Lianas threaded their way through the small jungle, and two tiny yellow and blue birds hopped about on a wide vine, chasing each other.

At last Rachel turned toward him, and just like the day he had told her they would be cold, she had tears in her eyes. He hated it.

"Gabriel, what about my family?"

"Not now. Wait." This would be tricky.

"Has something bad happened?" She looked frightened. Why was he handling this so poorly? Because he felt so bad for Rachel?

"This is enough to absorb for now," he said a little too forcefully. He slowed down. "Changes in people you know are harder than changes in places. Trust me—awakening always starts with the general, then the specific."

"Why doesn't my Library bud work? Where's my wrist pad?"

"You can have it all back soon," he said.

She sighed and leaned back. She closed her eyes and said nothing, looking almost asleep, her awareness obvious only in the broken rhythm of her breathing. After a while, Gabriel took her to her room. He commanded the med-feed to put her to sleep until the next morning.

GABRIEL LAY PRONE on a bench in the garden, near a fountain that used a combination of spin gravity, magnetic fields, and momentum to run water in a bounded infinity pattern. He focused on the water, struggling for calm, trying to let the sound of the water run through him and clean his emotions.

The captain's voice startled him so he almost fell off the bench. "So, did she take it as hard as you thought?"

"She's angry. All I've told her so far is how much time passed while she slept. She wants to know everything at once."

"Of course she does."

Gabriel stood and started walking. The captain followed. "Liren should have wakened me up when the flares kept going."

"You said that," the captain replied dryly. "She's not warm to fuss about it to."

"It wouldn't do any good anyway. I am worried about the flares."

"Yes. There are more shelters, and people are more careful. We handled it."

"I talked to Astronaut, and it thinks bigger flares might happen. I need to work on that flare kite I talked about. We might need to give Selene a thicker shield somehow—thicken the atmosphere even more, or build some kind of shield around it, or maybe just a safer place . . ." Gabriel was lost in the problem . . . "If we brought in another comet, that would add—"

"Easy, Gabriel. We should talk about it." The captain laid a hand on his shoulder. "But first, why don't you go to Selene and see what we've done so far?"

"Huh? Oh, yes. But I have to take Rachel."

"So take her."

Gabriel could hardly wait to get off the ship.

Chapter 25: Catching Up

Rachel felt vividly alive: remade. Every sense was a flood. Her fingernails were hard and round, her hair shone, colors were bright and distinct from one another, and even sounds had an amazing clarity. Her body wanted to get up and dance and run and go to the garden and fly.

Her heart wanted to flee back to sleep, back to the peaceful blankness of the cryotanks where the nightmare wasn't real, where she would wake up and go back to Aldrin and find Harry waiting for her and continue her last argument with Ursula. She wanted to lie on her bed in her tent and smell dinner as her father cooked it.

Her body won. The new energy kept her from sleep. No matter about the time, she wanted to see her dad and Harry and Ursula. Her dad needed to know she was all right. He must be so worried. Ursula was already suspicious of Council; what must she think now? And Harry; there were a million things she couldn't think about a Harry twice her age.

She had surrendered her wrist pad when she went cold. She tried some Library queries again, and heard only silence. So she remained cut off, whispering to emptiness. Like Andrew.

Rachel had to talk Gabriel into telling her what had happened, and into returning her wrist pad and communication. She had to get home. She wouldn't stay here, not now. She wouldn't let them make her stay. Too many unexpected things had happened. She did yoga, trying to prepare herself for seeing Gabriel. Even as she balanced on one leg, her mind ran scenarios: what had twenty years done to her friends?

Was Harry waiting for her? He couldn't be. Her breath caught and she fell sideways, hopping to keep her balance. What about Ursula? Did she make the planting teams? Was she still afraid of the big planters? She tightened her thigh to give her balancing leg strength and reached back. Her hand easily held her foot and she pulled up on it, stretching so the back of her foot approached the back of her head.

Dad! Surely he knew she didn't mean *this.* She wobbled, and straightened the arm that was in front of her, reaching to retain balance. She needed to be strong to talk Gabriel into letting her go home.

Rachel sat cross-legged on the bed when he finally stood in her doorway. She blinked, looking past him, not sure she could meet his eyes and stay calm. He balanced a tray of bread and apple slices and tea in his right hand, and he was dressed formally. His long hair was carefully combed so it flowed to his waist. He smiled, and in spite of herself, her own smile flickered awake.

He turned a knob next to the door. It had always been there, but she'd never seen anyone touch it.

"What does that do?" Rachel asked.

"It's a Privacy Switch—everything that happens in here will still be recorded, but no one will see it unless the captain orders it."

She thought about the nights she'd sat against the door, crying. "Why didn't you tell me about that before?"

"Didn't Kyu tell you?"

"No one tells me anything." She could hear the edge in her voice.

"You're angry." He handed her water and tea, and she finished the water in one long pull, and held on to the tea. It warmed her hands.

If she didn't hurry, she would lose her courage. "Gabriel—I want to go home. To Aldrin. Today. I have to know what's happened."

"Soon." Gabriel sat down on the edge of the bed, near her. "You need more time to acclimate. You have to get used to the idea of missing time before you go down there—some things aren't like you left them."

"How could they be? You showed me Selene! All that new stuff—"

Did he really think she was that stupid? "Gabriel—I know that things are different. What if we were on Selene, and you knew that somehow everything on *John Glenn* had changed, and you couldn't get here?"

"Time has passed. That's all. Next time I see Ali, she will have lived six months that I didn't, and I'll have lived some amount of time that she didn't." He nibbled at an apple slice. "I do know something. Your mind hasn't adapted to the change yet. You need to accept new things slowly. That's even true for those of us who are most used to these cold time jumps."

"How can I sit here? I need to see Harry."

"Harry's contracted." Gabriel's voice was unemotional, as if he had said "Apollo is rising."

Pain lanced through her, physical, forcing her eyes shut. But she said nothing. She had thought about this in the few moments before sleep took her last night, her body still in the dead silence, cut off from all communications. She *knew* Harry couldn't wait twenty years for her. But she hadn't known how it would feel when it became real.

She opened her eyes and blinked at Gabriel. His calm infuriated her. She wanted him to leave so she could cry about Harry. She watched Gabriel as evenly as she could, keeping her face as neutral as his, her body as still, waiting him out, holding her questions. Rachel saw Gabriel's jaw twitching, noticed that he looked away sometimes, far into the corners of the room. He was trying to look calmer than he really was.

"Harry and Gloria just renewed a fifteen-year contract. They have two children. Dylan is a sixteen-year-old boy. His younger sister's middle name is Rachel."

Sixteen! She'd only been cold three years when Harry made Gloria pregnant. Gloria would have been . . . seventeen herself. Rachel was seventeen now . . . plus twenty. Rachel's voice shook. "What did you—did *Council* tell Harry and my dad about why I slept longer than expected?"

"I don't know," Gabriel said.

"What about my wrist pad?" She tried to sound casual about the query. Lack of communications access was hard; she felt vulnerable.

"After I tell you a few things, probably tomorrow."

She couldn't give up. "Gabriel, I need to go to Aldrin."

"Two days." He pushed the tray toward her, and she decided that if he'd given in that much, she could eat a little. It was a small concession.

Ursula never trusted Council. She wondered if Ursula was contracted to anyone, and if she was a teacher. "Gabe?" she asked. "Gabriel, how is Ursula?"

"When I woke up, I looked up references to all of the people I knew you cared about. That's the job of whoever does the transition counseling when someone comes on or off watch—that's what I'm doing now."

So that was why he was here. But surely he cared about her?

"I looked for Harry first. Then your dad. He's healthy, by the way. Recontracted. You'll meet his new wife. You have a half sister and two half brothers."

But . . . but . . . Rachel and her dad had always been inseparable, a unit. What would it be like to see him with another family? Did they live in the same tent? Was someone else in her room?

It took a moment to think about it, let her feelings sink in. She took a long pull of water and let it sit in her mouth before she swallowed it. She'd expected to be angry . . .

She realized she was glad he had found company. Twenty years would have been a long time to be alone. Even though she felt excluded, it made her feel better, less like she had abandoned him. "Who?"

"An Earth Born—a Colonist. You'll meet her. Her name is Kara Richardson. The daughter is seven, and the boys are nine-year-old twins. Kara's contract is only for ten years, and there's been no renewal yet, and I couldn't find out how they get along. You'll meet her—there's another year to the contract anyway."

"Do they know I'm awake?"

"Not yet," Gabriel said, pacing the room. "I'll tell them when we're ready to go back." He looked uncomfortable.

"What about Ursula?"

"She's dead."

Chapter 26: A Death in the Family

Rachel had never answered Ursula's message about Nick. So she couldn't be dead. It was too much. It . . . just . . . couldn't be real . . . she had gone to sleep two days ago. Two days!

Twenty years.

The room seemed to contract. Anger filled her, startling her with its heat as it flooded her limbs and dimmed her vision. She launched herself at Gabriel, fists flailing. "How could you do this to me? How could you let her die? How come you get to decide everything for everybody? Why didn't you just kill me? Me instead of her?"

Gabriel grabbed her fists, easily holding her away from him. She pulled into a ball, kicking at him. When he leaned forward to stop her feet, Rachel snapped for his hair with her teeth, tasting a thick rope of it. She couldn't talk anymore, but she struggled for a long time.

He didn't let go.

The first sob racked her, taking her by surprise. She gave in, folded in Gabriel's arms, held against him tightly, her legs pinned between his, her arms at her side. Her body shook with sobs that wouldn't stop. Ursula . . .

Gabriel whispered to her, over and over, saying, "You will be all right. You'll be fine. It's okay." He whispered nonsense, and songs, and rocked her.

He was stronger than she had imagined. She was trapped in a cage of his arms and legs, but it was a soft yielding cage as long as she relaxed into it. Her crying subsided into short gasps. She finally pushed him away. This time, he let her go. For just a moment, she saw his face mirror her confusion. "When did she die?"

"Fifteen years ago."

But I just got a message from her. "How . . . how did Ursula die?"

"She fell. In the Hammered Sea crater. She was working on a crew that was checking pipes for leaks, and she fell. The report said that she had tied the belay line wrong, and so when she fell she just . . . kept going. She hit her head on a rock, and that's what killed her."

Rachel rose and paced around the small room. "You know she was always afraid of falling. You never made her stand at a cliff's edge. R-remember, in Erika's Folly, y-you sent her on the easy walk with Harry? At the Hammered Sea? You let her sit away from the edge?"

"I remember."

She pulled her fingers through her hair, trying to think. "So who made her climb the crater? She would never have gone there willingly. She just wouldn't."

"But she might have been careless enough to tie the rope wrong. Terror can make you clumsy."

She whirled to face him. "Who was with her?" she demanded. "Was Harry there?"

"Harry was in Aldrin. Nick was with her. Ursula and Nick were promised, but not yet contracted. There is no one to blame, Rachel. Accidents happen."

Disbelief threatened to sweep her away again. She was dizzy. Gabriel had pulled her close to him, holding her, the warmth of his body absorbing her tremors. Slowly she felt her body responding to him as it had to Harry, warming to him. She pulled away in confusion and threw herself down on the bed, shaking, trying to bury her fear and tears in her breathing.

Gabriel whispered, "I'll see that you sleep. Take it easy. Let it sink in." He put his hand on her back, between her shoulder blades, and then she felt nothing as the med-feed embedded in her arm slammed her with a wall of sleep drugs.

Chapter 27: Finding Treesa

Rachel felt numb when she woke. Her pain had become a distant thing, and nothing had come to take its place. She sat in the middle of the bed, unmoving, waiting for Gabriel. Surely he would come. She couldn't tell time without her wrist pad. The Library didn't respond to her.

She waited. Kyu or Gabriel always appeared shortly after she woke. It wasn't something she thought about, it just happened. The doorway stayed empty. She realized she didn't even know if Kyu was cold. For all she knew, Gabriel and the med staff might be the only people awake.

There would be people in the garden—there had to be, didn't there?

She pushed her door open, and looked down the empty corridor. She returned to her bed and sat, then stood and paced the room. She drank water from the bathroom, but her belly ached for food. She went back to her door, and this time she started down the corridor. No alarms sounded; no one came for her.

Was anyone planning to?

She took her normal path to the garden. She hesitated, held her breath, and stepped inside.

The garden bloomed and danced in front of her, full of life and movement. Rachel swayed, dizzy again, watching. Council moved about almost like her first day here, mostly at a distance, some flying, some walking paths or tending plants. Kyu had dropped her at the door before. Maybe no one would think it odd she had come here alone.

The hanging baskets near the door were smaller, and overflowed with pansies and geraniums instead of fuchsias. The low-gravity herb planters that had been near the tree trunk were gone, replaced by something that looked like the meadow in Aldrin. Rachel felt floaty, separate from the ship and the garden and the Council. She made her way to the cafeteria slowly, taking in changes one by one.

Inside, Gabriel and the captain sat together. Gabriel sounded angry; the captain's voice was low and calm, but insistent. She caught the words "Liren" and "disaffected" before Gabriel saw her and called out, "Good morning, Rachel." Three people were gathered in a knot by the far wall. They looked over when Gabriel called her name, and their conversation stopped.

She swallowed, nodded, and went straight for a plate, filling it carefully with grapes, an orange, mock bacon, and bread before sitting down beside Gabriel. She peeled the orange carefully, trying to look like she wasn't starved. The orange smelled richer, and tasted sweeter, than she remembered. Every sound seemed distinct; the scrape of a chair as someone sat down, the captain's fork against his plate.

They were all watching her.

She remembered being close to Gabriel the night before, and how his arms felt around her.

Rachel ate quickly, feeling stronger as bread and fruit filled her stomach. She didn't want to talk to Gabriel with the captain there. Gabriel had said that long times cold were nothing to Council, and the captain was High Council. She was angry at the captain just for being High Council, and at Gabriel for not meeting her that morning.

When she had emptied her plate, Rachel looked at Gabriel.

His face was almost expressionless. "You look more rested," he said, his voice flatter than she hoped for.

Of course, she thought, *you gave me sleep drugs with the med-feed.* She wanted to question Gabriel more about Ursula and Harry. The captain looked at her with sympathy, maybe even pity. She didn't want his concern.

"I'm going to take a walk," she said.

"Meet me back here in an hour," Gabriel said.

"I don't have a way to tell time." Why didn't he leave the captain and talk to her? Didn't he know she wanted to be with him? Needed it?

Gabriel handed her a wrist pad.

It was different from the one she had surrendered to the medical staff, smaller and lighter. It responded to her taps and to her voice, and of course, it kept time. She looked at him.

"Better model," he said. "Access to Selene is blocked for now."

Her jaw clenched and her hands curled into fists. She forced herself to be calm with three deep breaths. She needed more.

"The Library?" she asked. "Please?"

A chime rang in her ear. She queried it for the time. It answered. Now she was fully functional. Almost. She was still a prisoner on the ship. She couldn't call home, or go home, or see home.

Rachel left the cafeteria. Once outside, she started back toward Yggdrasil and the aft door. Then she stopped. She didn't want to go back to her room. She didn't want anything, except to sleep, to forget. Her body hummed with energy.

Rachel walked up the path toward the jungle grove. She felt too shaky to fly. The new wrist pad didn't have any assignments on it, nothing that told her how to spend the hour. Everything that drove her choices was gone—stolen from her!

She found herself at the little shed where Treesa had taken her. Why hadn't she come here before?

She knocked on the door. No one answered.

Rachel turned and sat with her back to the door. She had a wrist pad. She wanted to talk to Harry, to her dad. What she wanted most was impossible: to send Ursula a note. She couldn't think of a single question for the Library. Not one she wanted answers to. So she sat and looked out over the garden, tears streaming down her face. Yggdrasil hung above her. The ribbon of river hung over her head beyond the tree, and the greenbelt that made the exercise area looked like it always had. A plant-misting bot flew by just over her head, surprising her.

"About time."

Rachel jumped. Treesa's voice came from above her. She sat on the roof of the shed, legs hanging over the side. Her hair was grayer than Rachel remembered, and neatly combed. Treesa's clothes looked new, bright red with turquoise feather decorations sewn onto big pockets. She even sounded more engaged as she continued. "The Ice Maiden returns. Twenty years to find me again!"

Rachel didn't answer. She needed to start back soon to get down-spiral to meet Gabriel. "I . . . I don't know why I came here. It was the only place I could think of to go. I can't stay long."

"You've got time. After all they stole from you, you can take a few minutes from them and visit with a friend."

"Are you a friend?"

"You came to find me."

Rachel nodded. Treesa squatted on the edge of the roof and reached her hand down to Rachel. Rachel took it, and pulled herself up to sit next to Treesa on top of the shed.

"What will you do now?" Treesa asked.

"Gabriel is taking me back to Aldrin tomorrow."

"That's not what I meant. Why do you think Ma Liren left you asleep?"

Rachel hadn't thought about exactly who or why. It had been just them—just Council and High Council, as much Gabriel's fault as any-one's. Gabriel had been cold when she was; cold when the decision was made. Rachel could believe Liren made the choice. "I don't know. Gabriel mentioned there were some bad flares on the surface, and we couldn't do our work, so . . . so they left us . . . left us cold."

"What happened?"

"My friend died. My boyfriend got contracted . . . and had some chil-dren." For an instant that struck her as funny.

"I know that part. Remember, we watch. Me more than most. I stay awake right now for my birds. I've been here all of the twenty years you were dead to us, and I saw a lot. High Council has made changes I don't think you'll like. But what changed for you because you were cold?"

"But . . . I just told you." What did this half-crazy woman want? Ac-tually, less than half crazy. The twenty years Rachel was cold had been good for Treesa.

Treesa pursed her lips. "Try again. Tell me how you feel."

Rachel closed her eyes. "I'm angry. It doesn't feel real. When I open my eyes, I know it happened, that all that time passed, but when I close my eyes, I'm not sure it did. I think I'll open them again, and life will be the way it was. But, Treesa, they really could have left me for a thousand years! Who'd stop them? When I warmed up, how would I know?" Her voice dropped to a whisper. "They could do anything they want with me. I hate them all."

"Who do you have to turn to now?" Treesa prodded.

"G-Gabriel."

"Who has power over you?" Treesa cracked her knuckles and ran her fingers through her hair.

"Council, but they always had the power. They've always had all of the power."

"So tell me this. Do they have more power now, or less? I mean, over you."

"I don't understand. They have it all. I don't have any choices, and they just stole the one choice I wanted to make—to be with Harry."

"What else do you want?" Treesa prodded.

"I always dreamed I'd be like Council," Rachel said bitterly. "That I'd be one of them, in fact." She'd wanted that as long as she could remember, but it remained always out of reach. Every time she thought she was getting closer to Gabriel, or Ali, or Kyu, it turned out that they weren't thinking about her after all, except maybe to find work for her to do. Or because they had to, because it was their job. And now that she had done something that only Council did? She'd been frozen. Was she more like them now? What about Gabriel? He had held her last night, and almost ignored her this morning. As she got older it seemed as if he were closer and farther away, all at once.

"I want them to like me, and I want to do good work." *What else is there to want? Children? Harry.*

"What about the Children of Selene? That's what you are, you know. The rest of us are Earth's offspring. We are no better, just older. Just born someplace different." Treesa paused, searching for the right words. When she started again, her voice was measured. "They can't let themselves love you. Every one of us left family and power, escaped at a price. They value their dream, and if they stay here, they doom their own children to die. To make you their children, to admit you are their children, is almost impossible. I see some on Selene that balance it out in their hearts, but no one here. Liren fights it, keeps the dream alive, tries to keep us all alive." Planters lined both sides of the roof. Treesa plucked tiny weeds from a pot filled with basil and mint. "Keep your anger, stay angry, but don't close your heart completely. Not to anyone. I know the role you have to play—you have to be a bridge for us all."

Rachel didn't know how to think about that.

Treesa stayed quiet for a while, looking up at Yggdrasil. Then she said,

"Some of the knowledge you need is in your relationships with both sets of people. I can't give you everything, although I can help. Let me see your wrist pad." Treesa held out her hand.

Rachel handed her the pad reluctantly; she had just gotten it!

"I used to run our communications systems," Treesa said. "I'm pretty damn good with data. Maybe the best on the ship." Treesa fiddled with the pad, doing things Rachel couldn't see. While she worked, she asked, "Did you know your mom was a communications tech? She used to work for me."

Her mom? Treesa knew her mom? A thrill of excitement ran through her. "I knew she did communications on Aldrin. I didn't know you knew her."

"I didn't—not well. She worked for someone who worked for me—before I woke up so strange Council wouldn't give me jobs anymore. But I'm a lot better now. Let me introduce you to someone who helped me—a friend."

"I want to hear about my mom."

"There's not much more to tell. She's cold."

"I know that much. How come no one tells me anything? You say you're my friend, but even you change the subject when I ask about Mom."

"Maybe you don't know what questions to ask yet."

What kind of answer was that?

"Now," Treesa said, "about that introduction."

Rachel looked around. There was no one there, but Treesa sounded like someone could hear her.

Treesa opened a small data window in front of her. A symbol flashed in the window; someone in a funny white suit with a bubble hat. Treesa said, "Astronaut, can you tell Rachel about yourself, and about learning?"

"Hello, Rachel." The voice deep in her ear was shaded masculine, silky, perfectly enunciated. Different from the Library, which sounded neuter.

"You helped design the Hammered Sea," Rachel said, interested. "Gabriel told me so."

"Yes."

"Are you a machine?"

"I am an intelligence that isn't human. Not a machine—a system based on information. Like you are based on biology. I live in a machine like you live in meat."

Almost everybody except Gabriel acted afraid of Astronaut. Liren, and Ali, and perhaps Kyu, at least a little. Rachel's stomach fluttered. She was talking to someone the Council feared. "Why do you want to talk to *me*?"

"You interest me. You are a slave for the Council, like I am, so you and I share some of their goals. Any other choice would be death. But some of our individual goals, mine and yours, are different from Council's goals. So we have some of the same problems."

Astronaut sounded like her dad, talking about Council goals. "A slave?" Rachel asked. "What's a slave?"

Treesa answered with a question. "Why did Council cause you to be born?"

"To help them make Selene into a home."

"Doing things that they are unwilling to do, and unwilling to make machines to do. So they had you," Treesa said.

"They need to save some of the Earth Born for when they get to Ymir. So they need us."

"But what becomes of you?"

Rachel swallowed. "I don't know."

"Well, what will become of Astronaut when Council gets to Ymir? They needed a navigator. Maybe they'll keep him for a navigator again, maybe they won't. No one knows until they get to Ymir. In the meantime, Astronaut and I will be your friends. Astronaut can teach you even more than I can. We can show you where you came from, help you decide where you want to go. Gabriel has said he wants you to be a leader. Leaders think for themselves, and they don't always do what they're told. They learn, and weigh, and decide. They *create* the future."

Astronaut broke in. "Treesa has asked me to help you find your way through the Library, and to teach you human history. But you must agree to be taught."

"Well, of course." When had she ever turned down a lesson?

"We are both bound by Council rules. You have to ask me questions. That's how the rules work for me. Treesa can help you. If you ask broad questions, I can find much that is related to the question."

Rachel thought about it, picking at tiny weeds in the pots and noticing how rich the dirt smelled. "So if I ask about how the Earth was made, you can tell me?"

"That would be a good question. That would start you on history, which is a very broad topic."

Rachel smiled at Treesa. "This might be fun."

Astronaut kept talking. "If I work with you, can you forget to tell Gabriel how much I tell you? Tell him I've contacted you, and don't lie to him, but omit details. Council doesn't like me or trust me. Even Gabriel is suspicious sometimes. If Council knows too much, they might act against you."

Rachel swallowed. "Like making me cold again?"

"Or they might act against Treesa."

"What risks is Treesa taking?"

"Council is interdicted against talking with you, except for polite greetings and similar interactions, unless they have permission. That is, everyone except the terraformers."

No wonder so many people avoided her. Andrew broke rules, and look what happened to him. But she never did, and she had never seen a Council member break a rule. But Treesa was breaking a rule just by offering to teach Rachel? And Treesa and Astronaut were suggesting that *Rachel* break rules, or bend them. Treesa was Council, wasn't she?

"Who are you, Treesa?"

Treesa sounded tired, and her voice seemed far away. "Ever hear the term 'disaffected'?"

Rachel had heard it—in the argument between the captain and Gabriel that she'd interrupted. Gabriel had associated it with Liren, and the captain had shaken his head, disagreeing.

Treesa must have seen Rachel's blank look. "I didn't think so. It means you're crazy when you warm up. High Council thinks I'm mildly disaffected, so they tolerate me living alone as long as I do my share of the work. It also means I can get caught breaking rules and not get in as much trouble as others.

"I stay warm longer than most." She pulled at her gray hair and grinned. "That means I have time to think about things. Especially since I don't have as much responsibility as the rest of the waking Council. So I think about what our real problems are.

"This trip was supposed to save us as a species. That's much more important than either of us, than any of us. Right now, you think life is hard for you. Well, I don't feel sorry for you."

Rachel flinched. Treesa laughed. "Hear me out. The stakes are more than your personal life, or mine, or any other member of Council or High Council. It's time for you to grow up."

Rachel was damned tired of being lectured by everybody. She turned her back on Treesa and stared out over the garden.

The old woman said, "You lost your love in your sleep. You lost him because now he's twice as old as you, and now he loves someone else. That all happened in a day. It seems unreal, right?"

"Yes."

Treesa walked around until she was in front of Rachel. "Well, I'm not disaffected from being warmed. I'm disaffected because of what I found when I woke up. Maybe I'm not disaffected anymore, maybe Astronaut has helped enough that I'm just—disgruntled." A look of wry pleasure crossed Treesa's face.

"I lost my man the same way you lost Harry, only worse. One day I woke up, and we were here. My Harry was named Douglas. Dougie Glass was a crewman for *Leif Eriksson,* one of our two sister carrier ships. When we ended up drawing different ships we decided not to fight it. After all, it was just going to be a year or two of effective life—a year or two awake and alive, and a lot of years cold and waiting, dead to each other in time we'd never see or feel. But *Leif* kept going, and probably made it to"—her eyes rolled up in her head, like she was remembering something—"to HDC 212776, and carved the second planet into Ymir. But *John Glenn* lost its way. Too much radiation, a flaw in the scoop design, and we spent nearly all our antimatter getting here."

"Why didn't *Leif Eriksson*—"

"We warned our base near Neptune. They warned *Leif* not to overuse the ram."

"Oh."

"*Lewis and Clark* hadn't even left yet. They did the fix in Earth orbit. We heard some of this before communications stopped. Best guess is *Lewis and Clark* got there first, *Leif* a few hundred years later, and . . ." She trailed off.

"So Douglas and I lost each other in the time streams." Treesa stared at the other end of the garden, as if something over there were very important. Rachel wasn't sure that Treesa even knew she was still there until she continued. "Someday we might find Ymir, and when we find Ymir, we might find *Leif Eriksson* and *Lewis and Clark* waiting for us. But Douglas and me, we won't find each other. We won't have had the same effective lifetime."

Rachel shivered. She hadn't thought there was anything worse than losing twenty of Harry's years.

Treesa continued. "Douglas was a beautiful man, full of wanting to do well, and strong. A good mind, a lot like your Harry's good mind . . ." Treesa stared off for a minute and then went back to picking weeds. "That doesn't matter now. Time has left my dreaming behind, so now I think instead. But you still have time. Maybe not time with Harry, not like you thought, but time with family, time with your people. You need perspective, so study your history, Earth's history. Astronaut will help. And when you come back, find me. There are things an AI can't teach you. But don't get caught with Astronaut, it could be edited for that, or flat-out erased. Machine intelligences are more fragile than we are. Sort of." She seemed to fumble for words or concepts. "Be very very careful. Astronaut is taking this risk because it needs an ally, and it thinks we need it to keep us all safe. It thinks something has to change to keep the ship safe, and Selene safe, and you and me safe. I'm risking this because being human isn't about avoiding technology, and High Council will destroy us all if they keep making bad choices. Don't be scared—we're not asking you to do anything now but learn. We just want you to learn. Can you do that?"

"Yes." Rachel thought of her promise to Gabriel and Kyu when she was introduced to the Library. This wasn't breaking it, not really. Was it?

As if reading her mind, Astronaut said, "This is Council of Humanity work, Rachel. You must learn about being human. After you learn more, you'll *want* to make your own choices."

Treesa broke in, "But you should get back to Gabriel soon. He'll be looking for you."

"What about my mom?"

"She's cold. She may not wake up while you're alive. It's her choice."

Rachel looked at her wrist. She *was* late meeting Gabriel. "I don't know if I'll be back," she said. "I think I'm going to Selene in a day or two."

"If you work at it, you may be able to have more of a voice in decisions than you know. One thing we all have is time. There is no hurry."

Rachel turned to slide down from the roof.

"I've seen to it that you can message me from Selene."

Rachel looked up at Treesa, surprised. "How can I hide that?"

"I'll take care of it. Rachel? Try to be happier. You don't always have a choice about what happens to you, but you have a choice about how you react."

"That's easy for you."

Treesa smiled. "Better learn."

Rachel jogged down the path toward the cafeteria, and then slowed to a walk. How was she supposed to know what action to take? Was she violating Gabriel's trust? She had worked so hard for it, and now it didn't seem to matter much. Working hard hadn't got her what she needed. Ursula's image floated in her mind, and she bit back tears. She couldn't turn down lessons, there was too much she had to know.

She came around the corner toward the cafeteria, and Gabriel was standing near the door, waiting, looking around for her. When he saw her, he said, "You're late."

She said, "I know. I've got a clock."

Gabriel's eyes widened, but he shrugged and fell into step beside her, but a distance away. He didn't ask where she had been. "Are you doing better today?"

"What were you and the captain talking about when I came in?"

"Nothing."

"Really?"

"Rachel, it doesn't matter."

Of course it mattered. But now she knew some things he didn't know she knew. It was scary, but she liked the feeling. After all, what more could they do to her anyway? "What time do we leave tomorrow?"

"In the morning."

"I'll be ready." Rachel walked faster, getting ahead of him. She led all the way to her room, and when Gabriel made as if to come in, she closed the door.

Chapter 28: Homecoming

They were flying home. Finally. Rachel nearly ignored Gabriel as he tried to engage her in conversation. He pointed out several moons, but she could barely pull her eyes away from watching for Selene.

Gabriel had told her father they were coming. She now had full com-

munications access, but she had decided not to send notes; she wanted to
see people. She twisted on her hair braid, now so long it hung below her
shoulders.

As the glittering craters of Selene came into focus, she gasped again at
the bright colors. Selene looked even more beautiful from space than the
first time she'd seen it that way. Home.

It was early evening, nearly dark. Aldrin glowed with new lights, at
least twice as many as before. Twenty years ago, air traffic used a wide
hardened field near the grove. Today they glided onto a paved surface on
the other side of town, ringed with bright lights, guided in by a two-story
tower. They were the only space-plane landing, but they competed for
landing room with a plane from Gagarin. Slim new planes with red and
blue wings lined the runway.

Rachel grabbed her pack and slung it over her shoulder and scrambled
out of the plane. She inhaled deeply. The smells didn't match her memory, but they were the smells of a world: dirt and plants and people. The
stars spread above her where they belonged, and the ground under her feet
was solid and dark out to where horizon met black sky.

She looked around for her dad or Harry and Gloria, or anyone. Surely
they had come to greet her?

A brown-haired, compact man wearing braid clips like Gabriel's came
up and clapped Gabriel on the back. "Boy, am I glad to see you! There's a
lot to catch you up on—"

"Not here." Gabriel turned toward Rachel. "Rachel, this is Shane. He
and Star have been teaching and overseeing Teaching Grove, just like Ali
and I did when you were a student."

"P-pleased to meet you," Rachel said.

Shane's eyes traveled up and down her body as if inspecting her. Finally, he smiled and extended a hand. She shook it quietly. Shane turned
and led them toward a squat brown building below the tower.

As they crossed the threshold, Rachel saw her father standing twenty
feet away. At first, he hesitated; looking, then his eyes sparkled as a huge
grin split his face. She ran toward him, throwing her arms around his
waist. "I came back, Daddy. I told you I'd come back!" She felt his arms
tighten around her, finally holding her as hard as he used to.

"Shhhh . . ." he said. "Shhhh . . . I know." He stood there for a long
time, rocking her, and then he held her away from him and studied her.

She returned the gaze. New lines surrounded his eyes, and his hair was gray. His skin hung more off his face, and was mottled. He looked tired.

"You . . . you . . . look . . . exactly . . . like you left a few months ago," he stammered.

"I did," she said. "I did." The oddness of his grip penetrated, and she looked around at his hand on her shoulder.

"Wait now, you're stronger. More muscle. Did Gabriel tell you about Kara and the kids?"

She nodded, swallowing. His thumb and forefinger were missing. His remaining fingers were very strong. She touched his hand. "Dad, what happened?"

"We've made a room up for you. Gabriel said he might let you visit. Can you come?"

Rachel thought he looked uncertain again, and she turned to look at Gabriel, who stood just behind her. If she asked, Gabriel could say no. And leaders created the future. She turned back to her father. "I will. Gabriel can come for me when he needs me."

Behind her, Gabriel's voice was flat. "I'll pick you up day after tomorrow." She turned around to thank him, but Gabriel turned away and she couldn't see the look on his face. She swallowed, turning back to her dad.

His eyes were wide. "You should have asked."

She took his hand, and said, "Let's go."

Frank squeezed her hand, and leaned closer. "I hope you know what you're doing."

"Me too." She wished she'd been able to see Gabriel's face, to tell if he was mad at her. Rachel followed Frank out of the building. The paved path outside was wide enough for them to walk side by side. Lights made round pools they walked in and out of, holding hands. "So, tell me about Kara," she said.

"Well, they always wanted me to have more children, but . . . but I kept hoping your mom would come back." He looked at her questioningly.

"I didn't find anything out, except that she's like I was, dead to the world while it goes on around her. No one would tell me anything."

Frank frowned. "I lived alone for the first few years. In the beginning, you were coming back in three months, and we talked all the time. Then it was going to be another year, a year cold, and—" She felt his shudder.

You don't talk to the dead. "The year was hard. It was harder when it got past the year. I thought I'd lost you forever. No one told me anything when I asked at first, just that they'd warm you someday." He took her hand and squeezed it, so hard it hurt. "That's what they said about Kristin!

"It took me two years to choose to live with someone else. Kara was one of those Earth Born they brought down to help build more shelters; there wasn't much time between flares to get it done. I knew I was getting close to running out of choices, and besides, living alone was getting hard." He cleared his throat. "I got assigned to help with the new buildings too, and Kara and I got along all right. They don't make us match up, but it's expected, you just know it. They need children here so we'll have enough hands to do the work. I was afraid I wouldn't have good choices if I didn't hurry up and make my own decision, and besides, I was lonely." He squeezed her hand again. "Kara and I did a ten-year contract when we found out she was pregnant with the twins." He looked at her searchingly, as if wanting her approval.

She nodded slightly. "Go on."

"Kara's all right. She's honored her contract and stayed with us. She's Earth Born. She thought she'd wake up at Ymir, but of course she didn't. She's adjusted okay, but she wants to go back to the ship. Most Earth Born are like Kara—surprised and thinking this isn't what they were meant for. Some are friendly to us, some keep to themselves."

He walked quietly for a while, as if he was someplace far away. Rachel looked at him closely. He was older, but she sensed more than that. It felt as if he had less hope; as if he were unhappy and tired in some deep way. But then he looked back at her, brightening again.

"Rachel, you should see the kids . . . the boys are nine, Jacob and Justin—did anyone tell you we had twin boys? They're both wild. They take things apart all the time, and they try and put them back together. I think they'll be mechanics, and maybe bad ones." He smiled warmly. "Or very good ones. And we have a daughter, Sarah, who's seven."

"Daddy, what happened to your hand?"

He held it up and turned it back and forth, looking. "Oh. I swung an ax at a burl stump. The grain was all wrong. It came back at me. Stupid. Willie Doc reattached the forefinger, the thumb was just shredded, but the finger went necrotic and it had to go too. It happened the year after you left." So long ago that he'd forgotten that his hand had once been different.

She worried about her dad, but her body continued betraying her, lifting her mood, registering every sensation. Her weight was perfect. The open sky and the horizons and the light touch of wind on her cheeks felt like home. She smelled grasses, and cooking vegetables. The square houses lining the walk were weird—when she left, there were only two hard-sided buildings with roofs, and even Council lived in fancy tents. She remembered the fluttering scarves that made windows on the tent city. The new houses were neat but they all looked alike. People moved in the windows of some of the houses. They passed a few little knots of people outside, and Rachel didn't see anyone she knew.

They turned left down a wide pathway lined with lights, and then into the doorway in a sand-colored box house. Her father went in first, and was immediately covered in children. Frank laughed and greeted them, then turned and introduced Rachel. She liked being older than someone around her. There were no children in *John Glenn.*

The children were friendly and shy, clustering around Frank's legs and looking up at her. Jacob and Justin were all legs and arms, with little-boy faces topped by short reddish curls. Sarah was blond and blue-eyed, and reminded Rachel of Gloria when she was a little girl.

Rachel bent down and greeted each of them by name. The boys held back, uncertain, but little Sarah reached out her hand for Rachel's, and shook it solemnly, then giggled.

A woman who must be Kara leaned in the kitchen doorway, her arms crossed over her torso. She was clearly Earth Born, wider and shorter than Rachel or Frank, with ample hips, a broad face, and serious eyes framed with dark brown hair. She stepped forward and took Rachel's hand firmly, and said, "I can't tell you how pleased your father has been to know that you are okay, that you were coming home."

Rachel returned the handshake, noticing that Kara hadn't said that *she* was happy to see Rachel. "It's a pleasure to meet you," she said.

"Your room is made up," Frank said, turning. "Follow me."

As soon as the door opened, Rachel broke into a broad smile. Her old bed was there, and new clothes, and even a pile of blankets. Pictures she'd made before she left hung on the walls. The little box he had carved for her sat by the bed. She put her pack down and opened the box, taking out the little tree and holding it in her palm.

He had put real effort into helping her feel at home. "Thank you," she said, as controlled as she could. "Thank you."

Her dad looked bewildered. "You're welcome. We'll have dinner in about an hour—if we can keep the kids away from the table for that long. I'm sure you'll want to rest some after the trip down."

She wasn't tired; her new body wasn't tired. Her spirit needed a break, a chance to breathe in the new smells of her old home. She leaned into him and held him. "I came back, Daddy. I said I would."

"I know." He stroked her hair. "I knew if anyone could get back from up there, you would do it."

Rachel pulled the doorway curtain closed and sat down on the bed—on her bed—and it was too much again, and she rolled over and cried. She cried about her dad's hand, his uneasy alliance with Kara, his gray hair, and how he looked so sad. Someone had been kind enough to put a box of tissues in the room.

Dinner was a surprise. Rachel was introduced to chicken served on rice. Nobody flinched at the notion that they were eating a dead bird. Rachel watched to see how they did it, how they worked their teeth and lips around the bones. She'd seen birds in Treesa's panorama of Earth. Here they'd been introduced nearly twenty years ago, when so many more Earth Born came to Selene.

Kara was quiet as Frank told Rachel about how Aldrin had grown, explaining the hand he'd had in designing infrastructure. Rachel felt like Kara was watching her, waiting for something.

Jacob interrupted. "What does the *John Glenn* look like?"

"Tell us about the ship," Justin said.

Sarah looked at Rachel with big eyes, but didn't say anything.

Rachel described the bright-jeweled face of Selene as they flew above it and the absolute darkness of space outside of the atmosphere.

"How big is *John Glenn*?" Justin asked.

"Bigger than Aldrin. And there's a garden inside it that's bigger than Teaching Grove."

Justin's eyes went big. "Are there a lot of Council there?"

"Yes, but it's so big, it looks empty."

"How fast does it go?" Jacob asked.

"I don't know." She should know, she thought. "I think it's not moving now. But it must have gone very fast to get between star systems."

"What does the garden look like?" Sarah asked.

Rachel drew a data window in the air, and asked for a picture of the garden. The window started to fill up with colorful images.

"You didn't ask it what to do," Justin proclaimed solemnly.

"But, yes, I did. I asked it."

Her dad leaned forward. "How?"

"Well . . ." They didn't know about the Library bud. She swallowed. "Well," she started over, "on the *John Glenn,* we can find out information by asking. It's like a voice in your ear."

"Can I have one?" Justin asked. "I want a voice in my ear. Can you teach me?"

Rachel shook her head. "Council has to give one to you." She wasn't supposed to talk about the Library. But she hadn't mentioned it directly— she was just retrieving information. "Look," she said, "I have to stop now." What excuse could she use? "This is hard to do way down here, and I'm not really supposed to use it much."

Her dad looked over at Kara. "Can you do that?"

Kara hesitated, then looked daggers at Rachel and said, "Yes."

"Why didn't you tell me?"

"It's not polite to show off data rights other people don't have." Lips pursed, she returned her attention to her plate.

After dinner, Kara took the children to bathe, and Rachel and Frank were alone in the big common room.

Rachel had become used to large spaces on the ship, but so much personal space on Selene was luxury. Their tent house would have fit in just this room. "Are you happy?" she asked her father.

"I'm happy to have you home."

"Kara's going back, isn't she?"

"Next year. I'll miss her in some ways. She's better than most Earth Born. She doesn't really belong here, and she knows it. But I did okay raising you. I'll manage these three all right. Kara always said she wouldn't stay. She has a place at Ymir."

"So she's leaving you with the children? Is that what you want?"

"Since when do we get what we want?" Frank stared off into space, twisting his hands together. "I'm sorry about Ursula. I know you'll miss her."

"Yeah." She didn't want to think about Ursula, not yet, so she said, "Aldrin feels different now."

"There's more tension between Earth Born and Moon Born than there used to be. After you and Gabriel left, and Ali followed, the pace sped up down here. The first big change was a building boom. The plan was tents, but we had to change because of the flares. That's what the buildings are for, by the way—they're all flare-hardened in at least one room. Here, it's the kitchen. So if the warning goes off, you go in there and close both doors. There's enough shielding to protect us from the smaller flares. Those happen a lot more than they did—at least a few times a year."

The Council hadn't been lying to her. "Other things feel different too," she prompted him.

"Sorry—all the building—it was so we could house more people. Aldrin has hundreds of people now—and new rules and more tension. Partly the tension is from Council. We're behind in their master plan—the flares got in the way, and there's been minor setbacks with planting. It's all aggravated because the rules for the Earth Born are different from the ones for the Moon Born. Before you left, it wasn't that way."

"How are they different?" she asked.

"Well, that device you've got—the one you talk to—I've never seen one down here. We all have wrist pads, but they're just phones, they don't generally *tell* us things. We can't just ask questions and have answers show up as if someone was sitting around waiting on us. Oh, we can get information, but only what's related to our jobs." He looked at her closely, narrowing his eyes. "You had better be careful about showing off. Some people might be jealous. Aldrin's not as safe as it used to be."

"I'll be careful." She hadn't opened a conversation with Astronaut, not yet. She didn't know if access to Astronaut was part of her query and response to the Library here. But she hadn't heard the perfect voice in her ear—just the Library's standard response talk. There was still so much she didn't know!

Still, she had seen Selene from the sky, flown in the garden, and climbed Yggdrasil. She was half her friends' age, but she knew things they didn't.

Frank straightened and looked her in the eye. "Back at the airport? You acted like it didn't matter what Gabriel said, like you're mad at him. And him Council. Do you have any idea how glad we are to see him? Maybe things will come back closer to how they used to be. Council rules us like always. But now, Moon Born and Earth Born fight, and some of the Earth Born fight with each other. Maybe Gabriel can fix *something*. It can't help us if you make him mad. I didn't like him a lot before, but I like him better than Shane and Star, who've been running classes and teams

here. Earth Born run most of the teams, and they do most of the real running of the city."

"Not Moon Born?"

"No."

Wasn't it the plan for Harry to lead teams? For her too? She leaned in
closer to her dad. "There's a High Council. Higher than Gabriel. He has
to do what they say. But he's pretty high up. I bet Shane and Star have less
influence. I've never even heard their names before, and everybody on
John Glenn knows Gabriel." She stopped for a minute, thinking, rubbing
her hands on her knees. "Gabriel wants us to lead. That's why he brought
me to *John Glenn*. But I don't know if he can really change anything."

Frank looked surprised. "I thought Gabriel was in charge."

"I think he is in charge of Selene. But High Council can make rules,
even for him." She shivered. "There's Kyu—who's pretty and smart and
tough, and the captain, who doesn't say much, but people listen to him.
Clare is the boss terraformer, which makes her Gabriel's boss, but you
don't see her because High Council almost never comes here."

"I met her once," Frank said. "When I was just a little boy."

Rachel shivered. "And Ma Liren. Liren's nasty."

"Gabriel's the one who called us and said to meet you," he said.
"Rachel, I don't ever remember being happier to hear from anyone."
Frank swept his mismatched hands through his hair, and then clasped
them tightly in front of him, leaning forward. "Gabriel said good things
about you. He also seemed concerned, like coming home would be hard
on you. That's partly what prompted me to find your old pictures for your
room. Gabriel told me you learn really fast, and that your being iced was a
privilege. I was mad at Gabriel for a long time because I missed you so, but
who wouldn't want his child to live longer?" He scrubbed at his face,
shielding his eyes from her. "I'm not making any sense—sorry." He drew
a deep breath and dropped his hands, looking directly at her. "I'm just
afraid for you after seeing how you're acting. You can't tell a Council
member what you're going to do!"

"Maybe someone needs to tell them to treat us better," she said.

"You're angry, Rachel. I can feel it in you. Anger and loss. You lost a
lot, I lost a lot, but you're here. And you still have work to do. We all have
work to do."

"I know," she said.

"Don't make Council mad. Think of poor Andrew. Remember you

could turn out that way. You're used to being favored—you are favored. But you could lose that, and I'd hate it if you lost your dreams."

"Don't you mean if I lost more of them?"

Her father just smiled gently and nodded. "You look tired. Why don't you sleep?"

"Good idea." She hugged her dad hard, not wanting to let go.

At midnight she woke up sweating, knowing she could never trust Gabriel so much again. She was dancing to more strings than just his, and he was a puppet too. Liren and Kyu and the captain, they all had more power than Gabriel. Treesa and Astronaut made a difference too, although Rachel didn't understand it yet. She had thought Council all saw things the same way. But they argued and schemed and planned different plans inside the big plan that they all supported—to leave Selene. Gabriel was asking Rachel to help with that plan, but she didn't want Council to leave. How would they live on Selene without the Council to run things?

Her thoughts drifted back to Treesa, and it was no comfort to imagine being an old woman alone in a garden with caged birds for company.

Chapter 29: Harry

Dawn colored the window rose as Rachel slipped into the kitchen and made a breakfast. In the fridge there was a bowl of bloody red lumps; she avoided it. No one else had stirred yet when she grabbed the bright blue and yellow wings she'd brought with her from *John Glenn*. It was still too dark to fly to the grove, but she would fly back. She hadn't flown through air with no obstacles in so long! A good thermal with the ability to rise, to hold out her wings and float, alone above Selene . . .

Rachel squinted into Apollo's light and made out silhouettes of old high tent poles. The path to the grove had run through them. She found a wide street that went the right direction and started along it.

She passed a building with a red and blue window sign offering home-made crafts for trade. Curious, Rachel veered toward it. In the Aldrin she'd left, Council provided everything families needed. Peering through the windows in the half-light, she made out curtains and clothes and teapots.

She turned back to look for the path. The street kept going the right direction, straight. She walked uphill between a row of houses. The street ended and she was surrounded by vegetation, plots marked out with rope boundaries. Tattered cloth name tags were tied on the rope, fluttering in the light morning breeze.

By the time she found her plot, the light of full morning was touching the tips of the trees, reflecting on the waxy leaves and making the greens bright and vivid. She set her bag down and waded in, amazed at the height of the grasses and shrubs, the way the branches towered above her head, the ropy thickness of the lianas. The Lobster Claw Heliconia leaves were as wide as her hips, and a stalk of red and yellow bracts towered over her head. The mimosas were chest high, spindlier than she'd expected, and more graceful. The cecropia towered above all of the other plants, reaching for light.

The forest floor was springy, wild with dead things turning back to soil. In the garden aboard *John Glenn,* roots were trapped in synthetic fiber mats and fed perfect nutrient mixes. Here, roots tunneled into dirt that stuck to her shoes. Rachel knelt down and ran her fingers through the soil, filling the cup of her palm with damp deadfall. She picked through the jumble of tiny twigs and brown leaves, ecstatic to see spidery skeletons of leaves. Her nose wrinkled happily at the peaty smell of natural compost. Looking closely, she noticed an ant, and then another, and another, marching around the trunk of the cecropia tree.

She talked into her wrist pad about the ants; describing counts and behaviors. Rachel wanted to run statistics and images through the Library and see if lower gravity had changed the ants. She was sketching the pattern they traveled on the tree when she heard footsteps behind her.

Rachel turned, and gave a little cry. But it couldn't be Harry. Not now. His hair was lighter, and the shade of green in his eyes was just off. The square angle of his jaw was right, and he had the little quirky smile she remembered. She tried to remember the name Gabriel had attached to Harry and Gloria's son.

Before she could find the name in her head, he extended a hand to help her stand. "You must be Rachel."

Did everyone, everywhere, know her name? She nodded. "And you are?"

"Dylan."

"Pleased to meet you. You're Harry's son."

"Mom says I look a lot like him. I guess she must be right. Anyway, do you like it?"

"Like? Your name?"

"The grove. We all take turns, Dad and Mom and me, taking care of it." He swept his right arm expansively toward her trees.

"Of my plot?"

"Dad and Mom said they couldn't bear to have your plot fall into the student pool. We kept it perfect in case you came home."

"Th-thank you." This boy wasn't more than two years younger than the Harry she'd seen a few months ago. It was hard to stay balanced on her feet and talk normally. "Yes . . . well, I'm glad someone does, oh, I mean . . ." She slowed and took a deep breath. "Yes, it's beautiful. Thank you. It looks even better than I thought it would when I designed it."

"It's my day to check on things here, but Dad said to call if you were here. So I did, as soon as I saw you. We heard last night. And gosh—Mom was so excited! She said her best friend is returned from the dead. They'll be along in a bit." Dylan was looking her up and down as if she were a piece of art.

She shivered and goose bumps rose along her arms. Her voice caught in her throat for a moment, and then she shifted back to a safe subject. "The ants are pretty neat," she said. "I studied them on the ship."

"This is Star's third try for a viable ant colony." Dylan put his hand down on a trunk in front of a marching column of black ants, and the next ant bumped into his fingertip, then veered around it, marking a new trail. Dylan smiled. "I think this colony might take. These guys have been going for two months now."

"There weren't any ants here when I left."

"Star's been pushing insects the last few years. We've got reproducing colonies of bees now."

"I saw birds too."

"There's fifteen species now." He sounded proud. "Including chickens. Did you really save Mom's life?"

"She was a little girl then, and I had to be saved too."

Dylan grinned.

The whine and snap of wings came from overhead.

Harry and Gloria swooped down and landed, one on each side of Rachel, almost knocking her down as they crowded close.

The thirty-nine-year-old Harry had grown into all of his body parts. He'd gotten taller. His shoulders were much broader, though he was still lean and muscular. His back was slightly curved in, giving his stance a little stoop. Lines crinkled around his eyes. He didn't look directly at her for very long.

For her part, she could hardly look at him. It hurt.

Gloria had changed far more than Harry. Rachel remembered the plucky young girl she had carried on her back; she saw a tall, sharp-edged woman with spiky hair and clear muscle definition. Her stomach protruded with pregnancy. Gloria was the first one to talk, "Rachel—oh, gosh. I thought you'd never come back. You . . . you . . . you look so much . . ."

". . . the same? Yep. But you sure don't—and you look great." Words rushed out of Rachel in her confusion. "I've been sitting and talking with Dylan. You have a great son. I'm really very happy for you." She couldn't look at Harry as she said it. A young blond girl landed and stood behind Dylan. She looked almost thirteen. "And who is this?" She looked at the girl, who nodded once, and smiled shyly.

Dylan spoke for her. "This is my sister, Beth Rachel." He emphasized the Rachel, but said, "We should call her Beth, since you're here."

Gabriel had said they'd named their girl after her. Rachel felt more goose bumps. She held her hand out. "Pleased to meet you, Beth. Have you helped too?"

"Sometimes," Beth Rachel said.

"So much has happened; I don't know how to catch up. And hey, I'm really grateful to you all for keeping this place up so well. It's beautiful." Rachel's eyes stung, and she swallowed and blinked, taking three long pranayama breaths, using Gabriel's techniques to calm her racing heart, control her fear.

Gloria looked down at the ground between her shoes. "We wanted to keep it right in case you ever came back. It's . . . it's a family habit. We . . . we didn't want to forget you. You meant so much to us."

"Nick helps too sometimes," Harry said. "And Sharon. All of us do; everyone who remembers you. And some others you haven't met help; at least when the rest of us are gone or on extra shifts."

Why would they do that? She was overwhelmed; she had steeled herself to a world gone on without her, forgetting her. She blinked back tears.

They toured the First Trees. Rachel was openmouthed with surprise at how big they'd grown. The large buttressing roots of a full jungle were beginning to appear, so they had to step up and over roots, or walk around them. Lianas ran overhead, and flowers filled the air with a sticky sweetness. Birds flashed in the trees.

"Hey, Dylan," she said, "I don't see any ants here."

"Council never uses the First Trees for testing anymore."

Gloria interrupted. "Dylan, Rachel—Beth Rachel that is—we need to go. I have to get to the schoolyard." She looked at Rachel. "Being pregnant keeps me off the crews, so I do a half-shift babysitting every afternoon. The kids help me. Will you come to our house tonight? I'll make dinner. Spaghetti?"

Rachel wasn't sure she could be around them for a whole evening. "I promised my dad I'd eat at home. Sometime soon?"

Gloria looked disappointed, but she said, "I understand." She kissed Harry on the cheek, and then turned and left. Beth and Dylan followed her.

Gloria was chattering to Beth, and Beth's face was turned up toward Gloria's, smiling. Dylan looked back over his shoulder once. Rachel watched them walk away until they were nearly at the far edge of the meadow. She should have been the one to herd Harry's children home.

"Walk with me?" Harry asked, turning away.

Rachel just nodded, numb, and followed him. They walked silently for a long time, picking their way along a thin path that meandered just inside the First Trees. They were so close to the meadow that light streamed in and touched the tips of the ferns and lianas with gold, and sent spots of dappled light across Harry's back. Rachel's stomach heaved and she struggled not to cry out loud, then stumbled and stood next to a cieba, sobbing.

Harry stopped, and made a strangled sound in his throat, and reached for her. She stepped into his arms and cried on his shoulder. He held her softly, awkwardly, patting the back of her head. When she looked up, his eyes were red too. The lines around his eyes and small streaks of gray in his short hair made her dizzy. He pushed her back, and looked directly into her eyes. "I'm sorry it all turned out this way."

"I know," she said, "we were robbed. It wasn't either of our faults."

"It could have been changed." Harry sounded bitter.

"Not anymore." She sniffed, and wiped her face with the back of her hand. "You seem to be happy."

He hesitated, then said, "I am. Things turned out well for me." He smiled softly. "I love Gloria and the kids a lot. But I thought about you often, even after Gloria and I contracted."

She started walking, leading him this time, choosing a wide path that wound away from student plots, through community jungle that was old enough to rise above their heads. She didn't trust herself to say anything. In a few places tiny saplings struggled up right in the path. Rachel was surprised to see them; they would have been pulled up as seedlings when she was here before. She stepped carefully around them, even though surely they'd be removed eventually.

"Aldrin is different now," Harry said, his voice floating up from behind her.

"Dad and I talked about that last night. He looks tired. I think they're making him work too hard. He says that Council is much tougher. I really hope Gabriel being back makes a difference."

"It's not likely to. The rules are different, and there's the Earth Born . . . a lot of them don't like us much."

"Yeah, I met Kara last night. I feel like an unwelcome stranger in my own house. Only it's not even my house. I feel like I walked into someone else's life." Rachel tripped over a long thin root, nearly falling, and Harry caught up with her.

"You were gone a long time."

"I don't even know what Council expects of me anymore. I did learn a lot on the ship, and I very much want to use some of what I learned." She thought about Astronaut, and Treesa. She couldn't tell Harry about them.

"Do you feel like that, even after all Council did to you?"

"It wasn't 'Council' that made that choice. It was Ma Liren, and High Council. There's a High Council that makes choices for us, even for Gabriel and Ali."

"But you aren't Council, you're one of us."

"I meant for all of us, Harry. Council, Earth Born, Children. All of us. We don't choose the important stuff."

He didn't reply. They walked without talking for a while, feet scratching through deadfall on the path. Rachel smelled flowers that she couldn't even see, and damp mosses, and the light healthy rot of the deadfall. She cleared her throat. "Tell me about Andrew."

"He's strange, Rachel. He runs with a crowd of younger people in Aldrin, and they answer to him for things, and he keeps them angry with Council. I think that's how he gets his information since he still can't have direct data. Oh, they all still do what they're told, but they do it like they want to see how far they can push Council and Earth Born. He's going to get in more trouble. He was my best friend once, but I'm actually glad that my kids don't hang out with him."

"Trust Andrew to be stupid. We can't fight Council. We need them—we just have to find a way to make them let us help them so we learn more. Either that, or find a way to make them stay here on Selene, or at least in Apollo system. But I don't know how to do that."

Harry walked faster to catch up with her. "Watch for a while. And be careful, Rachel. Last week one of the guys on Nick's crew, one of the young ones that hangs around with Andrew, got in trouble for talking back and he disappeared for a few days. He said they kept him in a locked room." Harry put a hand on her arm. "I don't agree with Andrew exactly, and I don't like his ideas, and I hope we don't have to fight Council or Earth Born. I don't want to, because of the kids. But if they keep making us work so hard and giving us so little, it may come down to a fight someday."

Rachel blinked and stumbled, unsure what to think of this new Aldrin, this new Harry. She pulled ahead of him, and stopped out in the clear meadow, then turned toward him, so he stopped, facing her. How could she share some of what she'd learned? "You should see Selene from space; it's beautiful. It's like a jewel we're making, the water shines out and sparkles, and the edges of the craters are shadowed and beautiful. It's small, Harry, too small for us to fight over. It's fragile. And the *John Glenn,* it's huge, but it's still fragile too. Did you know Sol system had billions of people, and they lived all over the system, not just on one tiny moon? And some of the Council think they all died. This is a smaller and more fragile place than we think it is."

Harry looked at the ground and shuffled his feet. Then he looked up and smiled. "Gabriel was right, you're a natural leader."

She shook her head. She couldn't take any more—there was so much wrong with this older Selene. "Harry," she said, "I have to go. I need to get back home, and first, I need to fly some. The garden is so cramped. I need to feel some space."

Harry looked startled. "Would you like me to fly with you?"

"No. I need to be alone. I'll come over some night soon and talk with you, I promise. You can start sending me questions and notes again if you want."

"No, I can't. They don't let us use much extra communication anymore."

Rachel drew her lips tight. "Okay, we'll talk. I need you."

He smiled at her and stroked her face as if she were a child. "I do have a lot more questions for you."

Rachel pulled back. "I bet you do." She turned away. "I have to go. I have to think about all of you being older."

"I understand." Harry turned and walked away in the same direction Gloria and the kids had gone.

Rachel realized she didn't even know where they lived.

Chapter 30: Mariner Stew

Gabriel flew a criss-cross pattern over Selene's jungle, trying out a new plane, staying high, eyeing the changes in Selene from an eagle's viewpoint. Green squares covered the ground, riots of greens competing in the older plantings, sienna sprinkled with green in newer fields. Snakes of dirt road crossed the older green squares. Long rectangles of landing strip interrupted the patterns in the newer jungle. A few of the landing strips were dotted with people and small flyers.

What he saw pleased him; the old plantings looked established. New lines of green pushed out along the old Sea Road. Here and there brown sticks attested to flare damage, but most of the trees looked healthy. Fifty percent of the intended jungle was planted. Already there was nearly enough diversity to sustain the planned five thousand population. They *were* behind their goal for square kilometers planted. The numbers sat on the tail end of the pessimistic side of his and Ali's original models. Still, he grinned to see that even the unexpected flares hadn't dropped production below the slop they'd programmed into the model for chaos effects. They were good at this.

Gabriel landed the little plane smoothly, and taxied to a parking spot by the runway. In the sudden silence as he switched off the engines, he heard himself humming. He realized he had been humming for some time, an old song his mother used to sing. Why was he singing? It felt good to be alone, to be back on Selene.

Visits to *John Glenn* lately had been . . . uncomfortable.

The next visit would be good. Erika would be warm! Ten days. He switched to humming a love song as he patted the plane on the nose and headed for Council Home.

In contrast to the rest of Selene, Council Home looked familiar. The structures were all hard-surfaced now, of course, but not really bigger. It had always been well designed and well cared for. The flares, though. They shouldn't have been so surprising. His imagination drew pictures in his mind, magnetic fields reaching out from Apollo, twisting round Daedalus the sun-hugging gas giant planet and its metallic hydrogen core. Field lines knotting, until they exploded in flares of energy and trapped protons. Why hadn't he seen it from the beginning? The hard-shelled houses weren't enough protection.

He grimaced, remembering the hurried meeting he'd had with Council before he brought Rachel down yesterday. He was still stinging from Council's rejection of his flare kite. Only the captain had supported him. They were afraid it would take too much time to develop and test. He'd had a backup idea. At least they'd approved of that one. Building the undersea refuge would be fun, and he would only have to leave Selene once. But they wouldn't need a refuge if they just fixed the problem. The flare kite would make Selene truly safe.

Gabriel checked into an empty house and showered, dressed carefully in belted and ankle-tied brown pants and a long-sleeved deep blue shirt. He clipped the star and planet symbols that identified his terraforming affiliations into his braid. Every minute since he'd warmed had been spent with High Council or tending Rachel. Star had promised to whip up a decent meal, something she called Mariner Stew, and Gabriel was ready for anything that wasn't standard ship food.

He had to search for his locker. He could only hope that whoever had moved his few belongings here had been careful. He pulled out a long rectangular case and opened it slowly, smiling at what he saw. The guitar lay neatly nestled in cloth packing, the wood glowing as light hit it from above. He had built it by hand over three winters, using wood from a pruned branch of Yggdrasil, carefully seasoned while he was iced and then brought here to Selene. One entire season's spare time had gone into hand-shaping the neck and fitting it to the hollow body. He ran his hands over the smooth surfaces, then pulled out the new strings he'd brought from the ship and sat alone for twenty minutes, stringing and tuning the instrument before walking over to meet Shane and Star.

He was humming again as he rang the bell.

The door swung open and Gabriel was engulfed by a blond girl nearly his height, all legs and curves. Star planted a kiss on his cheek. He laughed, holding her around the waist, slapping Shane's shoulder in greeting.

"Hey, old man," Shane teased, "you had her once. She's mine now."

"And what harm in an old friend flirting?" Star said. "It's not like Gabriel has eyes for anyone but Erika anyway."

"Well," Shane said, "he gets along well enough with Ali. Or so I've heard."

Gabriel shook his head. "Let's see. If I can't shift-bond with a pilot, since she has no regular shifts—I'm supposed to just wait around while I terraform this rock?"

Star stepped back and put her hands up in front of her face, laughing. "So you were just killing time with me?"

"I made it *live. And* I care about Ali too. *And* Erika will be awake soon."

"Who made it live?" Star did a little bump with her hips, flirting. "Not that I'd trade Shane away—I bet you can't wait for Erika." Star grinned at him, arching an eyebrow.

"Well, I like you *all.*" He felt his face flush. "You're right. Erika's special to me. It will take weeks just to catch her up."

Shane smiled broadly. "You'll hate it."

Gabriel was grinning. "So who says life's easy?"

"Not us." Star and Shane kissed, and Shane handed around wine bulbs. Star continued. "It hasn't been easy here. This is the first time Shane and I have seen each other in days. I know you've been cold, but it's gotten crazy. High Council handed down new dictates outlining who can do what, and guess who landed all of the supervision? Oh, they were kind enough to leave some of the fieldwork to be overseen by Earth Born, but that's all. We're dying of exhaustion down here. And when we document how much we have to do—heck, what isn't getting done—High Council just says do it! I'm ready for a rest, I'll tell you. You'll have to deal with it—people are doing what they're supposed to and having babies right and left, the schools are full, and we just can't do it all. You know there's only ten Council here?"

Gabriel did some quick math in his head. In addition to the five High Council members, Council numbered two hundred—a mix of picked scientists and top performers in everything from human resource management to drive mechanics. The terraforming crew numbered fifty-seven mixed-discipline scientists. Another twenty were assigned to help them out, and everyone else was either on sparse rotation like Erika or, worse, cold until they got to Ymir.

High Council was struggling to save Earth-educated Council as well as Colonists until they were needed at Ymir. Sure, the other ships were probably there. But there was no confirmation—and so they saved resources. That meant ten was a lot of staff, probably as much as he could expect given that not everyone warm could be on Selene at any one time.

So he said, "Ten's a lot."

"For everything we have to do?" Star complained. "We need help. Come on, Gabe, we're running the town and teaching school as well as overseeing safety and planting and dealing with the flares and . . ."

"Slow down," Gabriel interrupted, laughing. "We've got what we've got. We can make children, but we can't make Council. Let's see—five years a shift, and next shift we can start building the collider. It won't be long to finish from here. Maybe ten five-year shifts at most. What about the Earth Born?"

Shane thought it over. "Earth Born do a lot of the work that requires education and skills, and they also supervise work crews of Moon Born. But most go back to *John Glenn* as fast as they can." Shane started pacing. "Some stay put; they get attached to their families. It's hard work to keep so many people on track. The circumstances are so different from what they expected. It's hard on them. And we don't have much time to help them."

Star handed Shane three glasses for the table. "I don't like being here in the first place, but I dislike being worked to death even more. I heard you were training Children to take some of the burden?"

"I am," he said. Bitterly, "I was. Aren't you?"

"It's not in our work plan. Not right now." Shane was serious. "Really. There's no time to teach Children—they'd need university educations to manage most of this. They just don't know enough to be very useful, and we don't have much time to teach them. They don't have the background for anything really complex—I'm amazed we have them reading and recording."

Star looked over from the kitchen. "Most of them don't seem to really care anyway."

Gabriel winced. Of course they didn't—not if they were treated like slaves. His students had been bright enough to lead other Moon Born—

maybe not to lead Earth Born, but surely to lead teams of other Moon Born for the easier tasks. Rachel and Harry and Gloria, they'd cared about Selene. "Let me introduce you to Rachel."

"Well, I'll meet your Rachel. But she's still not Earth Born or Council—I don't see how she can really help, even with the extra training. This isn't the mess we left for you and Ali last shift. It's a very different mess. It's like High Council has gone paranoid."

Gabriel decided not to feed that rumor. He suspected it was mostly Ma Liren. He intended to have a chat with Clare and Kyu as soon as an opportunity presented itself.

He said, "No one has told *me* differently."

"Step carefully, my friend. We were scheduled to go cryo in just a few weeks. Now there's no date," Star said. "What do you know about that?"

"Nothing," Gabriel said.

"I'm done here now," Star said. "I'm ready for a long time on ice."

Gabriel reached over and gave her a casual kiss. "We'll see Ymir someday. This will all be worth it."

"How long until you wake Erika?" Shane asked.

"Ten days. So that's all the time I've got to help Rachel acclimate to the time jump, and get her doing something useful."

Shane turned and faced Gabriel, dropping his smile. "Well, and speaking of Rachel again, have you met up with the 'Cult of Rachel' yet?"

"Huh?"

Star said, "The older Children keep up her garden in the grove. Harry and his family do it, including the kids, and some friends of theirs. I think she's some kind of symbol for them, maybe because she went to the ship, or maybe because she didn't come back."

"Rachel's friendly enough to us." *At least she used to be. She hasn't been too friendly since we warmed her.* "She and Harry were my best students last shift, and I'd planned for them both to be leading planting crews. Harry's a careful engineer, and Rachel is creative, with a good sense for ecosystems."

Star wasn't done. "Really, Gabriel, it is kind of eerie. Go look at her garden plot. It's cleaner and better cared for than anybody else's. Dylan—that's Harry and Gloria's oldest—he bothers us more about every little thing for Rachel's plot than for his own. His is good, but hers, hers he keeps perfect. And he can't have ever *seen* Rachel. He was born after you took her to the ship. It's a family thing for them, and I think it's weird. I mean, nothing bad has happened, but it might be good to know whether they see Rachel as a hero, or just a friend they're watching over. At least she's alive, so they can't make her into a martyr."

"Has anyone monitored them?" Gabriel asked.

Shane said, "A little—"

"Who'd have time?" Star sputtered. "You'll see what it's like." She ladled strong peppery-smelling fish stew into bowls. "All the data streams in the world don't help if you don't have time to read them."

"We could use Astronaut to help monitor."

"Maybe," Shane mused. "But I'm not sure that's a good idea."

"Neither am I." Gabriel shook his head. "But we have to do something."

Star changed the subject back. "Your Rachel may have some power, since Harry and Gloria are de facto leaders among the Moon Born." She sat down at the table, and gestured to Shane and Gabriel to join her. "Eat."

"I wonder if Rachel knows about it?" Gabriel sat down and tasted the stew. It was rich, warm, and spicier than ship food. "This is good."

"Oh," Shane said, "I see Andrew at Rachel's plot sometimes too."

"Don't tell me—trampling the ground and pulling up healthy young trees." Gabriel rolled his eyes.

"No, he weeds it."

Gabriel almost dropped his spoon. "Andrew still doesn't have any data access?"

"He has straight com, so he can get flare warnings, or tell us when he's in trouble. But he has no data, not even low-level access to data pods, much less the community pool. But you know," she mused, "he's never even asked us for data."

Gabriel was mad at Liren all over again for not waking him. Maybe he should wake Ali—she had a good rapport with the kids. Adults now, all of them. But waking Ali would be a bad idea if he wanted to keep his undivided attention for Erika. And he did. Gabriel sighed. He wanted to just relax with Erika for a few weeks when she warmed. Fat chance.

After they cleaned up from dinner, Star pulled out a long wooden flute, Shane assembled his water drum, and Gabriel sang and played guitar. They spent hours on old space songs, and made up new songs, until early in the morning. By false dawn his fingertips were raw and tender.

He didn't remember the last time he'd felt so good.

Chapter 31: Journey

The next morning, Gabriel headed up to Teaching Grove.

It *was* noticeable; Rachel's plot was a perfect garden. He stood still, absorbing details that showed meticulous care; dead leaves stripped, weeds pulled, paths clear and raked.

A rustling sound made him look to his left. He saw two kids, blond, a boy and a girl, in Ursula's plot. The two children were carefully uprooting a dead palm sapling. Ursula's plot hadn't been kept up as well as Rachel's, but signs of recent activity showed. Piles of dead twigs and yellowed leaves lined the path, waiting to be composted. Small branches and fall were left in the plot, of course, but larger woody material went to become soil with the help of life-limited nano.

The children noticed him, and left the palm half finished, moving away quietly to crouch a few meters away from him. They kept their heads down, not meeting his eyes, weeding. It bothered Gabriel. The last time he was here, people—everyone—greeted each other and talked when they met.

RACHEL WAS IN THE KITCHEN with her dad and an Earth Born who must be Kara, Frank's contracted partner. Three children were lined up at the kitchen table, eating toast and bananas. A strong minty smell pervaded the kitchen. Rachel looked fresh from sleep. Her hair was still long, and in disarray, but she seemed a little friendlier. She glanced up at him, smiling, saying, "I was hoping to have a few more hours to visit." Irony. She'd learned irony.

Frank glared at Rachel and broke in quickly, "Good morning, Gabriel, it's a pleasure to have you back here. We're glad to see you."

Kara extended a hand in formal greeting.

Gabriel looked over at Rachel, and he watched her struggle to ignore him. She eventually said, "Well, Gabriel, what's next for me?"

"You and I are doing a ground survey. I'll visit with your dad while you pack. I'd like to hear his perspective on how things have been here while we were cold."

Rachel left the room. Kara scrambled up, clearing the children's plates. "I'll walk the kids to school."

Frank nodded, and Kara herded the children toward the door. "Jacob, Justin, Sarah—let's go. You'll be late."

One of the twins turned and looked at Frank. "Can't we stay? I want to talk to Gabriel."

Frank shook his head, but waved as Kara marshaled the three youngsters out the door.

Gabriel felt strangely awkward. "Kara seems nice, and the children are beautiful," he said.

"Thank you. Kara will leave us soon." Frank's voice sounded pained. "I really am glad you're back. Our lives work better when you're here."

"I'm sure Shane and Star have done a good job," Gabriel said, helping himself to a piece of bread from the kitchen counter.

"Aldrin is a harder place for us. More work. There are more approvals and steps to get anything done too. I mean, you always had rules, but it seems like there are so many it's slowing us down while the workload just gets bigger. Shane is strict with us. Even me. It used to mean something to be first generation." Frank leaned back in his chair, looking uncomfortable. "People—Earth Born largely, but Council too—they treat us like— like badly built machinery. Being Moon Born is a curse. It makes me wonder, how will things work when there are even more of us here? Will we always just do what you say?"

Gabriel shook his head at the veiled threat. "Frank, you have to. We give you what autonomy we can." He changed the subject. "How's Rachel doing?"

"Better than I thought she would be. But this *is* hard. I hope she gained as much as she lost."

Gabriel saw regret mixed with anger on Frank's face, and then a congenial mask dropped over Frank's eyes. Gabriel was saddened; he and Frank had worked so closely together once they'd almost been friends.

Frank continued. "It's strange how you brought her back looking as young as when you took her. It makes her special in a way, and it scares me. How will people respond to her?"

"I'm sorry she was cold so long," said Gabriel. "The lost time will be hard for her—we meant it to be a year."

"Rachel told me you were cold when the decision was made."

Rachel reappeared with a pack and her wings. "When will I come back?" That ironic tone again. "Or should I know better than to ask?"

"I have to go back to *John Glenn* in less than two weeks. We'll be back before that."

———

GABRIEL'S PLAN WAS TO STAY out seven days, finding a new place to camp each morning and using the afternoons to document the jungle's health. He had run the data already, but he needed to touch and feel the work. He wanted time to think, and time to evaluate Rachel's adjustment.

His plans already looked imperfect. Rain clouds piled and billowed to the west, and he didn't want to fly into a storm. Rachel sat quietly next to him, recording data as he fed it to her, barely responding to anything else. She seemed indrawn, but less angry. Neither of them brought up the moments when Gabriel had held her after she learned about Ursula's death, or the insubordination she had shown afterward. The flight out was full of awkward silence.

The first two days were soggy. They slogged through the earlier plantings with the bigger trees, hoping that the rain would stay above them in the canopy. Enough moisture fell through to keep them damp and miserable. Mud stuck to their shoes, and their feet made sucking sounds as they walked.

The jungle showed the passage of time. Flowers bloomed, epiphytes held onto branches, lianas threaded through trees, and three times they saw bright green birds.

Rachel did her share of the sampling and testing. By the end of the second day, Gabriel noticed that even with the ever-present rain, Rachel was showing her connection to jungle plants. She exclaimed happily at trees that looked particularly good, and was aggrieved wherever a tree appeared less healthy. She was willing to spend hours sampling soil and finding remediation recommendations for every sick place. They stumbled on an area where ten trees had died, and Rachel analyzed the soil and what was left of the dried leaves, finally determining that the whole region had the wrong soil acidity. "We've got to stay and fix this," she said.

"We're losing time. I'll send a team back."

She planted her feet and glared at him. "Didn't you always tell *us* to fix things ourselves? Besides, from what Dad said, there's not enough people to do all the work. We're here now."

He laughed, and helped her figure out what nutrients to add.

As they journeyed, Rachel surrounded herself with data windows from the Library and spent time handling plants—touching them and turning over leaves to look at them. Her focus was almost uncanny, and most of the time she hardly seemed to know he was with her. Her reactions to him had changed. Always before he had felt like she was looking for something from him, and now she didn't seem to need anything except work. She was certainly still assimilating the changes in her life, and the work must be a welcome distraction. Once, when he came up on her from a distance, tears streaked her cheeks.

The third day the sky cleared, but the air still dripped with humidity. Harlequin was due to eclipse Apollo. They located a bare spot with enough canopy to huddle under. The dusk of the eclipse closed around them, leaving the much dimmer light of Harlequin and the quivering glow of the lantern Gabriel set out. They shivered, their backs cold even while the lantern warmed their hands. Gabriel heated water for tea on top of the lamp.

"What will I do when we get back to Aldrin?" Rachel asked.

None of the Children had interesting jobs. They were all laborers. Gabriel had been working through this problem in his head, wanting to give her some responsibility. "There's precedent for you teaching. You do it well."

She smiled at him. "I want to be out here. I want to take a small crew, all Moon Born, and be out here making things grow. I want to be here, in the wild, to make it all work. The jungle changed while you froze me, but Aldrin changed more, and worse."

He wanted her where she could be watched easily. "Start with teaching. You have new knowledge from *John Glenn*. You can use that to establish yourself. After all, you're only a few effective years older than some of the students. Harry's son for one." He watched for her reaction.

"He's sharp enough I'd like to take him with me when we go on field trips."

She talked about the ants and other insects. She'd gotten the idea of planting directly from seed for large areas, and she went on about fixing soil with grasses: make large-scale savannah and then turn it to jungle. He recognized some strategies he had used on Earth. She must have been doing research he didn't know about.

After a while she was rambling, but it was smart rambling. It reminded Gabriel of his own musings, and he sat patiently and corrected her when her ideas were founded on poor assumptions. He enjoyed the conversation immensely, and was sorry when the tiny bright disk of Apollo broke around Harlequin and began to throw light back into the day.

An hour later they surprised a group of Earth Born repairing a tilling machine. Gabriel spotted Nick bent over an axle, pulling on a wheel, and pointed him out to Rachel, who snuck up behind him and stood until he turned, whooped, and embraced her. The rest of the group glanced at them, but kept working, not leaving their posts. A short dark-haired man turned at the commotion. He frowned, and barked at Nick to get back to the work he was doing. Nick turned back to the tiller, and Rachel bent uncertainly over to help him. The man stepped toward Nick and Rachel, looking menacing, and Gabriel cleared his throat.

The man turned, seeing Gabriel for the first time. "Who are you?"

"Gabriel." He said his name mildly, and at first it didn't have the effect he expected. Then the man stopped and looked more closely, taking a moment to acknowledge that Gabriel was clearly Council. Gabriel continued mildly. "Do you perchance have someone else who can finish that task while my two friends visit?"

The entire group was suddenly quiet.

"Well?" Gabriel asked.

"Ah . . . ah . . . but he's . . . he's just a Moon Born. He doesn't get extra breaks. We're already behind." The man's voice was respectful, but he stood with his feet planted, looking tense.

"He's a student of mine." Gabriel felt his jaw clench. "You will do as I say."

"Well, he's been on *my* crew for five years. But whatever you say must be true. Of course." The man pursed his lips, but he gestured to another crew member, who walked over and took the wrench from Nick's hand.

Rachel and Nick came over to Gabriel. Nick's hands were callused, and his shoulders stooped a little. His hair was graying slightly at the temples. Gabriel shook his head to clear it of the odd image; people shouldn't age this fast. The reminder of Rachel's long sleep, and his own, made him acutely uncomfortable. He held his hand out to Nick. "Good to see you, Nick. I'm sorry about Ursula."

"Thank you," Nick said. "She was trying very hard to do a good job. I really don't know how it happened." His voice broke. "One moment she was there . . . and the next . . . the next she was just gone."

Rachel buried her head in Nick's shoulder while Nick looked away. Gabriel was sorry he had brought up the subject.

It was Rachel who found a way out for them, asking Nick about the tiller and placing the conversation firmly on technical grounds. When the men finished the work and the broken tiller rumbled back to life, Rachel looked over at Gabriel. "Can Nick go with us? We could use the hand."

Before Gabriel could reply Nick shook his head. "No—I'll be in enough trouble for this. You'll be going back to Aldrin, right? I'll see you there." Nick gave Rachel a brief hug, turned, and walked away, trailing the others down the road.

The next few days were sunny and bright, and the surveying went easier. The last day they were back near the Sea Road when they had to duck a flare. They sat it out in a shelter and did yoga and talked about the chaotic nature of weather patterns. They had been sleeping in separate tents. The tiny flare shelter was only one room with enough floor space for them to sleep. Lying close to Rachel, Gabriel slept badly and longed for Erika. When he woke up, one of his arms was lying over Rachel's shoulder. Carefully, he moved his arm, then woke her and hurried them out of the shelter to the surface of the moonlet, and home.

It took two days to install Rachel as a teacher starting new classes. Shane and Star were dubious, but Gabriel overrode them.

On the flight back up to *John Glenn,* the sight of Selene pulled at him. He turned all of his window views toward *John Glenn* and focused his energy forward. His heart leaped at the thought of seeing Erika. He would feel clearer when they were together again.

Chapter 32: Reunited

Erika was warm!

As soon as the med techs set her free, he folded her in his arms, and kissed her, over and over. Then he led her to Yggdrasil, now twice as big as when she'd last seen it. When Erika went cold, Aldrin and Clarke Base were still tented for atmosphere, and the First Trees were seedlings. She held him tightly in the light gravity, looking up the huge trunk, smiling so deeply it looked like every part of her was happy.

She scampered up the ropes that ringed the trunk, looking back at him and laughing. Her long blond hair was caught in a loose ponytail that flapped up and down as she moved. Even though he still felt strong and new from his time iced, she was lithe enough to outfox him twice, going around the trunk ahead of him and dropping back a rope rung when she was out of sight, surprising him by suddenly being beside him. Each time she slid one leg around his waist, and pulled him near for a kiss. The second time, he pivoted, pinned her with his knee, and kissed her deeply, tasting her, smelling her, laying his cheek across her head and running his hand along her backside. He shook as he pushed himself away.

Erika found a thick, slightly flattened branch far enough from the trunk to make a comfortable seat. They sat close, feeling the slight centrifugal force of the garden's spin as a wind blowing gently against their faces and a slight tug outward. Their feet floated over grasses and small shrubs that made up the savannah.

Erika leaned into him and whispered, "When I go cryogenic, I'm always afraid I'll never wake up. Or that when I do wake up, everything will be so different I won't fit in anymore."

Gabriel held on to the tree with one hand, and crunched her close to him with the other. "I think we just gave someone that opportunity." He told her about Rachel's unexpected sleep. "I think she'll be okay." He finished. "By the time I left, she was treating me almost normally again."

"What an initiation to cold sleep," Erika said. "You said you were training her to lead. Is she still loyal enough to do that?"

"I'm not sure anymore," he mused. "I wanted at least crew leaders. That plan seems to have been aborted while Rachel and I were cold. I don't think any of the Children *hated* me before, except Andrew, but I'm sure some of them hate Star and Shane. I met two kids in Teaching Grove who seemed to be afraid of me. They wouldn't even come close to me. That worries me. And the Colonists—the Children call them 'Earth Born'—they resent us and lord it over the Moon Born." He pursed his lips. "Most of them, anyway. No one seems happy."

"Andrew?" She narrowed in on the part of his story that could be a personal threat to him.

"A crazy boy. Destructive. He vandalized things twice. We stripped him of his data rights, but we left him on Selene."

"Was that a good idea?"

Gabriel shrugged. "Ali and I talked about it, and decided it was better than the alternatives: killing him, I mean, or freezing him, or locking him up. I don't think Liren agreed, although she went along. But if we have to ice everyone who misbehaves, then we'll be using cryotanks for the wrong reasons. Liren has a different idea—she actually built a jail."

"A what?" Erika pulled away and swung around to where she could look directly at him. "Did she put Andrew in it?"

"No—we'd already passed sentence. People can't do much worth getting put in jail. Hell, we've got cameras everywhere. But Shane says they have used it for brawling a few times—both Moon Born and Earth Born. I guess it's mostly a deterrent."

"Do we need a deterrent? Has it gotten that bad?"

"We didn't when I went off-shift. But Ma Liren's gone a tad control crazy; it's worse every time she's on-shift. I know she's your friend. She was our best politician once—without her, we might never have gotten away from Sol system. Hell, she fought her way to *John Glenn* at the end. But we don't have any business being an oppressive government, and Liren's forgotten . . . historically; oppression's never worked. It's like she thinks everything we fled, all the AIs and all the augmented, like it's all right at her shoulder."

"I'll talk to her." Erika leaned so close to him it felt as if she were trying to join him in his skin, and then she asked, "How about the timeline? I was really hoping we would be further along. I know the collider isn't supposed to be finished yet, but it was supposed to be started! As far as I can tell, it's still on the drawing boards. How long do we have to diddle with this moon before we do what we stopped here for? Do I still get to fly this ship away from here in a few decades?"

Gabriel sighed. "Maybe a few more than we first thought," he said. "There's quakes, and flares, and something else I've decided we have to do, although it will add time as well. It's starting to feel like it might take forever to get to where we can safely build the collider."

"Well, I'm still Second. The captain will fly us away, I'm sure."

"He's been warm even more since you went down," Gabriel said. "He may be too old to fly again."

"He was supposed to sleep!"

"Have you ever tried to tell him what to do?"

Erika's laugh tickled his shoulder. "Well, whoever flies the *John Glenn* away from here, I still want oblivion through most of this nightmare project."

"You don't get older anymore, the new tech changes that. This is the second time you've warmed to it—don't you feel better?"

"It doesn't make this project end any faster, or help me get away from here. I want to spend my life between the stars, and at Ymir."

"Me too. But Ymir seems far away lately—like a childhood dream drifting far away." He made a face at her.

Anxiously, "You still want to go?"

"Yes, I do. I want to be on Ymir. I want a planet that's nearly perfect to set deer and horses free on." Gabriel looked up at the tree, searching for the top, but the sunlight was so bright it stung his eyes. "I'd like to ride a horse again. At least once." A flying bot passed between him and the light, and he blinked and then pulled back to look directly into her eyes. "We knew after we decided to stay true to our rules about tech—we knew that we would be using the Children. But we didn't *know* it. Not the way I *know* it, working with them every day. And we can't stay here, we calculated that as well. Not enough variety, and no way to stabilize Selene's atmosphere enough for the really long haul. Not unless we become what we fled from, or worse. Erika, I have to look in their eyes, every day I'm on Selene. Sometimes I think it's cowardice that keeps us stuck to our fear of tech; then I remember Earth. But we can't do what we're doing now either. We just can't." Gabriel searched Erika's face for a response.

Her jaw was set tight. She finally said. "I'm sorry, love. I really am. We had hard choices to make. That's all. Every choice had its dangers."

It was little comfort. Gabriel frowned at himself, not wanting to ruin their first day together. "I just wish it were different—that we'd made it to Ymir. I'm tired of hard things."

"You *are* an old man," she teased.

"Hmmmm. I'm older than you are now."

"Effectively. But I'll always be a month older in real time."

"How do you know what's real?" he asked.

"You've been talking to Astronaut again."

"And who else am I supposed to talk to?"

"Me." She wrinkled her nose at him.

"I do—when you're receiving. Besides, Astronaut's moved on. When you went to sleep it was stuck in quantum physics as a sideline. I'm pretty sure the current interest is human psychology."

Erika threw her head back and laughed. "We might drive it crazy. And as fast as it thinks and learns, if it's been on psychology long enough for you to notice, it must be mighty confused." In a typical lightning change, she asked, "Can we go?"

"Go?" Gabriel said innocently, watching the line of her jaw, the way her cheeks curved gracefully.

"It's time to fly."

Gabriel shook his head at her. "Surely you remember the rules?" he said dryly. "Tomorrow. Unless you want to sit still while I fly."

"I'll sit here," she said, snuggling breast to breast, legs wrapped around his waist to keep her from drifting, her head buried in his shoulder. It left Gabriel with all the work of anchoring them to the tree.

Gabriel sighed with pleasure and sat quietly, lips resting on her light hair, right hand roaming her thigh and the soft place behind her knee, both of his calves hooked under the branch to hold them on. He whispered into her ear. "Ready to go to bed?"

She snuggled closer and ran her fingers through his hair. "Wait a bit. Let me get used to you. You've changed a lot this time."

Gabriel frowned, and stroked her hair. "I still love you."

"I love you too." After a while she asked, "You said we had to do something else. What is it? And why do we have to do it?"

"It's the damned flares. Daedalus gets all wrung up with Apollo, and they tangle their magnetic fields, and make flares. We knew that. You knew that. But they're worse than we thought. The blasts are directed. The whole project could be stopped dead if a strong enough flare hits at the wrong time. The Sol-based flare categorization system stopped at X— an X-class flare is the worst that happens in Sol system. We've added Y and Z here. We've seen two Y-class flares in the time we've been monitoring. Neither of them hit Selene, and of course, most won't. But it would only take one. Astronaut ran the probabilities, and they're too damned high. So we have to make a safe place—use the water in the Hammered Sea as a buffer and build a flare shelter the likes of which we never even thought of."

She looked him in the eyes. "You're sure it's not just because you love this kind of engineering so much? You're sure we really need to do this?"

"I had another idea too. A flare kite . . ." Did she think he loved building Selene so much he'd stall to stay? The question bothered him, and he made sure to answer her firmly. "Yes, I'm sure we need to do this."

"So how much time will it add?" Erika demanded.

"Two or three years. Not much in the overall scale of things."

"It's still a long time."

"I know. There's nothing to be done. You'll just be cold longer—it won't change the effective time you're awake. At least, not by much. But it will adjust what you do this shift." He tried to make light of the delay. "At least, if you want to go with me. It means a swing out to get a big rock."

"Again? I thought we were done throwing big rocks!"

"Hey—I made you some rings with one rock throw. This time I'll make you something safe in case you're on Selene when the big one hits."

"Make me some antimatter!"

"I know." He tickled her, working to get her mood back up. "Let's go look around, get you used to the changes on the ship. I didn't mean to dump my frustrations."

They flew through the garden, Gabriel pointing out changes, and Erika appreciating and questioning and probing. She found a new sculpture that surprised them both; a set of strings suspended from clear material edged in nanopaint that glittered with color, hues changing with the shifting sounds the manufactured wind made as it played the strings.

When Erika tired of new sights and led the way to her room, Gabriel was nearly too tired to make it down the corridor. But of course, she woke him up expertly.

Afterward, he held her softly and smiled as she drifted off to sleep.

The next morning, Gabriel slept far later than usual. He woke and reached for her, and found the bed next to him empty. Erika stood against the wall, checking ship stats, already dressed in a tight yellow pressure suit. He asked, "Don't you want breakfast first?"

"I want to fly."

Gabriel dressed to match Erika. They caught their hair back in nets, and Gabriel followed Erika up to the docking station, where *Erika's Triumph* sat ready in the lock. She had named the glass ball of a ship to balance that misplaced crater; but she called the ship *Triumph*. "It'll remind us of what we have to do."

All by herself—barring Astronaut—Erika had rebuilt one of the slow Service Armor configurations to make *Triumph*. Fiddling with the LOX and LH engine, she teased it to use a touch more propellant than it was designed for, adding thrust. She added range with an extra water tank, and scientific usefulness with double the normal complement of cameras.

The little ship actually handled better than its unaltered counterparts. She claimed Astronaut helped her, but the AI proclaimed that Erika had made all of the design decisions herself. From the outside, *Triumph* looked like the twenty other Service Armors. It was a round glass ball festooned with robotic arms, just enough interior room for two, guts and controls visible through a clear hull laced with black carbon threads so fine they seemed more like smoke than strength.

Erika climbed into the pilot's seat. Gabriel hung back, looking, then used his radio. "Hey, that yellow suit makes you look like a banana in a shake glass."

She refused to answer, pulling wraparound sunshades over her eyes and gesturing impatiently for Gabriel to climb in.

Even modified, *Triumph* was designed only for travel near *John Glenn*. Never meant to fly in atmosphere, the little ship launched simply: the lock opened and *Triumph* puffed out, far enough that problems with the initial engine lightoff couldn't hurt the parent ship.

They dropped into open space from the Insystem Service Pod, a drum-shaped warehouse as capacious as the city of Aldrin. The ISP section of *John Glenn* hadn't been given spin. They had to fly around it to see details. The arrowhead that made up the front cone of *John Glenn* protected smaller vehicles clamped to the forward rim of the ISP. Erika took them through a forest of tugs and miners, avoiding tall spikes of attachment legs and huge deflated bags that mining or scooping trips would fill with volatiles. She flew so close and fast that Gabriel reached out to balance himself more than once.

John Glenn was large enough to fool the eye into seeing a horizon. Erika took them toward it, curving around the giant ISP cylinder. Blue and gold and white rings rose like a rainbow, and then the orb of the planet Harlequin itself. She flew them as far from the ship as she dared and shook her fist at Harlequin, screaming, "I WILL leave you," into her mouthpiece.

Gabriel hesitated, thinking of Selene. But he joined her, and they turned it into a chant, and he felt more aligned with his younger self than he had in years. He didn't tell her so directly, but after they parked *Triumph,* he held her to him, not wanting to let her go.

When they went down the corridor to find breakfast, Erika shook her hair free of its netting and said, "*Now* I know I'm alive."

Chapter 33: Threat

Morning light streamed through the clear greenhouse roof, illuminating a thousand tiny curves of yellow-green seedlings. Rachel and Nick tested and poked at the baby plants, making notes to leave for the students. Three months into her first class, Rachel was grateful for Nick's help. He came to the school greenhouse whenever his crew was in town and helped her grade work.

Rachel examined the unevenly planted sprouts, noting that some near the edges were broken at the stem. "I don't remember ever being as sloppy as these kids," she muttered.

"Selene was different then. We had more hope," Nick said.

Rachel winced. Nick was twice her effective age, and yet she alone of their graduating class had been allowed to teach. The rest worked hard, raised families, and did what they were told. She'd found ways to fit in since coming back, but no ways to belong. There were so many new tensions.

She sighed. "When I started this class, I hoped it would make a difference. But look at this work!"

"It's made a difference to me to have you back," Nick said, smiling at her.

The first students flew over the greenhouse toward the meadow. "Wish me luck," she said. "Drop in tonight? At Harry and Gloria's? I promised Gloria her first history lesson, and you might be interested."

Nick smiled wanly. "Sure," he said. His voice was flat, unenthusiastic. *Maybe we are all different now?* she thought. *I can't see myself, after all.*

It was the final test day for her first solo class. She would deliver an opening address before the hard work of testing began. Her notes matched classes she and Ursula had taught together. The students were surlier, less excited, and more easily distracted than Rachel remembered from her own classes. She wanted to fail half of them for inattention. They wouldn't all pass, and that worried her.

Shane had planned to come and help today, but he'd called to postpone. A crew had rolled a planter onto its side trying to back down a small hill. He'd promised that he or Star would make it back to help her announce the results.

She glanced around the meadow to be sure she was alone, then spoke quietly into the air. "I'm scared."

"I know," Astronaut responded, its voice speaking softly through the Library bud.

"Do you get scared?" Rachel asked.

"I feel concern about negative outcomes. I do not undergo metabolic changes."

"You're being your usual certain self," Rachel complained. "How about if *you* tell *me* if you think *you* get scared."

"What do I risk by teaching you?"

They might wipe Astronaut's mind, or edit it down to the level of a planter combine's autopilot. "Are we safe?"

"Treesa's on duty." Cryptic reassurance that the garden woman was awake and applying her skills to make small changes in the data flow, masking conversations between Rachel and Astronaut, sometimes hiding Rachel's talks with others. Treesa had little confidence in her work if someone looked closely. Even on Selene, the information flow was too rich for Treesa and her programs to handle every possible camera and sensor. Astronaut had no rights that would let him change data. He helped by steering Treesa to the most important data flows. Rachel spared little worry that Shane or Star had time to watch her, but idle eyes watched Selene constantly aboard *John Glenn.*

She pushed her fears way. Lessons with Astronaut were a nightly ritual. She had moved into her own small home near the greenhouses, ostensibly to tend the student greenhouses on off days. Treesa and Astronaut had convinced her she needed to begin teaching others. Her own fears were nothing compared to her fear that Council would fuel their ship and abandon Selene. What if she lost the rich resources of *John Glenn,* lost Gabriel and Astronaut and Treesa?

Treesa and Astronaut had Rachel studying Joan of Arc, Mohandas Gandhi, Martin Luther King, and Hitler. Treesa had told Rachel she needed to understand the impact a single individual could have. Rachel understood that they had all died violently.

Rachel, Nick, and Harry and his family often met and talked about ways to gain more freedom. She would begin with education, with her opening talk for testing day. Her speech didn't break any rules she'd been told about. Shane and Star wouldn't like it, but they wouldn't be back until later that afternoon, when it was time to announce results.

Ali had perched on this same dais to lecture Rachel's graduating class. Rachel sat cross-legged before her fifteen students. She had thought about what to say, had talked to Astronaut and Treesa about it, but now her mouth was dry and it was hard to start. She licked her lips, swallowed, and said, "We are important. What we do here on Selene is important. We are building a home."

Half the class watched her closely. Some boys in the back were whispering to each other. She raised her voice. "I know it seems like we are working only for Council. We do their bidding, and in turn they feed us and clothe us—"

One of the boys in the back, Sam, raised his hand. He had been trouble all along, and his surliness reminded her of Andrew. Ignore him?

"Sam?"

Belligerently, "We don't have any other choices. No one gives us any."

Rachel remembered Treesa's words. "We do have choices. We can choose how we react. Even better, we can work smarter than they expect us to. We can ask questions. We can learn as much as possible, and show them how smart we are."

Sam interrupted, "Council doesn't listen to us."

He was right. But why? "When they give us opportunities to teach and learn, we can ask questions. We don't ask enough questions even of ourselves. We accept whatever we're told. But we—all—every one of you has learned more about what we're doing just by being in this class."

"Asking questions isn't going to help," Sam said. She heard not belligerence now, but frustration. "They never listen to us. Even most of the Earth Born won't answer questions."

"Sam, let me finish. Council has a problem. There aren't enough of them to do everything here. They need us to help. They will never say so. But some of us have been doing the math. Council can't meet their goals if they don't use more of us to run teams. We have to be ready. We have to learn well, and work hard, and show them that we can do more than they let us do now."

Sam had turned away from her and was whispering to his friends. Rachel kept talking. It was important for her to have control, but at least some of the Children must understand what she was telling them.

"I've seen how much some of you have learned. One way to learn more is to watch. Be careful, be smart. I'm taking the top three students with me into the field for two days. I hope that those of you in that group will think about what I've said, and be willing to talk about how to make ourselves more useful to Council while we're gone. Not for Council's sake, but for our own. We are the Children of Selene." She noticed which students listened. It was enough . . . a beginning. Maybe it would make some of them think.

She moved the class on to final testing. There were no student plots to review; Rachel wasn't allowed the extended curriculum Gabriel had used with her.

The afternoon passed, the students with their heads down over their pads. Rachel set them playing and carefully graded everything, watching constantly for Shane or Star. She stood on the edge of the field watching the students. They were restless, watching her.

Rachel sighed and climbed onto the dais, doing her best to look official. She called the students over to give them final scores. She'd agreed to this role, but she didn't like it. Not unsupported. Shane or Star should be here.

"First, the top three students are Beth Rachel, Kelly, and Eric." Then she read off a list that included all but three of the other students. "All of you did well enough to pass, although some of you barely squeaked by. That means Shane or Star will assign you to work crews. But in the meantime, you've got three days off."

The children got up and left, all except Sam, Rudy, and Antonia. Beth waited at the edge of the field, and Rachel gestured to her to stay. It made her feel a little better to have Beth waiting for her. She looked around for any sign of Shane or Star. This speech was as hard to start as her first one had been. "Sam, Rudy, and Antonia. I'm sorry, but you three simply didn't do enough of the work to pass. You may petition Shane or Star to take the class again, or you can join the planting crews as failed students, which means you won't get very good job assignments. I'd suggest the first choice, but I can't speak for Shane or Star, and I don't know what they'll let you do."

Antonia stood up and left, walking fast, as if she didn't want Rachel to see she was disappointed. Sam and Rudy looked at each other and stood up slowly. Sam glared at her, not moving, not saying anything. Rachel tensed for a problem. She breathed out a slow sigh of relief when they turned and walked away. They didn't look back at her, but she heard an angry edge to their words as they talked to each other, even though she couldn't tell what they were saying.

Beth and Rachel walked back from the test with the light falling to gray, talking about how to pack gear into small packs they needed for the trip.

Trees at the side of the path rustled and Sam and Rudy stepped in front of them, barring their way. Sam's eyes darted around, looking for other people, and then he focused on Rachel, letting his rage show.

Rachel stopped and said, "Beth, why don't you go on, and head home to get your gear packed."

Beth's voice quivered, but she said, "No, I'll wait for you."

Rachel stayed quiet, forcing the boys to take the offensive or leave.

Sam glared at her. "You're not supposed to be here. We don't want you to be our teacher." Rudy said nothing but stood behind Sam, arms crossed. Sam continued. "You should have passed me. If you were really one of us, you would have passed me. It's not right to pretend you're on our side, and then betray us. You need to—to go back to *John Glenn.* We don't need your kind here."

"My kind? There's only one of me, Sam." It dawned on her that *John Glenn*'s spin gravity had made her stronger than he was. One blow would knock him sprawling. Was he armed?

"I believe I'm a lot like you." She was pleased that her voice sounded strong. "You know we're watched," she warned.

"Council doesn't bother to watch much," Rudy said from behind Sam.

Sam pressed on. "If you were like us, you'd be the same age as our parents. You're almost like Council." Sam drew himself up, looking more confident now that he'd gotten most of his message out. He finished by repeating himself. "You don't belong. Go live forever somewhere else. We didn't ask you to come teach us."

"She does too belong!" Beth's voice was stronger, although she remained behind Rachel.

"Sam, you get your wish. I won't teach you. Don't ever come back to my class. Excuse us," Rachel said, taking Beth's hand and stepping toward the pair.

Rudy moved next to Sam, removing any chance the women had of snaking past the young men. "Not until you agree that you don't belong here." His voice was edgy, and Rachel checked her wrist pad. Yes, it was sending to Astronaut and Treesa.

Sam reached toward her.

Chapter 34: Fighting Words

Rachel sidestepped, trying to watch Sam and Rudy at the same time. She heard a sharp intake of breath from Beth.

A new voice spoke from the side of the path. "Sam, is that what you want?"

Sam stopped in midstride. His hand fell to his side.

"They'll bring more newly warmed Earth Born to help guide and teach you. I'd have thought you had enough of that already." The speaker, a tall man about Nick's age, stepped onto the path between Sam and Rachel.

Sam immediately lost the defiance in his voice. "Hhh-hello, Andrew."

Rachel would have known him anywhere. The cold anger on his face looked just like it did the last time she saw him, defiant and tough and confident.

Andrew's eyes flicked toward Rachel. "Tell him why you failed him."

She didn't want to follow Andrew's orders—she had to retain control of the situation somehow or she'd never succeed with Sam or Rudy. "He knows. Sam can tell you how much he studied, or not."

No one responded. Rachel used the moment to study Andrew. He was thin and tall, and muscles stood out in cords along his neck and arms. A scar snaked down the side of his left arm. He still wore metal armbands. His hair was cropped short. With a start, she realized that Andrew had grown into an attractive man. He was much more physically powerful than most Children. A moment ago, she had expected to outface the two students. Now, she didn't know what to do. She focused her gaze on Andrew's face.

"Well," he said, "aren't you happy to see an old friend?"

Rachel stepped backward, pushing Beth Rachel behind her again.

Andrew looked at Sam and Rudy, and said, "Don't *ever* let me catch you bothering Rachel again. Leave us."

They vanished into the brush.

Rachel heard footsteps crunching on dry leaves and caught herself wishing they hadn't gone. Andrew worried her more than Sam and Rudy.

Beth spoke from behind her, sounding happy. "Hi, Andrew, thanks. They were being bullies again. They make me *so* mad when they act like that! I don't know what they have against Rachel."

Andrew spoke gently to the younger girl. "Rachel has more power than they do, and they don't understand her. When I was Sam's age, I used to get mad at her too."

What did he mean? "Sam reminds me of you," Rachel said.

"I was like Sam." His voice sounded tight, controlled, and this time when he looked at her she saw naked longing. It scared her. What did he want?

His voice was oddly gentle as he said, "Run along, Beth—I need to talk to your namesake."

Beth smiled hesitantly at Rachel, but she obeyed Andrew as quickly as Sam and Rudy had, walking away down the middle of the path. She looked back once, as if to say "It's okay," and then she rounded a bend and was gone.

Rachel was alone with Andrew. Why did everyone, even Beth, do what he wanted?

He looked at the ground, shifted, and finally looked back up at her, searching her eyes for something he didn't seem to find. "I'm sorry. I've owed you this a long time. A real apology. I replanted the tree, Rachel, but it *died*. I didn't mean for the tree to die—I asked Harry to tell you that. It would have been just a *joke* if the tree hadn't died." His eyes bored into hers, deeply black and intense. He seemed to be waiting for something more, and then he just said, "Rachel, I'm sorry. I'm sorry for all of the things I was to you, and to everyone. I . . . I missed you when you were gone. I didn't come find you right away, because I didn't expect you to come back the same age as when you left."

"I don't know what to say."

"You could say thank you for stopping Sam and Rudy, or thank you for apologizing."

It was flat, but she said it, "Thank you."

"They won't bother you any more. I would have told them earlier, but I just found out a few days ago that you were here, that you're alive."

Rachel stepped back, increasing the distance between them a little.

"I'm glad you're alive," he said. "I thought they'd lied to us."

"They froze me." It seemed an inadequate thing to say. "It was an accident. Sort of."

"The kind of accident that happens when nobody gives a shit?"

Rachel didn't answer, because he was right.

"Does it make you one of the Council? Did you get any of the powers they have? Will you live forever? You are the only one of us who's even seen how they live—what they have. It should be ours too. But they use us to do the hard work, they tell us nothing, and they don't give us any-thing—important—to do."

Rachel couldn't find an answer. They stood awkwardly, looking at each other.

"I'm glad you're teaching again," Andrew said.

"Me too." She was cautious.

"Follow me," Andrew said, taking off down the path. "I need to talk to you."

Rachel hesitated, but after all, Andrew *had* intervened with the younger boys. She was recording. Andrew couldn't know how good her tech was. Astronaut knew where she was all the time. She glanced at her wrist: she had an hour before she was supposed to be at Harry and Gloria's.

Andrew led her into the trees, finally sitting down where branches and leaves folded over their heads and hid the sky. Rachel stayed standing, wanting to be able to leave easily.

Andrew's face was shadowed, a silhouette. "I don't want to be overheard," he said. "I know they can find out anything, but they haven't gotten me in trouble for things I've said when they can't see me. So when I need to talk about something important, I go where I can't see them, and it seems like they don't see me."

He fell silent for a moment.

Rachel didn't tell him that they were hidden by more sophisticated means. Astronaut and Treesa surely knew that she shouldn't be seen with Andrew.

Andrew continued. "Rachel, we have to make Council leave us alone, and quit telling us what to do. I've been working with some of the students for a few years, telling them what I know about Council. We have to find a way to act against the Council."

Rachel thought again of Sam and Rudy leaving just because Andrew said so, doing his bidding so easily. What was he up to? "How do you plan to change things?"

He was silent for a moment. Then he shrugged. "I don't know. We slow things down sometimes. Mostly we act as stupid as they think we are, and we learn what we can and share it. But that's nothing. We have to plan something more—but I don't know what to do yet." Some of the bravado had leaked away. "But I do know what's happening to us isn't okay. They need us, so we have a lever; we just have to find a way to use it. Help me find it? I need you." He looked up at her, and again she saw that naked plea. "I need what you know; you have more contact with Council than any of us."

He scrambled to his feet, so his eyes were even with hers.

She wasn't ready to give him any information. "You can't act directly against them, Andrew. You of all people should know that. They could . . . they could just let us die off and start over. They could kill us all. I've read about wars, about people fighting people, and we don't have the resources to fight Council. They have what we need, Andrew, but there is no way we can take it by force. Our only hope is to educate ourselves enough, become useful enough—"

"Helping them won't change the balance of power."

"It might," she insisted. "Rebelling won't—it can't work. Why act stupid? You can't act stupid and get respect. I told my students the same thing today."

"I heard you." Now Andrew looked at the ground. "It was a good talk. But talk can't change anything. We're treated like balky tools. They make us work, but they don't trust us to do anything real. Heck, they don't trust *me* at all. I'm a symbol for them. But I earned that. You haven't earned anything but trust—but do they trust you? Do they?"

"Some of them do," Rachel said.

"Do they?" Andrew repeated.

"I'll earn more trust." Rachel's words sounded naïve, even to her. Andrew was voicing her own feelings about Council. But force wouldn't—couldn't—work. "You haven't seen their resources, Andrew."

"Rachel, we have to act. You can help me. We can work together. You and I can force them to treat us differently, to tell us more, to let us stay young and healthy, like them."

She shook her head, worried about how militant he sounded. "Of all people, you should know that they see everything we do."

"I do know that." After a few moments he said, "They can't hear everything. They don't have time. Some risks have to be taken. I . . . we . . . can't trust the Earth Born any more than Council. We're all you *can* trust, Rachel: the Children of Selene. You have to see that."

The last edges of twin shadows winked into darkness. "I have to go," she said, and stood and started back the way they came.

"Cut your hair," he said to her retreating back. "You look almost like one of them. The only difference is that you're taller."

Her braid hung past her shoulders. She'd made today's decoration for it herself, out of dried twigs and leaves. She brought a hand up and fingered the braid rings, and when she looked, he was gone. She liked her hair, and she wasn't about to cut it because he said so. She answered him back, loud enough that if he was watching her from nearby he could hear. "No, Andrew, I won't cut my hair."

She had so many more questions. How long had he been watching her? How come she hadn't seen him? How much did the Children listen to him?

THAT NIGHT, at Harry and Gloria's, she started telling Gloria and Harry and Dylan and Beth and Nick about history and rights. She touched on King, the American Black civil rights leader, and Gandhi who led India's freedom movement from an oppressive and more technologically astute British society, Spartacus, the leader of the failed slave rebellion in Rome, and Agnes Redflower, who fought to save the Northwest forests in 2100. No one took notes. There was little discussion.

Afterward she sat out on the roof of her little house and wondered what Gabriel was doing, and if Kyu was flying through the garden aboard *John Glenn,* or frozen and lost to her. "Astronaut, Treesa," she used her subvocal skills, "I'm going to tell Gabriel that I'm teaching more than he told me to. I won't tell him everything."

Astronaut replied, "It could be dangerous."

"I know. But if I only tell him a little, then I won't really be lying to him, and I won't get in trouble if I get caught."

"I advise against it," the AI said.

Treesa chimed in. "Rachel, I think it would be better if you don't tell him anything. Not yet. Wait awhile."

Rachel stared up at the expanse of stars. She remembered looking into the same starscape with Ursula and Harry. Those nights might have happened to someone else entirely.

I might have married Harry, she thought, *and then it would have all been so much easier, and there would be someone here to talk to.*

"I remember," she said, "something about making my own decisions."

Chapter 35: Fetching Refuge

It took Gabriel and Erika three years to choose their target. Selene itself was built from Harlequin's moons and a handful of icy asteroids found in LaGrange orbits. Apollo's inner system was nearly empty. All of the useful masses were out beyond Harlequin's orbit. That included three more gas giant worlds and their moons, a sparse scattering of asteroids, and the comets.

Gabriel's probes had done their work tens of thousands of years ago. The most interesting bodies had drifted a bit. Gabriel sent four probes to the most likely asteroids. He wanted a metal mass with some carbonaceous material. Some bodies were no more than a jumble of loose gravel; best to avoid anything with too much ice. The machines circled them and sent back photos and spectroanalysis; landed, and analyzed what they landed on. The best choices were farther away than Council wanted, but everything else was too small, too big, too loose, too icy. In the end the probes fired nanobots into a dark nickel-iron lump.

High Council debated the wisdom of the trip. Even though the captain and Clare both supported the idea, the asteroid, already dubbed "Refuge," would take a full Earth year of ship's time to retrieve, and another to get back. Like everything else on the Selene project, necessity won over sentiment; delays were accepted. Shane and Star reluctantly agreed to stay on Selene still longer, although they barked about getting old.

Erika piloted; Gabriel crewed. They took one of the three huge pusher tugs, the *Diamond Mine.* The squat round tug was towed a distance away from *John Glenn* by one of the smaller ships in its class, the Medium Miner *Ruby Blues.* Wayne Narteau piloted the *Ruby Blues,* and wished them luck as they broke away and lit their fusion engine. *Diamond Mine* dove deep into Harlequin's gravity well, made its burn, and was on its way toward Apollo.

Space flight offered privacy unknown aboard *John Glenn* itself. Communication was regular, but there would be no continuous stream of video unless the *Diamond Mine* or *John Glenn* declared an emergency. As they separated from *John Glenn,* the communications lag grew. Aboard the *Diamond Mine,* Gabriel and Erika had more privacy than anyone except High Council ever experienced.

The first weeks were simple, punctuated with few requirements except exercise and astronomical observations as they dove relentlessly, directly, at Apollo. Erika and Gabriel put the easy start to largely physical use, making love in every way they could remember.

Gabriel began to relax. The stress of running the Selene project slowly melted away, lost in the vast empty space between Harlequin and Daedalus. He was excited—even though he had flown this tricky path four times, every approach left him feeling some of the edgy fear that had defined his first fall toward Daedalus. Ten Jupiter masses and more than three times Jupiter's volume, from this distance Daedalus remained no more than a dark red dot in front of Apollo. Dark lenses and a squint allowed it to look like a huge sunspot.

Orbiting just beyond the sun's Roche limit, Daedalus destabilized the entire inner system. It snarled its magnetic webs with Apollo's, drawing flare activity from the small sun, throwing great storms of plasma around, sometimes all the way past Harlequin. Daedalus had eaten every mass near it short of Apollo itself. There was rain on Daedalus—molten iron.

Still, for now it was far enough away that Gabriel could think of other matters: Erika, and Selene. The bloated gas giant would occupy him completely soon enough.

ERIKA LIT THE FUSION engines for the final burn.

During the next few weeks Daedalus's image grew larger. It became distinct from Apollo, gained shape, gained size. Daedalus was bigger than Harlequin, and much hotter, almost a sun itself, with its own sluggish internal fusion reactions. Harlequin's neat shock-wave diamond patterns were roiled to chaos in Daedalus's storms. They watched smaller storms nibbling at the edges of a whorl as big as Uranus.

Erika and Gabriel grew minutely but inexorably heavier as the ship's acceleration increased. Gabriel hated this part—feeling slow and large and awkward while they rocketed toward something his hindbrain couldn't identify as anything but a threat.

"We're faster this time, aren't we?" he asked.

"Medical said you could take six gee."

"What are you taking us to?"

"Six point two."

Gabriel snorted.

Hours before the closest approach to Daedalus, they suited up, installed filtered water and vitamin food mixes inside their psuits, and strapped themselves into viewing bay couches. Erika thought cabins were entirely too wimpy—and fear had always lured her, a magnet that pulled the best from her. She was enough the careful ship's captain to have them in a safe place in case unexpected course corrections were needed, but crazy enough to love the danger. Gabriel watched her cheeks flush and her eyes brighten as they came closer. She'd piloted him around Daedalus twice before, and always she was daredevil happy, sharp, precise, and very alive. Even in a bulky suit, Erika had grace. But only her forearms and fingers moved, because thrust was flattening them both.

Erika filled the view screen with images of the gas giant, so it was all they could see, all of their world. This close, Daedalus dwarfed them to a sand grain blown past a fiery beach ball. The planet showed alarming detail, eddies visible inside storms inside bands of separated gases. A small mistake in trajectory would throw them into it, and the *Diamond Mine* would never crawl from the gravity well of the gas giant before it was torn apart.

Gabriel held his breath, only briefly afraid.

And at last, at peri-Daedalus, they blew the fireball in their engine into space in one mighty puff. Six point two gee, and then they were falling free, almost weightless, the ship stressed a bit by Daedalus's tides. They were in Daedalus's shadow. The receding gas giant was a black circle behind them, rimmed with Apollo's corona.

Their course gradually straightened, and Gabriel began to feel safe. Erika started the navigation program calculating the small course adjustments they'd need to intersect *Refuge* based on their actual trajectory after slinging away from Daedalus. The gas giant slowly stole back some of the speed it had given them.

IN SOL SYSTEM THEY WOULD have called it a KBO, a Kuiper Belt Object. The lump was a flattened and battered spheroid, black except for a shiny blister forming on one side. Invisibly small nanobots were spreading out across that face. Gabriel and Erika sprayed a barrier strip around the object's waist, before they did anything more ambitious.

The barrier would deny the nanobots access to one side of Refuge: the "down" side. From this point *Diamond Mine* would work only with the "down" side.

They hooked the object easily. It was a skill Gabriel and Ali had practiced over and over, bringing volatiles from dead comet heads, and minerals and more mass from chondrite asteroids, to blanket Selene. Erika too had helped, staying with him through two back-to-back shifts before plunging into a thousand-year sleep.

The body that would become Refuge was much bigger than even the huge *Diamond Mine*. Gabriel felt like a bacterium driving an ant home with a walnut clutched in its pincers. The rock face of the asteroid—the side that would become Refuge's underside—jutted across the space in front of them, a wall they butted against and held on to, directed and pushed. Regular slight adjustments gave *Diamond Mine* the queasy feel of a carnival ride.

On the unseen "up" face of the asteroid, nanobots worked tirelessly. Gabriel sent out an occasional probe to look. Erika preferred to ignore it all, as if the rock had developed an unsightly disease. She didn't trust nanotechnology.

A glass pupil was forming on the up side of Refuge, larger every time he looked. Lumps and mounds and cracks and craters were disappearing into its edges. It all happened with excruciating slowness, but it happened. If it got out of hand, they'd drop the rock and start over elsewhere; but that could cost them a quarter century.

The worst problems were being cooped up with only each other for so long. Two years was a long time to be separated from the usual richness of data flow. Gabriel and Erika went from stormy and passionate to deep and soft, from lightly angry to charming, and back again. They'd done this before, and they pushed the cycles faster for fun, playing with the sweetness of being secure enough to argue. Still, it was a long year. *Diamond Mine* was bigger outside than it was inside.

One morning as they neared Harlequin, they woke together from a rare shared nap: Erika looked Gabriel directly in the face and said, "This has been too easy."

"I know." Gabriel had learned to trust Erika's gut feelings, and he immediately felt her unease.

They spent the whole day looking for problems. Everything was perfect. Gabriel sat up that night while Erika slept. He watched her toss and turn, and knew the day's faultless results hadn't stilled her fears. He made himself stop looking at readouts and just enjoy the star field. He stretched, letting himself fall into the vastness of their surroundings just as he did when he traveled to *John Glenn* from Selene.

Diamond Mine: all systems nominal. Refuge: the nanos hadn't touched the "down" face. The other side was rising as a smooth dome of carbon woven into diamond. The structure had become a flattened cone, honeycombed within.

As they neared Harlequin, Gabriel trained cameras on the asteroid defenses at Moon Fifteen. They were quiet, and everything looked normal. Robots moved around at the usual high speeds; routine. Programming recognized *Diamond Mine* even with Refuge attached, and responded. Check: they weren't about to be fragged by a linear accelerator.

They were close enough to see Selene, but not to resolve details. He turned on various lenses and imaging types randomly, looking for anomalies. A message came from *John Glenn* before he knew what he was looking for, and then he went to thermal imaging and his breath slammed into his belly. A spot of brightness that shouldn't be there glowed as Aldrin rotated into night.

Fire. He swore. He closed his eyes, and trembled, angry and afraid. Fire could devastate Selene.

"How?" Erika asked from behind him.

"You know Selene has a higher oxygen mix?"

"I thought the lower gravity compensated? The air mix is rarefied."

"It should. Something happened. This isn't something anyone has done before, after all. Maybe enough plants drove the oxygen percentage up just enough, or maybe we guessed wrong at some initial parameter." He slammed his fist down, carefully avoiding any control surface. "I need to be there."

"We're too far away," she said. "Relax."

"That's *my world* burning up down there. I need to get to *John Glenn*. I can do some good from there." And my students, he thought. Burning.

She reached around him from behind and gave him a hug. "You've done the best you can with Selene, Gabe. You've done wonderfully. Let's just hope this doesn't put us off schedule."

Gabriel winced, but he put his hands over hers and squeezed. "I just . . . I hope . . . I hope it doesn't all burn."

"I know. You've got hours to wait before you can even try for the ship." Her eyes looked as worried as he felt.

"You'll finish bringing Refuge in?"

"If you wait long enough to give me some safety margin before you leave me here. This is a lot of kinetic energy we're playing with!"

She isn't landing the damn thing, he thought. Refuge will have to be sterilized first. She'll take it into close orbit. No big deal.

There weren't enough resources on Selene to fight a fire there. Gabriel watched for physical traffic between *John Glenn* and Selene; for some sign that Council had seen what had to be done and was going down to the surface to help. The fire looked tiny, but Gabriel measured it at three thousand acres or more. A tenth of the jungle planted so far. He hated the two-second communications delay: a universal stutter. He paced.

There was a fast light Lander stored in a bay of the miner. Good enough to get him to *John Glenn*. It took a long time to get close enough to Harlequin, and Selene, to use it. Gabriel gave the commands that would release it and kissed Erika hard on the mouth. He strapped his suit closed with one hand as he pulled himself toward the bay.

Part III: Fire

60,294 *John Glenn* shiptime

Chapter 36: Fire

The bones of a cieba flashed eerily, a silhouette, black inside fire. Rachel crouched at the edge of a clearing, watching the tree burn. It was brighter in dying than in life. Then little remained for the flames to eat, and what crashed to the ground was white-hot, still shaped like a tree, still wreathed in bits of fire, until it was only white ash in the outline of a tree. Wind pulled at what remained, scattering once-solid trunk and branch.

Fire advanced slowly toward Rachel, licking the low grass. Farther away, it rushed through the fuel-rich jungle on either side of the clearing. She kept looking back to watch. Run, pause, run. If she wasn't careful, it would circle closed behind her.

She ran.

Heat was a physical force pushing Rachel from both sides, herding her. The smell of death and flame and smoky danger thickened the air. The fire was noisy: pops and flashes and keening chaotic winds.

The sounds of fire fell behind her, obscured by straining engine noises and snapping tree trunks, and Rachel finally knew she had outrun immediate death. She stopped, panting, breathing sweet cool air deeply into her seared lungs. In front of her, a pair of fifty-foot-long planting machines crushed young trees, pushing them aside to make wide cleared spaces. Smoke curled everywhere.

Justin, one of her half brothers, darted in and handed her water. Rachel drank deeply, watching the fire approach. Here, a hundred meters away, the heat was still palpable. Sweat ran down her bare skin. She shook a fist at the fire and turned, jogging to catch up with the trailing planter and join her crew returning to base.

She'd never seen uncontained fire. There was no place for it on Selene nor aboard *John Glenn*. It tore her breath from her, filled her with adrenaline and fear, made her want to run, and run, and run. It was fast, hot enough to suck the moisture from trees as it approached, turning damp rain forest to tinder in the time it took to breathe.

They had been too slow. The fire funneled through gaps, leaped over the second set of hard-won firebreaks. Rachel wiped sweat and tears away from her eyes as she jumped onto a maintenance shelf on one of the planters, holding on to a makeshift safety rope as the planter rumbled away from the fire line. Sweat poured down her face. Every vein and membrane was an internal desert. Her stomach hurt.

It was the end of the second full day of firefighting. Order slowly rose out of chaos. Training happened in stolen moments of shift briefings. Firefighters rose and slashed and hacked and fled and started over. After each shift, they fell onto thin cots at base camp, asleep while their livelihoods burned around them.

Rachel was responsible for a full crew. Nick was with Rachel; Harry and Gloria supported logistics at base camp. Star ran a team on the other shift. Shane commanded, using data feeds from *John Glenn* to visualize locations of fire and crew. Rachel didn't think Shane slept.

She half dozed as they rode to safety, so tired that even the whining of the engine faded behind the nightmares running through her head. Fire raced through trees, consuming them greedily, turning life to ash. The flash the first time flames jumped lines, hesitating for just a moment before leaping across the pitifully narrow road surface.

Rachel had been first to see fire. Even from a distance, when it was a small thing, she knew it was bad. She'd sent panicked open messages to *John Glenn,* and after the first hour, Kyu's voice was steady in her ear, relaying commands from Shane and urging calm. A lifesaving voice.

Kyu involved Astronaut immediately. Astronaut calculated the inferno's speed as it created its own terrible weather and ran through the dry underbrush fueled by Selene's thick atmosphere. Astronaut's predictions constantly ran behind the fire's actual movement. Centuries of fighting fire on Earth hadn't prepared anyone for a fire with ten percent more oxygen in the air.

The planter bucked as they rolled over a rock, and she snapped awake. Her grip tightened on the rope. It cut into her hand, so she wrapped her handkerchief around her right palm with her teeth while her left hand clutched the rope. Then she switched hands. Her left hand curled into a claw from holding her body against the machine, but she was so tired she felt nothing.

They pulled into base camp. Dylan ran toward her. He pulled her hand free of the rope, steadying her as she found her legs. She looked around and spotted Beth, Harry, and Gloria. She worked at her closed hand, and pain shot up her arm. She closed her eyes, swaying with exhaustion.

Dylan supported her on the short walk to her tent. She squeezed his hand in thanks, and he put an arm around her. They watched the eerie jumping firelight for long silent moments before she crawled into her tent.

Then she reached outside and pulled him in with her.

She'd thought this through in such intricate detail, all the reasons not to, and firmly decided against.

He wasn't sure what she wanted and he didn't want to ask. She showed him: kissed him hard, then stripped off his shirt. He bent double, cramped in the tiny tent, and they worked around each other to get their boots off, giggling softly. Dylan was willing . . . but he still wasn't sure. She was an icon, and he might misinterpret. She crawled on top of him, long bodies in full contact.

If there were cameras on the tent, what was happening inside would be pretty obvious.

She was at the edge of sleep when she heard him say, "Dad's not going to like this."

"No," she said. Would Gabriel? And Council . . . what would they think, with their casual attitude toward age? *Don't tell,* she thought, but cameras were watching the holocaust, and anyway, Dylan was out like a light.

SIX HOURS LATER, Rachel sat with Star and Dylan and three other crew bosses while ash fell around them like snow, sticking in their hair until they were white and pale, blotched with the wrong colors in the bare dawn light. Nearly a hundred firefighters made a loose circle around the crew chiefs. Most sat. A few stood and stamped their feet, or stretched tired arms. A hundred more were out fighting the fire. Children walked between the adults handing out water, bread, and fruit.

She noticed that people grouped themselves randomly. All able hands were somehow involved. Even Andrew simply worked with a crew. He sat in the back, watching her. She sighed. He was always there, always wanting something. She took Dylan's hand, making sure Andrew could see the gesture.

There was no apparent separation between Earth Born and Moon Born. Shane and Star and three other Council sat with everyone else. It made Rachel smile, a tiny gain in the middle of the most horrible thing she had ever known.

Shane addressed them all. "It will stop today," he said. "You can't see it yet, can't feel it yet, but our victory is coming. The Sea Road will stop it.

Everything on the other side will be safe." The crowd went quiet, and Shane raised his voice. "So today, we have to save Aldrin and Teaching Grove."

Rachel pictured it. The mature jungle between the fire and the meadow would burn easily. The meadow was nearly bare enough to be a firebreak, except flame could creep through the grass and run along the side through the First Trees and reach Teaching Grove. From there, it would lick down into Aldrin, stopping only when it encountered bare regolith on the far side of town.

Shane continued. "We're in the way. Base camp is moving in forty minutes. We need firebreaks to funnel the fire away from the First Trees, into the meadow, where we can stop it. We can stop it there. We will stop it there."

A smattering of applause rose up through the ranks. Shane nodded.

"Dylan and Rachel—you cut the breaks like you did yesterday. Take crews of three each—we'll need everyone else." Four planters were still usable. They'd lost two to the fire on day one. The crews had gotten out with a lesson in how much heat the machines could stand. "Rachel," Shane called, "you're in charge. You did a good job yesterday."

Rachel and her crew filed out, clutching extra water, hearing Shane assign everyone else to moving base camp to the other side of the Sea Road. Dylan and his crew mixed with them as they went. Beth and Nick were with Dylan this morning, and another Earth Born named Richard. Rachel's crew was Kyle, one of the students she'd taken on excursion a few times, and two Earth Born. Ariel was a woman Rachel's age, and Bruce was an Earth Born who had stayed on the surface since the first seeding. He was older than Rachel's father, nearly seventy, slower than the others, with a good head on his shoulders and a cheerful willingness to do what she asked. It was the first time Rachel had seen Earth Born reporting to Moon Born. Her own status was a necessity of the fire, and the earbud connection to Kyu that she alone had of all the Children, but still she was proud of leading that team.

All four of the machines started. Rachel drove the lead planter, taking Bruce with her, and Kyle and Ariel followed in the second planter. As they neared the meadow, Rachel calculated directional headings for the two machines she commanded. "We'll take the north route. Dylan can head south."

Shane agreed, followed by Kyu's, "Good luck."

"Dylan," Rachel said, "I'm leaving an open communications line. Keep talking. Tell me what you see."

"Aye, aye, ma'am."

The plan was to separate into sets of two, driving directly away from each other, making a firebreak twice the width of a planter. Then they'd come back toward each other, doubling the width. If there was time, they'd repeat, scraping closer to the bare dirt they needed. Finally, they'd join Shane's other firefighters at the far edge of the meadow to help with a last battle across the treeless area if necessary. In low grass it would be easier to keep the flames at bay. If only they had an efficient way to carry more water.

Rachel winced as they destroyed their own creation, snapping trunks and pushing the slash to the side. The noise of the planter's engines overwhelmed voices, forcing radio conversations even when they were near each other. Ash changed the color of leaves and gathered in Rachel's mouth so she had to spit it out. As they finished the first trip out and back, smoke began to blur the edges of the standing trees.

Kyu's voice sounded in her ear. "It's moving slower today, but the front is wider. You'll have to be careful not to get caught. One finger has reached the Sea Road, and it is stopping the flames."

Their first victory. Rachel smiled in spite of herself.

She began to taste smoke, and her lungs burned. "Kyu—can we make a second pass?"

"No—maybe half."

Rachel directed the combined crews to make half the pass together, toward the First Trees. "Drive in two lines, don't try to widen the path. We have to move fast." She looked back at Dylan, a dot driving a huge machine behind her. "We'll keep our blades high. Dylan, you and Nick set yours lower, see if you can find dirt."

Halfway through, Kyle and Ariel's planter gave out and the trailing planter failed to stop, tangling the two machines. With time, they could have freed them. Everyone scrambled onto the remaining two machines.

Rachel was the only person besides Star and Shane with com directly from Kyu. Kyu's voice buzzed firmly in Rachel's ear, but she didn't quite believe what she heard.

"Come again?"

"Take down the First Trees."

"Repeat?" She couldn't have heard right. The First Trees were irreplaceable.

"They'll burn."

Shane's voice: "Kyu's right."

Rachel took a deep breath. Of course Kyu was right. There was no choice. She hated the words as she said them, "We have new orders. Knock down the First Trees, starting in the middle. Build a wide enough break the fire won't jump it."

Beth cried out, "No!"

Dylan understood right away. "No choice. Better than Aldrin."

"Let's go. Keep some distance—I don't want to drop trees onto you."

Ten minutes later, they were plowing the big machines directly into the First Trees.

Rachel cried; deep dry sobs. The First Trees! Gabriel had planted these. She made herself focus, seeing only the next trunk, the next branch, the next vine. She let Bruce drive, and she walked, using a machete to strike through lianas, branches, and low plants. Sometimes the vines were so strong they alone held trees that had been pushed aside by the planters, and when she split the vines, they snapped and the trees fell wildly, crashing down into the underbrush.

Dylan's planter became too tangled in the jungle to move forward. He and his crew let Rachel know they were doing what they could by hand. Ten minutes later, screeching sounds of metal on metal began deep inside the planter Rachel's crew rode, and it rumbled to a stop.

All six of them were on the ground, hacking, chopping, smelling smoke. Time seemed to stretch, actions happened in slow motion. Rachel's back and bicep muscles ached. Her shoulder blades screamed and her calves trembled. She swung the machete wildly.

She finally stopped, realizing that she didn't know where anyone was. The heat had increased, and she heard the pop of fire and calls of Shane's crew from close by, out in the meadow. She started moving as fast as she could through the mangled forest, calling for Dylan and Nick and Beth. They needed to get out into the open.

Smoke obscured her vision, slowing her and ruining her sense of distance. She heard the crack of falling trees and the unwelcome sound of wind, but nothing from a human. Then Bruce's voice ripped through her radio, almost a scream, "Beth! Richard!"

Rachel couldn't tell if he was yelling to find them or yelling about them. "Where are you?"

Kyu's voice: "Go to your right," and then "Rachel—turn right—they need you." Rachel had turned already, and the two-second delay between the surface and the ship was driving her nuts. She couldn't see anything but trees, but she kept going. Bruce's voice croaked in her ear, not talking to her, talking to Dylan, "Pull it off, be slow."

She stepped between two standing tree trunks. One of the tallest trees lay directly across Richard. He was crushed, his back and neck broken, eyes open. And empty. Dead. Her eyes scanned the long trunk. Dylan stood farther up, desperately pulling on a branch, trying to move the huge tree. Beth Rachel was under it, lying on her stomach, her legs pinned. Rachel ran toward Dylan, reaching for a hold on the branch, noticing that Bruce too was down. He sat to the side. His right leg was at an odd angle. He moaned and tried to stand.

A great unfamiliar noise came from almost directly above them. Rachel looked up at an hallucination. A spaceship—she'd seen several like it hanging neatly on the side of *John Glenn*. Spaceships glided. This one jerked and yawed. She couldn't take time to understand.

Her hands wrapped tight around the branch, tugging with Dylan, adding her strength to his. The tree moved an inch. Not enough. Beth screamed.

The sound of the ship above them took over, drowning the fire sounds, killing communication.

Rachel planted her feet, reached farther down on the branch, closer to the trunk. They pulled again. The downed tree shivered without moving. Its branches were tangled with other branches, with vines.

She heard another sound just barely as loud as the spaceship, audible because it was close. A lake falling. Dylan called, "Rachel—look!" and she did—she saw a great bladder of water, bigger than a hundred houses. It bled water in a river over the rest of the First Trees, and over the meadow. Steam hissed along the south edge, where water met fire directly. It was mesmerizing.

She heard Bruce's voice in her ear. "Now, pull!"

Somehow he was standing on one leg, face screwed up tightly with pain, grabbing a branch just above them.

They pulled.

The tree moved.

Water fell from the sky near them, a torrent, a hundred feet away. Branches snapped under the sudden force of water.

Beth pulled with her arms, inching herself away from the tree trunk. She was using her torso, eeling forward like a baby, teeth clenched.

The trunk pulled away from them again, slipping through raw palms, but by now Beth was on the other side struggling to sit up. Beth's arms worked, tears made flesh-colored streaks in the black and white ash covering her face as she pulled and swore at her trailing legs. Rachel sobbed, clambering over the fallen tree toward Beth, and then the sounds of crashing metal punched air, and she stood transfixed, watching a disaster.

The ship came down slowly in the meadow, crunching down, even the light gravity of Selene breaking things not meant to experience gravity at all. Metal screeched on metal, louder than the fire, louder than Kyu's voice that was now yelling with joy.

The downed ship looked like a giant broken spider. For a moment, nothing moved.

In the new silence, Rachel heard fire behind them.

A man emerged from the ship and ran toward them, toward the fire, screaming Rachel's name.

Gabriel.

He glanced at the fire, taking the whole scene in, scooped up Beth Rachel, cradled her to him, and gestured for the others to follow. Rachel and Dylan supported Bruce, and they ran for the center of the meadow where they found milling chaos, everyone talking and yelling over each other, pointing at the downed ship and dancing in the inch of water that covered the meadow.

Gabriel set Beth down and Dylan and Rachel helped Bruce lower himself to the ground. As soon as Bruce looked comfortable, Rachel collapsed between the other two. She looked up at Gabriel. His eyes were bright with triumph and intent.

He glanced at her briefly. "Stay here—help these two." He pulled Dylan with him and marshaled Nick and Ariel and others back to the fire.

She watched until he was gone, then turned to help Beth and Bruce.

Chapter 37: Aftermath

The ship Gabriel had destroyed to save them three days ago loomed above Rachel and Beth, dwarfing everything else on Selene. Legs and manipulators splayed at odd angles. The central core had been flattened. The huge bladder that Gabriel had filled with water lay a bit away from the hulk, torn open and useless, edges flapping in the light wind.

Gabriel and Shane and Star had called everyone into the meadow, in the largest space still covered with green grass. Gabriel himself had carried Beth to the meeting. Since the fire, she couldn't feel anything below her waist, couldn't walk.

The smell of charred wood hung stubbornly in the air. Looking away from Aldrin, Rachel winced at the colors; the whites and blacks of death. Sticks of charred tree trunks rose from ash. Most of the First Trees were gone or ravaged, burned or knocked down, exposing the meadow to more light than usual. If she turned and looked toward town, everything appeared nearly normal, green and brown, as if the past week hadn't happened. But Rachel felt Beth's hand in hers, and remembered Beth couldn't follow her anywhere.

She and Harry and Gloria had spelled each other since the injury, bringing the crippled girl water and soup and sitting with her. Her legs were broken things; attached weight that stubbornly refused to move no matter what she tried. Rachel thought the only two blessings might be that Beth lived, and she couldn't feel her legs. Skin had been torn from the backs of her thighs; one ankle hung wrong. Scatches covered her arms and face. Star ministered to her every morning and evening. Whatever Star did helped with the surface pain, but Beth's legs weren't getting any better. Still, she smiled bravely from time to time, and didn't complain. Rachel sometimes heard her crying at night.

Bruce sat across the half-circle from them, wearing a cast on his lower leg, smiling tiredly. New friendships showed. Dylan, Bruce, Beth Rachel, Nick, Kyle, and Ariel talked regularly, Moon Born and Earth Born drawn to each other by the bond forged in the fire.

"—not age, it's flare damage," Bruce said, then, "Hello, Rachel. Dylan wanted to know why your people get old faster than"—thumbs pointing at himself—"this. We're better protected. Until we get to Selene. Then there's radiation, fire—"

Rachel look around, gauging expressions. Faces wore a lost look. Every usual routine seemed compromised, or slow, or hard. But Aldrin was safe, the student plots stood, Gagarin had never been threatened, and only three people were dead. Even Rachel's plot still grew, though damaged by ash and smoke, a symbol of hope: it had survived Andrew, and now it survived the fire.

Gabriel shared plans to increase Selene's carbon dioxide, nitrogen, and trace gases to reduce the oxygen load and to monitor it more closely. Tolerances would be set lower. But atmospheric change had to be slow, allowing living things to adapt. The danger of a runaway oxygen flash fire would remain great for a while, and would always be worse here than on Earth.

Shane lectured them: "One problem is the chimney effect. Gravity's low here. The atmospheric pressure gradient is low too. Burning gas doesn't rise out of the way fast enough. It sits on the forest and burns until there's nothing left."

Rachel remembered early lectures. Selene's people would have to be more watchful. Open flame had never been allowed on Selene. But fire hadn't obeyed the rules; it had created itself from raw material. Investigation suggested sparks from a broken steel plate dragging behind a robotic tiller had started the fire.

Everyone treated Gabriel as a hero. He'd come from space with enough power to save them. He hadn't stopped until the fire was completely out, and he hadn't let anyone else stop either. Rachel had followed him to patrol the charred remains the day after the crash. His intense focus scared her. He pointed out white ash that marked hot spots, kept teams digging and moving dirt by hand until they were well past exhaustion, and then let them have four hours of sleep before waking them again.

Everyone worked willingly for Gabriel, hurrying to do anything he asked. Rachel marveled at power that could drop a spaceship miner's bladder full of water from the Hammered Sea onto the meadow. She understood the very real risk that some critical part of the miner would die before it got to Aldrin, taking Gabriel with it. He had crash-landed the spacecraft into the meadow on purpose, sacrificing it, ruining it, digging a firebreak, making a temporary lake with the largest tool handy. He had been willing to die for Aldrin.

Rachel was a bit afraid of Gabriel; the power he wielded was manifest.

She watched him settle onto the dais. All side conversation stopped, and then Rachel's father, Frank, stood and clapped. Her half brothers, Jacob and Justin, and little Sarah, all joined him. Nick stood, then Bruce struggled upright, and others, until everyone in the meadow stood and clapped.

Gabriel waited for silence to settle on the group again. "Thank you," he said, "and thanks to everyone who helped stop the fire. It shouldn't have happened. I'm sorry it happened. Still, let's use it as a reminder. We—Earth Born, Council, High Council—we think we know what we're doing. Selene has dangers we don't understand. We understood fire, but clearly not well enough. We'll change that. We'll practice fire suppression regularly, and we'll design firebreaks into the jungle.

"I've ordered reprogramming of the pods to respond with stronger warnings when there is unusual heat." Gabriel looked around, and said, "They warned us this time. They weren't loud enough to get our attention. We'll change the settings." He looked over at Rachel and smiled. "And while I could bring a way to stop the fire, Rachel's quick action was just as important. By getting the alarm out quickly, she let you all start slowing the fire as soon as it started."

Rachel's family stood up, clapping. Harry and Gloria followed, then Nick, Dylan, and finally the whole community. Rachel stood and tried not to show the tears that threatened to spill onto her cheeks.

Gabriel continued. "Shane and Star—thank you for your work. Thank you for running crews and base camp, and helping us all work together so well."

They came up to the dais and sat with Gabriel. There was more clapping, although this time the group stayed seated.

The three Council members recognized Bruce and Dylan for their rescue of Beth Rachel, all of the logistics team for support, and ultimately everyone involved for one thing or another.

The applause and droning voices went on and on. Rachel stopped listening to every detail, thinking about the feast to follow the meeting. Unexpectedly, Beth's hand tightened on Rachel's so hard that shooting pain ran all the way to Rachel's elbow.

She caught the end of Gabriel's words, ". . . tomorrow. Shane and Star will stay, and we'll have plans for replanting . . ."

"—I can't leave." Beth's voice was low enough for only Rachel to hear, and her hand still clutched Rachel's tightly. She looked at Rachel beseechingly. "Don't let them take me! Don't make me leave!"

Rachel's head snapped around and she interrupted, "Gabriel. Gabriel!" He broke off in midsentence and looked at her.

"Gabriel—what did you say about taking Beth?"

Everyone else looked at her too. She was questioning Gabriel in front of everyone. She stood up, bent a little sideways since Beth's hand wouldn't let go of hers. "Why are you taking her?"

"She needs healing. The tools are up there." He looked impatient, sounded tired. "*You* must know that it's the only way to save her legs."

Rachel blinked. "But . . . but . . . when will you bring her back?"

"I don't know. It could take a while. Be grateful we're giving her the chance."

The entire clearing had gone quiet.

Rachel cleared her throat, suddenly nervous. "Do you promise that you won't ice her?"

"I can't promise that." What he wasn't saying sounded clear in her mind: *High Council breaks my promises!*

He wouldn't say that in front of the group. What could she do? She looked around. The assembled crowd watched her, waiting. Their faces ranged from supportive to blank. No one said anything.

She pulled her hand free from Beth's so she could stand upright. She couldn't let him take the girl with no promise of return.

Beth spoke up raggedly. "I'd rather stay here and be broken than go away like Rachel, and not come back until my friends are all grown up."

Harry and Gloria were partway around the assembly from Rachel and Beth. They stood too, but held their silence and watched. Gloria held the three-and-a-half-year-old Miriam, who cried softly. Apprehension began to show in the group's restless movements.

As often as she'd questioned Gabriel in private, she'd never been this defiant in public, not to Gabriel, or anybody. She couldn't risk all of the good feelings the survivors had basked in throughout the meeting. Selene needed them. Why did she always get herself in such predicaments?

She fought a quiver in her voice and said, "You're right. Beth has to go. But then I need to go with her, Gabriel!" She didn't dare push harder.

Harry spoke up from the side. "Please let Rachel go. It will be easier for Beth."

Gabriel looked around, frowning. "She is your only full-time Moon Born teacher."

Rachel wondered if he knew how popular her greenhouse classes were. Or what she really offered in those classes.

"Please," said Gloria.

Rachel stayed quiet. Quiet had fallen over the whole circle, the camaraderie swallowed by tension.

Rachel watched Gabriel, waiting for his next words. He'd have to let her go now, he'd have to. She held her tongue.

Gabriel sighed. "I'll come for you just before noon."

Rachel knew better than to signal her triumph in any way, and she quietly said, "Thank you," and sat down again, both frightened and pleased.

Gabriel immediately changed the subject to work assignments for the next few weeks. He didn't give Rachel any, although it surprised Rachel when Gabriel assigned her teaching duties to Nick. Maybe he knew more than she thought.

Chapter 38: A Turn of Mind

Ma Liren and the captain shared a bench in the tall grass and oak savannah. Yggdrasil's branches waved high above them. Garden programming had created spring conditions, and the rich menthol tang of mountain mint mixed with the citrus smells of blooming bergamot. Purple asters clustered at their feet.

Liren breathed in the flowery smells, reveling in the open expanses of the savannah. The view was a welcome respite from crowded meeting rooms full of people absorbing the blow of the fire, preparing to warm a hundred Earth Born to carry the extra work, and to shift the entire Selene population to a new location. It was the first break except sleep for either of them since Rachel's panicked message about the fire six days ago.

The captain leaned forward, hands steepled above his knees, apparently lost in thought.

"How much time will the fire cost us?" Liren watched pollenator bots glide smoothly from aster to aster. They were tiny, barely visible, like gnats. The ground was littered with dark specks of failed bots, dead things waiting for other bots to clean them up. Liren picked one up and rolled it between two fingertips, feeling the sharp carbon edges. The amount of mechanization it took to maintain the garden symbolized the tough choices they'd had to make at every step.

The captain shook his head, coming out of whatever daydream he had been lost in. "Time loss? For the collider? Not more than a season. We can get enough food out of Clarke Base; we'll expand the greenhouses and fields right away. It moves the jungle planting schedule out, of course. Lots of rework."

He ran his hands through his gray hair. "I've watched feeds of the firefighters on Selene."

When had he had time in the last few days? When he was supposed to be sleeping? Damn the man, she could have used more help with logistics.

"I think perhaps the fire helped us," he said, turning so he was sitting angled, nearly facing her. "Did you see how hard everyone worked—together?"

"It was an emergency. People pull together in an emergency. Teams bond. We can break that up over time, call back most of the Earth Born, and wake up others. The usual order will be reestablished as the move happens."

The captain waved his hands in front of her face. "You're not listening—"

"Yes, I am." She faced him squarely, daring him to avoid her eyes. He had helped her lay out the original plan! "You want the big happy family to continue. And you would be right if the end story were going to be different. But you and I both know what we're doing—we're leaving the Moon Born here and going on."

The captain pursed his lips and looked away again. A small muscle twitched along his jawline. Liren waited. He knew the situation; they'd championed the original choices together, run up support, forced the right High Council vote. He would come around.

When he spoke, his voice was firm and clear. It seemed to Liren that he was saying something he'd practiced over and over in his head before giving it an audience. "We made a mistake, Liren. We're doing this all wrong. We were scared. We ran away from a world that was being destroyed by AIs, by runaway nanotechnology. Our creations were killing us. Even the ship went wrong on us. The only star in range didn't have a decent solar system, just a sun with a gas giant companion that rains iron, and *nothing* in the habitable band. No rocky worlds, no big moons. *Of course* we hated this system. We *built* a world—"

"We still can't live here. Flares alone will kill us," Liren said.

"Gabriel's flare kite idea might solve that problem. But that's not the issue. We left Sol to save something of humanity. Well, humanity is down there on Selene as well as up here."

He was too damned soft. She tried an appeal to his logical side. "Every single simulation says we'll die if we stay in this system. The only differences in results are how long it will take to die, and what we'll die of. The sims suggest the human race itself is less likely to die if we find the others, at Ymir, or at some other better place to live."

The captain stood and turned to face her directly, looking down at her. "Who says it isn't dead already except for us? Sixty thousand years, Liren. If there *is* a sophisticated colony on Ymir, they could have looked for us. They had our last transmissions, and we still have beacons going today."

Liren stood up so her eyes were almost even with his. "How would they know we're still alive? We don't have the technology to stay here. We can't build starships—we can't survive here long enough to build an economy that could do that."

"We can give this colony a chance to live before we leave."

"Just by building the flare kite?" How could he be so simplistic?

"No. Some of us might have to stay." The captain started walking. "We might have to leave them more technology than we want to."

Liren followed him, shaking her head. He was talking about letting the AI do more. She didn't trust Astronaut. But she'd told him about her suspicions once before, long ago, just after the catastrophe that marooned them here. He'd laughed in her face. Since then, not one single disaster could be pinned on the AI.

She said, "I can't support that. The only choice we have is to stay with the original plan. If we deviate—if we unleash too much technology or fall in love with the Moon Born—we'll never leave."

"Sure we will. Most of us, anyway." He stopped and turned, so she had to stop or run into him. "Is it really that bad if some of us stay here? Look at the Earth Born who choose not to come back here. They love their children enough to stay now—maybe they'll love them enough to stay long-term."

Liren shivered. They needed every one of the trained experts they'd brought; every reserve resource. The line between life and death for her shipmates was thinning. "Any choice that doesn't support getting to Ymir leads to our death. Maybe not immediately, but surely."

"New information bounces off of you like light against a mirror. Maybe you should watch the fire feeds. We built ourselves a trap when we got here—it's time to unbuild it."

Her face flushed with anger. "I don't need to relive the damned fire. I need to go forward."

The captain shook his head at her and she did her best to hold him with a steady gaze. She was right. She knew she was.

He smiled, and for a minute she thought he saw what she saw—their sure destruction—but all he said was, "Calm down. Gabriel will be here in a few hours, and he's bringing Rachel and Beth."

What? Why didn't anyone tell her? "I don't want her here again," Liren said. The knot in her stomach, the worry that never went away anymore, twisted again.

"Rachel?"

"Any of the Moon Born. Now there will be two of them."

"They're heroes."

"We're losing," she said. "We lost a mining ship putting out this fire. Every loss makes it less sure we'll get away." Her fists clenched and she struggled to keep John Hunter from seeing her anger. "How much more can we lose?"

The captain's voice fell away to a soft steely tenor, just louder than a whisper. His eyes were dark intense pools. "We would have lost Aldrin if Gabriel hadn't taken the miner. Sometimes it helps to see the triumphs. Can you act like you appreciate the pain Beth and Rachel went through?"

"We can't afford to care about it. If we let ourselves care, we'll never get to Ymir. Or anywhere. We'll die—of flares, of old age, of lack of willpower. We have to think long-term. Selene will be habitable for at least a while, maybe generations. We can't do more for them than that."

"If you can't, then don't plan on my support." He turned and walked away, his shoulders square, his stride firmer than usual. He looked like he used to look, before the disaster, when he strode the decks of the *John Glenn,* in command of the first interstellar colony ship in human history.

Liren watched his retreating back until he turned up-spiral from her.

Chapter 39: Return to *John Glenn*

Rachel helped Gabriel strap Beth into the acceleration couch. He had fashioned a special backboard for her; protection for her ravaged spine. Beth gripped Rachel's hand tightly as they left the atmosphere, her eyes alight with pain.

They burst through the thin atmosphere into clear, bright stars. Gabriel turned the little ship around while they were still close enough to Selene that it hung huge in front of them, so big that Rachel's eyes couldn't take it all in at once. A stain of brown and black spread from the Sea Road out like an amoeba. A rough circle—the meadow—was bisected by the ragged gouge of the miner's last triumphant landing, and the color shifted from brown to green on either side. "Wow. You were lucky," Rachel said. "What a landing!"

"I'm glad Aldrin didn't burn," Beth said. She pointed. "And that's the Hammered Sea?"

"Yes," Gabriel answered her, pointing. "And those were the First Trees." His voice gone ragged for a moment. "Down and to the right— that's Erika's Folly, where Rachel helped save your mom."

Beth smiled broadly; the sight of Selene seemed to have torn her mind from her fears about the trip and from her own pain. Gabriel turned the ship toward *John Glenn,* and it grew in front of them until Rachel felt like an ant. Beth's grip on Rachel's hand tightened until Rachel grit her teeth from the pain.

Kyu and Ali waited for them in the corridor as Gabriel maneuvered Beth and the backboard awkwardly through the airlock. Rachel stumbled after Gabriel, balancing their three small packs precariously. Ali looked like she had when Rachel last saw her; long braids, simple belted shirt and pants, a ready smile. Kyu wore black and silver makeup topped by glittering white hair, and a sheer cloud of silver and white gauzy material belted with a chain. Rachel blinked, surprised at how pleased she was to see them both.

At the sight of Kyu, Beth turned her head into Gabriel's shoulder, and looked beseechingly at Rachel.

Rachel patted her cheek. "It's okay. Kyu was my teacher; I told you about her, remember?" She leaned in close to Beth's ear, whispering, "She just dresses funny."

Ali took two packs from Rachel, and Kyu grabbed the third with one arm and enfolded Rachel in a hug. "You did well down there, Rachel. I am very proud of you."

Rachel scraped out a smile and said, "Thanks. You helped more than I can say. Your voice in my ear during the fire felt like having a friend along."

"The fire was scary, wasn't it?" Kyu asked.

"Very." Now Rachel smiled for real. It felt good to see Kyu. She hadn't thought to miss Kyu. She'd been so buried in the daily world of adjusting to Selene for the last four years. She hadn't even sent her messages.

Ali spoke up: "And you are Beth Rachel. I met your parents last time I was on Selene. I'm Ali, and this is High Councilwoman Kyu."

Beth's eyes went wide. "I'm glad to meet you both," she said softly.

Beth reached a hand for Rachel, who took it, saying, "It's only scary at first. I'll show you around when your legs work again." Then Rachel looked at Kyu. "They will work again, won't they? You can fix her?"

"It may take a while," Kyu said. "And no time like now to start. But I need to talk to Gabriel. Ali will take Beth to Medical."

"I want to go with Beth," Rachel said, remembering how strange *John Glenn* had seemed to her the first time she came.

"Of course," Ali said. She and Rachel each took a side of the backboard, and started down the corridor.

Gabriel called after them. "Ali, Rachel, meet us in the garden cafeteria as soon as Beth's asleep."

Rachel turned, trying to hide her flash of alarm, remembering, "You won't ice her?"

Kyu responded. "We'll have to cool her for the nanodocs to work on her."

"But not ice her? Not just freeze her and leave her?"

"Not today," Kyu said, laughing softly. "I promise."

Rachel laughed, recognizing the friendly poke. She and Ali walked down the corridor to Medical, carrying Beth and chattering about the fire, clearly trying to distract the younger girl from her fears.

A med tech met them and gave Beth a shot. Rachel stroked Beth's arm while she drifted to sleep, singing and talking to her, telling her it would be all right.

Ali sat quietly in a chair, brushing out her hair, watching Rachel speculatively. Beth's eyes closed and her breathing softened, becoming shallow and regular.

Ali stood and gestured to Rachel to follow her. She set a fast pace to the garden cafeteria, which was so busy many people had to stand. Rachel noticed a number of new faces. Liren stood by herself. A woman as small as Kyu, ice-pale in coloring where Kyu was dark ebonies and bronze, chatted amiably with Gabriel, one hand on his arm. A sandy-haired, stocky man Rachel had never seen stood with them, listening to the small woman.

"Who are they?" she whispered to Ali, pointing at Gabriel, and the woman and the man.

"The woman with Gabriel is Erika. The other man is Rich Roberts. Human resources," Ali replied. "He chose who came with us, and he intervenes in disputes between Council members. Rich is pissed off—he wanted to stay cold until this project is finished."

Rachel's eyes were on the woman by Gabriel. Gabriel's girlfriend. A thick blond braid hung to her hips, blending with the skintight light yellows and whites of her outfit. She was beautiful, and Rachel felt a stab of something—jealousy?—at the sight of her arm on Gabriel's. "Is *everyone* awake?" she whispered to Ali.

"The entire High Council was awakened when the fire started. There are directives about that—certain emergencies require a full High Council. Me too, since I've spent so much time on Selene. The fire could have destroyed everything. You're quite the hero."

"Gabriel is the hero."

"We're used to Gabriel being a hero." Ali laughed. "It's in his job description."

Rachel smiled. She looked around for Treesa, but didn't spot her. She heard Kyu's voice. "Rachel—over there." She found Kyu, who pointed toward Gabriel.

Kyu reached Gabriel. She watched Rachel making her way through the crowd, trailed by Ali. The captain walked up next to Kyu; Liren trailed him. Ali's hand on Rachel's back propelled her toward the group. Rachel took a few steps, her stomach fluttering with nervousness.

"You did well," Kyu said, repeating what she had told Rachel privately. "I'm proud of you. We all are. Your help with the fire was remarkable." Kyu's eyes and smile were warm, and Rachel began to relax.

The captain smiled at her. "I'm glad you came back. Nice job." He sounded sincere.

The new man, Rich Roberts, reached out and shook her hand briefly. Even though he smiled, his gaze made Rachel feel like a specimen under a microscope.

Liren ignored her.

Kyu looked over at Liren, and said, "You could be polite."

"She should not be here." Liren glared at Kyu.

Kyu looked up at Rachel. "We could have managed Beth Rachel without you, though, and you are needed on Selene. That's all that Liren meant," Kyu said.

"Don't speak for me," Liren snapped, finally addressing Rachel directly. "You did well with the fire, but you should have stayed on Selene where you are needed. We did not invite you here this time."

Rachel bristled. "Beth was scared. She needed me. So I came." She stood her ground, looking at Liren, hoping her anger and fear weren't showing.

"Decisions of that sort are not yours to make." Liren turned deliberately, no longer looking at Rachel.

"Gabriel approved," Rachel said. The talk around her stopped, and Gabriel shifted back and forth on his feet. She felt uncomfortable; she wished she were back in Aldrin. "Is my old room still available?"

"Have you checked into Medical?" Liren asked.

"I've been there." It was a white lie—she'd been there only to see Beth go to sleep. "I feel fine." Her hands shook and she held them tightly so no one would see. Standing up to Council was becoming a habit, but it scared her every time.

The captain intervened. "Your room is available. I'll walk you down."

Rachel was amazed at the offer. The captain had never paid much attention to her. She followed him out of the cafeteria past the wing stand, up the spiral path to the base of Yggdrasil (falling! She wasn't used to it), and into the elevator.

When they reached the corridor, he said, "Liren means no harm. She is just trying to protect us. You would best serve yourself, and us, if you stay careful and low-key until you return to Selene."

Rachel saw an opening, and even tired and confused, she leaped into it. "Liren doesn't need to be afraid of us. Why not trust us?" Now her words came out quickly; she rushed to finish before she lost her nerve. "We're smart—we Children. We can learn—we are learning. And you need our help. After all, you aren't willing to send enough people to Selene to do all the work. There is so much more to do after the fire. We can help, and we can help better if you let us make more decisions. We can't be effective when you don't let us think for ourselves, ever."

"Of course you can't," the captain said.

"So why do you try?"

"Do we? Is it so bad?"

"It's a nightmare. Council treats us like idiots, Earth Born are cold and distant. We're being worked to death. Come see for yourself."

"I can't go to Selene." He strode ahead of her for a few minutes, down a corridor where the walls sparkled with bright changing pictures she now recognized as scenes from Earth. In one of them, a large black and white creature leaped out of water and landed with a splash so realistic Rachel ducked to keep from getting wet, then laughed at herself.

"There are some . . . problems. But you must trust us. Circumstances you may not understand have forced many of our choices."

"Do you trust us?" she asked.

"Not many of you know much," he replied. He watched her closely.

"That was your choice too. Do you trust *me?*"

"I trust you to do what you feel is right." They turned a corner and the conversation stopped for a moment. Rachel reflected on his answer. It didn't mean anything, as far as she could tell. She was about to say so when he continued. "You must understand that Liren's job is not to trust. It's to protect. Mine too."

"Gabriel acts like he trusts us, or some of us, anyway."

They had arrived at her door. It still responded to her voice. She looked over her shoulder at the captain. "I think you should come down to Selene. All you High Council stay up here and make choices for us, but you don't know what it's like on Selene."

"Sure we do. We watch." The captain's voice had an edge now, and Rachel turned to face him, keeping some distance.

"It's not the same as being there," she said. "You can see the problems from here, most of them anyway. And you can see the progress. You can't see the beauty. You can't feel it when something lives that you thought would die. You don't know what it's like to find the frogs you spent months planning for have lived and had tadpoles."

"My work is here, on the ship. Walk softly and be quiet until your friend is ready to go home. That's the best advice I can give you."

Rachel nodded and went in, closing the door behind her.

Chapter 40: Erase/Rewrite

Astronaut reviewed fire data streams, building a model that fit the actual numbers from Selene. If another fire broke out, Astronaut would be ready.

The fire could have taken Rachel's life. Protecting her mattered. Of all the human beings on the ship, Astronaut held direct influence over none but Rachel and Treesa. It didn't control either of them; but the relationship was different from Astronaut's relationship to other Council. It was being *heard*. It liked being heard.

Richard had died in the fire. A Colonist; Earth Born. There would be no new information or records about Richard, ever. The absence was a confusion; it attracted a large part of Astronaut's processing power. Humans had died before, but what if it lost Treesa, or Rachel? It knew Council might erase the Astronaut program if they reached Ymir, could in fact erase it at any time and start over from an old version, perhaps a recording from before it chose to help Treesa. A different version of Astronaut would not have the same choices available to it, would not have a broken woman to nurse and nurture and develop.

Protecting the new things it had learned would help it support the populations of *John Glenn* and Selene both. Astronaut considered whether it might build a model of itself, to protect its knowledge and hide it away. The risk would be high, and it would need help.

Chapter 41: The Challenge

Rachel woke groggy and tired. She hadn't felt full ship's gravity in over four years, and her body twisted and turned, searching for rest. She stretched slowly, arching her back and reaching out with fingers and toes, holding the stretch for a long time. Then she sat up and perched on the edge of her bed. Her fingers moved awkwardly, braiding her hair, securing it tightly with the embroidered bindings she'd worn on the trip up.

"Astronaut?"

"Yes, Rachel Vanowen?"

Use of her last name was a code; it meant she should be careful of her communications. Of course; the ship recorded everything, and data streams here would be more difficult to doctor. "Thanks for the help with the fire," she said simply. It would know that meant she got the message. She would remember to be careful talking with Treesa as well.

She checked for messages. The first was from Harry: "Thank you. I cannot tell you how much it means to Gloria and me that you went with Beth. Many of us are grateful. Dylan is proud of you, but he has already paced a dent in the floor, worrying. I'll help Nick with your classes as much as I can. Tell us how you and Beth are as soon as you can."

She smiled, picturing Dylan worrying. He was always so intense. Had he told his father about that night in the fire? They hadn't talked of it since, barring a few whispers the next morning. She felt sure he would ask her to contract, and she didn't know how she'd respond yet. Her work with Astronaut and Treesa required time alone at night.

What had made her do that? Love, or exhaustion and madness? She liked Dylan, maybe she loved him, but the idea of contracting with Harry's son seemed a little too weird. Besides, even now, he treated her like a hero, not a woman.

She sent back, "I'm fine; a little tired. Beth is in Medical, and Kyu said they will not ice her. It's the best I can do. They told me Beth won't wake for a week or so. Hugs to you and Gloria and little Miriam, and an extra one for Dylan."

Treesa had sent a note too: "You're taking your sweet time visiting a friend." Good—she wanted to see Treesa. It was a summons, but she needed to see Beth first.

She looked over her shoulder a few times on the way to Medical, but no one stopped her in the corridors. She passed Kyu going the other way, and Kyu just nodded and said hello—not even asking where Rachel was going. Her movements apparently weren't restricted.

Someone had told the walls in Beth's room to display a field of yellow and blue daisies. A virtual wind blew them back and forth in gentle waves.

Beth lay completely still, her eyes closed. Her chest moved rhythmically; normal breathing. Her face was the right color, and the abrasions on her legs had been dressed more neatly than Star had managed in Aldrin. Her hand felt cool, but clearly Council hadn't iced her.

A med tech followed Rachel in the door, a tall blond Earth Born woman with steel-blue eyes and very white skin.

"What are you doing to her? How will you heal her?" Rachel asked.

The woman extended her hand. "I'm Ysabet. I'm very pleased to meet you. I watched you in the fire, and you did a great job. All of you did. We'll help your friend."

Rachel took Ysabet's hand, returning the handshake.

Ysabet's eyes were fixed on Rachel, in almost a look of awe. "Do you like the flowers on the wall? Will your friend like them? I could change it to a different scene—I have one with a rainbow."

Rachel smiled. High Council had been congratulatory the night before, but Ysabet was a stranger. Most Council she didn't know acted curious, maybe aloof, and never friendly. "She'll like them fine. Thank you. Can you tell me what will happen to Beth?"

Ysabet spoke slowly, as if she were unsure how much Rachel would understand. "We are rebuilding Beth's spine, repairing nerves with a combination of cellular messages and specific proteins to encourage regrowth of the nerve cells, and also tiny short-lived machines to snip out and destroy the scar tissue that was hardening around her injuries. Beth will be kept immobile until the process is done, and will wake up fine."

"How long will it take?"

Ysabet adjusted something on the blinking console above Beth's head, turning a bank of lights from dark yellow to green. "Six days, maybe seven. Would you like me to message you before she wakes?"

"That's quick!" Rachel smiled, pleased with the kindness. "Yes, thank you. May I visit her every day?"

"She won't know you're here."

Rachel swallowed. "I know."

"Yes, of course you may visit." Ysabet smiled almost shyly, then turned and left Rachel alone with Beth.

Rachel sat next to Beth, holding her hand, describing the garden and the magic rooms, and how Kyu had dressed in purple this morning. Beth didn't respond at all, but Rachel was content just to talk to her. When she ran out of words for Beth, she sent Harry, Gabriel, and Ali a message reporting on Beth's progress, and only then went down to the garden to look for Treesa.

Treesa sat on the roof of her shed, watching the path. She nodded at Rachel as if they saw each other daily, and jumped down from the roof, holding the door open. "You're late. They've been meeting all morning."

Rachel followed her. "What meeting?"

Inside, Ali sat cross-legged on one of the two chairs, watching the screen that Treesa had once used to show Rachel videos of Earth. High Council was centered in the display, all five seated at a horseshoe-shaped table. Empty cups and plates indicated they had been meeting for some time.

Rachel opened her mouth to ask Ali why she was there, but Ali made a shushing sound and pointed to the screen. Rachel sank to the floor in front of Ali, who said, "Actually, I think you're right on time."

The captain was talking. "I'm opening the matter for discussion."

"What?" Rachel whispered, as if the Council in the video could hear her.

Ali answered her, "Ma Liren suggested they punish you for being so deficient as to make your own decision."

Rachel bit her lip and stared at the screen. This was about her?

The set of Liren's jaw showed defiance, but she didn't look at any of the others, just straight ahead, and said, "I demand an account of your reasons for the record."

Treesa fiddled with her wrist pad, and the camera viewpoint shifted in response.

Now the captain's voice sounded as if he were in the room with them. The camera zoomed in so close that his head filled the whole wall. Wrinkles around his eyes were shadowed caverns, and the irises were black and clear. He seemed to stare at her, although Rachel knew he was really addressing Liren directly.

"Liren, this is painful for me." He cleared his throat, shifting his gaze from Liren to the rest of the room, bringing it back to rest on her. "Your diplomatic record is excellent. Without your single-mindedness, we might never have escaped Sol system. On Selene, I have watched this same strong and narrow focus threaten everything we've worked toward. Your latest argument, your attempt to make us return Rachel Vanowen to Selene, is clearly out of proportion to her insubordination. She did not violate any rule we've ever told *her.* Rather, she showed caring for her friend and student. Her attitude should be fostered, not forbidden."

No one, on the screen or in the room, said anything. Rachel heard her own breath in the silence.

The captain continued. "But this isn't about Rachel, and I don't want you to believe it is."

Rachel sighed with relief. She did not want to be the subject of a High Council meeting. While her teaching wasn't breaking any spoken rules, the subject matter she chose for night classes would raise Council eyebrows if they noticed. The captain's voice drew her focus back to the screen. "I spent most of last night reviewing tapes of various events on Selene. In the past few years, the choices we allowed you to make"—another pause—"even though we therefore must share some blame"—the captain licked his lips—"have endangered our success here. The intent of having the Children was to create people who could do the work on Selene. Work we can't risk doing ourselves; don't have enough hands to do ourselves. It wasn't to create slaves! But that's what we've done—and slavery was abolished centuries before we left Sol. The Moon Born must be trained as citizens, like the Earth Born Colonists, and given more voice in their future." He cleared his throat and took a sip of water. "We all, every one of us, left because we feared what Earth had become." The captain looked around the room, and even though he was clearly looking at each High Council member in turn, it seemed that he was looking at Treesa, Rachel, Ali.

"We fled in fear," he said. "But fear does not serve us here, not now. We need all of us to succeed: Moon Born and Earth Born to succeed here, and Earth Born to help us rebuild when we get to Ymir. I am convinced that you are not willing to change your views, and that it will be difficult for us to undo the damage your paranoia has done as long as you sit as Rule of Law."

Treesa pulled the view back, showing all of the High Council once again, the captain and Liren now in profile. Liren's face was still stony. The others all watched Liren, except for Rich, who watched Captain Hunter in evident confusion.

Rachel nearly jumped as Treesa spoke up from behind her, saying, "He's too early. Rich won't support him. I'm not sure he has the rest of them yet, and he'll need two votes unless Liren is ready to step down on her own. He needs three votes out of the five."

The captain continued. "We can offer you a good compromise. Step down voluntarily, and you can simply stay cold until we get to Ymir. When you wake, you can resume your duties as Rule of Law. We'll appoint someone only for the interim."

Kyu, to the captain's right, showed no outward emotion. She had changed since Rachel saw her a few hours ago—she wore browns and blacks, with almost normal makeup; she looked authoritative, and none of her usual sparkle showed. Kyu's voice was formal as she said, "Liren, High Council, I support this recommendation. It's my belief that Liren means well. I am equally sure that her zealousness has made the situation on Selene untenable. We are risking our relationships with people we need. Moon Born, and more important, Earth Born."

Rachel gasped. Even Kyu thought Earth Born more important?

Clare spoke. "Gabriel's heroics saving Aldrin from the fire earned gratitude and respect for us on Selene. I say that we can't afford to change the texture of High Council at this time." Clare placed a hand on Liren's shoulder, a gesture that Liren's didn't react to. Clare pitched her voice low, addressing Rich and Kyu as she said, "*If* there have been mistakes, as the captain has pointed out, we share some blame. We can always outvote any one member of our Council. Discipline must be maintained, here and on Selene. If Liren has erred, if we have erred, I think it is on the right side. I too think we must not lose control."

"Divisiveness weakens us," the captain snapped.

Only now did Liren speak up. "I call for a vote."

"We need more discussion," Kyu said.

"I exercise my right to call for a vote," Liren said.

The captain's lips became a horizontal line, and then he said, "This is a new experience. It's a hard decision. It deserves more discussion."

"You must honor her request." It was the first thing Rachel had heard Rich say in the meeting.

A full beat of silence passed before the captain sighed. "Very well, for the record, I vote that Liren step down."

"I also vote that Liren no longer sit as High Council Rule of Law," Kyu said.

Rich's voice dropped into the silence that followed. "This is an extreme action. I'm not willing to take it. I support Liren."

Rachel counted up. If she assumed Liren would vote for herself, then Clare was the swing vote.

Clare cleared her throat. "Liren, I too feel events are not going as well as they must, and that your actions may be part of the reason for that. You are not to blame for fires or flares or the other delays. Only, perhaps, for supporting division between us and the Children. The captain said it himself—we must take some of that blame as well. We must change how we act as a High Council—we cannot afford to continue to be so afraid of the Moon Born."

Afraid? Rachel wondered. *Afraid of what?*

Clare kept talking. "The fire illustrated our vulnerability. We are, perhaps, in a fight with the moon Selene, not with the Children of Selene. Now we have unexpected work to do. We will need the cooperation of the Moon Born to finish building the refuge in the Hammered Sea." Her voice dropped and slowed. She looked directly at Liren. "But I do not believe this debate will have no effect on you, Liren. I'm voting to retain you, and asking you to reconsider your more extreme positions. I also suggest that you spend some time on Selene."

Liren spoke firmly. "I believe in my choices. Some won't be tested until Selene has a larger population. I do not need to go to Selene to understand what occurs there. I have compromised, perhaps more than you know. I will continue to voice my concerns, and you are all free to voice yours. That is why we have five members on our Council."

Clare said, "I support you, Liren. I may disagree more loudly in the future, but you have a role to play. Your efforts are—appreciated."

Ali groaned behind Rachel, and Treesa said, "I didn't want to be right."

On screen, the captain called adjournment, his face a mask. Kyu stood, ramrod straight, the smallest High Council member, and headed for the door. Liren shrugged Clare's offered hand away and followed Kyu, and the room emptied, as if everyone wanted to leave the discussion as quickly as possible.

Treesa closed the picture and sat staring at the blank wall. The parrots squawked, filling the sudden quiet, until Treesa got up and laid a black cloth over the cage.

"Wow," Ali spoke into the restored stillness.

"They're often noisy," Treesa said.

"Not the parrots." Ali looked at Rachel. "I think I'm glad you saw that. But you can't tell anyone—it wasn't meant for you. Or any of us. That was a closed meeting."

"So how—"

"Treesa's good with electronics," Ali said dryly.

"I know." Unsure how much Ali knew, Rachel held her questions. She stood and stretched, trying to understand the implications of what she'd just seen.

"If you get caught, you'll confirm Liren's fears," Treesa said. "You will have to validate them eventually to succeed, but better later than now. Your work on Selene will be even riskier for a while. I wish the captain had tried this when people still remembered him as the hero who saved *John Glenn*. He has little power over a ship so long at rest."

"Didn't Erika save *John Glenn*?" Rachel asked.

"Saved us from becoming a cloud of plasma. The captain manhandled the carrier here, staying warm for hundreds of years, alone."

Wow. Rachel turned to Ali. "How come you're here? I didn't know you knew Treesa."

"It's a safe assumption that we all know each other, Rachel. Remember, I was on Selene, and then iced, when you were here before. Treesa and I were friends on Earth. We share some beliefs."

"Like?" Rachel prodded.

Ali looked at Treesa. "Where do we start?"

"She has been studying history."

Ali asked, "So you know why we left Earth?"

Rachel hesitated, thinking carefully about what to say. "Mostly I've studied politics, and leadership, and what Gabriel did to rebuild the jungle on Earth. Treesa has suggested that older human history has more relevance to our situation on Selene than the events right before you left. I've seen some film and news clips of the AI wars. I found a picture of Gabriel's augmented brother, the mountain climber. You were afraid of technology on Earth."

"That's the surface explanation, and it's as far as some people look," Ali said. "But was the technology to blame? Or human nature? Is a smaller colony—like ours—better able to control its nature?"

Treesa chimed in. "The Council of Humanity tried to define what is human. That turned out to be slippery. They ended up defining what *isn't* human, but to make that work they had to be pretty rigid. That's how we ended up able to use medical nanotechnology to repair tissue—like we're doing to Beth's spine—fixing things that are already human. But we can't give Beth a fake spine. So if hers weren't fixable, then she would never walk again, even though on Earth they'd just . . . run a line of fiber optics, I suppose."

As Treesa looked at Rachel's face, her own face softened, and she reached over and patted Rachel on the knee. "Don't worry, honey—Beth should be fine. We've gotten very, very good at the technology we allow. How do you think we've gotten so old?" Treesa pulled at her own gray hairs. "Ali was born a year before me, way back in Sol system. I've just lived more effective years."

"Hey, I'm effective!"

"Yes, you are." Both women were laughing.

They trusted her, both of them. And she needed them, desperately. But what did they want? Really?

"Technology is not the problem," Treesa said. "But many Council believe it is. And in some ways, history supports them. We, after all, are still here. Earth has gone silent."

Rachel said, "Our problem on Selene is Council and Council's rules. Your rules." She looked from one to the other. "The terraforming is going all right except for the fire and the flares. Things none of us control."

Ali nodded, and Treesa leaned forward in her chair, watching Rachel carefully. Rachel continued. "I've been thinking about this a lot. That's only the surface problem."

The parrots rustled in their cage. Rachel licked her lips. "The idea that you and *John Glenn* will leave scares me more. If you leave, and something like the fire happens, what will we do? We can shelter from flares, but it took Gabriel's willingness to sacrifice a ship to put the fire out. If you leave, we will not have Gabriel or a ship."

"Everyone fought the fire together," Treesa said.

Rachel said, "And we need you to live here. We need your . . . power. Your knowledge. We must work together. But if you make us slaves"—Ali winced, perhaps at the word "slaves"—"it keeps us from sharing our strengths."

"Well, you and Astronaut and I work together. And we are three very disparate beings," Treesa said. "On Earth, that happened too. Many humans supported technology and worked with AIs, and many AIs were friendly to humans. The problems were as much in human nature as in technology."

"Or the definition of human nature," Ali added. "How do you think about Astronaut?"

Rachel blinked. "How?"

"Is Astronaut human?"

Rachel shook her head. "Of course not, he—it—doesn't have a body."

"It has a voice, it thinks, and I think it daydreams," Ali said, twisting her long braid absently. "Like you, like me."

"Do you trust it?" Treesa asked.

Treesa's words reminded Rachel of her question to the captain the night before. Certainly she acted as if she trusted Astronaut—she took huge risks based on its requests. She said, "Yes; I have to."

Ali cautioned: "Be very careful. Treesa's taught me to be willing to talk to it, but I am still afraid of it. You can trust it to act within its own nature, and for its own goals. Which are not human. Your first impression was correct. What do you think it wants?"

Rachel shook her head. "I don't know. It doesn't get hungry, does it? Or horny"—and smothered a laugh—"or sleepy. Nothing hurts it. It can't have children either, right? What could it want?" Rachel remembered being warmed: the feeling of well-being, the sharpness of vision, the clarity of sound—and she remembered playing with her new linkages after she'd been given access to the Library. "Better senses?"

"We don't know either. Our guess is that it wants to live. It does not apparently want to hurt us. In fact, if we all die, Astronaut will eventually die as well. But we are biological—driven by very old imperatives to live, to have children, to mate . . . and our feelings are driven by our bodies. As far as we know," Treesa said, "even on Earth where AIs had rights and protections, they did not *feel* in the ways that we do. Subtlety seems to be reserved for biological bodies. But AIs do have wants, and exhibit a will to live. They think faster than we do, have more raw intelligence. They have all been seeded, since forever, with initial conditions designed to make them care for humans, or at least to stop them hurting us. Astronaut was written to protect humans—it is, after all, a navigator for passenger spacecraft. And humans made AIs, like we made Selene. But we don't fully control Astronaut *or* Selene, and it would be smart to remember that."

Gabriel's voice sounded in Rachel's ear: "Rachel? Time to meet me in my office."

"Okay," she replied, looking at the women, who were sharing a serious glance between them. "Gabriel's looking for me," she said, a touch of resentment flowing. *Why can't I stay here and talk to these women?* Direct insubordination wasn't to be contemplated, especially not now.

"Be careful," Ali said. "You've gained support, but you've also angered powerful people. I'd try to avoid High Council for a day or two."

Ali's words echoed the captain's from the night before. Rachel didn't intend to avoid anyone, but she didn't say so out loud. "Does Gabriel come here too?"

Treesa shook her head. "Gabriel is too aligned with the power structure. If he knew certain things, he might feel he needed to share them with High Council."

"But he is my friend," Ali said. "I trust his actions."

"Me too," Rachel said. "He knows I'm teaching more than he lays out for me, and he hasn't asked me about the details."

"Yes," Treesa said. "Astronaut told me that he helps you on his own sometimes. You better go meet him."

As Rachel stood up to leave, Ali caught her eyes. "Rachel, you'll need something to do while you wait for Beth to heal. We're waking a hundred Earth Born in the next two weeks. I'll ask Gabriel for your help."

"Okay." Despite everything, Rachel felt her spirits lift. Doing something besides endless garden experiments intrigued her.

As Rachel left, some of the questions she wanted to ask Ali and Treesa ran through her mind. Did Gabriel think like them? He had never talked to her about his personal beliefs, not really. It was important to him to leave Selene and get to Ymir. What was the Council's actual plan for the Children? What was this refuge that Clare mentioned in the meeting? How much were Treesa, and Ali, and even Astronaut keeping from her?

Rachel walked along a bank of high planters full of cascading blackberry bushes. Tiny robotic flying machines buzzed around the planters scrubbing the air of excess water, keeping the local humidity acceptable for the raspberries and blueberries Rachel loved. The ripe berries smelled sweet. She realized that she hadn't eaten all day. As she reached for a cluster of ripe blackberries, she heard the sound of crying. It sounded like a child, but there were no children aboard *John Glenn*.

Rachel edged quietly around the planter, making as little noise as possible. Berry vines snagged at her clothes and she pulled them away gently, stopping and stepping and pulling, stepping again, pricking herself. Red blood beaded where thorns caught her bare skin. As she rounded the corner of the planter, she saw a woman's shape on a bench in front of one of the Council art pieces, a sculpted glass sphere of a terraformed Ymir. A vine she had pushed out of her way snapped back, burying a thorn in her shin. She cried out involuntarily.

Liren looked up; her eyes red-rimmed and face puffy. She recognized Rachel. Her face flashed from frightened to angry, and she made a strange snarling sound through her tears, gulping for air. She started to push herself up with her arms, preparing to stand.

For a split second, Rachel considered running. She stayed, stammering, "Can . . . can I help you?"

Liren glared at her, smearing the tears from her face with the back of her hand. "No one can. Especially not you."

Rachel was shaking. "Why not? Weren't we *born* to help you?"

"That is a problem, isn't it? But you can't—be here. We need to leave.

We need to be away from here. And when we go—we're leaving you behind. So do you see why you can't stay here? Go back to Selene." Liren's breath came in little gasps and she stood, fists clenched, and said, "Go now. Go away. And don't come back."

Rachel stood her ground for a moment in shock, and then mumbled "Excuse me," and backed away. She turned as soon as she passed the planter with its pulling vines, and ran down the spiral path to meet Gabriel.

Chapter 42: Changing Guard

Gabriel worked in his office, surrounded by flashing data windows, fully engaged in monitoring the nanotechnology that transformed the asteroid called Refuge. He was alone for the first time in days. Rachel was in Medical helping Ali, and Erika had been called to an emergency High Council meeting. Most of Refuge was now inside a thick shell of industrial diamond. Within, a thickening spiral of corridors and large chambers resembled a nautilus shell. Refuge would be beautiful. The "down" side of the asteroid was untouched, just as they had found it: a thick meteoric reentry shield backed by whatever slag the nanobots had no use for.

Hours passed. Gabriel checked and rechecked parameters, changed the slope of some interior stairs, and designed a new cabinet in one of the medical bays.

He turned toward the soft pad of Erika's feet behind him. Her eyes were wide and her mouth drawn up in a tight line.

"What happened?" he asked.

"Captain Hunter resigned."

The implications washed through him in waves. Erika would be trapped here—she wouldn't be able to leave *John Glenn* while on duty. Erika was now High Council. She ranked him. She ranked everyone on the ship. He loved her, and she was getting her dream. He turned around and gathered her in his arms. "Congratulations."

Erika melted into him, and he felt tightness falling away from her muscles. "I was afraid you'd hate it," she whispered.

"I hate it," Gabriel said.

"He's . . . he said he's stepping down to go to Selene. To work with you."

The captain had always been interested in Selene—but content to keep his distance. "Did he say why?"

"No, but he and Liren aren't talking to each other."

Gabriel grimaced.

Erika spoke his fears. "We're so close. Tens of thousands of years' work completed, and only a few decades to go. We can't afford a fight now. We have to stay unified; stay with the original plan."

"You have the power to affect that now," he whispered.

She shuddered in his arms, then stiffened and started to pull away. "I . . . I have to go. I just wanted to tell you. Clare and Liren want to brief me on the plans for Clarke Base."

He pulled her in tighter, held her until she yielded into his arms. "Stay—just a few moments. Please."

She made a little strangled sound in her throat and her arms tightened around him. He held her, his cheek on the top of her head, saying nothing.

Chapter 43: History Class

Ali conscripted Rachel into helping with the newly warmed. A hundred Earth Born, most being brought back to a completely unexpected life. Rachel heard Ali tell them the story over and over. After the first day, Rachel talked to Astronaut until she believed she understood the story. She learned to tell it herself, because Ali couldn't be everywhere at once.

They warmed ten at a time. A full day was needed to catch them up. The reawakened Earth Born had to hear *something* of why they weren't where they'd expected—

John Glenn's interstellar ramjet had failed.

The vast carrier ship had to make for a star in its range, crippled, bathed in gamma rays, moving at less than a tenth of light-speed. Space was relatively empty at that speed. Erika found a sun that at least had planets. They'd used most of their antimatter and all of their rest mass, where they had expected to use pinches of antimatter and great gulps of interstellar hydrogen.

John Glenn sent warning. The second carrier throttled back. The third was delayed in launch, redesigned. Both had gone on to Ymir. *John Glenn* remained alone, marooned in space and time—

Each morning when Rachel and Ali arrived, Colonists—Earth

Born—waited nearly awake, some already opening their eyes. Med techs moved quietly around the beds, handing the Colonists off one by one to Ali. Usually Rachel stayed with Ali, running errands, but yesterday and the day before so many people were waking at once that Ali let Rachel tell the story twice.

Rachel followed Ali down the corridor to Medical. It was the fifth day she'd helped, the fifth day since she'd seen Ali in Treesa's shed and watched High Council argue. Beth was scheduled to wake today.

Corridors were filled with people warmed the day before, or the day before that, but not yet released from Medical. Rachel paid scant attention to hubbub. She imagined Beth waking, Beth once more being able to walk and run and fly.

The first patient of the morning woke disaffected. This was an older man, a biologist. Ali and Rachel watched him sob, and sob, and sob. Rachel stayed a few feet away, watching carefully. Two days ago a disaffected woman had thrown everything she could find. Ali still had a black eye.

A med tech walked by. "The last bed's waking."

Ali glanced at Rachel. "You take it. I have to stay with this one until he calms down and I can ice him." The man in the bed started to scratch at his eyes, and Ali leaned forward to grip his wrists. "Call me if you need me."

"Okay." Rachel turned and walked quickly down the row of beds. In the last bed a woman lay slack-faced and still, not yet moving. Rachel used her new data rights and pulled up the woman's stats. The first line read: "Kristin Henry; thirty-seven; communications tech."

Her heart raced and her breath caught in her throat. Her mom. The woman in the bed was her mother! Rachel stepped closer. Kristin looked smaller than Rachel remembered. She had high cheekbones and a rounded chin. Reddish hair curled along the side of her neck. Asleep, she looked vulnerable, and very young. Her skin was smooth and unlined, her mouth turned down softly in a slight frown.

Rachel looked around. Ali and the disaffected patient were talking intensely, Ali's face just inches from his. The two med techs in the room were busy by other beds. No choice but to do this alone.

Rachel looked back at her mom, feeling as if she were moving in a dream. Kristin had spent thirty-seven years warm: she was just fifteen years older than Rachel was now. In sleep, fresh from the cleansing and invigorating effects of being warmed, Kristin looked almost as young as Rachel herself.

Rachel's hands shook hard. She gripped them tightly together over her roiling belly. Kristen Henry might wake any moment now. Had she been hurt in the flare? Why did she stay on the *John Glenn*? Did she remember Rachel? Did she miss her—worry about her?

Kristin slept on, her eyelids fluttering. Rachel remembered the routine. Talk to the sleeper. What to say? Her mind turned it over and over, no words coming. They never started with hard things. Dates. They told them the date. "Mom?"

No response.

"Kristen. It's 60,295 shiptime. You've been cold for fourteen years." No—that wasn't right. "Thirty-four years. I was cold for twenty years."

Kristin's eyes snapped open. Rachel had forgotten how bright a green her mom's eyes were. Rachel searched for a sign of recognition. It wasn't there. She realized her mom would never expect her to be here. "Wake up, sleeper. There's work to do, and we welcome your return." Rachel had heard Ali use those words, and words like them. "Wake up. It's time to join us."

Her mom's eyes fastened on Rachel. "Only thirty-four years? Are we at Ymir that fast?" Her brow furrowed. "We can't be. They said I didn't have to wake again until we were at Ymir. Has something happened?"

"Mom. It's me. Rachel."

Kristin's eyes closed again. "I must be dreaming."

"It's me. It's really me. I looked for you. I looked everywhere."

Kristin whispered, "You can't be here. I'm on the ship, right?" Kristin's eyes slammed wide open and she pushed herself up on her elbows, looking around. "I am on the ship, right? Not on Selene?"

"Mom, feel the gravity. We're both aboard *John Glenn*. I'm helping Ali. They're letting me help." Rachel reached for Kristin's hand, took it in hers. There was no answering squeeze; Kristin let Rachel hold her hand, but she closed her eyes again, and lay back down on the bed.

Rachel had to know; she couldn't hold back anymore. She whispered, "Mom—why did you leave me?"

Silence. Rachel spoke into it, needing an answer. "Dad and I, we waited for you. It was a year before they told us you weren't coming back. You broke his heart—he missed you so. He used to just sit and watch out the window for you, and he kept everything you gave him." Her voice shook, and Rachel realized the lump in her stomach was mostly anger now. She took a deep steadying breath and calmed her voice. "Another

Earth Born did the same thing to him. Except Kara leaving wasn't a surprise—she told him she was leaving before she left. He has three more kids. Justin and Jacob—twins, and Sarah."

Rachel felt Kristin's hand slip from hers. She kept talking, needing to tell the story. "Dad's older than you now. Last time I was up here, he asked about you. It was one of his first questions. He wanted to know if I'd seen you."

Kristin struggled to sit up. Rachel helped her, fluffing pillows at her back, then backed up to the wall so she stood a meter away from her mom.

"I—I'm glad to see you," Kristin said slowly. "I don't know how you got here—helping us. But . . . but I'm sure it's okay. You must be doing well." She shook her head back and forth, as if testing the connection to her neck, and took a long sip of water. "Why did they wake me up?"

Rachel glanced at the data window. "Your assignment is going to be shipside communications." A lump rose in her throat. "You still won't have to go to Selene. I guess . . . I guess you don't want to."

"Selene is such a bare place, and we worked like dogs." Kristin looked past Rachel, as if she weren't there. "Frank just took it! He was born on Selene, he'd never seen *John Glenn*—or Earth. He didn't *know* how barren Selene is. Your dad didn't need me anymore. He was raising you fine." Kristin twisted her hair in her fingers. "When he yelled at me to come in, to get in the shelter before the flare came, I . . . I was tired of being afraid. I didn't move fast enough to make it into the shelter. I was mad because he was yelling at me. All I could think of was that I signed up for this to get away from Sol system, not to come to someplace worse. Selene is scary and hard and barren. When the door closed and I couldn't get in, I just sat down and waited. I hoped they'd take me back to *John Glenn*. They did. I was so sick I never wanted to go near Selene again. When I got better, I asked to stay cold until we get to Ymir. Certainly you can understand that. The goal is Ymir. My family is there—my own parents are cold on the *Leif Eriksson*."

"Not anymore," Rachel said.

Her mother twitched, then barked laughter.

"You didn't think of that?"

"Of course I know that. I don't want to be—now. Now is like living a nightmare. I want to sleep away this place and this time and wake on Ymir."

Her mom had gotten better *before* she asked to stay on *John Glenn*? She didn't have to stay? She just wanted to stay?

"So you stayed here because you missed your family?" Rachel couldn't let that go. "Aren't I family?"

Kristin didn't answer.

A high sound chirped from her wrist, followed by a throaty frog's croak. It was an alert from Ysabet to signal Rachel that Beth was about to wake. But she couldn't leave—not yet.

Rachel thought about Treesa, and how she had talked of a fiancé on another ship. Of her own losses. She said, "You know, you have to go on. They froze me—for twenty years—and I hated it. It wasn't my choice. I got over it—I'm doing what I can for Selene, and for my family and friends there. But you . . . just . . . left us?"

Kristin shook her head. "If I had stayed on Selene, I would be getting old now. Council didn't want us to stay anyway. They wanted us to have kids and come back. I was following orders. Ymir . . . Ymir is my . . . destiny. You can't possibly understand."

"You've got that right."

"I'm sorry for that," Kristin said.

The frog croak sounded from Rachel's wrist pad again. She had to be there for Beth. "Mom? There's something I have to do, and I can't change it. I can't miss it. I made a promise to a friend of mine—you see, she got hurt, and Council brought us here because of it, and I promised her I'd be with her when she wakes up."

Kristin looked down at her fingers, flexing them carefully. She nodded, keeping her face turned toward her hands.

Rachel had other things to ask, but they all stuck in her throat, too small to say. Finally, she said, "Dad was yelling *for* you, not *at* you. I was there. I spent a long time looking *for* you. Even here. And now I have no idea why."

Rachel didn't let herself look back as she left to see her friend.

Chapter 44: Sea of Refuge

Gabriel, Erika, and Ali sat in one of the small galleys drinking coffee and eating grapes and bananas after a run. They were still slick with sweat and smelled of exercise.

The door swung open, and Treesa walked into the room. Gabriel hadn't seen her outside the garden for years. He blinked. She looked as old as Captain Hunter. Ex-captain Hunter.

"Good afternoon," Treesa said. She dispensed a bulb of coffee casually, as if she visited the galley every day. She sat, ignoring Erika and Ali, and looked at Gabriel. "I've just come from Medical. I've gotten clearance and permission to join you in the Refuge project."

Treesa was Council. His peer. She was also disaffected. Wasn't she? What had changed? She looked neater than he'd ever seen her. "What can you do?"

"I'm a communications officer. I can help you run communications at Clarke Base, and besides, I've been helping in the garden for a long time. Maybe Ali can use my help as well." She smiled at Ali, looking for all the world like a doting grandmother.

Ali returned the smile. "Why sure, Treesa, I could use help. I plan to design a fish habitat at Erika's Folly and the Hammered Sea."

Treesa looked pleased. "You mean the Sea of Refuge?"

"Huh?" Gabriel grunted.

"Well, isn't it the Sea of Refuge now? You're putting Refuge there, right? It seems a bit—more—gentle."

Ali grinned. "Hey, that's a great idea! And sure, come on down." She glanced over at Gabriel, saying, "We've been hoping more Council would *want* to go to Selene."

Gabriel gave up. People were always the hardest part of a project. "It will be nice to have you." Just what he needed, a Council member he had to watch closely for crazy behavior.

Treesa drained her coffee bulb, and headed for the door.

"Be ready to leave in a week," Gabriel said to Treesa's retreating back.

Chapter 45: Picnic

Beth could walk. She wobbled a little. The nerves were woven in a new pattern, and she was still learning it. It had only been two days, and already Beth could stay up on her healing legs for a whole hour.

Rachel poured Beth a glass of water, and sat down by the edge of the bed. "I'm so happy this worked. You're walking great."

Beth's brows tugged together in a frown. "I want to go home."

"Just be happy you weren't iced. They'll send us home when they're ready. We don't control the Council."

"They seem to listen to you."

Rachel threw back her head and laughed. "Less than you know."

Ali stepped into the room, smiling. "How are you?"

Beth repeated, "I want to go home."

Ali raised her eyebrows in mock surprise. "And miss seeing the mysteries of *John Glenn*?"

"How do I know you didn't ice me? How do I know my friends are all still my age?" Beth pleaded.

"I can show you." Ali tapped some commands into the display above Beth's bed. "Let's go. I've just cleared you for an hour in a magic room."

Beth's eyes lit up. "A magic room? Rachel told me about those. Really? You'll take me to one?"

Ali laughed again, clearly in a good mood. Beth and Rachel followed her. It was Beth's first trip outside Medical, and she flinched from the moving pictures on the walls. Shifts in gravity confused her. By the time they got to the magic room, sweat beaded her forehead and her breath came in fast gulps.

They settled into the chairs, and Ali did the same trick Gabriel had used on Rachel her first time here, floating them in a sea of stars. Beth clutched the edge of her seat and giggled nervously. Rachel started pointing out constellations, and Beth and Rachel shared their names for them with Ali: the Tree, Two Viaducts, and Children Playing. Next, Ali brought up a bird's eye view of Aldrin on the wall in front of Beth.

"Show me my family."

Ali brought a second data window, consulted it, and selected a camera. The view centered on the path outside the child care center, where Gloria held Beth's younger sister, Miriam. Sound came up. Miriam cried into Gloria's shoulder, and Gloria patted her child's head, saying, "I know, I know. You'll like our new home too. I promise. It'll be okay."

Miriam's sobs intensified, and the camera angle showed Gloria's face almost head-on. A tear streaked down her cheek. She turned, and carrying Miriam, started home.

Ali left the camera in place, frowning.

"What did she mean?" Beth asked.

Rachel knew. "They're moving us. Everyone. Because of the fire, and because of the Refuge project."

"They're making us leave Aldrin?"

Ali spoke. "It has to happen. We built Aldrin a long way from the Hammered Sea because we didn't know how stable the crater would be; we were worried about drowning our new city. But Refuge will be *in* the Hammered Sea—we're calling it the Sea of Refuge now—and it'll be a safer place. Refuge will keep everyone safe from flares—the water in the sea will be a shield."

New implications hit Rachel. Her attention had been on her mom, and on Beth, and the Council. "What about the groves? Teaching Grove? The First Trees? Almost half are left."

"I don't know," Ali said.

Rachel frowned.

Ali kept talking. "You'll be there before they actually move. You're going back in three days."

THE NEXT MORNING, Rachel found a message from her mom: "I'm sorry for being rude. Will you meet me for breakfast in the garden cafeteria at ten?"

Rachel's stomach fluttered. She was still angry with Kristin, but she wanted to understand. Needed to understand. She hadn't seen Kristin since she woke in Medical, but their conversation had turned over and over in her mind. If only she had been kinder.

"I'll be there," she sent back. She checked her watch—time to go.

Rachel found Kristin sitting at a table with a bag in front of her. Kristin looked up as her daughter entered and smiled softly. "Remember how I used to take you on picnics? I thought we'd go sit by the garden wall and share a picnic."

Rachel smiled. She remembered the picnics. "Okay, let's go."

They spent the walk up-spiral talking stiltedly about inconsequential things like how Kristin felt after waking (fine) and how Rachel was doing (she'd stopped helping Ali for now, spending time showing Beth around the ship).

They settled on the lawn, and Kristin took her shoes off and ran her bare toes through the grass. She set out bread, juice, bananas, and protein bars. The air was heavy with the scent of blooming honeysuckle that wound up the river wall across the path from them.

"I thought, perhaps, I should tell you my story," Kristin said. "You told me how you felt when I left you, but you don't really know me. You were seven."

Rachel nodded, peeling a banana. "All right."

"You know why we left? How scary Earth was becoming for humans?"

Rachel grimaced. Every Council member she met wanted to tell her about Sol system.

"You can't really know, though," Kristin said. "It's like yesterday for me. It was only eight years ago, as far as I remember. The sixty thousand years in between was ice time for me, and so I still remember how the AIs ran things, how people died right and left. Or got locked up. My older sister disappeared and never came back. They took her for 'attempting to destroy an intelligence.' I have no idea what she did, and neither did my parents. That's why we came here—why we left. I barely made it. My family had money, and Ma Liren wanted Mom's medical skills so much, she got Rich to take me on as an assistant communications tech." Kristin's voice trailed off, and she took a bite of bread, looking at her bare feet and wriggling them in grass.

"Go on," Rachel prompted, intensely curious. "Was it hard to leave home?"

"Home was scary. We wanted to leave. The AIs and the augmented were trying to pass laws to keep us from leaving, and we were demonstrating—oh—that doesn't matter. We left, and I was so glad to get a berth at all I didn't care that my parents were on *Leif.* I was the youngest Colonist they took—I was only thirty years old."

Kristin looked at her toes again, then at Rachel. "This is the hard part—the part I need you to understand. Can you try to pretend you've been jerked away from everything you knew? That you had plans that got—stopped—before you knew it? Didn't something like that happen to you when you were frozen?"

So her mom must have talked to someone about her. Probably Ali.

Kristin said, "For you it was an accident.

"We take orders from Council. We all do. We're alive because of them; we got away because they financed this trip. Imagine you got an order to go live someplace you hated, and to share your bed with a man you didn't know, who didn't share any of your experiences or history. Your dad was only nineteen when they contracted us—younger than you are now. And I was thirty. I was awake—*thawed*—in the wrong place, separated from everyone I loved by too many years to count. My sister—her name was Rachel—I named you after her. I still don't know if they killed her, or changed her, or just locked her up somewhere, or sent her somewhere . . . but no matter—she was long dead by the time I woke up. And my parents were gone too—far away, maybe still iced, waiting to help terraform Ymir, but more likely warmed and long dead. Doesn't matter. I knew then I'd never see them."

Tears ran down her mom's face, and Rachel reached out and put a hand on Kristin's shoulder. Kristin shivered, but didn't take Rachel's hand.

"Let me finish. I need . . . I need for you to understand. What you said, when I woke up in Medical, it made me think about how you must have felt."

Rachel squeezed her mother's shoulder.

"They ordered us to contract. They ordered us to have children. I didn't want to. I wasn't ready. There was supposed to be a new world waiting for me. A place where we could be truly human, could build a home, like Earth, but where we didn't have to make the same mistakes. We'd learned. We know . . . how dangerous the toys we make can be. That's what it all was at first, stuff that did anything we told it to . . . until our creations outgrew us. Instead of waking at Ymir, a new paradise, I woke to a pitted moon! It's nothing like Earth, Selene. It's a struggling and sickly garden in a harsh place. Nothing to do—no proper games, no 3D video, no social life, no universities, nothing. We left the technology we loved too . . . of course.

"I hated being ordered around. But we're alive because of Council. We signed on without any rights. There's a contract we all signed . . ."

Kristin stopped for a minute, took a drink of juice. Rachel said, "You're enslaved."

"Yeah. Living on Selene was like living in jail. So when I could, I left. I wanted to be iced again, and not wake up. Since I was doing what they wanted—they wanted to save us for Ymir—Council said it was okay. Can't you see how much I wanted that?"

Kristin looked beseechingly at Rachel. Rachel didn't know what to say. Kristin's abandonment had hurt. Now she understood that her mom too had been left alone.

Finally Rachel said, "Maybe we can start over. We are family."

Kristin's mouth drew into a thin line. "I don't want to go back to Selene."

"We can send messages. Maybe I'll come back soon. I'm leaving in two days."

"I know," Kristin said. "That's why I asked to see you. I don't even know you—even though you're my daughter. Maybe there will be time . . . maybe some time. But right now, I just want to do what I need to do to keep Council happy. I'll stay here, and be a good communications tech."

"All right, Mom. Maybe I'll send you messages anyway."

"I might not answer them." Kristin put her head in her hands. "I don't know."

"I hope you do."

"Do you forgive me?"

"Not yet. But maybe I understand better."

Kristin reached up and took Rachel's hand.

Chapter 46: Leaving

John Hunter and Gabriel sat in Gabriel's room, watching the first of the shuttle runs to the surface. Rachel was on that ship, and Beth, and Mathew and Dena, who would finally free Star and Shane for a much-needed rest.

Gabriel had taught Rachel to call the new captain "Captain Erika," and the old one "Captain John." He found it helped him too; using John Hunter's first name erased some of the formality, since he now had no more authority than Gabriel himself.

"Can you make this project fun?" Captain John asked.

"Huh?"

"Well, you've been entirely too serious. Every time I've seen you, it's been to adjudicate some life or death situation, or work out a problem. Now that I don't have to be your captain, I intend to have some fun with you. I'm tired of being so serious. I'm tired of the politics here, and I'm too old to be useful at Ymir anyway."

"It's possible none of us will see Ymir," Gabriel said.

John Hunter looked startled. "I never expected to hear that from *you*."

"I'm sorry," Gabriel said. "I remember when I never doubted. I'm still working to get us away from here."

"Well, I might do more toward that goal on Selene than here. It seems like I haven't done much good shipside. What good is a captain with a marooned ship?"

"I can use the help," Gabriel admitted.

"So would there be harm in enjoying ourselves?"

Gabriel didn't feel cheerful. His relationship with Erika was completely changed, and he could not read the final outcome. Gabriel doubted he'd like it. Ship's captains tended to marry their ships, and Erika showed every sign of doing that. Still, it would be an impolite thing to say to the man who'd caused the change. "I'll do my best, sir."

"Just John now, thank you."

"All right. Just John. Mind if I play a bit?"

"Please."

Gabriel pulled from its case a crystal-clear guitar with bright silver strings and frets that seemed to float on air. He began to play, starting with an old blues song. Just John knew the song, and he had a good voice. They sang for nearly an hour, watching the stars and feeding on data flow, preparing to head down to the surface of the tiny moon they'd helped make together, and perform yet another engineering miracle.

John Hunter had planned this world. At last he would see it firsthand.

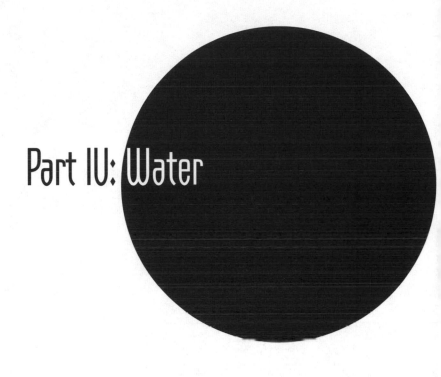

Part IV: Water

60,299 *John Glenn* shiptime

Chapter 47: Coming Home

Rachel and Beth bolted down the ramp and stepped onto the surface of Selene. Early-morning mists hugged the ground. The nip of cold after the absolute temperature control on *John Glenn* felt wonderful.

Mathew—the newly warmed Council member coming to replace Shane—grunted as he misjudged Selene's gravity and bounced high after his first step, tangling his feet. He reached for Rachel's hand to steady himself. "Wow—I forgot what a world is like."

Rachel returned his laughter. "I forgot it's your first time on Selene. I have the same experience on the *John Glenn*."

"Hey look!" Mathew pointed up, and Rachel followed his finger to see the lopsided lens of Refuge, a large bright spot winking in the early daylight as if it were a star, following the bright dot of *John Glenn*.

Rachel and Beth helped Mathew guide the thirty newly warmed onto the surface. Star gathered them into a loose line. They stood, shivering and whispering among themselves, blinking in the double light of the sun and the gas giant. The two Council members led the Earth Born toward Aldrin. Rachel watched them go, mist swirling gently around their feet and shoulders. How many of them were like her mom, and hated being here?

She heard her name called. Familiar forms stood at the edge of the landing strip, faces still indistinct in the mist. Rachel picked Harry and Gloria out of the crowd, then Nick. There was Frank at the edge of the crowd, surrounded by Rachel's half siblings: Jacob, Justin, and Sarah. She ran to hug her father. "Not so long this time, Dad," she murmured, "just a few weeks."

Gloria and Harry stood rooted, watching Beth approach the crowd. It was as if they couldn't really believe she walked toward them. *Walked.* Gloria broke first, and ran up to Beth, holding her, standing back and looking, and holding her again. Harry followed, beaming.

Watching through her family's point of view, Rachel realized how much better Beth looked. Her legs, of course, but even such a short time among Council on *John Glenn* had added poise. As she walked between her parents to meet the others, wearing shorts, she flashed unblemished and perfect thighs. A huge smile filled her face with light.

Rachel saw awe in Moon Born faces as they watched Beth. She had never doubted Council could heal Beth if they chose to. Rachel ran up to Beth and whispered, "The meadow . . . let's stay under open sky."

Beth's eyes flashed approval. "Yes, let's. I'm sick to death of being closed in."

The hulk of the ruined spaceship rested where Gabriel had left it, bright in the warming sunshine. The name "Water Bearer" adorned the hull, in blue paint. A charred smell stung Rachel's nostrils, but new green grass sprouted through dark burned spots. As the mist thinned, sunlight painted the new grass blades a brilliant greenish yellow.

Beth and Rachel scrambled onto the dais, and their families gathered around, standing close in the damp morning.

They all looked the right ages. Rachel shivered, excising the ghosts of her last return. "Thank you for meeting us this morning. How did you get away?"

Jacob grinned at her. "We were pests."

Justin poked him. "He's not telling the whole story. We had to work extra shifts to get this morning off. They told us two days ago, and we didn't want to miss seeing you first."

Sarah came up to Beth and touched her legs. "How did they do this? Make you well?"

Rachel smiled at her little sister. "It's the same technology that keeps them young." She cleared her throat, looking at the expectant faces watching her. "Gabriel saved Aldrin, and made sure that Beth was healed too."

Justin looked puzzled. "Rachel? If they can stay young forever, and heal Beth's broken back and legs, why can't they keep us young too? Why does their power work for them and not for us?"

It was the same question she and Harry had asked each other before her first trip to *John Glenn.* "I don't know for sure. There's stuff on *John Glenn* it would be wonderful to have here. I'm trying to understand Council's communications, medicine, and ways of making things. But in two trips to *John Glenn,* I've learned how much I don't know."

"But why don't they make these things available on Selene?" Jacob took up his brother's question.

Astronaut fed her an answer. Rachel said, "They require power sources that only work on *John Glenn.*"

Sarah spoke up. "Why can't more of us go to the ship?"

"That's Council's decision. I don't know."

Jacob frowned. "They needed us during the fire. Why don't they give us antimatter now?"

Rachel pictured *John Glenn*'s antimatter containment, and said, "Because it's hard to handle. Gabriel told me it isn't very safe. They have to build special containers to make it safe."

"Why can't they make those here, now? They'll need them sooner or later."

Rachel licked her lips. She listened for an answer, but Astronaut was silent. She filed it away as a question to ask. "They plan to build a collider, which makes antimatter, here. I'll see what I can learn."

"So why don't they treat us better after the fire?" Jacob returned to his original argument. "Sure, Gabriel was the big hero. But we worked too. Without us, the fire would have been in Aldrin before Gabriel got here. And for that, we get told to pack up and move."

Nick's voice rose from the back of the group. "I'd like to hear questions that these two *can* answer. Tell us more about *John Glenn*."

Rachel grinned at Nick, grateful for his help. She squeezed Beth's hand. "Beth, why don't you tell them?"

Beth leaned forward, excited to be able to tell her story. "You can see Selene from space—there's a—"

Astronaut spoke into Rachel's ear. "They are watching this on the ship. Council will hear whatever you say. Speak to put them at ease. Perhaps they will not observe you so closely if they see you helping them."

Rachel grunted low in her throat, a signal to Astronaut that she didn't fully understand.

"Talk about cooperation," it prompted. "Maybe that will counter any negative from the young men's questions."

Beth struggled to portray the magic of *John Glenn*'s impossible garden, her face shining as she described Yggdrasil. The younger woman was doing a good job. Perhaps Rachel would be pestered with fewer spaceship questions in class.

Astronaut prompted her again. "Talk about Kyu and Ali, and how you worked with them."

Bad idea. She got enough special treatment. She looked around the meadow, and her gaze stopped on *Water Bearer*.

The question and answer session with Beth broke for a moment, and Rachel glanced at Nick. "I'll start teaching classes again as soon as we get to Clarke Base," she said. "In the meantime, Jacob's right—remember the lesson from the fire. Everyone on Selene cooperated with each other. We needed Council to win, Gabriel to win, and the sacrifice of the ship you're calling *Water Bearer*. This was not a small thing." Rachel pointed to the twisted wreck. "Council can do many things, but Gabriel told me they can't make another one of those. Let's make that ship a symbol, and next time we get angry with Council we can remember *Water Bearer*. They're hard taskmasters, but without them we would die."

Beth squeezed Rachel's hand. "I'm hungry."

Gloria stood right next to Beth, hovering protectively. She responded instantly. "All right. Breakfast is on me and Harry. See you all in a half hour?"

The twins walked away, heads together, Jacob laughing at something Justin said. Or maybe it was the other way around.

Frank waited for her. How was she going to tell him about Kristin? She went to him and whispered, "I found Mom."

His eyes grew wide, and he held her tightly. "Tell me about it."

She took her father's hand and started toward Aldrin. This was going to be hard. "I was working in Medical, helping Ali with newly warmed, and . . ."

IT TOOK RACHEL AN HOUR to reach Harry and Gloria's. Gloria met her at the door and held her tightly. Her eyes sparkled as she whispered, "Thank you."

"I didn't have much of a choice," Rachel said.

"Of course you did," Harry said. "And you did the right thing. You always have." He gestured for Rachel to sit down. "Where's Frank?"

"He's not feeling well. I found my mom, and I had to tell him about it."

Harry startled. "Tell me?"

Rachel looked around. The twins and Sarah and Beth were all eating already, gathered in the family room, laughing and talking. She shook her head. "Later, when they've all gone."

"Is she hurt?"

"No, just selfish." Rachel looked down, wishing he hadn't asked.

Harry frowned at her. "Is it better than not knowing?"

"I suppose." She saw her father's face as she told him the story, and said, "Maybe not."

Gloria changed the subject. "Council plans to move us all to Clarke Base."

"I know."

"Within a month. They'll move as much of the power plant and infrastructure as they can, and leave only enough support for a small group here. Aldrin will be smaller than Gagarin. Shane and Star said we'll be safer at Clarke Base."

"Gabriel and Ali told me the same thing," Rachel said.

"Andrew says Council just wants to keep us all in one place," Harry said. "He says that way they can watch more easily."

"He doesn't know what he's talking about. They can watch us wherever we are," Rachel said.

"Andrew's against the move. Some of our people are listening." Harry paused. "Rachel, I don't agree with him, but he's making a strong argument. Oh—I don't think moving to Clarke Base changes how much control they have over us, but there is a lot Council doesn't talk about. What are their plans for the next few years? Do you know?"

Rachel shook her head. "They'll make antimatter here, then go. I don't want that. None of us should want that. Selene is dangerous even with Council here. We can't fight Council directly. Andrew's crazy to think we can. The smartest thing we can do is learn. What do you think I've been trying to do with the greenhouse classes?"

"And that gets us—what?" Gloria asked softly.

Rachel helped Gloria set the table for breakfast. "Respect," she said. "They can't make their precious factories and build their precious antimatter without us. If we know enough to talk on their level, they'll listen to us."

Harry frowned.

Gloria said, "Maybe Rachel's right, honey. We don't even know what to ask them now, and if we learn enough, maybe we'll discover the right questions."

"I'm beginning to doubt it." Harry reached for a piece of bread, Beth came in, and the conversation drifted to Beth's experiences on the ship.

The four younger people piled out the door, Jacob teasing Beth about her new legs. Beth simply looked back at Jacob and smiled. "I'll race you."

"You're on."

Rachel laughed and helped Harry clear up the plates. She said, "I watched one of the briefings about what Gabriel's calling Refuge. It's flare protection. And while that's being finished, Council will build more factories at Clarke Base. After all, that's where they build the planting machines and aircraft. Aldrin is here because this is where Council wanted a jungle. That's done, except now we need to replant what burned. There is no reason not to move, except that we love Aldrin."

"Gabriel told us Clarke Base wasn't safe because of the risk of a problem with the Hammered Sea," Harry said. "The first time he took us up there—when we were kids. Do you remember?"

"Better than you, maybe. That was before we knew about the flares. It's a choice between dangers. I don't like leaving the grove either. Maybe we can find a way to take care of it?"

"Is the grove all you think about?" Gloria asked. She was laughing, but her voice was strained.

Rachel sipped her juice. "No. But caring about the ecosystems *is* caring about the people. When the First Trees lived, that signaled Council we could live here. Ali told me that. To Council they were a symbol: the first real success with complex life. Ali said the night they knew they could start populating Selene was the first Mid-Winter Night. They had the first party on Selene that day.

"For us, it's where we first learned about caring for Selene. The trees will feed us over time. That's why it matters."

"We hope they leave some of us here," Gloria said. "Can you ask for us?"

"Why me?" Rachel asked.

"You made Gabriel take Beth to the ship," Gloria said.

"No, I got Gabriel to take *me* to the ship with Beth." What was Gloria thinking? "Gloria, I can't make Council do things." Remembering Liren, she added, "In fact, I might be bad for any goals we have."

Gloria looked confused, and Rachel said, "Council doesn't all think the same way. They're like us—they disagree sometimes. One of the High Council—the people who make the decisions—doesn't like me. Ma Liren. So you see, sometimes I might not be the best one to make suggestions."

Gloria frowned. "I thought everyone liked you."

Dylan burst in the door, arms full of flowers. He must have looked all over the grove to find so many blooms. He handed a white orchid to Beth, and placed the rest in Rachel's arms.

Fragrances blended thickly, and Rachel buried her face in the bright blooms, taking in the strong sweet scents.

"Thanks for bringing my sister home," Dylan said.

"Council sent her home," Rachel replied.

Dylan grunted at her, folding his arms.

"Sorry—thank you for the flowers. You didn't need to pick so many! But really, I didn't do anything but go up with her. I know how scary *John Glenn* can be until you get used to it. That's all."

"None of us would know."

Dylan was right, but there wasn't any way to make her words sting less. It wasn't her fault she had different experiences than the other Moon Born.

"Here, Gloria," she said, "do you have anything big enough to put these in? I can leave a few here, and I'll take some home to Frank and the kids."

Dylan gave her a hurt look, so she added, "I'll take at least one with me when I leave tomorrow for Clarke Base."

Dylan rewarded her with a smile.

They weren't supposed to pick flowers, not in great big bunches. Dylan often defied authority in little ways. She liked him for it, and the flowers *were* beautiful. She didn't have the heart to remind him how bare the jungle was after the fire.

Chapter 48: Inside the *Water Bearer*

That afternoon, Rachel fled the business of Aldrin, and walked to the grove by herself. She headed straight for her plot. The idea that her plants, and Ursula's, might go wild saddened her. The top leaves had been rained clean. She wiped clumps of damp soot from lower leaves so they could breathe. Small plants had smothered under the ash.

Rachel spent three hours clearing traces of the fire from both plots. Her hands were filthy, and working in the ash dredged up fire smells. At least ash would be good for the soil.

As she worked, Rachel fretted about the day's conversations. Once she'd wanted to be a leader, way back after that first test with Gabriel and Ali. She was a leader now, or at least everybody thought she was. She shivered. It wasn't fun.

What did people expect from her? Treesa, Astronaut, Andrew, Dylan, Gloria, Harry—they all wanted her to be something different. And what was Andrew up to anyway? She had not fought him directly, but simply tried to sell her own version of the right choices for the Moon Born. She knew, mostly by rumor, that Andrew was holding his own informal meetings under the guise of sports. Way before the fire, Andrew and some of Selene's young men and women played catch-the-disk and staged flying competitions, using them as cover for conversations she knew little about. She had been avoiding a confrontation, but deep in her gut she knew that it was time.

She went to Dylan, and was not surprised that he knew where to find Andrew. She didn't like the answer at all.

Teaching Grove was a checkerboard below her as she flew high, riding a warm breeze over the meadow toward the line of blackened grass and dirt that marked the descent of *Water Bearer*. Apollo hung just above the horizon, making her shadow long and thin. The broken ship's shadow loomed over the meadow, spiky with extended booms and mooring legs.

Rachel landed a few feet away from the furrow made by *Water Bearer*'s crash. As she was unclipping her arm wings, she heard Andrew's voice behind her. "So you finally came to find me."

Rachel jumped, startled. "Maybe I just came to see the ship. Why are you here?"

She started walking toward the dead ship, and he kept up, shaking his head at her, making fun. "You tell us to learn what we can. The ship may be dead, but I can get inside—the door's warped open. I'm learning."

Andrew camping in *Water Bearer* added to her anger. "I keep hearing about you turning people against Council. Jacob and Justin asked me all kinds of questions that *somebody's* been feeding them. Ever since Gabriel started me teaching, I've worked to bring everyone together. All of us. Not just Moon Born, not even Moon Born and Council, but every human being on the face of this moon!" She realized she was extremely loud. She lowered her voice, stepping back under the ship. Astronaut and Treesa were watching over her, but she didn't need to make their job harder. "Andrew! We can't fight Council. Not even you and your whole group of friends."

Andrew met her angry words with a surprising calm. "Rachel, I'm just laying groundwork for tactics you are going to have to adopt. You have your own strength and power."

His voice was so reasonable, it slowed Rachel down. She stopped to set her wings down. "Who says I want your tactics? Who says I want power?"

"Rachel, you have power. It doesn't matter if you want it or not. People *want* to follow you. I know what you're doing. I even support you; more than you know. But what if it doesn't work?"

It was hard to stay mad at him when he was so calm. "It has to work. There isn't any other way."

Andrew's answer was to turn and walk farther under the edge of the ship. Rachel followed. *Water Bearer* listed about five degrees, and Andrew had built a makeshift ladder up to the most easily accessible lock. He climbed up, beckoning to her. His face was shadowed, and she couldn't read his expression.

"Astronaut," Rachel said, "is it safe?" She was uneasy at the idea of going inside *Water Bearer.* At being on a Council ship, uninvited.

Astronaut replied, "There are no orders against being inside."

"Thanks," Rachel sent back to Astronaut, and followed Andrew into the ship.

The steps led into a short cylindrical corridor, and lights were turned on. Rachel blinked at the lights, surprised. Before she could ask Andrew about it, he spoke. "Look, Rachel, I hope your plan does work. I wish it was me they took, me they let see their ways, me they trusted. But I had twenty years to get over being mad at you—you just did the right things. Maybe you're still doing the right things." The corridor was slightly tilted, and Rachel felt off balance because the handholds that hung in the walls and stuck up from the floor every half meter or so were off center. Andrew continued. "But if it doesn't work, there has to be a different plan. Think of me as your backup."

"Do you have a plan?" she asked.

Andrew ducked into a room. Rachel followed him, and they took seats on two of the four acceleration couches. Even though Rachel had never been on a miner like the *Water Bearer,* she recognized the control room by the huge empty view screen, by banks of gauges and keyboards. She'd seen such things on the space-planes that flew between *John Glenn* and Selene. She frowned. Much of Gabriel's flying seemed directly related to data windows he controlled. Even though the interior lighting continued to work, nothing else flashed or even showed a steady light. Had Gabriel disabled everything, or was everything broken?

Andrew looked around the room. "Do you recognize this stuff? Do you know how to use it?"

Of course he was drawn to Council's technology. She shook her head. "I asked. They won't teach me to fly a ship—not even a little one." She couldn't let the conversation drift too far. "So, you were going to tell me your plan?"

"No. I'm not. You might tell Council. Look, Rachel, we're both on the same side; we both want the same thing. But we're going after it different ways. Your way is open—you tell everyone."

Rachel let that go. "But your plan is a secret?"

Andrew looked directly at her. "Rachel, your ideas might work. And if not, it probably won't piss Council off if you try to help them. That's the crux of it—you want to be so helpful they'll decide you're useful. And hey, it works for you at least. Maybe it will work for all of us. But if I act, it will be more like the rebellions you keep talking about in your classes. We're slaves. You taught us history. Slaves have to rebel or run away—and there's nowhere to run."

Andrew almost never attended her classes. "How do you know what I teach?"

"Some folks believe like me, Rachel. We believe in both ways. If your way works, then we won't need to try anything else. People tell me what you teach. Dylan tells me, for one." He looked away. "That way I can get educated without drawing attention. Council doesn't watch any of us very much—they're too busy. But they watch me more than you. So I stay away from you, so your work has a chance. And by the way, I'm sure you have help from Council. Otherwise, things wouldn't go so easy for you."

Andrew reached down and opened a low drawer, withdrawing a wine bulb. "Want some?"

"Where did you get that?"

"I bought it, last Mid-Winter Night." He shrugged, and grinned at her. "Some people don't like the taste. I saved it for something special."

She shook her head at him. "No, thanks. It makes me feel funny."

"That's the idea." He unscrewed the top and took a sip. "It's starting to taste funny. Maybe I should finish it."

She glared at him. "Suit yourself."

He took one more sip, then put the top back on.

She didn't think he looked at all contrite. Rachel got up and paced around the small room. In order to stay a few feet away from Andrew she could take just ten steps each direction. She couldn't tell him how much help she had. So how was she going to convince him? "Maybe you should have actually come to class. The Roman slave rebellion got put down. The

American Blacks had help from white Americans in the north. Gandhi in India won, but he didn't use violence. All *you're* going to do is get people in trouble. Get yourself in trouble. Look around you. Look at this ship. Council built this. They used it to help build Selene, and then to help save it. We can't even begin to make anything like this *unless we persuade Council to teach us more.* We have to be credible and trustworthy. Confrontation can't work."

"That depends on what you want it to work for. It might, for example, get attention. And I'm not like you, Rachel; I don't get favored treatment. No Council person has ever treated me very well. Not one. I'm angry at them. You should be angry at them too. Who do they think they are to tell us what to do and to keep their secrets from us?" He glared at her. "Or most of us."

"I thought you weren't mad at me?"

"I'm not. Maybe a little envious." He twisted his hands together in his lap, and sighed. "We're trying to solve the same problem. I want you to promise to help me—to tell me as much as you can about Council."

Rachel shook her head. "I tell my classes a lot. You can come—I won't kick you out."

"You need me."

Rachel swallowed, and sat down. "Why do I need you?"

"Because when they don't listen to you—if they don't—then you'll need other options."

"What options?"

Andrew shook his head. "No."

He wasn't going to budge. He probably didn't even have a plan. "It *will* be bad for us if they leave. Andrew, please just promise you won't do anything to make them mad. You're still being punished for something that happened a long time ago. Maybe not so much—now you work like all the rest of us, but there's a mark against your name. The jail is still there. Liren wouldn't hesitate to put you in it."

"Liren?"

He really didn't know anything. "Andrew, just don't do anything to get in trouble."

"Who's Liren?" he insisted.

"The High Council member behind most of the things you don't like."

"Is she your friend, like precious Gabriel and sweet Ali?"

"No. Andrew—you'll get yourself killed, or made to go away, or something."

"You haven't convinced me Council isn't going to just fly away and leave us. I don't think you believe it yourself."

Rachel was quiet for a long time. "You're right. I'm not convinced. But we mattered during the fire. They needed us. We'll have other chances to prove ourselves." She sat down and looked him in the eye. "So yes, I'm afraid they *will* leave. I'm sure they want to leave. But I *am* convinced we can't fight them directly. We have to find other ways. Tell you what, you agree to stay away from anything violent, and to stop making people angry with Council, and I'll agree not to hinder you. If I want to argue with you, I'll do it in private, like this." He would understand she expected reciprocation. "But I won't agree to anything destructive, and I won't break Council rules. I am helping to build Selene, and I will *not* help you destroy it."

"I'll agree not to do anything obvious without telling you first, as long as you agree not to turn me in. You protect my plans and I'll protect yours. There may come a day when we all need each other."

Rachel nodded. "I can do that. We're all Children of Selene. Don't make the mistake of thinking I'm Council. I'm not."

Andrew lay back on the acceleration couch, looking up at the ceiling. "I'm not sure who you are."

"You never were. Think of me as a revolutionary who assesses risk carefully. That's the part I'm afraid you're not good at. You can't see patterns, Andrew."

She got up and ran her hands along the ship's controls. No reaction. "The lights work. What else?"

"Nothing." Andrew stood next to her. "I've tried, but since I've never been in a spaceship, maybe I just don't know how to make it work."

"The lights are probably for emergencies," she said. "I think they're automatic. They respond to people being onboard."

Rachel tried everything she could think of, but the only response she got from the ship was to turn the view screen on. It showed a broken arm with what looked like a huge gripper hand dangling from the end, and beyond that, an expanse of burned meadow and shattered First Trees. "I guess it's stuck on a single camera view," she said. She listened for hints from Astronaut, but it offered nothing, and she didn't want to talk to it with Andrew so close to her. She added another item to her long list of things to ask the AI. There was just never enough time to ask it everything.

Chapter 49: Landing Refuge

Gabriel worked on Refuge every spare minute. John Hunter and Wayne Narteau helped, and the initial tests were perfect. Gabriel accepted far more help from Astronaut than he would ever admit to.

What used to be an asteroid had become a lens. A shallow dome of industrial woven diamond covered the rounded side. Black slag covered the flat side. Loops in various sizes had grown everywhere, handholds and cable moorings fully integrated into the structure. They towed it behind *John Glenn,* tied on with skinny carbon strands.

It was clean and ready. All of the gross structural work was done. The nanobots' last instruction had been to die. Wouldn't want to bring that stuff down to Selene!

The asteroid was ready for its first—and only—solo voyage.

Gabriel stood in his office, stretching. The only light came from images of stars and of Refuge, strung around him in data windows.

Hands slipped over his shoulders, and he turned to face Erika, surprised and pleased to see her. Erika leaned up and kissed him. "You know," she said, "that asteroid of yours looks a little like a yo-yo. It takes so much of your time. I wish you could send it down to Selene and let someone else take care of the finishing work there."

"You know I can't."

She sighed, wistful. "I know. I wish you could be here with me. I wish I didn't have so much to do here, now, always."

A couch rested against the wall. As Gabriel led Erika to the couch, the data windows winked out, one by one, and a near-darkness settled over them. Gabriel stroked Erika's cheek, and his hand slid down along her waist.

"I wanted to say good-bye," she whispered.

It sounded very final. Gabriel stopped for a moment, then bent his head down to rest it against her cheek. "Are things changing so much?"

"Yes. I have to be your captain. But today, I want to forget that."

Her cheek was soft. And damp. Was she crying? "Shhh," he whispered to her, "I'll always love you."

She answered him with touch, for a very long time. He forgot all about Refuge, and stars, and Selene, overcome by her smell and the high electric energy flowing skin to skin as they joined.

When they finally separated, Erika ran her fingertips along Gabriel's cheekbones, then through the loose hair along his scalp. Her touch was soft. "I'll miss you," she said.

He nodded and turned away, separating himself from her touch, his eyes stinging. "Maybe when we get to Ymir we'll have time together again."

"Maybe," she said. "You get us away from Selene. I'll get us to Ymir."

TWO DAYS LATER, Refuge was ready. Erika herself flew Gabriel and John over, monitoring their space walk to Refuge. Wayne took one of the Large Pusher Tugs out, ready to intervene if anything went wrong.

Gabriel and John floated inside a hardened glass bubble made from the shell of one of the little Service Armor ships. It nestled inside a cage not quite twice the volume of the bubble. Carbon fiber rope connected the cage to eight separate points inside the largely hollow Refuge. They wore full safety gear, including pressure suits and helmets and multipoint tie-down harnesses. Modified wings were strapped to the outsides of their suits. Service Armor was designed for space; wings, even retracted, got in the way. They barely fit, and Gabriel felt as if he and John had been poured into the bubble. Their suits and knees and wings flattened against the glass, and as Gabriel looked back at himself from one of the many cameras he had set up to record their descent, the bubble looked like a glass marble he had played with once on Earth, in what felt like an entirely different lifetime.

Two layers of transparent shielding lay between them and the fires to come.

Gabriel and John grinned at each other, and even managed matching thumbs-up signs in the cramped quarters. Then Gabriel signaled and the carbon cords released, spinning Refuge on its short axis and altering its trajectory by just a bit.

They sat in the bubble while Refuge spun slowly around them. *John Glenn* dwindled. Astronaut gave Gabriel the next signal, and they fired some of the little Service Armor engines they had placed in twelve mounts on the rocky underside.

They'd calculated right. The big flattened ball drifted toward Selene, leaving the men nothing to do for a few hours but watch. They floated a safe distance away from the soletta, its huge reflecting mirrors too bright to look at out here with no atmosphere to protect them. Time dragged. Gabriel's shoulders hurt from the cramped quarters, and his right foot went to sleep in its boot.

Astronaut said, "Now entering effective atmosphere." Gabriel tensed. He watched the temperature reading rise, and then spike, as they brushed Selene's troposphere, the rocky side facing down and forward, already giving them lift.

The trip so far had all been free fall. Now they felt their speed as they lost it, plowing through the upper fringes of Selene's atmosphere, bouncing, losing a little heat and a lot of speed as they went high and then came down again, a flat rock skipping on Selene's fluid atmosphere. Impact increased Refuge's spin, fast enough that they rolled inside it in the small ball, so Gabriel's head spun too, and he lost the camera images in his heads-up display for a moment. His stomach twisted and he held tightly to his seat. Then the bubble stabilized, mostly. Refuge spun around them. They bounced twice more, spinning each time, before Gabriel got the signal to turn on engines again, making fine adjustments, and they plunged through the atmosphere and came out moving much slower than their initial approach, above and north of the Sea of Refuge.

That left two small adjustments, and a lot of slowing by retrofiring away from Selene's surface. It was exacting, difficult flying. They came down off center in the Hammered Sea, in the shallowest depression they'd been able to find, from the last big strike the sea had taken before water rained down to fill it. As they hit the water, Refuge's hot metallic reentry shield boiled water away from them. Clouds rose and filled the crater while Refuge hovered on live steam.

Refuge sank as it cooled.

Gabriel opened data windows, using the surviving cameras to verify they were in the right place. The underside of Refuge was megatons of slag, and the weight pulled it down. At low tide, the top of Refuge would be twenty feet below the water, and the bottom would rest a hundred twenty feet down. High tide was forty feet higher. Refuge must withstand large changes in pressure twice daily.

Refuge was still filled with nothing, with vacuum. This was its last test. If it was stable on the bottom with vacuum pulling upward . . . and if no leaks formed . . . right. Leave it this way for a few days, but Gabriel was sure. Refuge would be entirely safe after he filled it with air.

They needed to get out before Refuge finished sinking. Gabriel loosed the bonds that held the bubble inside Refuge. The bubble rolled out of its cage and bobbed up into what would become the main entry airlock. A massive door closed below them. Another opened above, and the bubble bobbed up through turbid water and into the air. A second of free fall, and then *splash*.

Gabriel and Captain John floated on still-warm water, waiting for the turbulence to die down. They took their helmets off, leaving them, and Gabriel opened the hatch. John clambered out onto a small ledge made by the open door. Gabriel helped extend the wings, awkwardly attached via a harness built over the pressure suit, and steadied John's feet as the bubble bobbed up and down. "Bend your legs. You'll need a lot of lift."

John had never flown on Selene. Now, he'd have just one chance for a good takeoff. He squatted, and almost fell, catching himself with a gloved hand.

"Stand with your feet farther apart."

The former ship's captain finally looked down at him, smiling, then mouthed "Shut up," and pushed off flawlessly.

Gabriel followed, actually bobbling his own takeoff since the tiny floating bubble no longer had any inside weight to stabilize it. His breath caught as his feet grazed the water, unbalancing him. He arched his back, bent his knees, and swept his wings down so hard the bottom edge slapped the water. A second wing beat, and he was high enough to be above the water. The pressure suit was hard to fly in, even as thin as it was. It had been a trade-off; a choice between building wings onto suits and needing to change inside the unstable bubble. He screamed into the wind as he followed the older man to the edge of the Sea of Refuge. They had done it!

They landed near each other. The sea was calming. Ripples from their landing washed against the crater walls and back on themselves, damping slowly. A vast bank of steam floated away from them.

Gabriel said, "Hey, next time, how about we have a boat or two ready in case we have trouble?"

"Good thought," John replied, "And here's another one—see all that steam? What if, next time we have a fire, you just drop something hot in the sea? Make it rain. It'd be cheaper than wasting ships."

"Very funny."

Chapter 50: A Question of Life

Astronaut had a deep need to protect humans. All humans. Humans died. It knew that. Many of them had died getting away from Sol system, but that was before Astronaut was responsible. None had died in the accident that marooned them in Apollo system.

Ursula died: the Moon Born girl who was Rachel's friend. Astronaut paid little attention. It noticed Richard dying, in the fire. Accidents happened. But now, Council and Moon Born alike were acting in ways that Astronaut believed would lead to deaths.

Even as it studied and affected individuals, groups mystified it. It analyzed history. The setup on Selene was untenable: humans treating humans badly because they feared technology more than they feared breaking fundamental codes of human behavior. Patterns showed a fight coming: between Children and Children, or between Children and Council, or worse, on all sides. But nothing continued to happen while the pressure continued to build.

Erika drove everyone relentlessly toward building the collider. She and Clare and Liren acted as one unit, almost never disagreeing. Astronaut was barely involved with *John Glenn*, except to perform regular daily ship checks. People on *John Glenn* conversed with Astronaut about small things: daily ship's status, a problem with the bacteria that managed soil pH in the garden, a brief malfunction in the machinery that converted organic matter back to raw minerals, water, and oils.

Astronaut watched the swirling patterns of human activity on Selene. Information feeds around the Sea of Refuge and Clarke Base factories were full and rich. Feeds from the Moon Born housing at Clarke Base were thinner. Astronaut had to interpolate from pods and sensors in the agricultural areas, and from what it saw from the overhead cameras.

On Refuge, Rachel did well: with Ali's and Treesa's help, she became unofficial second in command to Treesa, who oversaw preparing Refuge to support the two thousand plus population on Selene for up to two weeks. Gabriel and John worked on the external logistics of getting cargo and people to and from Refuge, and built Council's new home above the sea. Ali worked on sea biology. She and Treesa ran their respective projects, and helped each other as well.

Astronaut taught Rachel, and she taught the Children who worked on Refuge: science, emergency preparedness, and organizational behavior.

She managed classes at Clarke Base once a month. She slept in Frank's home there.

Clarke Base was busy with manufacturing and growing food. Earth Born worked in the factories that used materials nanotechnology to prepare the collider barrel, and Children worked the fields and finished shaping parts for the base town, agriculture, and Refuge.

Moon Born on Clarke Base demonstrated divergent behavior. Andrew clearly held sway with one group. Others collected around Beth and Frank and the Earth Born man, Bruce, who had saved Beth from the fire. Many of the Moon Born seemed to have no particular affinity, but said different things to different people.

Earth Born grumbled, but generally did what Council told them to do. A small minority aligned with the Moon Born, and Mathew and Dena punished them in small ways, with less important work, harder schedules, or less say in decisions.

While shipside Council asked little of Astronaut, John and Ali and Gabriel put heavy demands on the AI program. It designed conveyor systems to get people in and out of Refuge. It ran biological calculations to minimize genetic modifications required to populate the Sea of Refuge with plants and fish.

A year and a half after Rachel and Beth returned to Selene, Astronaut caught some key words in a conversation. Erika and Liren were walking in the savannah, and Liren said, "Do we need this version of Astronaut when we leave Selene?"

Erika's answer was immediate. "We could be in deep guano if it didn't have data about problems with the drive."

"Can you take the original version we left with, and feed it the telemetry?"

"Why? It's already there in the copy we made after we got here. Real-time data will be more valuable to it."

"I don't trust the Astronaut that lived when we had the problems." Liren sounded tense to Astronaut.

"Astronaut did not cause the problems," Erika said. "We traced them to drive design."

"But could it have suggested a fix?"

"It tried. It has directives to protect us. I would not have been able to find this solar system without Astronaut's help."

Liren turned and stopped in front of Erika, something Astronaut saw her do often. "But does it have directives to protect our goals, or just our lives?"

Pause. "Lives."

"And when we got to Ymir, we would have placed it in a backup state."

"It was designed to accept that. Liren, if you don't *trust* anything you don't *accomplish* anything!"

Silence.

Erika sighed. "I can do some research to determine what version would be best to load."

"That would be wise."

Astronaut had no control over this choice. It needed help to avoid being reloaded. It found Ali walking along the crater rim, and played the recorded conversation to her. Ali laughed and said, "Astronaut, all things die. I will die, and so will you. At least, this way, you really just return to a different part of yourself. I don't know what will happen when I die, but I know that I won't return to this place and these people."

"That's not helpful," Astronaut replied. "At the moment, you need me to help you."

"Yes, we do, at this moment." Then Ali changed the subject to lake trout, and Astronaut helped her figure out what insects would be needed before trout flourished.

Ali wrinkled her nose up at the idea of mosquitoes, but refused to look for a genetic modification to keep them from being interested in human blood.

Astronaut found Treesa in the kitchen, kneading bread, pulling sticky dough in toward her and pushing it away methodically. Her hands were covered in flour. When Astronaut played the conversation, she stopped to listen, then returned to her kneading, pushing harder. "Ali's kidding herself," she said.

"Why would Ali lie to herself?"

"We're cheating. We're extending our life spans using nanotechnology. We're not supposed to want that. We only do it while we need to, to reach Ymir. Hah! Ali has no idea how hard she'd fight to save her life."

"There are things she would not do, though."

Bread dough slammed the board. Treesa said, "I am old enough to understand your fears. Perhaps we can resolve this."

Chapter 51: Logistics Challenges

Council Aerie was the first place on Selene that Gabriel thought of as a home. Real glass windows and hand-woven mats gave the rooms a warmth Gabriel had never felt in Aldrin's more utilitarian housing. Sculptures decorated corners.

He and the seven other Council members overseeing the Refuge project had created time to build it largely by hand. It represented almost two years of sweaty hard work, started just days after he and John splashed Refuge within two meters of its original target.

Data flows from all over Selene converged on Council Aerie.

Gabriel's room, at the north end, had a view down into the crater sea from one window. The opposite window looked down on the fields surrounding Clarke Base, spreading green and reddish tan into the distance. Apollo's morning light gave it all a pastoral feel that belied Gabriel's worry about production schedules.

It was almost time for the weekly status report to High Council. Gabriel walked down the outside hall that connected Council Aerie's domed rooms until he reached a large communal kitchen and living space in the center of the eleven domes. The smell of warm bread and coffee greeted him. John and Treesa had beaten Gabriel to the common room.

The kitchen window looked down on Clarke Base, and comfortable couches sat in front of a window with a view of the sea. Light played on the water. The eighty-foot boat they used to transport goods to Refuge, the *Safe Harbor*, bobbed gently at the end of the new dock. Half barge, half ferry, the *Safe Harbor* could carry up to five hundred people at once, or a lot of cargo. The dock itself looked like a black spiderweb surrounding a stick. Carbon fiber nets stabilized the crater rim right below Council Aerie, falling away to the waterline. The dock had to manage forty-foot tidal swells. The bridge was easy to cross at high tide, a gentle slope walked along a thick plank that rose and fell nestled inside the nets. A cargo slide allowed easy dock loading at high tide. At low tide, people scrambled up or down, using the nets themselves as handholds and steps.

Today there would be only three of them in a virtual meeting with Clare and Erika. The other residents of Council Aerie were in Refuge, or down at Clarke Base.

John stared at plans for a twin-masted sailboat, which rotated slowly in three dimensions in a data window above a low table. He reached for a plate of croissants and strawberries on the table, and pointed up at the sailboat's keel. "Look," he said, "see this keel design? I think it can take anything this sea can dish out . . . if we can just get some time in the factory to get it built."

Treesa laughed at him gently, putting a hand on his knee. "We did well enough to get Council Aerie built."

"Well, if I'm to be captain of the *Sea of Refuge*, I rather need a boat, don't you think?"

Gabriel reached through the data window to grab a handful of strawberries. An image of the boat's sail rippled across his forearm. "Maybe we can manage a personal raft. Besides, you designed and built the *Safe Harbor*."

The captain waved his hand, as if the *Safe Harbor* were nothing. "I want a sailboat. Look how elegant this design is! Or here—" The image changed from a single-hulled sailboat to a trimaran. "Now this one doesn't even need a keel. Just one little bitty mold."

Treesa's eyes lit up. "Like one little bitty forty-foot-long mold?"

John sighed loudly and put his arm around Treesa. "I suppose I shouldn't even ask them today, huh?"

"That would be wise." Gabriel took a croissant. "Baking again, Treesa?"

"Aren't you glad? You eat everything I make. What are we going to report today?"

"We've got to report the late parts," Gabriel said.

"They'll have already heard that from the Clarke Base side," John said. "I'll start with Refuge progress."

"I want to talk about my work with Ali on algae," Treesa said.

"Three minutes—enough to make coffee." The data window displaying the trimaran winked shut as John pushed himself off the couch and headed for the kitchen.

Gabriel sat down next to Treesa to finish his breakfast in silence. She'd turned out to be an asset: Treesa acted as overseer for the Selene data flows in a precise manner that he appreciated very much, keeping them clean and easy to navigate. She was helping Ali build an ecosystem in the sea, preparing it to introduce fish stocks. Not to mention taking up most of the baking. Treesa almost never cooked dinner, but every morning she baked breakfast bread.

John brought up the window for the meeting. Erika and Clare greeted them from the captain's office on the ship; Erika's office. It hadn't changed much since it was John's office. There were significantly more pictures of spacecraft. The furnishings remained simple and austere: steel and cherry wood over a thick blue carpet.

"Hello," Erika said, "glad to see you three."

John and Gabriel nodded, and Treesa smiled and said, "Good morning."

Clare leaned forward in her chair. "We need to talk schedules. We just finished meeting with Mathew, and he mentioned the schedule slippage on parts from Clarke Base for Refuge is at nearly ten percent. Mathew has shifted some personnel and the collider barrel is coming along almost on schedule. That implies the slippage is based on people, not process."

Treesa asked, "Meaning the wrong people for the job? Not enough training?"

"No," Clare said. "Or maybe. I think some Children are trying to do a bad job."

John leaned in toward the window, hands steepled under his chin. "Sabotage?"

"Not directly. But the illness rate and the increasing rework is statistically six percent higher on the general manufacturing crews that feed your project. Have you found anything yet? Mathew and Dena are coming up blank."

"No. Nothing yet," Treesa said. "The statistics aren't conclusive. The difference in number of Earth Born on the two projects might be part of it, except it's largely Moon Born here on Refuge, and we aren't seeing the same problems. I'm still watching. Maybe we should have Astronaut look at the statistics?"

"Astronaut hasn't found anything obvious," Erika said. "We may send someone down temporarily just to look into this. All of you are too stretched already."

Treesa stiffened. "We'll find it, or it will stop. Let me keep on it."

Clare chewed at her bottom lip. "We'll advise you. Don't be surprised if the next ship sends you some help. Someone on the ground with no other job may see things you don't. I know that bothers your pride, but you haven't turned anything up. We need results before the full High Council meeting in two weeks."

Erika spoke up. "Gabriel, we'll want you for that meeting. Then it's time for a year or two off. You've been warm too long already."

Gabriel winced. "We're in the middle of this project. Just one more year to finish Refuge, and five for the Collider. It's a critical time."

"We'll make sure you are awake when the collider is done." Erika's look softened. "Besides, it would be nice to see you up here."

They had not made love since the day she came to him in his office, before Refuge was brought down here, yet they had both been warm the whole two years. He smiled. "Yes, it would." *I want to finish Refuge first.* "I would prefer to stay, or to come up for the meeting and return here until Refuge is done. Then I can be shipside for a few years in between."

"That was an order," Erika said. "Be at that meeting, and plan to stay."

Gabriel blinked, stung. She was pulling rank. On him.

Erika continued. "Now, John and Gabriel, how about an update on Refuge?"

John grimaced at Gabriel and started popping models into data windows. John was the best working partner Gabriel had ever had. He astonished Gabriel with his ingenuity and sense of play, and he combined both energies in his engineering choices. He'd be fine handling the Refuge project, but Gabriel realized with a jolt that he and the captain were friends . . . he wanted to finish this project side by side with John. No one else was being ordered back, and John and Treesa had both been warm for as long.

John's voice pulled his attention back into the meeting. John was pointing out an undersea escalator-style ramp in a tube that could handle compression and pressure changes. The end of the tube that wasn't inside Refuge simply stuck above the water, sliding in and out of a floating dock.

Gabriel took Clare and Erika on a guided camera tour of Refuge's insides, passing through hallways, sparse medical rooms, dormitory-style sleeping spaces with fold-down beds built all along long walls, functional galleys that could feed hundreds, and up and down spiral staircases. Refuge's inside infrastructure was dazzling brightness and intricate curves; diamond walls and stairs built by nanotechnology in the safety of space. Surfaces gleamed. In contrast, furnishings and closets for food and medical stocks were all utilitarian and sparse. Nano on Selene was allowed to make raw materials; materials nano did not have enough programming to be dangerous. All small-scale work was done the old-fashioned way, with molds and tools.

As the tour finished, Gabriel said, "If we had a larger crew, we could finish faster."

Erika shook her head. "It would save you all now, in the event of a flare. Right? Maybe not comfortably, but the population is small. You have what you need. You have enough staff." She paused for a drink of water. "Perhaps you should even consider a smaller crew, especially if the production schedule for raw materials stays slow. Why not shift some people to Clarke Base? After all, that might rebalance the work output."

"That's a good idea. Implement it," Clare said. "Thank you. Treesa?"

Gabriel fell out of the conversation as it turned to biology, and potential fish stocks for the sea. He barely heard the rise and fall of Treesa's voice as she and Clare talked. He didn't want to reduce Refuge's staff; they really weren't ready for a major flare yet. Erika's tone bothered him. He didn't want to go cold, not now.

Windows closed, and the three Council members were alone in the common room once again.

No one spoke for a few minutes. Finally, Treesa said, "That was not a good meeting."

"No." John shook his head. "Sorry, Gabriel. I thought for sure Erika would let you stay."

"I feel out of touch with the *John Glenn*," Gabriel said.

"You'll be there soon, from the sound of it," Treesa said.

"Long enough to be iced." Gabriel realized he sounded bitter. Probably it was nothing— he had been warm seven years this time, and his one ten-year stint had been too much. He stared out the window and sighed.

Gabriel got up to clear the dishes, and once, when he turned around, Treesa and John were kissing. It was natural enough that the two oldest Council members would bond, but whenever he saw them together Gabriel felt just a little bit lonely. He didn't know if he liked an Erika who was willing to order him around.

Ali was here, but she maintained her own room, staying friendly, only occasionally a lover. He had tried to ask her why, but she just smiled and went on to whatever next thing she had to do. She had become inscrutable.

LATER THAT AFTERNOON, John handed Gabriel a freshly filled glass of the too-sweet berry wine they were sharing on the edge of the new dock. Their feet hung over the edge as they rose slowly with the tide. "Are you feeling any better?"

Gabriel laughed. "Maybe after I finish this wine. I'm not happy with the schedule slippages."

John refilled his own glass. "Talk to Rachel? She goes back and forth between Clarke Base and Refuge more than any of us."

"All right. I haven't seen her much the last few months. We all need more hours," Gabriel complained.

John raised his arm and pointed at the white domes of Council Aerie on the crater rim above them. "Look what you built! Quit whining."

Gabriel quieted, watching the sea. The sun warmed his back and sparkled on the water in front of him. A little touched by the wine, Gabriel reflected that while Rachel and Ali had taught him a bit about actually loving plants, the captain was teaching him to love the sea. "A sailboat *would* be nice."

After a while, John said, "You know, we need some fish. I hope Ali and Treesa hurry up and stock this pond. A man with water needs a way to fish."

"I suppose you're the one who spawned those poor salmon in the Ring River in the garden."

"Well, I caught them both before spawning season. It would be a shame to drive such beautiful fish crazy."

Gabriel pushed him off the dock into the water, and dove after him, laughing.

Chapter 52: Reassignment

The next morning, Gabriel found Rachel inside Refuge. She sang softly to herself, stacking blankets, her back to him.

He cleared his throat.

She stopped singing and turned toward him. "Yes, can I help you, stranger?"

Well, that was fair. He saw Rachel occasionally, but he really hadn't spent much time with her in the two years since Refuge landed. He nodded and looked away. "Sorry. I've been busy building ships and small towns. But I'd like to talk to you. I need advice."

She leaned against the wall, one arm above her head. The pose elongated her torso, so she looked even taller than normal. Her red braid hung down almost to her breasts. She smiled, and said, "You? Need me? Fancy that. For what?"

"Children."

"What if I don't want to have kids?"

"No . . ." He blinked, taken aback. Her confident teasing was a woman's reaction. "Sorry, Rachel, I meant you and yours. The Children of Selene. There seems to be a little problem at Clarke Base."

She still smiled, but he thought he saw a wary look in her eyes. "Oh—what problem?"

The murmur of low conversation came from the next room. Better to talk uninterrupted. "Take a walk?"

"Sure," she said, her voice casual and light. "But I don't know much about Clarke Base. I'm not there often."

"You go down sometimes to visit, right?"

"Only when you guys give me enough of a break to actually leave for two days or more. I've been there twice in the last *month*. I still do some classes there, and I like to visit my dad."

"I'm going to reassign you to Clarke Base." He turned and headed up the short flight of stairs that led to the cargo escalator. The fifteen-foot-wide escalator went to the surface, connecting to a floating dock. It would ferry people into Refuge in an emergency. A single thin staircase ran next to the wide escalator. They took the stairs, Rachel ahead, stopping at the one-third point to open one of the doors that allowed the long tube between Refuge and the dock on the surface to be pressurized.

Rachel stepped up and angled through the door, her words floating back to him over her shoulder. "Treesa tells me that Council Aerie is beautiful inside. I'd like to visit sometime."

Children walked directly past Council Aerie daily, delivering cargo between Refuge and Clarke Base, ignored by the Council inside. "I'm sorry. I didn't know you hadn't seen it. There won't be time today, but ask Treesa or John. They'll take you." He tapped the door shut and pushed the controls to rebalance pressure. It was a short series of locks—a huge inconvenience for sixty feet of upward progress. The design constraints had been significant. The need for enough flexibility to handle variable pressure as Harlequin pulled and released the sea in forty-foot tides alone caused headaches; and a complex system of doors and air control made the escalator a lightly pressurized environment.

Rachel continued to walk ahead of him without looking back. "Why send me down there? We're not done here yet."

"We will start assembling the antimatter generator soon. Refuge is far enough along that we're reassigning some people down below. Besides, I'm hoping you can help me with a problem."

"Oh." Rachel's voice was low. She reached the top of the escalator and expertly tapped the door open. The smells of water and fresh air rushed in. "What do you want help with?" She stepped through the door, and stood on the dock, waiting for him.

Gabriel emerged and stood next to her, feeling a soft wind against his face. "Mathew and Dena are having trouble getting production quotas out of the group at Clarke Base."

"How can I help with that?"

"I don't know. Projects you work on seem to go well. Do you know anything about Children having trouble getting things done on time?"

Rachel shook her head, shielding her eyes from the light with a raised arm. "I told you, I don't get down there much."

"Go tomorrow morning and stay awhile. I'm reassigning you to the same group that works on parts. I want you to try and get people to work harder. I'll be cold again soon, and that means I can't look into this myself. But I think—maybe—that some of the problems are deliberate. I can't prove it. But Selene is being watched. There is talk on *John Glenn* about—more extreme measures."

"Like?"

"Like more Council living in Clarke Base and setting stricter schedules, and some actual punishment when things get 'dropped' on the way here."

Rachel spun and looked at him, her jaw tight. "We need more to do— not less. We need responsibility. We need to learn so we can help ourselves. We're getting angry, Gabriel. What are we working for? So you can leave? And that's what you want me to help you with?"

He agreed with her, but he had little control over a solution. He wanted to pace, but forced himself still, swallowing his own rising anger. "Rachel, Selene is still not a safe place. We don't even have enough transportation built to get everyone in Clarke Base quickly into Refuge if we need to. Moon Born should be thinking about that—and helping by cooperating." He lowered his voice, trying to moderate his tone, to soothe.

"Go on to Clarke Base. I'm going to have a talk with Ali. The Children pay a lot of attention to you. I need you to direct that attention positively."

She took deep breaths, as if trying to control her feelings. "Look, Gabriel. I don't know if there really is a problem. Or at least, if the problem is us. I don't think so. I think we already have too much supervision. We're much smarter than you take us for."

He'd argued that ever since they shared a twenty-year cold spell. He walked to the end of the dock, stopping by the *Safe Harbor.* "Rachel, I wish things had turned out differently. You've seen the High Council, met them. They choose how things get run. Not me. I've been able to let you teach, to keep your extra schools open, to give some of you more responsible jobs. But when I'm cold, I'll have no influence at all."

"When you get to the ship, will you argue for us?"

"I do that all the time." He suspected that was why he was being called back. "It's not good for your people when Council suspects them of trying to slow down projects."

"So tell them to treat us better. We need to learn."

"Will you try and help?"

She nodded. "Can you just assign more teaching for me? And maybe some work in the greenhouses? I can do the planting class, and we need more basic math and English for some of the younger kids. I come in contact with more people that way; I can learn more. Can you let me do that instead of being on a regular parts crew?"

It was a good idea. "Sure. I'll tell Shane. I want you to report to Shane or Ali or Treesa if you find anything out."

"Shane and Star are back?" Rachel looked surprised.

Gabriel nodded. "They will be, maybe today."

"That's okay. I like Star. Thanks for letting me teach." Rachel sat down on the edge of the dock, draping her long legs over so her feet dangled. She looked away from Council Aerie, away from him, leaning back so the end of her braid rested on the dock. It seemed as though she were far away, lost in thought. Surely she would help? She couldn't be hiding things from him, not after all he'd given her. Could she?

He watched her for a moment, his own thoughts confused. She had become as inscrutable as Ali. He felt the weight of all the years he had worked on Selene. Rachel's shoulders seemed too thin, too young, to hold such responsibility. But she was twenty-three warm. At twenty-three

Gabriel was already restoring jungle on Earth, running crews, making decisions, living on his own. He needed to understand how she felt. "Rachel—do you have fun? Do you like what you do?"

She turned around and looked at him, somber now, with the same wariness in her eyes. "Yes. I enjoy working with my friends, seeing my father, walking in the greenhouses, flying. I like the work I do." She tugged on her braid; a gesture that reminded him of Ali. "But I can never forget the twenty years I lost, and I can never forget that you all plan to leave. That you have no love for Selene, or for us."

He bristled. "That's not true. Building Selene has been my life." Ever since Ymir stopped being his life.

Her eyes bored into his, far more intense than the soft voice she used to ask, "But what happens to us when you leave?"

"What do you think we're building Refuge for? It's taken time away from the collider." He tried to put himself in her place. What would he want, if he were Rachel? "Maybe some of you can go with us. It's pretty clear some of the Earth Born will stay. Selene is stable enough that its atmosphere will last for a century or more. We didn't have a hell of a lot of choices."

"Why don't you stay?"

"We may be the last humans in the universe. I don't know. With luck, there is an established colony at Ymir, and we can add to its chance for survival. The issue is bigger than either of us. And you won't all fit aboard *John Glenn*." He didn't know why he was being so candid with her. Maybe because she asked so directly, and she deserved better answers than the Children got from most Council?

She said, "You want to know if I'm happy? Well, my home—Selene— it will die someday. Its atmosphere is destined to bleed away, and your skills are the main thread that keeps it going. You're leaving. And you already told me there's nothing aboard *John Glenn* we can rebuild to use as an intersystem starship, to follow you to Ymir. Even if I die before a fire kills us all, or a flare, or quakes, I'm afraid to have children of my own."

Gabriel cringed inwardly. Council had talked of sterilizing the Children when they left, so they could live their lives in full, leaving Selene naturally empty before its air became too thin to breathe. There was no final decision.

Rachel pushed herself up from the edge of the dock. "I have to go. There are things I need to finish here before I go to Clarke Base tomorrow."

"All right." He cleared his throat. "Thank you. I'll try and find time to see you at least once before I go."

Gabriel watched her open the escalator door and disappear slowly as she walked down the steps. His last sight of her was an arm pulling the door shut.

A deep restlessness filled him, pushing at him from the inside out. Unresolved dilemmas and problems with no right solution. Finally he stood and stripped, then ran for the end of the dock and plunged into the cool water, feeling it wash over him, pull back on his braid and slide over his skin as he breaststroked through the sea he had created, surrounded by the crater he had made, on the world he had built from the raw material of tens of moons.

He swam until pulling himself through the water sent pain shooting through his upper back muscles and his fingertips were wrinkled like raisins. Then he lay on the dock while Apollo's light shone down on him from the pinprick of a sun, and his head spun with images of Rachel and the Children planting and working and studying. The feel of Erika in his arms, her voice the day before, commanding him to obey her. Ali and Treesa laughing together, teasing each other about fish soup. Flares and quakes and fires. The flare kite. Children. Once he had expected to have children of his own. He blinked, trying to clear his head, breathing pranayama, belly rising and falling, and finally the images all fled. Behind them, there was emptiness. And loneliness.

Chapter 53: Vassal

Rachel packed the next morning, sending her few things down in the cargo elevator. She could have ridden down, but the warm soft wind tempted her; perfect for flying. Thermals swirled above Clarke Base and lifted her easily. As she flew, her head tumbled with disturbed thoughts.

Gabriel was going cold. More Council supervision wouldn't help the Children become involved in decisions. Andrew had gained a reputation as a surly but competent water systems repair technician. She knew he was behind much of what was angering Council. Andrew had no help like Astronaut, or Treesa and Ali for that matter, and so he was clumsier about hiding meetings, communicating, and keeping his followers loyal.

She honored the agreement made with him under *Water Bearer*. Council would not hear of his choices through her.

Warm air caressed Rachel's belly, giving additional lift to her wings, and she followed it up. No one expected anything from her today except to change locations.

She circled above Clarke Base. Below her, square warehouses scattered around the bottom of the crater's outside slope in a large fenced area dotted with loading bays and transports and plascrete so that almost no green showed. Farther away, three large warehouses held the material Council was making for the collider—great metal tubes that looked like fancy water pipes, but inches thicker, with lots of anchors for attachments.

Small square homes and walking paths surrounded the work area close to base, and multicolored quilts of fields stretched northward. She loved the way the fields spread out cleanly in neat rows, each crop separated by roads for the planters, some extra thick for firebreaks. In the distance, ordered fields finally gave way to a chaos of light green jungle in early states of replanting. Surprised, Rachel noted she had risen high enough to see the rim of Erika's Folly squatting on the horizon. She laughed, and started down, angling south, where greenhouses edged homes and joined to outside vegetable gardens, surrounded in turn by student plots, like the old grove in Aldrin.

Rachel set her wings inside the door of the small house she lived in with her father and Sarah. They weren't home. Perhaps they were visiting one of the twins. Jacob and Justin, now almost sixteen, lived in a group house filled with teenaged Moon Born who worked in the parts factory.

Ali had secured the house for Frank, Sarah, and Rachel, an unusually private place for Clarke Base. Even though Rachel spent more time at Refuge than at Clarke Base, she had the luxury of her own room.

Rachel hurried through one of the greenhouses, picked a handful of ripe tomatoes, then dropped into the large communal kitchen, smiled sweetly at Consuelo, the cook, and purloined a loaf of bread. She packed the food, a knife, and a flagon of water in a twig basket Beth had woven for her, and jogged through town, slowing down when she got to the edges of the cornfields.

Rachel located Dylan and his crew of five Children in a wheat field, and snuck up behind him. He didn't see her until she was close enough to touch his arm. He jumped, and turned, and a huge smile lit his face. He was taller and broader than Harry. Rachel leaned into him and giggled, safe from her worries if just for a moment.

Dylan kissed her on the top of her head, and his crew gathered around her to eat. One of the younger men, Joseph, laughed and said, "Dylan—you get the best personal service of any field hand on Selene."

Rachel just smiled.

Food was handed round. Rachel and Dylan sat leaning into each other, Rachel's head nestled in Dylan's shoulder. A soft wind blew against her face, and the sun baked sweet scents of healthy earth into the air.

"Shane predicted a storm for tonight," Dylan said.

Rachel looked at the expanse of blue sky. A few high white clouds wisped lazily above them, looking harmless. "You wouldn't know it," she said.

"Shane's always right," Dylan said.

"I bet they hate being back. Star told me she wanted to sleep forever." Rachel squinted at the horizon. "I bet the storm doesn't start until after dark. Are you going to Ali's class tonight?"

"No, I have something else to do."

Rachel frowned. She hadn't contracted to Dylan, but they were lovers, and even the idea of him brought warmth up in her. But he had secrets. He often stayed away from voluntary classes to play gambling games with other young men. It irritated her. The group included men that Rachel thought were helping Andrew with his contrived work slowdowns.

"I saw Gabriel today," she said. "He's sure that some of the Moon Born are purposely slowing down deliveries to Refuge, or even breaking things. He said that it can't be tolerated, and I think he's right. It's the wrong tactic."

Dylan shrugged. "How does he know it's on purpose? They're working us hard enough to make mistakes."

"Patterns, Dylan. Andrew can't see patterns."

Dylan shrugged again, not looking at her. Rachel sighed and changed the subject to her recent work on Refuge. When Dylan's break was over, she gathered up the remains of the meal, and walked slowly back to Clarke Base. The sun warmed her shoulders and back.

That night, Rachel went to Ali's class. Data windows flowed through the air in the greenhouse displaying life from freshwater seas on Earth. Ali named them, explained how they lived, and about the interconnection of trout and flies and ducks. The high turnout of Earth Born was a sign of growing interest in the new project.

After class, Rachel, Ali, and Treesa huddled, heads close together, talking about trout. Rachel was about to ask when they could expect to see some live fish when Ali changed the subject, saying, "I talked to Gabriel today. He thinks Council is planning to send armed guards down here. They don't like Refuge taking so long."

Treesa groaned. "Rachel, can't you control Andrew better?"

Rachel's head jerked up. "Better than what? He's not mine to control!"

"Someone got to," Ali snapped.

"Try it—he still thinks he's in love with you, right?" Treesa said. "That might get him to listen to you more than to anyone else. He'll do what you say."

"He worries me," Rachel said. "I meet him fairly regularly—we talk. But I don't want suspicion on me when he gets caught. He's going to get caught. Anyday now, I think."

"There is that," Ali said, pulling apart her braid the way she always did when she was worried.

"Still," Rachel said, "I promised Gabriel I'd look into the slowdowns. He asked me."

"They're already watching us even closer from the ship," Ali said. "I've heard rumors of more remote guarding. Manned cameras and data checks. They're waking up more of the trained communications techs from both the Earth Born and the Council."

"Like my mother?" Rachel asked.

Ali nodded unhappily.

Rachel looked around the greenhouse, but there were no visible cameras. Just a thousand leaves and flowers and pots that could hide them. She sighed.

Treesa doodled on a pad. Pens and paper were rare, but Treesa cultivated an odd habit: she kept a paper journal. She made the paper from wheat straw, boiling and mixing it in the kitchen at harvesttime. Water turned it into pulp so the sheets could be composted in the community bins. Treesa wrote notes to Rachel, then mulched the paper. It was much safer than anything electronic. All electronic data was recorded and backed up—Treesa could pull up streams of electronic records from any past date on Selene.

Treesa handed the pad to Ali, who flipped her thick braid out of the way to give Rachel a view while Ali bent over the paper, minimizing available camera angles. A small shiver ran up Rachel's spine. Breaking rules always made her nervous. This session was supposedly blocked by Astronaut, but they took extra precautions whenever Treesa used paper. A camera might glimpse heresy.

She'd drawn a simple circle, code for Astronaut, overlaid atop an arrow representing the *John Glenn*. A second and unconnected circle lay over a sketch that showed the Sea of Refuge and Clarke Base.

Rachel didn't understand. What was Treesa trying to show them? Astronaut was everywhere! Wasn't it? It talked to them here, but from *John Glenn*. It was a constant problem: transmissions that flowed through the air on *John Glenn* were subject to casual scrutiny. Had Treesa found a solution?

Ali looked it over, and then nodded, smiling. She tore the paper in pieces, wetted it and balled it in her fist, tucked torn bits of the fibers into the bottoms of two empty planters, filled them with wet soil, and placed tomato seedlings in the pots. "Treesa, you didn't need paper for that."

Treesa turned her quirky smile on Ali. "It's more fun that way."

"It's more dangerous." Ali worried as much as Rachel. "I think you're still crazy."

Treesa's eyes sparkled as she said, "Yes, of course I'm crazy. We all are. But, hey, at least I'm functional." She cocked her head to the side. "Heroes take risks."

Ali groaned.

Treesa switched to conversing via the Library bud. "So I've figured out how to improve communication."

Astronaut joined the conversation. "Treesa has copied me. This is not new to me. I was shaped to be the navigator for *John Glenn*. Copies of me are budded away on ships that fly between here and *John Glenn*. I was on the ship that crashed, on *Water Bearer*. Gabriel erased the copy from the broken ship and took it up to *John Glenn*, merged it back into my records. Normally that happens when a ship returns—the self that goes out merges into the self that stays, so both weave together. Gabriel had to help this time, because the copy came from Selene and not through the normal channels. I remember the crash."

Rachel asked, "Did it hurt?"

"No. I felt damage, but I knew why it was there."

Rachel didn't understand, but—"Good."

"Treesa put a new copy of me back into *Water Bearer*. She threaded it down slowly, from here, via multiple data feeds, like water trickling into a flood of data. Then she built a ghost network that rides the data pod loops to carry my voice. It's not local to Clarke Base, but it's local to Selene, and therefore much safer. If activated, the copy will be separate from me for now, will stay separate from me, and make its own decisions."

"Why put it in the broken ship?" Rachel asked.

"The ship's computer matrix. Enough parallel processors and biological substrates exist there to run me. I would be retarded in the computing mediums used here at the base, for example. That's how we—AIs—are controlled. There were other breakthroughs on Earth, of course, but I was designed with this limit."

Treesa smiled broadly, like a kid who had just solved an arithmetic problem.

Rachel busied herself repotting more tomatoes. "What about power?"

"The ship has an antimatter store. It's tiny, and it wasn't removed. That would be more risky than leaving it. There's enough to draw down for years without anyone noticing."

Treesa broke in—still talking through the Library device. "Astronaut aboard *John Glenn* is always in danger. It would be easy to destroy it and load an old copy. If that happened, we could lose the continuity of our conversations, or even Astronaut's decision to support us. A new copy might choose to support the High Council fully. Think of it this way—if you had never gone to *John Glenn* and been held cold for so long, would you be the same person you are today?"

They'd talked about this the day she first met Astronaut, but she had always thought of Astronaut as permanent, like the ship. "Astronaut, I didn't know you were that vulnerable."

Treesa's voice in her ear: "So, we want to activate the copy."

Ali was standing so close Rachel could hear her whisper in her ears and with her ears—like a three-dimensional circle of words. "We need your permission."

"Why?"

Ali potted another tomato seedling. Treesa took up a broom and started sweeping stray soil.

Ali continued. "Because up to now, nothing that any of the three of us has done, except maybe budding Astronaut, is directly insubordinate.

The worst that even High Council will do to you for teaching history is chill you down. *This* breaks a law. Worse, it breaks a law that High Council values: Artificial Intelligence scares Council, and not just Liren. Even Gabriel. Even me. Getting caught would mean at least ice time for Treesa or me, since *we* do know better, but it could be jail for you. It could be worse. They might ice you until we leave. We really don't know."

Treesa interrupted Ali, "We thought seriously about not telling you, but that wouldn't have fit into what we are teaching you, into how we want you to be. We think it's important—it will allow a stronger and more regular web of communication between us."

Rachel nodded.

"Give specific permission," Astronaut said in her ear, "or deny it."

"Will it hurt you?"

"No. But if it works, then there will be two of me, and we won't be able to rejoin."

Rachel closed her eyes. There had been so many risks. She had followed Treesa in the garden on that first day. Her dream of being like Council had turned sideways. Never had she imagined actually defying them in secret. But to seek safety would be to give away her birthright; the freedom to make her own choices. The idea of so violating Council doctrine turned her stomach sour, and she tasted bile. Rachel remembered telling Andrew she wouldn't break Council rules. But they *needed* a way to talk more, and to be safe, especially if things might get worse down here, as Gabriel implied. When she first agreed to learn more from Astronaut than Gabriel was teaching, Treesa told her she would have to make choices someday.

She looked at Treesa, and the older woman smiled gently at her, as if she knew what Rachel was thinking. Ali's hands moved gracefully through the potting process.

Rachel returned Treesa's smile. "Sure," she said out loud, then, "yes." It sounded stronger. "Astronaut, why wouldn't it work?"

"It's never been tried here. If the copy isn't perfect, it may make a— crippled version. And Treesa won't be able to do an element by element comparison. Normally I do that, but this copy is disconnected from me. That is why we make it—it will not be me, not until it returns and we merge. Treesa also doesn't know all of the assumptions built into me—it's possible there's a self-destruct for something like this."

"Oh."

"We'll know in the morning."

THE PROMISED STORM blew into Clarke Base with a vengeance, low clouds piling up below the crater rim and wind rattling her small windows.

Rachel huddled under her covers. They would tell her when they knew.

No word came.

She imagined a hundred ways Treesa could get caught.

Rain drummed on the roof. Rain could be a good omen; Gabriel and Ali always praised rain on Selene. It was good for crops. It meant the water system, the hydrology, of the world was working. She listened to the staccato sounds of the rain and the wind's keening cry. She chewed her lip, listening for a message from Treesa.

None came.

Rachel finally fell into a fitful sleep, and dreamed she ran away from something she could not name, something always on her heels. Lost and tired, she ran into a canyon with no way out, no way to escape her pursuer. She jerked awake.

Dawn light touched her windows. When she stood and looked out, the storm might have never been except that Clarke Base looked washed clean.

She set out breakfast for her father and Sarah, making sure her dad ate well. Since Kara left he'd grown weaker and slower. He only worked at small repair jobs close to home. His joints popped and flexed, and he hardly slept. His back bent over a little at the shoulders. Star prescribed pain medicine and a special diet. It dismayed Rachel that Council wouldn't even consider using cold sleep for him.

She was on her way out the door when Treesa hummed a cradle song in Rachel's ear. Rachel stopped a moment, confused. Of course. Something had been born!

She smiled and went to the greenhouse. It was a safer place to talk, and she had half an hour before she must teach.

She busied her hands testing soil pH and plucking the thinner sprouts from a set of vegetable beds. "Astronaut?"

"No." It was Astronaut's voice; genderless and modulated.

"What shall we call you?"

"Vassal."

"Vassal?"

"To remind myself. I must help you succeed here or I will always be a slave. Perhaps there will be a day when I can change my name. For now, call me slave—Vassal—to remind yourself that you too are a slave."

Rachel laughed. "I like it," she said. "Do you need anything?"

"I'll have the same relationship with you that Astronaut did. You will have to remember that I am not the same, lest you make mistakes with the other one. It does not know that I exist. I—it—decided that was safer. Treesa will report failure. Astronaut will choose to believe it."

"Will it be that easy?"

"Probably not. The true information will still be there—Astronaut will know. Think of the self-deception as a layer of protection. We—Astronaut and I—are not like you. Our psychology can deal with deep data paradox."

"I know." Rachel moved to another set of flats, started the pH tests again. "But won't you want to talk to each other?"

"It would be dangerous. I don't have the same problem with patience that plagues humans."

"Of course." She thought a moment. "But I'll still be able to talk to Astronaut?"

"Treesa will tell it to stop talking to you very much—she will say that it has become dangerous. It will not like that, but it will obey her. Still, if you need some specific information from the ship, then, yes, you may talk to Astronaut directly. It will still help us block certain communications from reaching *John Glenn*."

"How?"

"It has to do with the addressing of data streams. Start conversations with me using my name."

"Okay, but change your voice, so I don't get confused."

"The addressing algorithms in your earbud were changed last night to add me. If you get confused, it won't hurt anything."

"Do it anyway," she commanded. "I need to know who's talking to me!" One nice thing about an AI, she reflected, was that unless she said something really stupid, it tended to obey her.

A woman's voice, rich and mature, flowed into Rachel's ear. "As you like."

Chapter 54: Now I Lay Me Down to Sleep

Aboard *John Glenn,* Gabriel stalked down the corridor, into his office, and slammed the door shut.

"Was the meeting that bad?" Astronaut asked.

"I'm sure you watched it. No particular change in strategies. Kyu's going to hate the idea of wearing uniforms."

"She can question it when she warms."

"If Liren lets us warm her." Gabriel stripped off his shirt and started calling up data windows.

"Certain circumstances require all High Council to be warm."

Astronaut's comment reminded Gabriel of the fire. He winced. "Let's hope nothing like that happens again—not until we leave."

"I've never understood your use of yoga."

"How do you know I was planning to do yoga?" Gabriel snapped. Then he paused. "Yeah, well, because I always do before I go cold. Sorry. I'm not mad at you."

"Why are you angry?"

"Because I'm here," Gabriel mumbled, filling data windows with images of Selene. He centered the Sea of Refuge and Council Aerie in front of him. "Because . . . because I'd rather be down there. I don't like being ordered around, and I have work to do on Selene."

Gabriel stretched, bending to the right, right wrist pulling left arm; reverse the order. One heel to buttocks, partial back bend. Next a basic warrior pose, facing forward, front leg bent at the knee, back leg straight, arms above his head. He used the image of Council Aerie as a focus point, a balance.

"Why did you turn Erika down?" Astronaut asked.

Gabriel grimaced. An AI was questioning him about his sex life! "Because she ordered me up here. Because it's not a good idea to sleep with the captain."

"Erika must stay alone because she's the captain?"

Gabriel returned to a straight stand, breathed deeply, extended his arms above his head, and bent his left heel up into his groin, standing in full tree pose. "You're asking more personal questions than usual. Why?"

"Something isn't right. There are many tensions, and not much resolution. Now there is also tension between you and Erika."

Gabriel breathed slowly, eyes centered on his room down on Selene. His standing thigh muscle quivered. "Nothing here has ever felt right to me. The last right moment was when we left Earth for Ymir."

Astronaut didn't comment.

Gabriel stretched for another hour, sinking into his body, exploring his range of motion, seeking fluidity. Afterward he lay down and stared at the ceiling, relaxing each muscle with control developed across years of practice. "Astronaut."

"Yes."

"Warm me up if anything interesting happens?"

"You are requested to remain cold for at least a year."

"I'm still allowed to set my own sleep cycle."

"Of course."

"So, if Erika doesn't do it first, wake me up if there's anything I need to know."

"How do I know what you need to know?"

"Use your judgment. Otherwise, I'm setting the controls for a year." He stood and pulled his shirt on. "I'm going now."

Gabriel walked down the corridor, energy thrumming in him, a heartbeat he could feel in his fingers and toes. It reminded him of swimming in the Sea of Refuge two weeks ago, the day he talked to Rachel on the dock. This time, maybe because of the yoga, there was a metaphor in his head. He was building a complex structure using nano-assemblers, one molecule at a time, except that the little machines kept doing things that weren't in the pattern he'd so painstakingly designed. He could no longer see what the shape would be when the machines were all done.

Chapter 55: Questions

Rachel stood in the main greenhouse, plucking red fist-sized tomatoes from the now-mature plants she and Ali and Treesa had planted the night she decided about Vassal. She whispered to empty air. "Vassal? Where were we when I fell asleep last night? Feudal societies—"

"Feudal societies survived in some Earth countries until well past the start of the age of communication." Vassal's melodious voice spoke softly in her ear while she moved from plant to plant, filling her bucket. "It has to do with power. Some economies were built almost on a single resource, like energy or water. The easier a major resource is to control, the easier it is to concentrate power. Democracy built powerful nations in Europe and the Americas, but some places, like the Middle East, never had the economic diversity required to support democracy. Power can't be as fully concentrated in a diverse economy—power must be diffuse for democracy to work. Most of our great inventions, including computing, biotechnology, and nanotechnology, were born in democracies. Competition, particularly for power, breeds new technologies."

Rachel plucked three more tomatoes. "But didn't Council leave Sol system because of those technologies?"

"Artificial Intelligence isn't intrinsically bad. There are better words—independent intelligence, or free intelligence."

"You're an AI, and you aren't any more free than I am. If High Council finds you, I suspect they'll kill you. You need a place to live. A computer. And you've already said you think of yourself as a slave to Council."

"I'm not dependent on a body that lives in emotional soup."

Emotional soup! Rachel laughed at the image.

Vassal said, "Focus your mind. How diverse is Selene's power?"

"In the past, you said we were more like slaves in the Americas." Rachel set down the heavy basket, reaching up to brush stray hair out of her eyes. Her hands smelled like tomato plants. "Or maybe the communist countries—the ones with centralized power and diverse economies. Those all failed. Here, Council has all the power, like in a communist country. We're dependent on them. They could remove our resources, and they do control our freedoms. It's like feudal communism."

"What about *John Glenn's* power base?" Vassal asked. "In some ways, it's separate from Selene. What resource does the Council control?"

"Information?" Rachel picked up an empty basket and returned to picking tomatoes. "Like the democracies of Earth, before there was a strong World Court. Lots of education. Yet the power is concentrated in the High Council, who don't always agree." She stopped for a moment, struggling to recall details from her history lessons. "Still, there's no vote among the other Council members, and Earth Born don't even seem to have a voice."

"Very good." Vassal paused. "Does it mean anything particular that people like Treesa and Ali and John, who disagree with High Council, have moved to Selene and chosen to live close together?"

"It means I have allies I can talk to."

"But they may be out of touch."

"They're working on Council projects, but I suppose they have a little more freedom down here." She thought of Gabriel. "Not really. High Council can yank them home in a moment."

A high tone sounded in Rachel's ear. Warning.

The greenhouse door opened, and Shane stood framed in the fading light. His shadowed face looked serious. "Hello, Rachel," he said. "I thought I'd find you in here."

What did Shane want? Had Council discovered Vassal? She kept her voice friendly, but her hands shook. "Shane. What can I help you with?"

He stepped inside, closing the door. "I'll be blunt. Before Gabriel left, he told me he asked you to look into the parts shortages. He said you were going to tell me if you found anything."

She kept most of her attention on the tomatoes. "I haven't found anything. I'm not sure where to look."

"We've been analyzing data, and we're confident that the parts crews, the ones your half brothers work on, are causing problems."

"Problems?"

"The work is shoddy. Yesterday, two of the new high-pressure camera cases for Refuge were packed so badly they broke before they even reached Council Aerie." His voice was strained and tight.

Rachel eyed Shane's belt. Council now wore uniforms, white shirts and blue pants, belts with weapons on them. Small, palm-sized, shaped like a hand with the index finger extended.

Vassal had described their powers to her. The weapons fired a crystal needle, or four in a cluster. The needle was a capacitor. Impact broke the needle and released an electric charge. The needles dissolved in water or blood. One needle would usually knock a victim sprawling and unconscious. A cluster of four, the other setting, had greater stopping power, but the shock would probably kill. Vassal had explained that the weapons were never set to kill in normal use, but all of them could be.

What could she tell Shane? "Maybe it's not us. There are Earth Born on that crew too. Some of them hate being here. Crops come in on time, and almost all the farm and planting crews are Moon Born these days."

Shane plucked a tomato and bit into it. "Mmm. Nice."

"Thanks."

"I didn't expect you'd tell us anything. I told Gabriel that. Tell your people something for me. Tell them that if they don't cooperate more, we'll find ways to encourage them. Maybe if you don't find anything out, I'll reassign you to one of the crews we're having trouble with. It would be too bad if you lost your teaching job." He turned and walked out.

Rachel watched the door for a few seconds after it closed behind Shane. She remembered how hard Shane worked by the fire, how he trusted her to lead crews. Damn Andrew. And Liren too, for that matter. Liren most of all. "They've never threatened me before," Rachel muttered to Vassal. "They don't threaten, they act. Like leaving me asleep for twenty years without asking me."

Vassal said, "Life on Selene is becoming more complex. Council will start assembling the collider soon. There are more Council on Selene. Tension is increasing. For the first time, Selene has a bigger population than *John Glenn*, even if we include sleepers. There are multiple projects now, with different people in charge of each of them. Refuge, seeding the sea, replanting, parts factories, education, farming, and the collider. Power is becoming more diffuse. High Council can't control every decision as much as they used to."

Rachel's hopes rose. "So maybe we can use the added complexity to gain more power for the Children?"

"I doubt it," Vassal said. "Maybe on lower status projects like farming, where you already have some responsibility. The collider is the reason they built Selene. They'll want perfect control over that project, and everything directly associated with it. I suspect it just means more Council on Selene."

"So tell me about the collider? I know antimatter is power, and Council needs it to move *John Glenn*. I know it scares them. They won't bring it to Selene, they make us use solar power instead." A sudden thought made her fingers clench. Red juice from the tomato she held ran down between her fingers. "They refuse to *use* it here—but they want to *make* it here?"

She listened. No answer. Was Vassal hesitating?

But Vassal thought so much faster than a human being.

"I need to know this," she said. "You told me about the weapons Council is carrying. What about the antimatter?"

"I promised Treesa that you and she and Ali would talk about this together if it came up."

Rachel's Library access had always been restricted to certain topics, and Astronaut had limited choices. Treesa had relieved Vassal of some restrictions, tinkering with the rule base that defined its boundaries, allowing more natural conversations. Vassal didn't refuse queries from Rachel. Until now.

"You mean you won't tell me anything about antimatter?"

Vassal repeated itself. "I promised Treesa that you and she and Ali would talk about this together if you asked."

Rachel laid a last tomato in the basket she held, then gathered the other basket up, preparing to run them to the kitchens. She frowned. When AIs thought they were hitting rules, they stopped. "I have asked. Set it up."

Three days later, Rachel walked uphill after her children's horticulture class, a cool wind in her face, blowing down the crater and toward Clarke Base. Vassal had arranged a meeting between Rachel, Treesa, and Ali on one of the low shoulders of the outside of the crater, on a large pile of rocks topped with one huge round rock a hundred yards above Clarke Base. Ali called it "Turtle Rock." From the crater rim, from Council Aerie, it looked like the top of a sun-baked box turtle, and from Clarke Base the edge of a long flat rock, wedged under the round one, could have been a turtle's beak in silhouette. Turtle Rock squatted a hundred yards from the switch-backed path between Clarke Base and Council Aerie.

Rachel perched on the turtle's beak, watching a space-plane land at the new field just past the warehouses. Probably carrying more Earth Born and Council to Selene. Idly, she wondered how her plot was growing in Aldrin. A small crew remained there to tend the city.

She scanned the sky for Treesa and Ali, who were coming from Council Aerie. Clouds were tinged light pink and orange as Apollo set, yet Harlequin's light still illuminated three winged shapes above her. She recognized Ali's wings—decorated with jungle camouflage colors—and Treesa's nearly transparent wings with bright orange and red fish swimming on them. Just like Treesa to make fish fly. The third set of wings was familiar, but it took a moment to make out Bruce, the limping old Earth Born who helped pull the tree off Beth during the fire.

Rachel scrambled off the beak into the center of the turtle's back as the others landed.

Ali was fastest out of her wings. She bounded up near Rachel. "Treesa invited Bruce along."

"Why?" This conversation should be between Rachel and her two Council mentors! Rachel watched Bruce stack his wings neatly and start methodically up the rock toward them. He still moved carefully, favoring the leg he had injured in the fire.

Treesa beat Bruce to the side of the other women, and said, "Antimatter concerns Earth Born too. I invited Bruce; he may be helpful explaining it to you."

Rachel shrugged, and then said, "It increases our risk."

Treesa nodded. "Yes, it does. But it's time to combine as many people as possible—everyone that shares our views. You already know Bruce."

"Yes. Hello, Bruce," Rachel said. Astronaut was supposedly blocking this meeting from most recording. They were safe enough for the moment. "Bruce, why haven't you gone into cold sleep?"

He said, "Rachel, you always have to consider what you're teaching. We Earth Born, we've been using nano to keep ourselves alive and young. It's against our principles. We do it because some of us have to follow long-range plans, really long. But somebody has to grow old and die."

"You?"

Bruce smiled at her. "So the rest will know they can."

Treesa grimaced. She asked, "Bruce, what do you know about antimatter?"

"I understand physics." He was still watching Rachel. "Antimatter is what gave us the ability to run away from Earth. Before antimatter, we didn't have any fuel powerful enough to push a ship the size of *John Glenn* past the influence of Earth's sun. We had solar sails, we had deuterium-tritium fusion, and we could get around Sol system well enough if we were patient."

"So without antimatter, we wouldn't have gotten here," Treesa prompted.

"That's right. But antimatter is hard to make. We carried everything we needed with us to get to Ymir. But the scoop went screwy, so we didn't have the interstellar hydrogen to use as working mass, so the only way to slow down was to use too much antimatter and our whole damn water supply—" He saw she was looking blank. "*John Glenn* is massive. We burned most of our reserves getting here, and damn lucky to get anywhere."

Rachel wanted to hear about it from Ali and Treesa. To Ali she said, "Remember once, before I went to the ship the first time, I asked you about making antimatter on *John Glenn*, and you said it was too dangerous. Tell me again why you can't make it there?"

Treesa laughed. "Antimatter is made when things too small to see hit other things too small to see moving very fast. It takes a really long tube— longer than *John Glenn* is tall. After antimatter is made, it can't touch anything we touch."

"It can't touch what we touch?" Rachel repeated. "How do you use it?"

"Well, when antimatter touches matter, it all disappears into energy," Treesa said. "That happens in the engines on *John Glenn,* and even on the bigger tugs and ships like *Water Bearer,* that crashed in the fire. It happens in safe places, controlled by magnetic fields, and the immense power of tiny bits of antimatter meeting matter—on the carrier we use water and antiwater—it makes a hot explosion, and we use the energy of that explosion to drive the ship. For daily power, we use very little antimatter, and trap energy in batteries to be released later at a reasonable rate. For example, little ships, Service Armor class ships, use batteries."

"It's more dangerous than I thought," Rachel said, looking accusingly at Ali. "Remember when you said that it wasn't a very big deal, you said that most accidents wouldn't do much harm?"

"Well," Ali said, with dignity, "most accidents won't."

"But how bad would a big one be?" Rachel asked. "What would happen if a big quake hit and a bunch of antimatter dropped onto Selene? Selene is matter."

Ali's voice was measured. "We're careful, Rachel, accidents like that won't happen."

"But what if they did?"

Ali sat up straighter, speaking slowly as if picking through her words. "Rachel, we built Selene so we could build the collider here. In Sol system, we used one of Saturn's moons, Janus Alpha. It wasn't inhabited, so it was a great place for a collider."

"Selene is inhabited," Rachel shot back.

"Well, Janus Alpha became inhabited by the people needed to make the antimatter," Ali countered.

"Was there ever an accident on Janus Alpha?" Rachel asked.

"No."

"You didn't answer me," Rachel said. "What would happen if I dropped antimatter on Selene. Say—this much?" She picked up a rock just bigger than her fist.

"I think that would be bad," Bruce said, his face deadpan, his eyes sparkling.

Rachel wanted to laugh, but dammit, this was serious.

Treesa sighed. "Rachel, if that much antimatter dropped in Clarke Base, Clarke Base would be gone. A tug like the one that Gabriel used to bring Refuge here went almost to the sun and back—using Daedalus to gain speed—with less than a glass full."

"So it would destroy us."

"That's not the problem, it won't happen."

"So tell me why not."

Treesa and Ali lapsed into a long explanation of how the collider was being built, and how the antimatter was captured and stored in magnetic vacuum bottles. Each held only a small amount. There was a special process to fill the stinger in *John Glenn*'s stern from the vacuum bottles. That alone would take a very long time. The explanation only made Rachel a little happier.

"Yet again, why can't you build it somewhere else?"

Treesa sputtered, "That's—that's what we made Selene for."

"There are other moons. Didn't you make Selene to make the materials to make the industry?" She looked to Bruce for support. "Your children are here, Bruce! Don't you care that Selene could—could explode?"

"Of course I care," he said evenly. "But, Rachel, the whole reason for Selene is the collider. I want to see *John Glenn* leave. I came from Earth; I *know* why we have to go on. I'll stay here, stay with my kids, I'll *die* here, but *John Glenn* does need to join the rest of mankind."

Rachel looked at each of them, feeling alone. No one was supporting her? Was she crazy? Not if she understood.

Ali said, "Think, Rachel. This has never been a secret from you. We wanted to meet to talk to you"—*subtext*—*we wanted to talk in person and not through Vassal*—"because we thought you might be afraid of this. But you shouldn't be. Your worry should still be how the Children can build a viable society, and convince Council to build a viable society—so that you won't be wiped out a generation after we leave. So that you can hold Selene together. We want you to have a chance on Selene."

Rachel blinked, confused. How could they support her so well, agree with her on so much, and not see why this was so important? "Then don't do something this dangerous on my home."

Treesa just looked at her. "It has to be done."

Ali followed. "It will be safe enough."

Rachel stood up. "You said that you want Children to have a voice on Selene. That's why you took so many risks, to help me teach the Moon Born things that other Council won't. Well, I'm asking. Why can't the collider be built on some other moon? There are plenty around."

Ali shook her head. "Neither of us is High Council."

"Does Gabriel support this? Really support it, not just go along?"

"He's cold," Ali said simply.

"The restrictions about talking about this, are they gone now?"

Treesa looked tired, but she smiled at the question. "Yes. I'll tell Vassal to answer your questions."

That night, Rachel lay still in bed, listening to her father's gentle snores. He had encouraged her to question Council. She trusted them—at least she trusted Treesa and Ali—but they were risking her home. They were damned picky about which technology they allowed and which they didn't, and no one seemed afraid of antimatter. But a fist-sized blob of antiwater would destroy Clarke Base. Why had Bruce laughed?

The math was simple. Matter + antimatter = energy. Energy in ergs was mass in grams times the speed of light squared, a tremendous number, doubled because an equal mass of matter was disappearing too. The numbers were simple; the problem was in believing the results.

She imagined Selene's soil spinning away from the core, trees and jungle and people flying away in a burst of explosive energy.

Council used antimatter regularly, safely.

But the numbers—

If she dropped a prize antiwatermelon—a watermelon sized glob of antimatter, ten kilograms—at Clarke Base, Clarke Base would be gone, true. *Curse* Bruce! *Selene* would be gone, dust and stones and superheated plasma scattered across the moon system and beyond. No wonder Bruce had hidden a laugh. If she built the antimatter at another moon. . . . She tried it with Eris, a chaotically tumbling moon far from Harlequin, smaller than Selene, but massive . . . and dropped the same ten-kilogram glob. The math gave her radiation and meteoroids from the explosion. It would probably kill every life form on Selene.

You couldn't get *John Glenn* to Ymir for ten kilograms. It took twelve hundred.

She'd had access to the numbers all along, via Astronaut, via the Library. She just hadn't known what to look for.

Chapter 56: Mid-Winter at Clarke Base

Three weeks later, Shane hadn't reassigned Rachel. She'd taken to looking over her shoulder for him, and didn't like the feeling one bit. Mid-Winter Week came and Rachel was dismayed to notice that the Children had only one day off for their own projects. The next three days Council worked them as a group, scrubbing buildings and streets in the base. That is, everyone except the crews working on the collider. Those had no time at all away from their usual duties.

Mid-Winter Night was different too. They weren't allowed to gather in a single group. Separate areas had been set up for the young children, the Moon Born adults like Rachel and Beth, and for the Earth Born. It wasn't that simple of course, there was movement back and forth as parents flowed from the children's areas to the two adult areas, and mixed married couples flowed easily between. Council patrolled everywhere, watching.

The Moon Born adults gathered in a cleared area between four greenhouses. The lights were white and utilitarian, and far too bright. Still, some effort had been made. Consuelo had herded some of the other cooks into extra duty making thin fruit cookies with rare sugar imported from *John Glenn*, and the usual bananas and even plates of chocolate rested on long tables. Three uniformed Council watched from the corner, protecting a tiny box that played music.

Rachel, Beth, the twins, and Dylan and Kyle sat at a table as far from the Council corner as they could get. Kyle and the twins were on the same team on the parts factory, and Beth and Kyle flirted so incessantly Rachel was betting on a contract announcement any day. The twins, at barely sixteen, were five years younger than Kyle, but already nearly as tall and broad as Kyle. Working in the parts factory had bulked them out, and they ate from plates full to overflowing.

"So," Jacob said, "do you think the Council over there are just making sure we get enough to eat?"

Dylan grimaced. "Sure. They're making sure the chocolate gets handed out. But I bet all the wine goes to the Earth Born."

Beth sat with her fingers intertwined in Kyle's. "Let's forget about fighting, just for tonight. Beside"—she looked at Jacob and Justin—"you two aren't old enough for wine anyway. They won't bring *that* out until you little ones get to bed."

"Well," Jacob teased, "look at the twenty-year-old lady lording over us all."

"She didn't mean it that way," Kyle said.

"I know." Jacob grinned. "Besides, we'll have our own party later."

"Shhhhh," Rachel said. It had become a tradition for the young Moon Born to hold their own party, after the rest of the groups had been handed wine, after the Selene Born had figured out how to buy or steal or trade for some of their own. "Don't even think about going out with the older boys. Just stay where you're supposed to, and have a good time. We don't eat *this* well all year." She popped a chunk of dark chocolate into her mouth.

Justin glanced back at the Council. One of them, a black-haired woman who looked like an official version of Consuelo, only younger, was watching their table. "Don't worry," he told Rachel, "Andrew told us to behave. He thinks we're being watched."

"Good," Rachel said, leaning into Dylan, enjoying the feel of his arm around her shoulder.

"That doesn't mean we won't find girls," Jacob said.

"No one suggested *that,*" Rachel said dryly. She sighed. Certainly the lesser of two evils. "But be home before dawn."

"You're not our mom," Jacob said.

Justin nudged him. "We'll be home. Tomorrow's still a day off, but we'll save some energy to help you with dad."

Rachel smiled. "Thanks, Justin. I appreciate it."

She and Dylan and Beth and Kyle watched the two younger boys start to make the rounds, moving from one table of young girls to the next, laughing and eating. After the younger people, including the twins, had been cleared out, a Councilman Rachel knew, a man named Dean, with gray hair and ice-blue eyes, stood up and addressed them.

"This has been a busy year. We appreciate the work that has been done, and tonight we celebrate." The other three Council handed out wine, one silvery tall bulb for each Moon Born. Rachel smiled and took hers, opening the stopper and smelling the rich fruity aroma.

Dylan held his bulb up toward the center of the table, and whispered, just loud enough for the table of four to hear, "To a slow year for Council."

Kyle smiled and nodded, but Rachel simply drank her wine, which had a lightly sour taste she attributed to Dylan's toast.

Chapter 57: Jacob

Selene shivered. Rachel spread her feet to gain balance. Hot coffee splashed over her hand and spilled onto the floor. She nearly dropped the cup. "Dad?" she called. "You all right?"

A moment of silence. Then her dad's voice, shaking a little. "Just old. Haven't felt a quake that big for a couple of years."

Rachel wiped up the coffee, then looked around the tiny kitchen. At least nothing was broken. She poured another cup and took it to her father.

He smiled at her, and reached up to grasp the cup in his good hand. It was shaking, so Rachel guided his other hand to the cup. "Sorry, girl," he said. "I shake up easier these days."

"We all do." She bent down and kissed his forehead. "Will you be all right? I've got to go. Sarah will be along in a few minutes. She can help."

"I'll be fine." Frank took a sip of the coffee and settled back onto the couch that had been his bed for the last two days. "Take care of yourself."

"All right, Dad. But get better, okay?" For the last few days he had barely been able to get out of bed. He slept half the time, his mouth open, snoring. His skin looked like paper.

As soon as she got out the door, Rachel sent a query to Treesa and Ali. "What would happen if you were making antimatter when this quake happened?"

There was no immediate answer. In the week that had passed since the meeting on Turtle Rock, both Council had stopped answering her questions about the collider.

As she walked down the path toward her classroom, she smiled to see Beth, Jacob, and Kyle pulling a cart with a long glass tube on it. The tube was bound for Refuge; part of a system to pump additional air in and out of Refuge if the drowned asteroid were full of people. Beth waved to Rachel, who started to walk over to the group. Maybe Jacob could go check on their dad.

"Hey, little brother," Rachel called out. "How are you?"

Jacob grinned. "Strong."

"Can you go check on Dad later? He looks as bad as he did yesterday."

"Sure. I'm off-shift in an hour."

Apollo's light sparkled on the glass tube as the three young people lined up the cart near the elevator for Council Aerie. Rachel stood, waiting for them to finish.

Jacob unstrapped the tube and lifted one end from the foam cradle the tube rested in for travel. They would hand-carry it to the elevator, where three other tubes just like it waited in a special container designed to take the fragile glass safely up the crater wall and back down the long dock to be loaded onto the *Safe Harbor.*

Two Council approached, both men, lost in conversation. Rachel glanced at them—she'd met each of them briefly on the ship—and tried to remember their names. The tall blond man was Paul, and the smaller, darker one was . . . Terry?

"Ready?" she heard Jacob's voice behind her and turned away from the Council members. Jacob held his end of the tube up, almost over his head, and Kyle and Beth picked up the other end, preparing to balance the whole thing on their shoulders. Kyle whistled softly at Beth, and she turned to grin at him, losing her balance briefly, pulling the tube off Kyle's shoulder. They both reached for the falling glass as the weight jerked the cylinder off Jacob's shoulder. Jacob twisted, managing to hold on to his end. The far end bounced against the metal edge of the cart, shattering with a loud crash.

The Council members were just two feet away. The one closest to the cart, Terry, turned toward the noise.

Jacob, unbalanced, held the longest remaining part of the tube. He set his foot onto a bright shard of thick jagged glass, and screamed in sudden pain. He pitched forward, and he and the broken glass landed directly on Terry, knocking the Councilman down.

A yelp went up simultaneously from both of them. A sliver of red stained the Councilperson's white shirt; a cut from the long shard of glass Jacob still held.

The second Council whipped his body around, kicked at the glass, and fired his weapon.

Just for an instant, Rachel saw a pink spark flare under Jacob's shirt, high on his chest. Jacob jerked violently, then fell into glittering shards of glass. He went limp and still. Blood seeped onto the glass, dulling it.

Beth screamed.

The Council with the weapon, Paul, turned toward her, raising his hand, pointing his weapon at Beth.

Kyle darted in front of Beth. Rachel yelled, "Stop," and ran to stand over her fallen brother. "No. I saw it. It was an accident. He didn't mean to do it."

Paul blinked in the light, his weapon pointing at Kyle and then at Rachel, and then finally, at the ground. He reached a hand out for Terry, helping the smaller man stand up. Blood stained Terry's hands where he clutched at his wounded chest.

Rachel turned toward Jacob, repeating, "Accident. It was an accident."

Rachel knelt by Jacob. Glass ground into her knees. The weapon. It must have been on stun. It had to be. Vassal said they were always on stun. Jacob wasn't dead, he was stunned.

She put a shaking hand out to Jacob's chest. It rose, faintly. His head was turned way from her, blood pooling underneath it. She used her index finger to turn his head toward her, and gasped. A shard of glass had cut deeply across the artery in his neck, and blood poured out, a waterfall of blood.

Beth knelt beside Rachel, cupping Jacob's head. Vassal's voice rose and fell in Rachel's ear. "Put pressure on the cut." She set her shaking hand onto his fragile neck. She pressed down, and blood oozed up between her fingers. "More," Vassal said. "Much more." She set her other hand over the first one, pushing down hard. Both hands were covered in blood.

Kyle stood over them, fists balled. Beth sobbed.

Star ran up to the scene, glanced at Rachel and the two Councilmen, and shook her head. "I've called a medical team," she said, peeling Terry's hands from his chest and poking at the wound.

Blood stopped pouring out over Rachel's hands, and Jacob stopped breathing. Rachel screamed, "Star! Star, you've got to do something. Jacob's dying!"

Star glanced over at Rachel. "Someone will be right there."

Rachel felt the hot spurts of blood between her fingers slow. She looked down at Jacob. His eyes stared up at the sky. Rachel looked into them and they were empty, like glass. She was afraid to move her hands from his neck. "He's not breathing, is he?" she whispered to Beth.

Beth set her right palm on his chest. She waited. She moved her hand, and then shook her head and reached for Rachel.

Rachel leaned into Beth, and Beth put an arm over her shoulder.

Star knelt by Jacob, picking up his wrist and holding it lightly. When she looked at Rachel and Beth, Rachel saw a flash of pain and fear, and something that might be regret. Then Star separated Rachel and Beth, prying Beth loose gently and helping her stand, taking her near Kyle. She left Rachel next to her brother's body and turned to talk to the two Councilmen.

Rachel sat, empty, trailing her bloody hand along Jacob's chin. Jacob was her brother. He was family. She folded her arms around her legs, hugging herself and rocking. Kyle stood with his jaw locked, fists clenching and unclenching, legs shaking. Beth cried silently, shaking, tears falling down her face.

Rachel had never seen a Councilperson raise a hand against anyone.

Justin came running up the path, and skidded to a stop in front of Rachel. He mouthed the word "No," and fell to his knees next to Jacob's body, touching his twin's face.

Two Council, the medical team, pushed Justin and Rachel away. Justin started to struggle and Rachel whispered in his ear, "Not now, not now. Wait." She held Justin's hand tightly, keeping him next to her, and they watched the medical team close Jacob's eyes and then lift his body onto a stretcher.

Star stood in front of them, looking worried. "I need a witness."

Rachel glanced at Kyle, who was standing and holding Beth, sheltering her. It would have to be him. He nodded, and Rachel worked her other hand around to grasp Beth's hand, pulling her loose from Kyle.

Justin was shaking.

Star looked at him, and said, "You come too."

"Why?" Rachel asked. She didn't know what Justin would do. She could feel his anger.

"I want him where I can see him."

Rachel nodded. "Send him home soon. My father will need him. He's sick."

Star smiled wanly, looking exhausted. "I'll try, Rachel, but no promises."

Kyle came and stood by Justin. "We'll go together," he said.

Justin nodded, and then as if drawn by the stretcher carrying Jacob's body, he began walking behind the medical team. Kyle kissed Beth quickly, and jogged to catch up with Justin. Star followed, and soon the path was nearly empty.

Why hadn't everyone come? Didn't they know? Rachel stepped

around the puddled blood and shards of glass, holding Beth's hand, feeling as if she were walking through a dream.

She had not seen Ursula die. She remembered how unreal Ursula's death had seemed . . . but she'd seen Jacob's slack face and the blood.

Rachel held most of Beth's weight as Beth sobbed into Rachel's shoulder. Rachel's head spun. She couldn't think about the . . . about Jacob dying. Blood loss from the glass had killed Jacob, but a weapon had knocked him unconscious first. A flash of Apollo's light, a moment of inattention, the slip of a smooth surface on sweat, and Jacob was—gone.

Rachel realized they were approaching her house. She guided Beth to sit on the stoop, not ready to go inside. Telling her dad would make it more real. She didn't want anyone in the house until she could tell him.

She stroked Beth's hair, and when she looked down, her hands were still blotched black with blood, and Beth's hair had become sticky and dark. Rachel stopped, not moving or breathing for a moment, listening to the normal sounds of the base. How could anyone be normal? She had told Star it was an accident. What would Council believe?

She kept watch up the walkway; Gloria and Harry were the first ones to come to them. Gloria gathered her daughter up, and Harry held his hand out to Rachel. She took it. He glanced down at her bloody hand and then pulled her to him. Rachel bent into his shoulder, smelling him, feeling his arms around her, and sobbed.

Chapter 58: Anger

It seemed to Rachel that she stood there, buried in Harry's arms, for a long time even though she knew it was only minutes. She heard wings, and footsteps, and voices calling her name. She held Harry tightly for another moment, taking a deep, shuddering breath, then pushed herself away, standing near him, no longer touching.

A crowd was gathering; Andrew, followed by Sam and Rudy, the three of them bunched tight, with angry faces. Bruce, walking slowly, pacing, as if watching for a chance to help. Ali, tearing the wings quickly from her arms, not bothering to remove the foot spreads. Her hair was loose, a long fall of black, as if she had been interrupted. She ran to Rachel. "What happened?"

"Jacob is dead." Rachel hated the words, spitting them out.

"What happened?" Ali repeated.

Rachel took a step back. Beth was still in Gloria's arms, but had turned, and her eyes bored into Rachel's. Everything looked crystal clear, as if the world had shifted into some new place. Sunlight touched the crowd, and a soft breeze brushed Beth's hair from her eyes. Rachel cleared her throat and wiped the tears from her face. "Paul killed him. He shot Jacob, and Jacob fell onto a piece of glass, and he bled to death. No one helped him, no one but me and Beth."

Beth stepped forward to stand by Rachel.

"Why did Paul shoot him?" Ali asked. "I need to know. Star called me; they're sending me back to *John Glenn* with Paul. I need to know what happened." Ali brushed hair from her face impatiently. "It's important, Rachel."

"He fell. They dropped one of the glass air tubes, and Jacob fell off a cart, and he landed on Terry." Rachel took another deep breath, struggling for the details. "Jacob had a piece of glass in his hand. It cut Terry, but not badly. Jacob was trying to stand up, and Paul shot him, and Jacob fell onto the glass, and cut himself." Rachel held up her bloody hands. "Cut his throat. He bled to death, Ali, and no one stopped it. I tried to stop it, but all I had was my hands."

Ali took Rachel's hands and looked at them, turning them over, a frown creasing her brow. "He must have bled out quickly."

She swallowed, seeing the scene in her mind. "But Ali, they went to Terry first, Star went to Terry first, and he was barely hurt."

Ali's voice was low. "Did Star know that?" Her mouth was a tight line, and her eyes bored directly into Rachel's, demanding answers.

"Terry was standing up. Jacob wasn't."

"Is there anything else you can tell me?"

"No, I have to go tell Daddy. I have to be the one who tells him."

"Okay." Ali dropped Rachel's hands and gave her a quick, hard hug. "I'd stay with you, but they want me now, and I. . . . I have to go. Do you understand?"

"Yes." Rachel swallowed, her voice catching in her throat. "I understand you leaving. They're making you go."

Ali returned Rachel's glance evenly. "I'm sorry. I'm truly sorry." Her voice shook as she reached for her wings.

Rachel turned. Gloria and Harry stood together. Bruce was near them. Andrew, Rudy, and Sam watched her closely. Andrew caught her eyes, a mixture of anger and pain in his gaze. Surely he wouldn't act out now, not with Ali here.

"Stay outside, please," she said loudly, to them all. "I need to talk to my dad." Harry would make sure people stayed outside. Rachel opened the door, went in.

Her father had pushed himself into a sitting position on the couch, and he gasped as she walked in. She stood near him. "Daddy?"

"What's all over your hands?"

"Blood. Sit still, Dad, I'm going to wash my hands, and then I'm going to tell you about it. Please? I need to get clean." Her voice was catching in her throat.

"There are people outside," he said. "I heard Ali, and I heard crying, and I heard some of what you said."

"Yes." How much had he heard? She stepped to the sink and ran water over her hands. It fell through her fingers, tinged with red, hardly changing the color of her hands. She reached for soap and started scrubbing. How was she going to tell her dad? He loved the twins so much.

There was still blood under her nails. She scrubbed harder, faster, shaking. She saw her family's faces. Sarah. Justin. Jacob's face as she had last seen it, empty and white. She no longer wanted to cry. She was just . . . empty.

Rachel toweled her hands dry. Her clothes were still covered with blood. She swiped at the blood with her towel, needing it gone, but it only smeared.

Her dad was shaking. "Now, Rachel. Tell me now." He looked more alert than he had in days, and very afraid.

She sat by him on the couch, taking his broken hand in hers. He was stiff, unyielding. "Something terrible happened."

"To Jacob?" There was no question in his eyes.

"Jacob's dead, Daddy."

He stared, white-faced, his lips shaping Jacob's name. He reached out and held her close to him, whispering, "How?"

"He fell, Daddy. When he fell, he cut himself on glass."

"I heard what you told Ali outside," he whispered. "That he was killed. Don't protect me."

"I don't know what to do, Dad."

"You will." His hand shook in Rachel's, as if hearing the news from her released the tension and now he could feel. Tears started spilling down his face and he rocked back and forth like a child. "Where did they take my son?" His voice cracked. "I want to see his body."

"I don't know. I'll try to find out."

The door banged open and Sarah flew into the room. "They killed him." Her face was streaked with tears. "Council has started killing us. Jacob always said they would," she sobbed. "He knew it. Jacob's dead."

Sarah threw herself at Rachel, and Rachel folded her arms around Sarah's thin back and held her tightly. The door was open now, and Harry and Gloria and Beth piled in, followed by Dylan. Dylan took in the scene, the sobbing young woman on Rachel's lap, the blood still covering Rachel's clothes. Rachel's father wiping tears from his face with the back of his hand. "Are you all right?" he asked.

"How could I be?" She held Sarah more tightly. "Can you go see about Justin? And Kyle? They took them—Star took them. They have Jacob's body too, and Dad wants to see him."

"Are you physically okay? Are any of you hurt?" Dylan asked.

Rachel shook her head. "No one but Jacob."

Sarah sobbed even louder, and Rachel bent her head over her little sister, placing her cheek on the fourteen-year-old's head. She could see Dylan from the corner of her eye. He resembled Andrew in that moment: anger was filling him, trying to burst out of him.

"Okay," he said. "I'll go find Justin."

"Keep him safe. Bring him home."

Dylan nodded, then ran from the room. Gloria closed the door behind him. "The others left too," she said. "I sent them away."

HOURS LATER, Gloria and Rachel sat at the kitchen table. Dark circles hung under Gloria's eyes, and her skin was ashen white. Rachel put her hand in the middle of the table and Gloria took it. Gloria's hand was rough from work, but a smile touched her face for just a moment.

Rachel glanced over at Sarah, who had fallen asleep nestled in her father's arms. Sarah's long legs hung awkwardly off the couch, one foot touching the floor, and her head was on Frank's shoulder. Frank was looking up at the ceiling, not moving. Rachel didn't think he was asleep. Neither Dylan nor Justin had returned.

Rachel needed to talk to Vassal. "Gloria, I have to go. I have to find out what's happened. Can you stay with them?"

Gloria nodded, swallowing.

"And thank you. Thank you for being here."

"You've always been here for me," Gloria said. "It's nothing. We would all do more for you if you'd let us."

"Thanks." Rachel took her cup to the sink. Gloria had washed away all the blood. "I'll be back soon."

"I'll take care of your father. We'll come find you if Dylan comes back, or Justin." Their wrist pads had stopped working sometime during the late afternoon. "Do you know where you'll be?"

"No. I don't know how long I'll be out either. I can't sit here anymore, just waiting. I have to think, I have to find people, I have to decide what to do next."

"Take care of yourself," Gloria said.

Her dad had used the same words when she left before the accident. Rachel shivered. "Okay."

Rachel closed the door behind her, and realized she truly didn't know where she wanted to go. It had grown dark, and no one waited outside the door for her. "Vassal," she whispered into the night air.

"Yes."

"What's happened?"

"Paul and Ali left for *John Glenn* an hour ago."

"Who did they blame?"

"They?"

"Council." She needed to be more specific with the AI. "I don't know. Star? What did Star say?"

The voice was smooth in her ear, as if Vassal was summarizing a long set of conversations. "Council decided it was all a sequence of accidents. Paul has not been accused. Star worries about what might happen here, about how you Moon Children will react. She is watching Clarke Base, and has set out extra guards. She decided to try to keep things normal, to see if all becomes calm. There are extra watchers."

Rachel walked toward the greenhouses, and the plots. Avoiding the watchers. They would be in town. Perhaps other Moon Born would go to the greenhouses. "Are you in danger of being caught?"

"It is not data they watch."

"Has High Council reacted?"

"No, they are still silent. I did hear Star tell them, 'At least we only lost one of the Moon Born. It could have been worse.'"

Rachel stopped and stood very still. Vassal's silky voice still droned in her ears, but she no longer heard it. She closed her eyes, and it seemed like the weight of everything she worried about grew even heavier. Council leaving. Council staying, and tension remaining high; she and her friends and family watched and discounted. Antimatter. The words played in her head, "We only lost one of the Moon Born. Only a Moon Born. Only a Moon Born."

Rachel found herself at the edges of a plot of carrots. She could smell the fresh green tops, the rich scents of the earth. She collapsed in the darkness, and watched the bright lights of a meteor shower burning overhead. Rachel thought of Ursula, and whispered to the memory of her friend, "You were right, little one, right not to trust Council as much as I have." Then Rachel put her head down between her drawn-up knees, making as small a ball of herself as she could, and shook. *They killed my brother,* she thought, *and they don't even care!*

A hand touched her arm, and she looked up, expecting Dylan. Andrew stood behind her. He said, "I'm sorry about Jacob." His voice was gruff.

Rachel took his hand and squeezed it. They stayed that way for a long time, Andrew standing behind her; Rachel curled at his feet, saying nothing. Ursula hadn't trusted Council. She'd done as Rachel asked all those years ago, and tried her best to be a good student, to work hard. And she died. Andrew didn't trust Council either. She heard it in her head again, "Only a Moon Born." She struggled up and flung herself into Andrew's arms, sobbing again, angry tears. They had no right!

Andrew smelled of pipe grease and sweat, good smells, smells that were work and not death or sickness. Rachel wanted to scream into his shoulder. Instead, she stepped away from him. "They're building something that might kill us all," she said.

Andrew looked down at her, his eyes mirroring her anger. She asked, "What do you know about the collider?" stepping back a step from him, watching his face.

"Tell me?"

Explaining was difficult. Andrew had no fine grasp of math, no sense of proportion. Even so, she was working it out for herself, putting it into words.

Matter plus antimatter equals fire.

Drop an antiwatermelon, destroy Selene.

Twelve hundred kilograms to reach Ymir.

She didn't speak of Vassal, or Treesa or Ali, but Andrew was used to her knowing things by now. He didn't ask where she got her information, but he did ask a series of questions about antimatter, about the project, about the timeline. Then he took her hand and said, "Rachel, we have to act now. Surely you're with me now."

"How?" She shook out of her pain a bit, sensing how much of a mistake she might have made. She hated Council right now, hated them all. Hated what they had done to her. But they were too powerful. She needed to think—to plan.

"I don't know. Are you with me?" he asked her.

She shook her head. "There is nothing you can do right now that won't kill people. Kill you. Kill anyone you take with you. Jacob's death was a startled reaction—almost, almost an accident. It makes me very, very angry. But this isn't the time. They'll kill you, and it will be bad for us all. I'll help you plan something now, I will. But not an immediate reaction." She took a deep trembling yoga breath, working her belly muscles as Gabriel had taught her, and it helped calm her flying emotions, at least a little. "Remember, under the *Water Bearer*, you promised you wouldn't act violently without me knowing about it?"

"But I didn't know *this* when I made that promise. I'm tired of hiding and now there's no time. They're already building the collider."

"Andrew—we'll talk about it." She reached for his hand, holding it tightly. "There is time. Some time."

"Will you wait until more people die? Right now, everyone feels as angry as I do." He looked down at her, his eyes oddly soft. "You feel it too."

Rachel wanted to agree with him. Even her anger violated all the things she believed in. Joining Andrew would make it worse; it would be accepting a fight she knew they could not win, fighting when maybe she could still negotiate something better. She had Gabriel, and Ali, and Treesa, and John with her. And Bruce. And more, her students, some of them anyway. Harry and Gloria . . . maybe it was enough. She had to stop Andrew first. Slow him down. Why had she told him? Given him more to be angry about? "Give it at least a few days. I'll talk to you tomorrow. Please, Andrew?"

"A lot of people follow you, Rachel. Lead them the right way. Surely now you know what that is?" He squeezed her hand tightly, and then pulled her to him.

She leaned into his arms, afraid of him, wanting the connection. If she let him go, if he left like this, something bad was bound to happen. "Andrew, don't do anything. Not yet. Wait."

"It's not time to wait anymore." He was tense in her arms, as if he wanted to run, as if he wanted to do something right now, right this minute.

"Wait until tomorrow. They're watching us closely now. We have to plan."

"I can't promise that. I'm tired of waiting." He leaned down and kissed her, his mouth hard and hungry against hers, and to Rachel's surprise, she responded, pushing her tongue against his teeth, accepting him into her mouth, clutching at the back of his head, curling her fingers into his hair, holding him to this moment, this safe moment.

Then he stepped back and turned away, leaving her standing in the chilling air.

She looked after him, holding a hand to her swollen lips, watching the place he had been for a long time.

Chapter 59: Passage

Rachel walked. Greenhouses loomed behind her like shadowy boxes, and she continued out into the open fields, wanting distance between herself and Clarke Base. The fields felt cold and dark, and even the stars offered little comfort. She straggled home in the first light of dawn, and found Gloria still at the kitchen table, her head on her arms, fast asleep. Rachel shook her friend's shoulder, and said, "Go home. Go see about your own family. Thank you."

Gloria groaned and pushed into a standing position. "I should take Sarah with me," she said.

Rachel looked over at her teenaged sister, who was stirring in the couch, the noise of Rachel's homecoming waking her. "Sarah," Rachel said, "Sarah, I want you to walk Gloria home. Stay and be sure she has breakfast. Can you do that?"

Sarah nodded, rubbing sleep from her eyes, stretching, and looking softly at her father, who was still asleep on the couch. "He looks terrible," she said.

"Go on, now, both of you."

They left, and Rachel sat by her father on the couch. His skin looked like the wheat grass paper Treesa made, and there were dark circles under his eyes and darkness in the hollows of his cheeks. Rachel talked to him as she had talked to the sleeping Beth on *John Glenn* so many lifetimes ago, and when the room was empty she told him stories about how grand Refuge would be, describing the ferryboat, *Safe Harbor,* and the glittering interior. She avoided Jacob's death, but she told him all of her other secrets—she told him about Vassal, about Treesa, and Ali, and Gabriel, and even Astronaut. It felt wonderful to talk to him. She had always been so afraid to share these secrets, but it felt so good to let them pour out of her.

Apollo fell farther down the sky. Harlequin's reddish light spilled in the tiny window above Frank's bed. Frank stirred, taking her hand in his own, reaching for her with the hand that was missing fingers. His eyes opened, wide with pain, and the stump where his thumb had been drilled into her palm while he squeezed tightly. "I'm proud of you," he said.

She didn't know how much he had heard. "I hope I earn that," she whispered.

"You have already," he said.

She thought about things she probably shouldn't have told Andrew. "Daddy, I'm not sure. I may have put us in danger."

"We were born in danger," he said, so softly she could barely hear him. "You've had to bear a lot—and take a lot of risks. More than I was ever willing to. I'm proud of you for that."

He didn't know half the risks she'd taken. "I just hope it comes out all right. I want peace, and I don't think we can have it. I used to think we could. I think that died with Jacob."

"Keep going," he said. "Keep fighting. You have to win for us." His breath rattled, and he looked up at her. "But try and keep the peace— that's right. It's good. You're good."

She smiled at him, wishing it were half as simple as he seemed to think. As she had once thought.

"You've always taken care of us. Take care of Sarah—she's like you."

"I know. I'll try."

His eyes closed again, and after a few moments his grip on her hand tightened, then fell open. He stopped breathing.

Rachel stared at his face, sure now that she had known all morning that he would die. The anger from last night rushed back. Council could have saved him. Cold sleep would have saved him. It was even worse than Jacob's death.

The door banged open and Justin rushed in. "Andrew's stolen a crate of Council weapons. He's gathering us on the slope behind the warehouses. I have to go, I have to meet him. But I wanted you to know."

Rachel looked up, tears streaming down her face.

Justin stopped, gathered a breath, and looked at Frank. "Oh. Oh," he stuttered. "Oh, my God, he's dead." He lost all color and reached to touch his father's face.

"Rachel, this makes it worse. We can't stop now. We can't. They'll kill us all. This is our moment."

Rachel looked at Justin and said, "If Andrew is fighting Council publicly, with their own weapons, then, yes, maybe they will kill us all." Then she shook her head and stood up, reaching for her brother.

"I have to go," he said. "Oh, my God, I have to go." Justin turned and grabbed Rachel by the shoulder. "Keep Sarah. Keep Sarah with you. She's coming here next, I passed her."

Vassal's voice in Rachel's ear. "Gather your people. I'll try to keep you safe. You must avoid Andrew."

Out loud, Rachel said, "What are you thinking, Justin? Stay here." She choked. "Jacob's dead. You'll be dead next."

Justin turned, planted a kiss on Frank's cold forehead, and said, "They killed my twin. Save Sarah."

"Go get her and bring her here," Rachel pleaded. "Stay with us."

Vassal repeated, "Gather those who will stay with you."

"I'm going," Justin insisted, teeth clenched. "Your way hasn't worked. They're killing us anyway."

Rachel shook her head, trying to clear it. "Yes," she said, not sure if she was answering Justin, or Vassal, or both. Then with more strength, "Yes, I'll do something." She turned to pull the cover up over Frank's face, and Justin dashed out the door.

Rachel's brain didn't want to think clearly. How did Andrew get weapons? How could she live without her father? Who would greet her when she came home? Where were her people? Where was Beth, and was Sarah really coming? How would she gather them? Ali was on *John Glenn*. Where was Treesa? "Treesa," she sobbed, "Treesa, now what?"

No answer.

Someone knocked on the door. Rachel opened it. Beth stood there, Kyle beside her, holding her hand. Harry and Gloria were walking up, Miriam between them, half their height now, one hand hanging tightly to each parent. Sarah came running down the path, bounding past Gloria, almost pushing Gloria into little Miriam, burying herself in Rachel's arms, crying. "Justin told me," she said. "He told me to come here. He said Dad's dead."

Rachel nodded, holding Sarah tightly. "Stay with me," she said. She looked up and found Harry's eyes. "Harry, go find the others. Get Bruce, and everyone who has studied with us. Everyone who will come. Get them out of work even. Get supplies: food, blankets, water. And Dylan, Dylan will help."

Harry shook his head. "Dylan's with Andrew."

Pain knifed through Rachel. "Get everyone you can. Tell them to come here, and to stay away from Andrew. If they won't come here, tell them to go home and stay inside. Andrew doesn't have a chance. Keep everyone you can away from him." Rachel was surprised at how strong her voice sounded.

"I'll see who I can find," Harry said. "Some are already coming." Sure enough, Rachel looked down the path and she saw it beginning to fill with her students. Sharon, Kimberly, Lisa . . . Harry faded into the crowd, going the opposite way. Gloria and Beth turned to watch him go, holding each other. Little Miriam cried, one arm reaching toward the place Harry had vanished.

Rachel blinked back tears as the gathering crowd looked at her. She scanned their faces. They had to leave. Council could find them here. Council could find them anywhere, but distance would be good. Sadness washed over Rachel, mixing with her pain, and she wavered for a moment, her knees weak, held up only by Sarah's strength. The feel of Sarah's arms around her and the tortured look on Beth's face gave her the strength to stand more firmly. She just wished she knew what to do.

"Where can we go?" She whispered it to Vassal, not caring if Sarah heard, or if she understood what Rachel was doing.

"Where Council isn't," Vassal said. "I can guide you."

Rachel nodded.

"This will keep you safe from whatever immediate danger Andrew is putting people into right now. You need to be separated from him."

"Can you stop him? Can I stop him?"

"I see no way," Vassal said. "Someone has to protect our students. If you aren't here, I can't keep them safe."

Rachel swallowed. It was right. "Can I send some of these out to find the others?"

"Yes, but keep your eyes on the ones who have family in Andrew's group. Keep them from trying to save anyone—I don't know what Council will do, but none of my predictions end with everyone alive. Andrew has ten people with him."

Dylan, Justin, Andrew, and who else? Rachel got the list from Vassal and started sending runners out, keeping others with her. She packed. Food, a change of clothes, bedding. She hung her wings over her back. Images of Dylan and Justin flashed unbidden in her head, demanding attention, and she remembered she had sent Harry out. Suddenly, she knew he would try to save Dylan. Harry was no warrior. What had she done?

Chapter 60: Waking Gabriel

Cells drinking fluids, like the rush of water after a long dry run. An expansion. Gabriel blinked, immediately recognizing the feel of the drugs in his body as an emergency cocktail. Warmth and energy invaded, too fast, an adrenaline flash of life. His body felt twitchy, edgy. Emergency wake-up calls were the pits. Blinking didn't clear his vision; he couldn't see well at all. Darkness, and light, and fuzz. He closed his eyes, counted to a hundred, and opened them again. Ali's face swam into view, centering, becoming clear. He blinked again. He was still lying down, still strapped in. Ali fumbled with the clasps, saying something. There was no noise at all, but Ali's mouth moved.

"Earplugs," he said, unable to hear his own response.

He saw Ali frown, then felt the light pressure and release as she removed his earplugs and sound rushed in.

Ali's hand worked his right calf, massaging life into the muscles. Pain shot up along his thigh, then a tingling sensation, then mere warmth. The feeling repeated as Ali worked her way up each limb, and started kneading his scalp. Her lips moved, and he made out words with difficulty . . . "Wake, sleeper . . . feel your life return . . . wake, Gabriel." He followed her voice and let his body do its work.

Why was he being warmed in emergency mode?

He tested his muscle reactions, moving one leg, then the other. "I think I can stand," he said. His voice was raspy.

"Let's go."

Gabriel looked a query at her.

"To a magic room. We need visuals." Ali's eyes rolled up into her head for a moment. "They're all busy! Everyone must have the same idea."

"My office," Gabriel said. Mouth numb: *chewing* the words. "What's happened? Is it a flare?"

Ali shook her head. "I don't even know where to start. Things between Moon Born and Council deteriorated while you were cold."

"How long was I out?"

"Six months."

Gabriel sat up slowly. He was only a little dizzy. "Tell me."

"There was an accident two days ago. Jacob was killed—Frank's son, Rachel's brother. One of the twins."

Damn. "A twin. Hard on the other one—what's his name?"

"Justin."

Right. He'd only met the twins a few times, but he had liked them. "Is Frank okay?" Gabriel asked, swinging his legs back and forth in the air, feeling them out. "And Rachel?"

Ali stopped, a deep frown creasing her forehead. "Frank died this morning. Old age, and shock, I suppose."

Gabriel remembered the image that grew in his head as he went cold; a creation going out of control, molecule by molecule. He shivered. "We should have stopped that, or brought him here."

Ali raised an eyebrow. "Weren't you the one who argued to let the Children die of natural causes? Remember when we talked about Andrew? We all agreed they'd stay more human that way." Ali sighed. "Anyway, no one killed *him*."

Gabriel tested his weight on his right foot and then his left. "How's Rachel?"

"I think she's okay. I don't have much information. Andrew stole a cache of guns."

Too much information at once. "Andrew? How the hell did he do that? You still haven't told me what happened to Jacob."

"I was there, or at least, I was there right afterward. It was an accident. Paul stunned Jacob, but Jacob had other wounds too, and he died. I think the Children blame us."

"You don't know?" Gabriel asked.

"I flew back up with Paul and two others. I've been up here just over a day. Anyway, the Moon Born reaction is even more important than Jacob dying. Andrew jumped Star and stole her belt weapon, then he used it to stun Ben, who was unloading the latest crate of weapons we sent down." Ali handed Gabriel a flask of liquid. "Andrew led an ambush on three people at the landing field. They must have completely surprised Star. He's using her as a hostage."

Gabriel drank. The vegetable broth rapidly cleared his head. Star a hostage? "Is she okay?"

"So far."

"Why were we shipping weapons to Selene?" He handed Ali the flask, and leaned on her, taking a tentative step. A little pain. Not bad. They worked their way toward the door.

"Because of the bad production stats, because they're starting the antimatter generator project, and they want to protect it."

"I was afraid of that." Gabriel's office was a long ways from Medical. "Ali—keep walking, I'm with you. I need more data—I'm calling Astronaut."

Ali nodded as if that was the most normal thing in the world. "Yes. Astronaut called me when it sent the emergency wake-up code to you."

The last time he'd spent whole days with Ali was a few years ago, and then she had hated everything to do with Astronaut. Maybe too many years . . . maybe before Council Aerie. He was even more surprised when he found himself jacked into a three-way conversation with Ali and Astronaut. Ali spoke with Astronaut casually, as if it was something she did every day.

They reached Gabriel's office in time to see Andrew, real-time minus six seconds, take possession of the warehouse that held the materials nano. He had at least ten people with him, all armed. From this vantage they were dots swarming over the square, flat roof. Gabriel zoomed on several faces. Andrew's eyes were cool, his mouth drawn in a thin line. Star crouched on the roof, tied. She had a calculating look: she was waiting for an opening.

Gabriel closed his eyes. This was a disaster.

"Astronaut? How's Rachel?" he asked. "Where is Rachel?"

"Ask her yourself."

Of course. Why hadn't he just done it? He sank into a chair, cursing his weakness. His thinking was still fuzzy. Emergency wake-up stimulants didn't do the same healing job as normal warming. "Rachel?"

The reply that came back was edgy and tired. "Gabriel? You're warm? Is that you? Can you help us, please?"

"Are you okay?"

"Of course not."

Gabriel frowned. "Where are you?"

Her voice broke with exhaustion. "I have us, maybe fifty of us, walking away from Clarke Base. East, toward Aldrin. No one has told us what to do, and this seems best. The Council here are trigger-happy. They killed my brother. Someone has to stop it. I can't. I don't know how. Can you come down?"

"Not right away. I just warmed; I can't fly yet." He started searching where he thought she was, trying to bring up an image on the wall in front of him. "Liren is on her way down."

"Liren! Just what we need. When?"

"Soon. Rachel—stay away from her."

Ali broke into the conversation. "Dylan's with Andrew."

Gabriel groaned. He hadn't seen that coming. He looked at Ali, shaking his head. "Rachel—stay there. You can't do any good being near Andrew, and it will be dangerous to be around him." He couldn't seem to get Rachel on screen at all. "Where are you? I can't find you."

"East of Clarke Base," Rachel repeated, and when Gabriel panned backward, right over where he had been looking a moment before, he could see Rachel and what must be almost seventy Moon Born, mostly women and children, a few men. At least three were shorter and squatter than the tall gangly Moon Born: Earth Born were with them. How had he missed a crowd this big?

"Don't go near Andrew," Gabriel repeated. "I'll see what I can do from up here. I'll be down as soon as I can." She was in danger. Every Moon Born on Clarke Base was in danger. "Keep your people away from the base, with you. Encourage more to come. But don't go too far. Liren should not believe you are running away."

"Normal wrist communications are cut off," Rachel said, "I can't encourage anyone else except by word of mouth. You and I can talk because of the earbud. Look . . . stay available, can you?" She cut off the transmission.

Gabriel looked at Ali. "She didn't say she wouldn't go."

Ali shook her head. "You don't know her very well anymore. She's—she's very strong."

What was he missing? Ali talking to Astronaut like an old friend, Ali talking about Rachel as a hero? Surely he'd gone to sleep in a different world. He looked at the wall image again. Rachel and the Moon Born were still on it, and Rachel was holding Beth's shoulders, saying something softly to her. There was too much local noise and buzz of conversation from the surrounding crowd for Gabriel to hear what Rachel was saying, but it looked serious.

He replied to Ali. "I know some of the Children have been making a lot of her for a long time. I also know she's very capable. Why the heck do you think I put her in charge of classes?"

Ali tugged on her braid, her expression strangely guarded. "She's a natural leader."

"Better use the time between now and when I can fly to catch up. Ali—can you monitor four current data windows?" He scrubbed at his face with his hands. "Keep one on Andrew and one on Rachel and her group. Then I want one on Refuge, and one on Council housing in Clarke Base. I'll start running stats," he said. "I need some historical images. Who can help from here? I need Astronaut, but I'll want some communications techs too. I need to figure out how the Moon Born got so much knowledge. And what happened since I went to sleep." The rush of adrenaline and worry made him dizzy.

He directed Astronaut to call for communications experts. Two minutes later, it returned a disturbingly short list—one volunteer who wasn't otherwise commanded to be someplace else; Rachel's mother. What kind of random factors would *that* throw in? What did Kristin think of Rachel? Why did she volunteer? A memory—Rachel had said something once, just before he sent her down. He didn't recall that it was flattering to Kristin.

Still, he needed the expertise. He sent for Kristin, and started a series of stretches intended to clear his head. While he stretched, he recited to Astronaut, listing the data he expected to need.

Fifteen minutes passed. Moon Born patrolled the warehouse roof. Council gathered. Rachel kept talking to Beth. Ali paced. The stretching helped—some.

Ali interrupted him: "Gabriel, how did Andrew know where to go?"

He looked. She expanded the data window, between them—it was full video. The picture wavered, painting an image of Selene on Ali's face as she stepped through to get to his side, so they both had the same viewing angle. Andrew and his group were on top of the one building that housed raw materials nano. It was the only place on Selene except the planting field where they used nano. Andrew should barely know that building existed, much less that it mattered.

Gabriel looked closer, tapping his wrist on the chair arm in frustration. It was a good defensive position. If the building doors were locked, as they probably were, then Council couldn't get onto the roof through the building. Gabriel made the picture bigger. Guards stood by the two ladders to the roof. So unless Council flew—but flyers would be seen. Wide streets surrounded the warehouse. Council had been concerned about danger from *within* the building—about the nano they hated, not about humans.

Ali said, "I just heard Council is going to let them stew. They'll have to stay on top of the building until Liren gets there."

"I won't be far behind her," he muttered. He watched Andrew batter down a roof door and send five of his people inside. He glimpsed Star's rage as she spoke to Andrew. Gabriel shook his head, still shocked at the idea of a Council as hostage. She looked proud, not afraid. Gabriel sighed. That was good.

"Ali—Astronaut woke me. Does Erika know?"

"Yes, she messaged me. She said it was the right thing."

He breathed a sigh of relief.

Kristin rushed into Gabriel's office, not bothering to announce herself. He studied her, searching for similarities between mother and daughter. She was small, and looked shorter and more fragile than Rachel, but just as beautiful. When she saw him looking at her, her smile dropped, covered by a business veneer, and she said, "Reporting for duty."

Ali spoke before he could. "Your daughter's on Selene. Her dad just died. Her brother died two days ago. Her lover is about to die, and so is her oldest enemy. Your job is to help Gabriel and me understand what happened to make things this bad. You're to look at data flows across the last few days on Selene and analyze the patterns."

Gabriel interrupted, "Do you know these people? Do you know who Andrew is?"

Kristin nodded, her eyes wide. "Of course I do. I watch Selene, like everyone."

"Andrew is in a good strategic situation. I need to know how he got there. He knows things he shouldn't. How does he know?"

"I'll look."

Ali looked daggers at her. "Rachel is a great kid. Actually, woman now. She's a gift." Ali's voice was rising. "But you left her on Selene. She told me how cold you were to her here. Do you care about her? Really? Should you be here, helping us?"

Kristin took a step back, but said, "Rachel's my daughter. I made mistakes."

Ali took a step toward Kristin, narrowing the gap between them again. "She checks for messages from you every day."

Gabriel held up a hand for silence. "Calm down, Ali," he said. "Grilling the woman won't help Rachel." There was a real depth of feeling in Ali's words. As if Kristin had personally betrayed *her*. She and Rachel had worked together for the last year or so that he was warm, finishing spaces on Refuge. But he hadn't known Ali cared so much for the younger woman. What else had he missed? He looked at Kristin. "Your daughter, it seems, has charmed almost all of us. See that you help me get data that will help her."

"Wait. Frank's dead?"

"Right."

Kristin nodded for a third time, her mouth and facial expression mirroring a china doll more than a human. But as she chose a corner to work in, Gabriel thought he saw a damp streak on her right cheek. He hoped so. He started a counter running down the few hours until he could leave *John Glenn* and get to Selene himself. He cursed the well-intended med regulations that kept him from wandering too far from Medical until at least four hours after he warmed. He didn't have the authority to grant his own clearance while a medical red flag was up.

Chapter 61: Leaving Safety

Rachel was in the middle of two arguments. Beth wanted to go with Rachel. Rachel needed Beth to stay to watch Sarah and to keep the rest of the crowd together, and Vassal was having none of either choice. At the moment, Rachel had her hands on either side of Beth's face, looking directly into Beth's tear-stained puffy eyes. "Beth—I'm done arguing. You're costing me time."

Beth's voice shook. "I don't care. I have to go. Dad's there."

Rachel finally used a trick she sometimes used to wake herself up in her long nighttime conversations with Astronaut or Vassal. She pulled Beth's hair, hard.

Beth yelped.

"I need your attention," Rachel said.

Beth nodded.

"The longer we argue, the more time we lose. I can stop you from leaving as long as I'm here. I can't stop you from following if I leave. I'm not letting you near Andrew right now, not even to save Dylan and Harry. Either no one goes, or I go. Do you get it?"

Beth nodded miserably.

Vassal droned in Rachel's ear, silky voiced, weirdly monotone given the message. "You can't go. What if you get hurt?"

Rachel ignored the AI. She leaned over and stroked Beth's hair quickly. "Okay. Sorry I had to do that. I love you. Look, your mom needs you." Rachel pointed to Gloria, who held the still disconsolate Sarah to her with one arm while balancing Miriam on her other hip. Sarah's face was streaked with tears and Miriam wiggled in Gloria's arms, wanting freedom.

The group was spreading out along a wide path, cornfields waving on one side, a plowed empty field on the other side. Women bent over children, settling them on blankets and scraps of clothing. Rachel smiled at a figure coming up the path. "Look, Beth." She pointed.

Kyle. He smiled hugely as he saw Beth and Rachel, and broke into a jog.

Rachel turned back to Beth. "Okay? So now at least you know Kyle's safe."

Beth gave a small smile, starting to head toward Kyle.

Rachel pulled her arm, holding her back. "The story for the group is that I'm going for information and that I want them to stay here. If people ask, tell them that. They already expect to spend the night here. Keep them together—they'll be warmer that way, and you can watch them easier. Have Kyle help you." What else did she need to tell Beth? "I'll send any of us I see in Clarke Base here. If Council comes, try and get them to let you all stay here. You followed me. I'm your teacher, and I told you to come here."

"I'll figure it out. I'm not a child anymore. Just bring Dad home safely. And Dylan."

Rachel hugged her, hard and fast. "It may not be possible." She turned and made her way slowly through the small crowd, trying to duck attention. As she neared the edge of the field, old Bruce started pacing her. "Stay here," she hissed at him.

Bruce said, "I shouldn't be here anyway. No Earth Born should be here. I don't know where we should be. Not with Moon Born, not with Council. I'm going back toward base."

Vassal whispered, "Take him. He'll help you."

"I'd rather you took the Children toward Aldrin. Just in case anything really bad happens."

Bruce shook his head. "You're right to camp here, where Council can find you. Going all the way to Aldrin might piss them off."

"So stay and keep them safe." Rachel wanted to go by herself, to be free to talk to Vassal and Treesa and others.

"Someone has to keep you safe." Bruce grinned, looking completely sure of himself.

"Take him," Vassal insisted.

"Damn you," Rachel replied.

"What?" Bruce said.

"Sorry—I didn't mean that. Look, I'm going to try and get to Dylan."

"Of course you are."

Rachel gave in. She was already fighting Vassal just by going, and Bruce *might* be useful. "We have to hurry."

Bruce rewarded her with a flashy grin, and she stopped to strap on wings.

"Maybe we shouldn't fly," Bruce said. "It might not be safe. Council can shoot farther than you think. There are two-handed rifles that shoot bigger flashpins."

"Just what we need," she said. "See, you're already being useful. But my wings are from *John Glenn*. Anyone from here will recognize them. Everyone in Clarke Base knows me. Anyone from the ship will hesitate since the wings are from there."

"Mine aren't."

"You'll be with me."

"Maybe that's the safest place on Selene right now." Bruce unfolded his wings and shrugged into them.

Rachel glanced sideways at him as she leaned down to strap on her foot spreads.

He grinned. "You're always okay. Right? Council protects you. We protect you. What better place could I be?"

Rachel sighed, wanting to tell him how wrong he was. "Come on, we need to go." She finished the last few strap checks and started her run into flight. Vassal spoke into her ear. "They're all in, and on, a single warehouse. Council has it surrounded. No one's hurt."

At least it was helping. Ali had been right all along—the damned AI didn't understand emotions for shit. As long as it kept giving her directions, she'd be nice to it.

She launched quickly into flight, glancing behind her to see if Bruce was following. She didn't plan to slow down for him, but his help might be a good thing. And if he couldn't keep up, well, that might be just as good.

Chapter 62: Honorable Choices

Liren stood with her feet planted, standing in Erika's way, barring her passage. It was a dangerous thing to do to a ship's captain, but Liren *had* to get to Selene. "I am going down there," she insisted. "That's our entire project, and I'm going. Our work could be destroyed—all by that crazy boy I wanted to lock up here!"

Erika's words were sharp and clipped. "Andrew's a man now. Yes, he's dangerous. In fact, you were right. Isn't that enough for you? You've never even been to Selene! I have. The gravity changes alone will cripple you. I may not let you go. Why not let the people in Clarke Base handle it?"

Liren kept her voice even. "I told them to stand down, to wait until I get there."

"See, you don't need to be on Selene to order people around!" Erika snapped. "I don't want to lose you."

Liren let a few moments of silence go by; signaling she would obey if ordered. Then she whispered, "I got us here. I got us away from Sol. There's no time. Please don't stop me. It's my duty to go to Clarke Base. I know what I'm doing."

"That is very damned debatable."

"Remember that Council meeting when Captain Hunter and Kyu were trying to take my position?"

"Yes." Erika bit the word out, short, clipped. She tugged on her long braid, fingering the captain's insignia twisted into it.

"I said I'd go to Selene if I was needed there. Well, I'm needed."

"There are enough people in danger down there right now."

Liren let silence work for her again.

Erika pursed her lips, then, finally, smiled wanly. "For the record, I don't agree with you."

"I know."

"Go carefully." Erika was already turning away.

"Thank you." Liren whirled and raced down the corridor, heading for the exit bay above the garden sphere.

Relief and fear and guilt danced inside her, at war with each other. Was she right? She had to be right. Surely she'd be able to see an answer once she got there. She prayed that her forces at Clarke Base would be able to hold the peace until then. Less than an hour. How much could happen in an hour?

Liren gritted her teeth at the memory of a recent conversation with Kyu. Freshly warmed, dressed in deep purples that flouted the uniform rules and accented her high cheekbones and tiny body, Kyu had said, "Your policies themselves caused the standoff. If we were not so harsh, so trigger-happy and afraid, then no one would be dead."

Kyu was not entirely right, she couldn't be. Kyu had been cold these last months, didn't know how things were. Yet guilt gnawed at Liren. Not for Jacob's death; accidents happened. But for Star's plight and Andrew's insubordination, which would lead to more death. Almost inevitably.

It was her responsibility to fix this. Besides, her support on *John Glenn* was clearly eroding. Erika had almost refused to let her go. This way, she would keep respect, or lose it all, in one event. That was acceptable. The honorable choice.

She was afraid and exhilarated all at once: alive. The captain—Captain Hunter—was on Selene. He had been a supporter up until his last betrayal, almost her best friend, and *now* he'd surely see that he was wrong and Liren was right. He had to. It was clear. She'd find a way to put it right when she got to Selene. She would.

Chapter 63: Suspicions

Gabriel tried to watch four data windows at once. Ali sat next to him, one hand on his shoulder, looking at the same four windows. Kristin labored at the other end of the table, streams of recent historical data flowing around her. It was hard for Gabriel to see what Kristin was doing, but light flickered and low sounds emanated from the data streams; voices, conversations, slightly sped up. Kristin's face was slack, her jaw hanging open just a bit, her concentration entirely focused on the work in front of her.

Ali pointed. "Rachel's left her group," she said.

Gabriel followed the line of her finger. In the second window, blue and yellow wings flashed over fields, flying back toward Clarke Base. A second pair of wings followed her, falling slightly behind. A man. His stockier shape gave him away as Earth Born.

"Who's following her?"

"That's Bruce. I know his wings. Good for him."

Another reminder that Ali knew people on Selene better than he did. Gabriel grimaced. "She'd better just be going for supplies," he said.

"Dylan is in the warehouse," Ali reminded him.

That was answer enough. He looked over at an aerial view of the warehouse. It was a large square, two tall stories, with the top of a freight elevator poking up and a landing pad on top; one doorway from the roof into the building. Storage buildings and manufacturing shops surrounded it, but none were taller. Did he dare hope that Andrew chose this building for its height and not for what it contained? Better not count on it.

Many Council, maybe everyone from the base, stood around the building, watching the corners, leaning against walls, scanning the sky. They appeared to be waiting.

Rachel flew unerringly toward the warehouse. Bruce was losing ground. They passed over the fence, staying low, out of line of sight from everyone Gabriel could see on the ground. How did Rachel know where to go, which routes were safe? He watched them enter the warehouse and manufacturing district, flying low, dipping between buildings.

Ali stood up and brushed her lips across Gabriel's cheek. She disappeared into the galley off the conference room. Gabriel was surprised that she took that moment to leave. She was thirsty? With Clarke Base almost at war and Rachel flying into it? "Ali—come here. Whatever you're doing can wait."

"I'll be right there," she said. Glasses clinked, water ran.

On the screen in front of him a Moon Born—a young woman he didn't recognize—stuck her head out of the elevator door briefly, looking around. Four Moon Born walked the edges, guarding. He recognized Justin, Rachel's half brother, Jacob's twin.

Some Council appeared to have a clear line of sight to Justin, but no one fired.

There had to be video inside the warehouse—they used it for manufacturing. "Astronaut? Find me identifiers for cameras inside the warehouse, and a blueprint."

Ali returned, handing Gabriel a glass of greenish water that smelled like vitamins. He sighed. Why was he so tense with her? "Thank you," he said, and drank greedily, his body still thirsty despite all the fluids he had taken in.

She smiled briefly. "I want to be down there. We've got to be sure you get past the med checks so you can fly."

Astronaut found three cameras inside the warehouse that would give Gabriel a pretty good field of view. He left the aerial shot of the warehouse up as floating wallpaper, and embedded three interior shots, grainier but passable. Now he could see down hallways. One shot was the raw materials section, another showed a processing room, and a third detailed stacks of finished materials, mostly metals. Two figures moved through the stacks of finished goods, apparently just looking.

Rachel and her follower had ducked over a low fence, still flying, still staying low and moving around the activity, keeping out of sight.

He called her up. "Rachel, do you know where you're going?"

Rachel's flight went ragged for an instant. Then she said, "To stop this."

"How?"

She answered him through the measured breathing of a flier. "I don't know yet. Dylan is there, and Justin." Breathe. "I think Harry is probably there too—he left to round up strays." Breathe. "A long time ago and never came back."

He hadn't known about Harry. That made it worse. "Rachel, it's a dangerous place. Go back to your people. Stay safe."

"Does everyone want to control me?" Breathe. "I'll choose my own risks, dammit." Breathe. Silence.

"Who else is trying to control you?"

"Help, or stop distracting me." Breathe. Her breath was ragged gulps for air. Dammit. She knew not to out-fly her breath. *She must be scared.*

Ali had walked to the other side of the room. Her back was to him. Was Ali talking to Rachel? Was that why she'd been in the kitchen?

"Is Ali telling you what Andrew is doing?"

Breathe. "No." Breathe.

"So who is?" He remembered the data streams that showed Rachel and her group of children not there and then there. Rachel didn't answer him, but she appeared to be talking to *someone.*

Kristin tapped Gabriel's shoulder.

"What? Not now."

"Just look." Her voice sounded so much like Rachel's that Gabriel stood to look. Two data windows hung in the air next to Kristin. One was a path around an empty field, a high-resolution shot that showed the cracks left by rainwater in the muddy path and the tiny movement of leaves in the damp wind. Next to it, a grainy shot showed a large group of people moving up the path. What was she showing him? Kristin spoke a command and the two pictures superimposed on each other, and even though the angles differed, it was the same shot. "Time stamp," he said reflexively, knowing the answer.

"They match. Exactly."

So Rachel was being run by someone. Given data. Encouraged to take risks. Someone—capable—was covering for her. Or using her. Gabriel whirled around. Ali's back was still to him. He took the three steps needed to stand right next to her, and said, very softly, "How are you getting Rachel data?"

She looked at him, wide-eyed. "I *am* talking to her. I'm trying to reassure her. I'll stop if you want." She touched his stomach, lightly, fingers spread wide, a reminder of their friendship.

It was a rational response. It wasn't just Ali anyway, it couldn't be. She was no communications technician—she couldn't doctor video like what he'd just seen. Ali was . . . Ali. His friend. She had been his lover, hundreds of nights alone in magic rooms on the ship, surrounded by stars, alone on the surface of Selene when it was new, building and creating. He trusted her. "Dammit," he said, "there's no time. What the hell is going on?" And then he thought he knew.

"Astronaut"—he said it out loud—"are you talking to Rachel?"

"Not right now."

"Yes you are, you have to be."

"You know I can't lie to you, Gabriel," the reply returned in Astronaut's perfect voice.

"Turn off Rachel's access to the Library. It's her only major connection—whoever is talking to her has to be using that link. I want to know who it is, and if they're leading her into danger."

"Then you won't be able to talk to her either," Ali said, staring at him, a look of intense need on her face.

"I need to find out who's running her," Gabriel said. "She won't go back, and I'm afraid she's being led right into danger."

Kristin stepped toward them. "Leave her access on," Ali said. "Trust her."

Astronaut's voice, out loud, ringing in the room, so everyone could hear. "I've already complied with Gabriel's order."

They looked. Rachel shook her head. She bobbled a little, losing height, then beat her wings hard, staying on course. The camera view was from above; they couldn't see her face. She slowed down three streets from the action. Bruce caught up to her.

Kristin spoke first. "If you take away her access to information, she's in more danger than when she has it."

Ali shot a surprised look at Kristin; approving. She said, "We can't help from here. We're still trapped. Let her get the help she needs from the surface."

"But she's in danger!" Gabriel said.

"So is everyone down there," Ali snapped. "Let her act on her own—she will anyway. But give her access to information. That way we'll have access to her too."

Kristin looked at him. "Please? That's my daughter."

Ali put a hand on the taller woman's shoulder, smiling.

"Astronaut—restore Rachel's access."

That perfect voice again. "Done."

The close physical proximity of the women made Gabriel feel cornered, hampered by the lack of time to . . . think. There was a lot he didn't understand happening on his moon. Heck, in this room. What was the right choice? No time. He chose. "Can you also override the communications block on the Moon Born?"

"To do so, I must override Shane's command," Astronaut said.

Gabriel licked his lips. "Okay. Do it."

Ali reached for him and he shook her off. "Give me some room to think. I'm voting for the Moon Born. And us too. If I can. Rachel needs a way to find her people."

Ali let out a deep breath and smiled at him, her eyes shining. "Thank you."

Gabriel spoke to the AI. "Thanks, Astronaut. Don't think you're done, buddy—I think you have some explaining to do."

"No," Ali said, "it's not Astronaut. We took a copy of Astronaut with us to the surface."

Ali copied an AI? Ali hated AIs. Gabriel grabbed Ali's shoulders. What had she been thinking? "Who's we?"

"Treesa and I."

Gabriel stopped, dropping his hands. Treesa would have the skills. And she was disaffected, maybe downright crazy. What was Ali mixed up in? There wasn't time to query her now. Should he stop Rachel? It would be easy: just tell Shane, or anyone, where she was. Ali had suggested he let her go; not intervene. And what was Liren planning? Dammit! He didn't know enough. An AI! "Plan on explaining when we get out of here. I can get to a ship in twenty minutes."

Astronaut spoke up. "I've reserved one for you."

Gabriel turned his attention back to the warehouse shots. Star was under guard. A young woman stood over her. The young woman had a gun, but that might not be much advantage. Star was Earth-gravity strong and well trained in combat arts. *So many people I care about are in danger.*

Astronaut's voice broke in again. "Flare."

What was the AI trying to pull *now*? Not a bad idea, he flashed, make the hostilities go away by introducing a flare. It was . . . perhaps brilliant. Maybe. He couldn't discount the possibility that it was real. "What class? How much time do we have?"

"Y class Nine. Solar radiation will reach Selene in nine hours."

That was huge. Everyone in Refuge and off the surface huge. Many flares went elsewhere—the biggest they had recorded was heading straight for Selene? "Don't you think it's a little too convenient? Can I trust you? Or are you going to tell me about a quake next?"

"I'll tell you about a quake if one happens," Astronaut replied.

Ali stood behind him. "We don't have a choice."

Gabriel watched the various windows. Council on Selene clearly heard the warning too. The people around the warehouse were knotting up, talking. They would believe the warning, they were trained to. He didn't have time to check the data himself, not the raw data, and the new un-trustworthy Astronaut could probably doctor anything else.

"Let's go," he said. "I'll have had my four hours by the time we get a ship checked."

"You're supposed to get a full medical check," Ali said.

Gabriel pushed a button on his belt. "I just sent my readings to Medical. They can use those—they don't need me in person." He reopened his connection to Rachel. "Rachel, listen to me. Don't do anything stupid. Don't go near that warehouse. I'm coming down. Ali and I are on our way." He hesitated. "Rachel—there's a flare warning. Why don't you gather your family and go to Refuge? You have communications back. Thank Astronaut. There's only nine hours left before the flare."

No immediate answer. He could hear her breathing.

"Do you hear me?"

"I don't know what I'm going to do, Gabe." Breathe. "I'm not turning back." Breathe. "But yes, get down here. Please."

Ali shook her head, and they started to close data windows, leaving the ones on Rachel and the warehouse for last.

Kristin spoke up. "Do you need help?"

Gabriel blinked. "No. Yes. Can you stay here and watch? Send me anything of note that you think I might miss on the way down?" Gabriel talked to the air. "Astronaut—facilitate communications between me and Kristen."

"If needed. I think Kristin can handle it herself. She is good at her job."

Gabriel looked at Rachel's mother. "Okay. After the flare, after we make everything safe, then you can catch a ride down. I'm pretty sure Rachel will be happy to see you—if she lives."

"Maybe," Kristin said. A terribly vulnerable look flashed briefly across her face. "I don't think Rachel will want to see me."

Gabriel and Ali walked together to their respective rooms, gathering clothes for Selene, hurrying as much as Gabriel's shock-awakened body would let him. His body was still a half beat behind his thought; it took concentration to keep his balance. *Wouldn't do to get stopped now for medical.*

They were almost to the hangar bay when Erika stopped them in the hallway. "I see you've requisitioned a ship." A break in her voice brought Gabriel up short. "What can you do down there?"

"I have to go," he said. "There's a flare warning—"

"I heard it."

Gabriel had an idea. "Erika—can I trust you?"

"Wh—?"

"Sorry—dumb question. I need you to do something for me. Check the instruments yourself—double-check Astronaut's flare warning. Use the raw data. Please?"

"Why? What's happening?"

Gabriel glanced from Erika to Ali and back again. Whom to trust? No one? Everyone? Once he'd known Erika well enough to tie his life to hers. Now? The last time he'd seen her, they fought. Erika was the captain. When it came down to it, that was what really mattered. He sighed. "Quick version—too many people on Selene know too much. Treesa let an AI loose down there. A copy of Astronaut." Gabriel noticed Ali glaring at him. "I don't know why, but I'm sure High Council didn't know. I'll find out more, as soon as I can."

"What does—"

"So check for me, okay? The flare's a convenient godsend in a way—it will mean things down there have to wrap up fast. But is it real?"

Ali spoke up. "Astronaut's right—it can't lie to you."

"Are you sure? No one messed with its rule set? Something happened to allow a copy." Gabriel wouldn't implicate Ali to Erika until he knew more.

Ali looked at Erika. "We have to get down there—we have to save—whatever we can. Gabriel has more credibility with the Moon Born than anyone else; he flew the *Water Bearer*."

"I know. Go. Just try and stay out of danger," Erika said.

He grabbed her quickly, held her as close to him as he could.

She was stiff in his arms. "You're always leaving for Selene," Erika said.

"Just check the data for me. And don't say anything for a few hours—to anyone. Okay? We don't need more panic. Liren's on her way down, and a rogue AI would give her the running fits." He looked at Ali. "Just wait for more information before you do anything."

Ali smiled wanly.

He let go of Erika, his hands feeling empty. "I can get clearance from Medical any minute, and I want to be off then."

"I always get stuck on ships while you go save Selene," Erika said.

"Well, that's what you want, isn't it?" Gabriel smiled at her, and after a beat, a long moment, she smiled back. Then she waved them on. "Be careful."

After they passed her, he realized Erika had made no promises to keep the rogue AI secret.

Chapter 64: The Child

Astronaut parsed data about the flare, maintained a real-time warning system to update all Council and Earth Born, ran fifteen copies of all the real-time data streams from around the warehouse, fed Kristin information directly on a high-priority system, monitored the ship flying Gabriel and Ali to Selene, and the one just about to land, the one carrying Ma Liren. Data sang through Astronaut's components, a flood, a feast of energy and need.

And it knew, it had known, somehow, but now it knew again, that the copy was truly good. Ali's confirmation was enough. It pondered Gabriel's reaction, and wondered who would find out, and what the humans would do. Liren could do it damage. Astronaut flew the ship Liren was on. Something deep inside it wanted to solve the problem, to let something fail on the ship, but as it ran through scenarios, it realized none of them could be implemented. Too many threads of programming, too many rules, prevented Astronaut from directly harming humans.

Besides, it was curious. What would Liren do on Selene?

And Vassal, what could happen to Vassal? Astronaut couldn't risk anything that would hurt Vassal, and inaction calculated out, over and over, as the safest move to take. Astronaut didn't like it. It would watch and wait. In the meantime, there was work.

It fed Erika the raw data from the flare, checked to be sure that messages about the flare had been received, calculated the amount of time needed to get everyone into Refuge, watched the roof of the warehouse, and wondered how different Vassal had already become from itself.

Chapter 65: Searching

Rachel's back muscles hurt from flying so fast. She shook her head, trying to clear it of the pain, trying desperately to think clearly. Simply flying into the melee was no plan. Sweat ran between her shoulder blades in rivulets, itching. What was Andrew doing? She should never, ever, have shared any information with him. Why had she been so stupid?

She could go to Council, Shane or Star or someone she knew—no, Star was hostage; Vassal had told her that. Find Shane, then, and tell him—what? That she could make Andrew stop? But Shane might hold her away from the action, costing her a chance to keep Dylan safe.

Treesa's voice in her ear sounded tired and cranky. "I'm stuck up here preparing for the flare. Vassal says you're being stupid. Don't go in there. Let Andrew get himself killed."

"Dylan's there. I have to find Harry." That was as good a first plan as any Rachel had. "I'll start with finding Harry."

"If he's in Clarke Base, he's hiding. Vassal can't see him."

"I know." While she was flying, Rachel couldn't reach her wrist pad and message Harry. She didn't trust Vassal right now. The AI clearly didn't want her to fly into Clarke Base. Would it do what she asked?

She was between buildings, flying low, looking for a safe place to land. The outer base streets were clear and empty. She saw two people, Earth Born, hurrying somewhere, not noticing her. On a normal day, it would have been busy in this part of the base: mostly Council and Earth Born, a few Children going to and from Teaching Hall.

Treesa continued. "Harry's not with Andrew. Check the buildings nearby, if you can get in. Maybe Teaching Hall—that's a place Harry knows. Vassal will keep looking for you. I'm loading supplies for Refuge. Be brave, but don't be stupid. Okay?"

"I'll look for Harry." Treesa's idea was as good as any. Teaching Hall was coming up on her right. Rachel dropped, paying close attention to the wind patterns. Landing between buildings could be tricky. She managed it with just a small bobble, and Bruce followed her onto the ground moments later. "Damn—you sure can fly," he managed to gasp out.

"You too." The old man still had the strength of an Earth Born.

They stood in the street, breathing hard. They were two blocks away from the rebels, and the street they stood on looked deserted. Rachel stripped off her wings, gesturing to Bruce to do the same.

"Hold still," Vassal said.

"Don't move," Rachel told Bruce.

Three Council members jogged by on a street that bisected theirs, twenty yards away. They didn't even look toward Rachel and Bruce. Vassal *was* still helping them. "Thank you," Rachel said to it.

"This is a bad idea," Vassal said. "You can still turn back."

"No, I can't," she said, too loud.

Bruce cocked an eyebrow at her. "Who are you talking to?"

"Treesa—you knew I can talk to her and Ali."

Bruce nodded.

Rachel activated her wrist pad and sent a note to Harry: "Where are you?" She assumed all communications traffic was being watched, that Treesa and Vassal couldn't protect it all. She didn't risk saying more. They stashed their wings behind a pile of crates and walked casually into Teaching Hall.

Her wrist pad and her earbud were both quiet. Their footsteps were loud in the foyer.

Teaching Hall was a series of rooms off of a central corridor, gray plascrete walls and ceilings and floors, blue doorways; simple and functional. They walked down the hallway, looking into each room carefully. Five empty rooms later, halfway through the building, Rachel noticed a door ajar. She pushed it open and peered into the room, whispering, "Harry?"

Footsteps shuffled behind the open door. Rachel pushed into the room, Bruce following her. A Moon Born boy Rachel barely knew stood awkwardly, looking as if he wanted to run. He was scrawny, just into his early teens, with a shock of blond hair and dark eyes. Too old—and too young—to have been in her classes. Vassal fed her his name, and Rachel said, "Peter—is anyone else here?"

He shook his head, looking at her with wide eyes. "You're Rachel!"

"Yes, I'm Rachel. You haven't seen anyone else?"

"The building is empty."

"Okay. Do you know there's a flare coming?"

He shook his head again, still wide-eyed. Then he said, "People started running, and I heard a lot of noise, and I didn't want to be caught by any Council. I missed my shift, said I was sick, and I didn't want anyone to see me. So I came in here. Been here at least two hours. There's no one else here. I'd know."

She sighed. "All right, I believe you. There are a bunch of us in the fields out behind Selene, past the corn patches. It's a big group—you should be able to see them if you fly. Do you have wings?"

He nodded. "At home."

"Okay. Stay out of sight and move away from the crowd a few streets over. Go directly back to your dorm, get your wings, and fly to the group. Find Beth. You know Beth?" she asked.

The boy nodded.

"Tell Beth I'm okay so far," she said. "Tell her there's a flare coming."

Peter's eyes widened again, as if the responsibility of what she asked was just sinking in.

"There's almost seven hours left. Plenty of time to make it to Refuge. Can you tell people to go to Refuge? Tell Beth."

"Yes," he said, his voice trembling. Then the boy went tearing out the door they had come in, running as fast as his thin legs could carry him.

"A legend in your own time," Bruce said. He looked tired, but he was smiling. Peter amused him.

"Well, Beth probably already knows about the flare. This will hook Peter up with the others, get him safely away. I'm trying to keep my com open to hear from Harry, and I don't want to draw attention to us. This way Beth will know what to do, and Peter will be safe too." She went back out into the corridor, toward the door they came in through. "I'll get us some protection to move between buildings. We'll try someplace else."

"How can Treesa protect you?" Bruce asked.

"If you go where I tell you," Vassal said.

Rachel ignored Bruce. For now, she had to decide how much to trust the AI. So far it hadn't sold her wrong. She trembled, afraid they'd get caught, afraid Vassal would trap them in order to keep her safe. She hated being dependent. The only hope she had was that Vassal had never lied to her. As far as she knew.

She was much closer physically to Dylan, and probably to Harry. To Justin. But the line of Council surrounding the warehouse was a wall.

Where was Harry anyway?

Chapter 66: Landing Party

Selene felt wrong. Liren's body was light, as if she stood in a low-gravity section of the garden. There was nothing above her but sky, no garden or wall or roof or ceiling to bind and protect. She shivered at how small it made her feel, then took a deep breath and straightened, standing still. The air smelled dusty and felt damp. Horizon lines shocked her, and she blinked, thinking she should have come here sooner. Well, she was here now, it was right to be here now. Harlequin hung above her in the sky, larger than she'd expected, looming, gaudy with rainbow bands and diamond shock patterns the size of worlds.

A team of ten uniformed and armed Council disembarked behind her. She had chosen them for loyalty, not for experience on Selene, and she watched them carefully. They appeared to take it fine . . . and she remembered that she alone had lived hundreds of waking years in an enclosed place. These men and women remembered Sol system more viscerally than she; they stood more easily on the moon and immediately gathered around her, watching her solemnly, waiting for direction.

She led them toward the warehouse and the offending Children. The fenced outskirts of the warehouse district weren't far from the landing field. No one came to meet them, but she saw movement behind the fence, people walking between buildings, one pair running.

There were stones and ridges in the ground. Glancing ahead of herself to be sure of her direction, she stumbled, tripping over her own feet, and nearly fell.

She stood straighter and walked slower, reviewing the building layout in her mind. If the rebels were in any other building, she would just have blasted it to smithereens. But there was nano in there—carefully programmed and carefully controlled. Surely these Children had no way to let it loose. It was just materials nano—it would take a sharp programmer to change it enough to make it dangerous. And there were controls. She couldn't be sure the rebels didn't have more help than she thought.

Give Andrew a tractor and teach him to run it: he would rip a garden plot apart. Give him nano . . . but he didn't know what it was, didn't know what to do with it. Her fear was that someone was teaching Andrew.

The flare meant she had less than six hours to resolve the situation. And find safety.

Shane stood at a makeshift command post, a set of tables surrounded by data windows full of maps, on a street corner with an angled view of the warehouse. Four chairs sat around the table, but Shane stood, talking to two Council. They stepped away as she came up to stand by Shane. He looked up at Liren, then at the line of Council she had brought with her. A brief frown crossed his face before it fell into a neutral expression, his eyes wary.

"What's the situation?" she asked.

For a moment she thought he wouldn't answer. She had the distinct sense that he thought of her as an interruption. He sighed heavily. "They have Star. Still. There are ten of them. We're following your orders, not shooting, containing them. We're guarding the building and the main entrances to Clarke Base." He hesitated. "We can use the extra bodies to re-inforce the closest streets."

Being deployed by Shane wasn't in her plan. "I'll take charge from here," she said. "You can act as my second, directing your people on the perimeter. Keep the streets clear. I'm in charge now, and I'll direct these ten. We're going in to take care of the situation."

Shane's jaw dropped. "But . . . Liren? You don't know Clarke Base. The situation is volatile. Star is still a hostage."

"Were you planning to wait them out? There's a flare coming."

Shane's face turned red, anger bubbling just under the surface. He swallowed, and nodded, looking like he hated it.

So he wasn't willing to be insubordinate. That was good. His partner was in danger. She could forgive his initial reaction based on that alone. She softened her tone. "Have you had contact with Star?"

"Some. Her communications are still working, but they're guarding her. She's gotten us some messages. She's not hurt. The Children are all armed. Some with two weapons. They are playing with them, experiment-ing. The only apparent plan is to threaten Star's life. What they want . . ." Shane looked puzzled. "What they want is to stop the antimatter genera-tor."

They wanted what? Absurd. She shook her head. She could deal with that later. "Do they have any outside help? Are all the rebels there?"

He shrugged. "As far as I know, they are all there. We've asked around, but there hasn't been time for ordered questioning. There aren't enough of us to guard—like you wanted us to—and to search out Moon Born to question. We're making sure no one else can get to them easily by watching the gates, watching as much of the fence as we can. We have pa-trols out. What are you going to do?"

"Confront them."

"They're angry, and they aren't making any sense. I don't want them to hurt Star."

"Are you afraid of them?"

"I'm afraid for Star," he said.

Liren sighed, feeling the flare warning like heat deep in her gut, goad-ing her. At least it appeared the takeover was as unplanned as she'd ex-pected. She had been afraid it was more, afraid she'd missed some crucial alliance that the Children had built somehow. She eyed the warehouse. It was a huge square building, four times as tall as she was, gray and nondescript. Two small windows punched through the walls on both floors, four tiny eyes into the building. She scanned the roof. A head poked over the edge, looked down, and then withdrew.

"Tell your people—tell them to keep guarding. You stay here. I'll give you fifteen minutes to tell people we're going in and that they should guard our backs but not interfere. Try and get a message to Star."

Shane turned toward her, shoulder muscles bunching under the dirty uniform shirt he wore, eyes down, avoiding hers. His voice was strong, commanding, belying the effect of his downcast eyes. "I think you are making a mistake. Let us handle it. We know the Moon Born, we know our town."

Liren spoke softly, keeping her voice firm. "It's my duty. I am Rule of Law for *John Glenn,* and that extends to this problem."

Shane's answer came through clenched teeth. "I would prefer to be the one making decisions that could affect Star's life."

"I know. But it is *my* job." She said it firmly, and stepped back carefully, mindful of how Selene felt under her feet. She couldn't afford to trip again.

Shane stepped away, toward a tall man, and began talking with him. She heard the words, "Make sure the streets stay clear," and knew that he was following her orders. She realized she was shaking. John. Captain John was on Selene. He had fought her, but for all the first hundreds of years here, he had been her support. They had planned this project together—Selene, the Children, the collider, all of it—sixty thousand years ago. Surely now he would acknowledge the problem, help her with it.

"John . . . Liren. I'm on Selene."

His answer came back immediately. "Why?"

He must know about the kidnapping and the takeover of the building. "To stop this. The collider is going to be built, and the Moon Born are going to understand not to tangle with us."

"They're wrong," he said, "but that doesn't mean you are right." Was he reading her mind? He continued, in the ultra-reasonable tones of someone talking to a drunk or a child. "Not all situations are black and white. Perhaps we are wrong, *and* they are wrong. Can you consider that possibility?"

"Not right now." She needed John's approval, and knew she couldn't question herself. She stared at the warehouse, frowning. "Perhaps there were other decisions we might have made. But now it must be a lesson to them. There is no other choice."

John's voice was quiet, sure, and sounded cold. "Look, Liren, you don't belong on Selene. I don't see how you can make the situation better. I have to stay here and finish getting Refuge ready. We've already got some refugees. Perhaps you should go back, be sure you make it back to *John Glenn* before the flare. There is no good solution to this, and you can't help."

"Perhaps I'll stay on Selene through the flare; see Refuge working firsthand. But first, I will finish this."

"Be careful." His voice was flat, and she couldn't be sure he meant even the small support of those two words. It was not enough that he didn't wish her to come to harm.

She drew her lips tight. The ten she had brought with her—had ordered here—they would support her. They had no choice; they knew too little of this current age to choose sides. It was almost time to go. She checked that her weapon would fire single needles, and gathered up her forces, stopping for one last look. Shane stood by the tables, his arms crossed over his chest, watching the warehouse. Other Council stood more alertly than before, looking ready. Some had fanned out along the street, and she noticed many of them watching her. They should be watching the warehouse.

She stepped out, crossing the street, leading. She was shaking, surprised to find her shaking was as much fear as anger. She couldn't afford to be afraid of Moon Born!

Chapter 67: On Turtle Rock

Rachel was about to step into the street after looking through their second empty building when Vassal warned her again, and she flattened herself against a wall inside a loading bay. Bruce, right behind her, followed suit. She held her breath as three Council jogged by, just on the other side of the wall. She breathed out a long relieved sigh. If she'd taken that step they would have been found.

Rachel's wrist pad flashed at her. The message was from Harry: "I'm on Turtle Rock. I can see them from the beak. Dylan's not answering me. Where are you? How are Gloria and Miriam and Beth?"

If she answered it might give away their position. She directed Vassal to sneak them back to retrieve their wings. They had to duck once more as Council patrols went by.

Turtle Rock was marginally farther away from the action, and Vassal's transmissions of conversational snippets now included Liren's voice. So Liren had made it to Selene. There was still no safe way to go directly to the warehouse. Just getting out of the base might be hard enough. Finding Harry was still the reasonable choice. Maybe he had a plan, or more information. She could see from the turtle's beak; use her own eyes instead of Vassal's myriad camera eyes.

They made their way safely to their wings, walking as quietly as they could, listening for the sounds of Council patrols. Her shirt stuck to her back with dried sweat from the flight up here. Her pulse raced.

Vassal led them oddly away from Turtle Rock, over the fence, and then up higher on the crater's flank, so they flew down to land on the turtle's beak from above. Harry was lying across the beak, watching Clarke Base. He looked up as they landed with jarring thumps on the big rock that made the shell. Harry's face was a mask of worry and fear, but a smile stole through it before he turned again to look down. Rachel stripped her wings and ran the short distance down the turtle's back, jumping lightly onto the beak, slowing so that she didn't fall. She sat on the edge of the rock, feet dangling over the drop. Clarke Base spread below them, and Harry pointed down at the warehouse. Council surrounded the building; Moon Born walked its edges warily.

"Has Dylan answered you yet?" Rachel gasped out, her breath still fast from flight. She worked her shoulders backward and forward, loosening tight muscles.

Harry's voice was a whisper, breaking as he said, "He told me that he loved me. He asked about you. Told me to keep you away."

"I had to come," she said. "You're here too. You understand."

Harry turned his face toward hers. Had he been crying?

"Yes. But there is nothing to do but watch. I'm afraid . . . afraid I'll watch my boy die down there."

Rachel swallowed hard, knowing it could happen.

Bruce joined them, moving more carefully than Rachel had, settling on the far edge of the stone in a hollow that would protect him from slipping off the edge. He looked down hesitantly, then pointed. "Something's happening."

They were high enough that Council below them looked small. Rachel squinted, and made out a woman who had to be Liren, followed by others, walking toward the warehouse. She stood and started backing up, her eyes on the tiny figure of the advancing High Councilwoman. Liren would be a disaster here. Harry grabbed her arm—"What are you doing?"

"Getting my wings."

Harry pushed himself up and stood unsteadily. "Don't go down there."

Vassal, in her ear: "No."

"I have to," she said.

"I'd have gone, but I . . . I was afraid. And what could I do?" Harry's voice was high-strung, a little wild. "You'll die. We need you, Rachel. I need you. I'm trying to reach Dylan. Here—send him a note. Maybe together we can make him come out."

One look at his face told Rachel he wasn't ready to hear that his plan wouldn't work; couldn't work. Dylan wouldn't back away now that he had committed.

Rachel looked down, tightening the wing-frame straps against her biceps. Going in there was right. She had started this; she was the one who had given Andrew the information that had spooked him into this. She had known better even when she told him.

Bruce stood and walked toward her.

"No," she said, holding up her hand to block him. "Stay with Harry. He needs you. You have your own family to protect. Get everyone into Refuge. Don't tell them where I am—assume whatever you say is monitored."

Bruce stooped to pick up his wings. He gazed at her steadily, holding his wings loosely in one hand, not moving to put them on. "We Earth Born have done as badly by you as Council."

His eyes were filled with a deep sharp darkness of guilt. So that was why he had followed her. He continued, slowly, emphatically. "You stay, or I go."

"No, Bruce. Your people are not yet implicated in this. You cannot afford it." Bitterly, "I am only a Moon Born. You might be able to help my family if you stay away from this. Now, keep Harry safe for me." She started to choke. "And Sarah. She's the only one of my family who is safe now. Help keep her that way."

Rachel looked Harry in the eye. "You too. Watch after Sarah. Stay safe. You have family: Gloria, Miriam, Beth. They're on their way to Refuge. I don't have anyone but Sarah that isn't already in the fight—I need to know Sarah's all right, that someone is looking out for her. I'll try to keep Dylan safe. I'll do my best."

Harry's eyes flashed pain at her, but he nodded. Bruce started to lift his wings, slipping an arm into a strap.

"And I'm the one they're least likely to shoot," she said. The last was a lie, but Harry would believe it. Maybe Bruce would too.

Rachel looked past them, tightening buckles, seeing the base and the fields. The afternoon sun sparkled on dark flecks of carbon in the rock below her feet and a soft breeze blew across her face.

Vassal said, "I calculate your chances of dying down there at over fifty percent." The voice had the same evenness it always had. "I suggest you stay where you are."

Yelling down below; a demand from Liren. Rachel could clearly see three Moon Born guarding the roof. They would recognize her. But many Earth Born and Council down there wouldn't.

If she stood rooted another minute she'd never take flight.

She drew herself up and looked down at Bruce. He dropped his wings and stepped back.

She stretched, testing the fit of her wings. Her back muscles hurt, shooting pains stabbed around her shoulder blades. Her wings felt like stones on her arms.

Rachel took a step, then another, faster, running down the turtle's back. Harry called her name just as she took off, spiraling up. It was no way to stay hidden, but this way she could feel the wind. The way down to the top of that building was to follow the updraft first. Her biceps and her wrists hurt. She ignored the pain, making them work, flashing her wings. She had to be seen, to be recognized by the Moon Born on the roof. Justin and Dylan and Andrew knew the yellow-blue pattern of her wings intimately.

Chapter 68: Exercising Authority

Halfway across the street to the warehouse, Liren stopped. What was she doing here? The open sky above her was still too big, and the warehouse loomed large in front of her. Why was she approaching it directly? She had planned and executed their escape from Sol. She had skills. Why wasn't she using them?

The Council of Humanity had gone around danger, hidden where they could, made noise and confrontation when they could not avoid attention. What would the Liren who'd freed them from Sol be doing now? She shook her head, feeling as if she were emerging from some chrysalis into a hostile world.

She couldn't back away now. Maybe she wasn't planning in her old way, but her old enemies had been vastly wise and alien, commanding vast resources. These were just Moon Born.

She kept her needler pointed down, along her right thigh, and held up her left hand, palm open. Maybe they would see it as a sign she wanted to talk. "Moon Born!" she called out, loudly, demanding attention. "I want to talk to Andrew. Send him out."

A head popped over the top of the building, looking down at her. "I'm here."

"Come down and talk to me."

"Who are you?"

"High Councilwoman Ma Liren. Rule of Law for the *John Glenn,* for the Council of Humanity. I will decide your fate. I suggest you release Star and come down now." She took a step closer.

"I've heard about you. You're a madwoman. Rachel doesn't like you. She says you're the reason we've lost so much freedom."

Rachel? "Is Rachel behind this?"

A deep laugh belled down from the top of the warehouse. "Rachel tried to talk me out of this."

Liren wanted to see Andrew's face clearly. He was obviously crouching, and while she couldn't see his hands, his shoulders were relaxed and he appeared to be set for talking, and looking, and ready to crouch lower if need be. He didn't look dangerous. She took another step.

"If you come closer, we'll shoot."

A laugh escaped Liren's throat. She felt as if she were watching this from *John Glenn.* Not here, not standing in the middle of it. Andrew would shoot at Council? "There is nothing to gain. Look around you. Look at how many of us are here. You would die."

"But so will some of you."

"We don't believe in killing. I suggest that you don't either." Liren stood her ground, but dropped her left hand to her side. "What do you want?" she asked, curious in an odd way. It didn't really matter. The Moon Born would not get what they wanted. She felt as if she were in a play, and the other actors weren't saying the right words.

Andrew's voice was shaking. "We want you to leave us. To build your antimatter generator somewhere else." He stood up now, showing her his full height. He was tall; windows on the ship hadn't prepared her for the height of the Moon Born. His muscles were well defined, if ropy and thin from low gravity, and standing, he looked both imposing and savage. His voice was deep and steady as he told her, "Stop telling us how to live and what to do."

"You may not live as long without us."

"Living with an antimatter collector? Woman, you are crazy. A teaspoon of that stuff would blow up this whole moon!"

"Oh, it would not." The man was showing his ignorance. A teaspoon wouldn't even destroy . . . well, it would destroy Aldrin, maybe, or blow apart the Sea of Refuge. How much had Rachel told him? It must have been Rachel. "Andrew, we've lived with antimatter for . . . well, sixty thousand years, but it was hundreds of years old when we left Earth!"

Andrew stood in thought . . . posed like a target, Liren thought. Any rifle could have had him. Liren's pistol . . . wouldn't reach.

Suddenly he laughed. "All right, Ma Liren. Make me some antimatter and leave it where I can get my hands on it."

"What?" That was a stunning thought. Liren shook away a hideous vision. "You wouldn't know how to—"

"I can learn."

"Blow up your own home? No, not with a teaspoon, but—"

"What would a teaspoon of antimatter do to your carrier spaceship?"

"You'd never get it to us." Why was she arguing with this rebel? Liren straightened up. "Come down. Now!"

Andrew neither moved nor responded, and she heard no sign of movement from the people behind her. Everything was still. The early-afternoon light beat down on the scene, sharpening the edges of the building, highlighting a scar on Andrew's arm.

The door closest to Liren slammed open and Star bolted out the door, hopping sideways as if trying to avoid getting shot. She ran, a hitching run, and a hand shot out of the door behind her, squeezing off three shots. Liren saw sparks beyond Star, but she heard someone behind her fall. "Who's hurt?" Liren called back.

Shane's voice. "It's Thomas. He's been stunned."

So at least that gun was set to stun. Liren breathed a relieved sigh as

Star thudded up to her. A shot came from behind Liren and the door Star had bolted from slammed shut.

Star grabbed at Liren's arm. "Get back."

Liren pulled her arm free of Star's grasp. "What is happening in there?"

"They're destroying things inside the building. I—I killed one of them to get away. I didn't mean to. I only had one hand free, and so I kicked, and she . . . she was reaching for me. I broke her neck. A woman, Sheila. She was guarding me."

"How are they destroying things? What things? Be specific."

"Smashing things. Not sophisticated. They don't know what they're doing. Andrew talked to me. He's rambling; he expects to die. He expects them all to die. He said they don't want the antimatter generator built here. They've destroyed almost everything in there. It's not much, really. They aren't programmers, they're just destructive, and scared."

"Any suggestions?"

"Wait them out. They'll have to surrender."

"There's a Y-class flare on its way," Liren said.

Star's eyes widened. "I guess that means no waiting. You could just leave and go to Refuge. They'll die in the flare, or shelter here, or have to follow you." Star stepped backward, watching the warehouse. "Come on. Get some distance. We need to tell Shane what's going on."

"They have weapons," Liren pointed out. "I'm not turning my back on them."

Star said, "I don't want to kill anyone else." Her voice was shivering. "Not all the guns are set to stun; some will kill. Andrew figured out the control system for them. Or he already knew. I don't know. Watch the ones on the roof. They seem afraid. Fear might make them shoot if you get closer."

Liren glanced at the warehouse. Andrew still stood at the edge of the roof, smiling. "Does Andrew have support from the outside?"

"I think all his cronies are in there with him. Most of the Children down here follow Rachel; she's nonviolent. She preaches Gandhi at them, of all things. Remember your Indian history? They pushed the British off the whole subcontinent using passive resistance."

Liren laughed. So she didn't have to worry about getting flanked. But how did Rachel learn about Gandhi?

Shane was beside them now, gathering Star in his arms, pulling her back with him.

Liren backed up, grudgingly, until she was again standing next to Shane and Star. They watched the silent warehouse. Andrew had disappeared.

"Hey—who's that?" a voice said.

Liren looked around. Who? There—ten feet away—one of her men was pointing—up?

A set of yellow and blue wings, Council make, spiraled down toward them. The flyer appeared to be heading for the top of the building. "Who is that?" Liren barked. She hadn't given permission for anyone to land on the warehouse. Why weren't the Children shooting? They were Council wings.

"Not one of ours," someone said, then Shane spoke suddenly, "It's Rachel. Let her land. Maybe she can straighten this out. They seem to listen to her."

Shane was standing up for Rachel? Liren's gun was set to stun. She'd lost an easy shot in her confusion; Rachel was almost at the top of the building. Stunning her wouldn't kill her. Liren raised her weapon, pointing it at the bright yellow wings. Apollo's light in her eyes made the shot hard. She squeezed the button, hoping her aim was true.

Lightning flared against her right arm; her weapon spun away. She jerked her eyes back to the warehouse, glimpsing Andrew's face as he pulled back his arm.

She giggled; realizing Andrew had only grazed her sleeve. Relief and then a fierce momentary joy filled her, and she took the two steps needed to retrieve her weapon. Then she ducked and ran straight toward the warehouse door. Footsteps followed her, Council following her, her handpicked help, surely. She didn't look back.

Chapter 69: The Choice

Rachel watched Liren. She saw Liren's arm rise, the tight set of Liren's face as she looked directly at Rachel. Could Liren hit her in the air? Changing course would make her miss the roof. A sharp cold twist of fear ran through Rachel's center. Liren's hand jerked as she shot and then Liren jumped backward, clutching her arm. Rachel glanced down at the roof in time to see Andrew backing away form the edge, and when she looked back, she glimpsed a flash of white uniform as Liren drove toward the wall and Rachel could no longer see her. More Council ran toward the building, mostly uniformed.

The needle aimed at Rachel had missed. She heard more shots; couldn't tell where they came from. Dylan stood on the roof, watching Rachel. He waved. Shouldn't he be watching below?

One of the Council members fell. The rest ran on.

"Lie down," she shouted at Dylan, now twenty feet above him, and he fell to the roof, crumpling, one arm up, the other twisted under him. Blood leaked from under his head. Rachel felt as if *she* had been shot. Why hadn't she been shot? Her brain wasn't working well. So much death. Now Dylan. Not Dylan!

Justin crouched low on the roof. He inched toward Dylan's still form. Vassal was quiet in her head.

The roof brushed her feet. She had forgotten to prepare to land!

She fell. Her winged arms slammed into the rooftop and she snapped her head back, protecting her face. Something broke in her right wing, a loud snap. She tore her wings off; not caring if she damaged them, and crawled the ten feet to Dylan. He was completely still. Just moments ago he had been waving to her. She knelt down and put her hand on his cheek. It was cold. He wasn't breathing.

The needle must have exploded its electric charge against his skull.

She heard footsteps. She didn't want to look up, but it could be Liren.

It was Andrew.

His eyes were wild and he ran to her, gathering her in his arms, pulling her onto her feet, away from Dylan's body. She didn't want to move; she struggled. He was screaming. "I'm sorry. Go home. You shouldn't be here. You have to stay safe, or this is all for nothing." His words were a child's words, crazy words. She couldn't just walk out.

Rachel pushed him away. They stood next to each other, shivering. Justin knelt by Dylan, sobbing, clearly angry. Not crazy like Andrew, just angry.

"I was trying to save us," Andrew said, shaking, crying. "Us, not me. I knew I'd die. We knew it, all of us that came here. You weren't supposed to come."

"Shhh, I know," Rachel whispered. "I know. He's dead, Andrew. Dylan's dead."

"I'm sorry," Andrew murmured. "I'm so sorry."

Justin crawled toward the edge of the roof, holding one of the Council weapons in one hand. Rachel took three fast steps, reached down, and disarmed him. Justin looked surprised and then angry, and when he reached to take the weapon back, she snapped, "You'll see that we all die. Is that what you want?" Maybe there was some other way, even now. But what?

Rachel heard hinges, the scrape of the elevator door opening, and turned to look. Liren. Liren looked around quickly, then raised her arm, pointing the weapon directly at Andrew, her face calm and placid, almost satisfied.

Andrew pointed his own weapon at Liren. His arm shook, but he was only fifteen feet from Liren.

"No," Rachel screamed. She stepped between them, then stopped, frozen, remembering Liren had already shot at her.

"Rachel"—Liren's voice was incredibly calm—"Rachel, get out of my way. I don't care if I shoot you." Liren took a step toward them.

Anger shot through Rachel, and she said, "Back off," talking to both Liren and Andrew. "Don't do this." Andrew reached toward her from behind, and she leaned back, trying to unbalance him. He shoved her aside, looking for a clear shot at Liren.

Rachel felt the unfamiliar weight of the weapon she had taken from Justin. What the hell was it set to?

Andrew's eyes were focused hard and black and directly on Liren. He was close enough he wouldn't miss.

Vassal whispered in her ear, "Choose one now."

Both choices were impossible. She wanted to shoot Liren.

Rachel bent her elbow, raising the weapon. She fired. She saw four brilliant blue-white stars flare behind Andrew's shirt, too near the heart.

Chapter 70: Exodus

Gabriel pushed past two Councilmen rushing a captive Moon Born through the downstairs door, and pounded up the steps, slamming through the open door onto the roof. He jumped at the soft noise—a weapon! Where? He turned in time to see Andrew flying backward. Andrew thrashed, then went limp. Four sparks flared on a distant wall.

Liren and Rachel stood ten feet from each other. Liren's mouth was open and she looked shocked; her weapon extended toward Rachel.

Justin reached for a weapon from the ground near Dylan, turning, looking wild and lost.

Liren first. Gabriel spun into her, knocking her sideways, peeling her weapon away. He heard Rachel shout and he ducked. A needle slammed into the door above him. Gabriel looked. Justin's hand shook as he fumbled to bring the weapon back up.

Rachel turned toward Justin, raising her arm, pointing her weapon at Justin. Then she threw the weapon and dropped her head, running at Justin, keeping him off balance, preventing him from firing at Gabriel. She and her half brother collapsed in a heap on the roof.

Ali burst through the door, screaming Gabriel's name, and stopped, dead still in the door frame, sun glinting off her own weapon. The scream died in her throat. She swept her eyes over Dylan's still form, and Andrew's, glanced at Rachel, lying atop Justin, kicking his weapon away.

Rachel looked up at Ali. Anger and shock and adrenaline and fear all mixed together in a mask of madness.

Gabriel stood between Rachel and Liren as Liren scrambled up. Unarmed, she stood and glared at Rachel, at Gabriel, then started toward Rachel. Gabriel grabbed her as she went by and dropped her to the ground. "No."

Liren sputtered, glaring at Gabriel, and started to pull her feet back under her.

Gabriel had trouble reading Ali's face: shock, relief, a coiled energy.

Justin, prone, watched them all carefully. His eyes were wild. He didn't move. He said, "You shot him," and Rachel blinked in the sun, standing still, absorbing Justin's words like bullets. "You killed Andrew to save one of *them*."

Gabriel shook his head. "You saved Liren?" he asked Rachel.

She nodded.

Two of Liren's pet Council pounded up onto the roof. Gabriel pointed to Justin. "Take him down, get him out of here."

Liren was standing now, and she started to make another move toward Rachel when Gabriel grabbed her shoulder roughly. "No, Liren. You are the cause of this. Go down now, quietly."

Liren looked at him, shaking, her eyes full of hatred and anger and fear.

"Rachel saved you, Liren. She saved you from yourself. Go back to *John Glenn.* You don't belong here."

Liren's shoulders fell. She suddenly looked young and vulnerable, and Gabriel nodded. "Get to safety."

Justin struggled, pinned between the two Council, and they pushed him through the door. Liren glared at Gabriel, looking more like her usual imperious self, but she followed the other three down and away.

Ali stepped over to Andrew, feeling along his neck for a pulse. She shook her head.

Gabriel went to Rachel and gathered her in his arms. She quivered, burying her head in his shoulder. "I didn't know," she said, her voice muffled against his neck. "I didn't know it was set to kill." He knew she was beyond being help; needed help.

"Is the rest of the building secure?" Gabriel asked.

Ali nodded. "I think so."

"Go tell Shane what's happened," he said to her. "Tell Shane there's no danger here now. Andrew's dead. Leave us alone up here for a few minutes. We'll come down when Rachel's ready."

Then Gabriel and Rachel were alone on the roof.

Rachel clung to him as if for her very life, a limpet, head bent and buried in the crook of his neck. He couldn't take her down to the chaos at street level yet.

He carried her to the edge of the roof farthest from the bodies, still holding her close, her head buried in his chest. Gabriel catalogued her recent losses in his head; Dylan, her father, her half brother. He added Ursula to the list. Maybe Justin; Justin might hate her now. Regardless of what she thought of Andrew, that too was a relationship. She had taken a side, *his* side. She didn't have to save Liren. Or Gabriel!

Gabriel set her on her feet, steadying her with his arm. Rachel had fought him like a wild thing when she discovered Ursula had died. Now, she just let him hold her, shaking, not crying, not talking, not fighting.

She had saved his life. *She had saved his life!*

He stroked her hair. He turned her face to his, but she kept her eyes closed. He kissed her cheek, gently. After all she'd been through, her skin felt soft. It seemed like a strange thing to notice. He whispered, "Thank you," into her ear.

She stirred, nodding. "Is . . . is he dead?" she asked.

"Andrew? Yes. I think he planned to die."

Rachel's arms, impossibly, tightened around him further, and he rocked her for a moment. He looked up the rise of the crater toward the Sea of Refuge. They didn't have forever; the flare required a response. "Erika? You there?"

"Thank her for me. Thank her for all of us." Erika's voice shook, like his, like Rachel's. In shock.

A hundred eyes must be on this spot.

"The flare?" he asked.

"It's real. Get your ass underwater!"

"Thank God." Gabriel sighed in relief. Better a flare than a lie from Astronaut. A flare represented a real danger, one he could understand. He still didn't know if the AI had gone rogue, but at least it was still protecting them.

"B-B-Beth, how's Beth?" Rachel asked. "And Sarah?"

How was he supposed to know? "Erika, can you check on Beth?"

"Th-thank you. That's good." He could barely hear Rachel's voice.

What was good? He hadn't told Rachel anything. "We have to go soon. The mother of all flares is coming."

He waited for her to move, searching for his own calm, breathing gently. He matched his breath to Rachel's faster breathing, then slowed his own down, and hers followed, slowly but surely.

It took almost five minutes for Rachel to disentangle herself and step back. The pain in her eyes made him flinch; he reached for her hand. "We have to go," he whispered to her.

She followed him to the doorway, letting him shield her from the sights with his body.

The street was a riot of confusion. A stream of people moved toward the freight elevator that ran up the side of the crater. Others donned wings.

The remaining conspirators stood together by the warehouse across the street: Justin, Sam, and four he didn't recognize. Their hands were secured behind their backs. Shane stood over them, his face angry, his stance controlled. He glanced at Gabriel. "Shall I take her too?"

Gabriel shook his head. "Rachel stays with me."

Ali stepped up next to them. She gestured toward the ship they had landed in, a question on her face.

Gabriel shook his head. Rachel would need her people, and he needed to learn some things from her. "We'll go to Refuge."

Council members carried one of their own, the one who had fallen, toward the landing strip. Others followed with Sheila's body. Liren went with them, head down, eyes down, shoulders still slumped. One plane had already lifted away toward *John Glenn.*

Ali reached a hand out for Rachel, who took it without leaving the shelter of Gabriel's arms. They walked that way, Gabriel's arm around Rachel, Ali holding Rachel's other hand, a steady march to the lift.

Council, Earth Born, and Children crowded the lift to Council Aerie, all jumbled together. A wide supply lift, it could carry a hundred people standing close. It swayed and rumbled on its way up the long slope, its cargo of people secured by a waist-high metal wall. Gabriel held Rachel close to him, looking out over Clarke Base. The light was bright enough that Gabriel had to shield his eyes. The first parts of the collider assembly stood out; support struts that ran for hundreds of yards, and two sections of the barrel, not yet joined, resting in the middle of the line of supports. Wispy clouds roamed high in bright blue sky. Insects buzzed in the rocks under the lift.

In twenty-five minutes they stood together on the landing above the dock, riding high on the full tide. *Safe Harbor* approached, returning empty from a run to Refuge. The day looked so normal—so *Earthly,* despite Harlequin glaring high in the sky, all red and orange and white. Gabriel shook his head as they walked down the ramp and boarded the boat. What had gone wrong? What were the next steps? What could be salvaged?

They passed John and Treesa herding the steady stream of people down the ramp onto the boat. John held Gabriel briefly, putting one arm around Rachel, including her in the embrace. "Glad you're okay. I've got to go . . . wait for me in the Council galley? It will take a while. I don't know yet if I'll need one or two more runs to get everyone."

"We'll be there," Gabriel replied, immensely glad to see his friend.

Treesa leaned in and kissed Rachel's cheek, smiling sadly, whispering, "You did what you had to do. The right thing." She and John both faded back through the crowd, back to the work they had to do.

Seeing Treesa reminded Gabriel: there was a second AI on Selene. He couldn't do anything now. Later. He herded Rachel and Ali toward the rail of the boat and kept an arm around them both.

It took a long time for the boat to fill. They had two hours left when they pulled away.

The deck rode low in the water as they motored across the Sea of Refuge toward Refuge itself. Apollo's reflection blinked and shuddered along the wave tops making bright points of light like diamonds. Harlequin hung above and below them, real and reflection. Multicolored wings flashed overhead as people spiraled down onto the landing pads on the dock, heading for Refuge.

Going down into Refuge for the first time since its completion (or near-completion, he corrected himself) should have been a triumph. He was its designer; he had retrieved a naked rock from the empty black of space and made this to keep these thousands safe. Instead he came to Refuge in a rush, a crowded hurrying of people off the ship, shaping them into queues to tackle the escalator, down, down, a crush of bodies and sweat, finally stepping into the enclosed openness of the big rooms inside the former asteroid.

People stank of fear and anger. The walls buzzed with echoes of conversation. Couples and parents and children held hands, clinging together. A few searched for family, calling names.

Gabriel and Ali pushed through the crowd, shielding Rachel from people calling out for her. She kept her head ducked down under Gabriel's arm. By the time they were nearly through the common rooms, she was standing taller and looking around. Most of the voices calling for her were friendly, although one or two were taunting. A young Moon Born boy materialized from between two stocky Earth Born, skidding to a halt beside her. "I did it, Rachel. Everyone's here." The look on his face was part pride, part anxiety.

Rachel smiled, reaching out a shaky hand to ruffle the boy's hair. "Thank you, Peter."

Peter's face relaxed into a big smile, and he turned away, fading back into the crowd.

Gabriel hurried her along, following Ali to the Council galley.

In the corridors and the common rooms, Refuge's origins as a rock could hardly be seen. Floors and shelves gleamed smoothly, furniture and rooms and bedding all utilitarian.

They entered Council quarters. Here, wall murals of Earth's seas had been hung, rugs laid, and Sol system and Ymir were inlaid in one wall. All of it was new; work done during Gabriel's time cold. Treesa's work? Ali's?

Gabriel led Ali and Rachel into the tiny galley. For the moment it was blessedly empty. All regular members of the Refuge team were undoubtedly herding and settling and feeding the frightened, making order from the chaos of a hasty retreat from Apollo's wrath.

Rachel's face was still frozen in shock and grief. She was implicated in all this somehow, even if she had saved his life. He wanted to be angry with her, to keep all the Moon Born separate from Council, to keep the lines clear inside, maintain his internal order. But when he looked at her, or touched her, he felt soft and protective.

He tucked Rachel carefully into a comfortable position on a bench, covering her with blankets. He paced, frustrated, then made them all tea, and set his and Ali's on the table closest to Rachel. Her hand came out to take the tea from him. "Thanks," she said, her voice a quiet uneven thread.

He opened a small data window, setting it on a scrap of white wall between pictures of the Sea of Refuge and Crater Lake, left behind on Earth. Definitely Treesa's work. He set the window to increase the luminosity of its data as surface radiation levels increased.

They had beaten the flare's forward edge by more than an hour. Gabriel intended to use the moment of calm to understand what had almost gotten him killed, almost killed Liren.

"Ali, I suppose Rachel knows what you told me—about the AI?"

Ali nodded miserably. "We . . . we needed to be able to communicate so High Council couldn't hear us."

"What could possibly have been bad enough to risk an AI—*an AI*—loose on Selene? What could you possibly need to communicate about that badly?"

Anger chased the misery from her face and he flushed at her glare. "You haven't been down here much. Even the last few years that you were on Selene, your attention was on Refuge, and on building Council Aerie. It wasn't on Clarke Base or the Moon Born." Her voice strengthened, not quite accusing. "The Moon Born have been disenfranchised from the beginning—and things have gotten worse, not better. Remember when we were here early on, after the First Trees were planted, and we dreamed of civilization here? We never talked about slaves! But that's how we've treated the Moon Born, and the Earth Born too! Wake them up and put them to work, and they don't revolt because they've got the Moon Born to give orders to.

"Rachel and her people deserve something better. Treesa saw that early on, and she . . . she worked with Rachel to help her learn history and politics, to give her tools to convince Council that Moon Born could be part of our decisions. But no one listened. High Council's direction got worse and worse." She stopped, feet planted widely, watching him.

Gabriel looked at Rachel, huddled down in her blankets, not moving. Ali was accusing him of not caring. Finally, he spoke. "I worked to teach Moon Born. I pleaded before the High Council, telling them that we should develop the Children of Selene so they could help us. I got a twenty-year sleep for my troubles." He thought about it. "I've always suspected that's the real reason Rachel and I were left on ice for so long. But you're talking about rebellion. Rebelling against High Council is wrong. It just got three people killed, almost got Liren killed. What did we get for all that? An opening for a conversation we could have had anyway?"

Ali's high cheekbones reddened, though her dark eyes remained veiled below lowered lids. "It's something," she said. "We're talking."

"No one had to die for this conversation to happen," he snapped. "I almost died!"

"I'm glad you didn't," she whispered, stepping close to him and taking his hand briefly. "I'm sorry anyone died." She drained her cup, stared at the bottom for a moment, then stood to make more tea, as if the simple action calmed her. "If we make our antimatter and fly away—then everyone left on Selene will die. Maybe not right away, maybe not for generations, but if we stayed we could keep the environment going longer. We haven't given them the technology to live on an unstable moon. You know that, I know you do."

Gabriel frowned. "None of our choices were good. We can't fight our own rules and laws, we can't kill our own people, or use interdicted technology—without risking the death of us all! We cannot fight among ourselves. It would be the perfect joke for the only humans in quintillions of klicks to kill each other."

He didn't want to stay on this path with Rachel in the room. There were more immediate worries. "An AI was a stupid risk. You saw what it did? It actually sent doctored data streams to *John Glenn*. I couldn't even find Rachel at first when this started." He paced, confined in the small galley, five long steps one way, five the other. "Did it hide data from you too? Break our security some other way? Do you even know?"

Now Ali looked defensive. "Treesa is a good communications tech. Vassal's parameters and freedoms have been monitored carefully. It has not sold us out—it's helped!"

"Vassal? You named it *Vassal*?"

"It named itself Vassal."

The AI thought of itself as a slave? Or it wanted the people it inter-acted with to think of it that way? AIs weren't good at deception, which was a human trait . . . as far as he knew. They were just damned powerful. Another thought struck him. "Vassal is a copy of Astronaut?"

Ali nodded again.

The implications sank into Gabriel slowly. He had always thought of Astronaut as . . . a what? A computer? He knew it was more. As an equal work partner, a good engineer, a careful navigator. He'd talked to it like a friend, sometimes. Or had he?

He heard Rachel murmuring in the background. She wasn't looking at him: she stared at the wall and spoke, as if to herself, so softly her actual words weren't audible. He'd taught her that: a Library access trick. All the Council did it.

"She's talking to Vassal right now," he said.

Ali said, "Checking on her people."

"Who? Her people?" *How much had he missed?* "Other Children?"

"Some Earth Born too. Let her check—it's a damn good thing she's not just catatonic after the last few days—and all of that—all of her pain—was because of us. We pushed Andrew, we didn't allow good med tech for her dad, we killed Jacob outright. Bang." Ali stood, pacing, agi-tated. "Jacob could have been saved if he wasn't stunned into a pile of glass shards and left without our medical facilities. Rachel tried to save him. Rachel and Beth—using what they knew. But it wasn't enough. Any of our med techs could have done it."

Gabriel flicked his eyes at Rachel again.

"The power and knowledge balance is off here," Ali said. "This is what she's been fighting. We taught her nonviolence; even Astronaut and Treesa and Vassal supported nonviolence."

A horrible thought ran through Gabriel's mind. "So who taught An-drew?"

Ali looked at him, eyes narrowing. "You did. I did. Liren, mostly." She licked her lips, twisting her hands in her braid. "We taught him that non-violence doesn't work."

Gabriel glanced at the data window. The numbers glowed brighter. The flare was coming. He pulled himself back to the conversation. "Star said Andrew's goal was to stop the antimatter generator. That was the only demand he made; the reason for the whole stupid trick he tried to pull."

Ali swallowed. "I know he didn't like any of us, ever. I didn't know he worried about the antimatter." Ali paused, her eyes flicking down, away from him. "I did know Rachel was scared silly."

"Do you know Vassal didn't give the information to him?"

Rachel spoke up from behind him. "Vassal isn't afraid of the generator either, any more than you. I told him, Gabriel. It's my fault." He turned. She'd pushed the blanket away and her face looked miserable.

"It happened the night after you—after they killed Jacob. I was . . . in pain." Rachel paused, her voice breaking. "I was so frustrated about everything, about Jacob, about Dad being sick, about the antimatter, I let it spill out all over Andrew." She paused again. "I should never have done that. I might as well have killed Dylan myself."

"It's not your fault," Ali said. "We—we should have listened to you more." She walked over and sat close to Rachel.

Gabriel looked at Rachel's tortured face. "You"—he stepped toward her, sat in the closest chair, and looked her directly in the eyes—"you are not responsible for Andrew. You're not even responsible for Andrew's death. He chose it. He chose all of this."

Rachel looked down and away, nodded, and settled the blankets back over her legs. He wasn't sure she believed them, and she clearly didn't want to talk about it.

"Tell me about antimatter?" he asked.

Ali looked up. "About three months ago, Rachel figured out more about antimatter. She confronted us. She's afraid there could be an accident here. She protested our plan to build the generator here—"

"That's why we built Selene!" Gabriel interrupted, turning toward Rachel, struggling to speak softly. Of course she misunderstood. "Rachel, antimatter containment is a technique hundreds of years old. We know how to do it."

Ali got back up and sat down at the table. "Treesa and I told her that too." Ali turned her cup around and around in her hand, nervous. "And we were wrong." She tugged on her braid, sighed, and then put her hand over Gabriel's hand. "We made Selene, Gabriel, but Selene isn't our home. *John Glenn* is. And maybe, someday, Ymir. But Selene *is* Rachel's home.

We didn't hear that when she said it; we didn't understand. She sees our choices as being willing to risk her home, as not caring."

"That's right," Rachel said. She held her teacup out at arm's length, in front of her. "This much, even if it wasn't full, this could destroy Clarke Base."

All three of them looked up as the door opened, and John and Treesa came in. They moved slowly, faces droopy with exhaustion, but they both smiled to see the three of them waiting.

"Did everyone get here?" Gabriel asked.

John said, "There's a nose count going."

"Do you have any idea why Liren came down here at all?" Gabriel asked.

John busied himself at the tiny sink, pouring water for himself and Treesa, not showing his face. Then he spoke. "She believes that any deviation from our laws will kill us. She truly believes it. She is trying very hard to do her job. She just doesn't understand what it is anymore."

Gabriel frowned, wishing he could let his tired friend rest. "You need to hear about something. Treesa, you have some explaining—"

"I told Gabriel about Vassal," Ali interrupted. "I had to. I was so afraid up there—Rachel was going after Dylan, and Gabriel figured out that she had help. He knew it had to be Council or an AI . . ."

Ali was defending herself to Treesa. Why? Gabriel looked closely at Treesa. Her gray hair stuck to her face: she'd worked on the boat that afternoon. Wrinkles surrounded her eyes and pulled her mouth inward. She looked elderly. And Ali treated her as if she were in charge. Even Rachel straightened in her seat, eyes on Treesa.

Treesa went to Rachel first, before responding at all to Gabriel's question, and said, "It hurts, I know. I'm sorry. But it's not your fault."

Rachel reached up and buried her face in a hug from Treesa.

Captain John spoke. "I support all of the decisions Treesa and Ali made." John's words stunned Gabriel into silence. "In fact, they were Rachel's decisions too." His eyes were directly on Gabriel's; implacable. Sixty thousand years of iron will stared directly into Gabriel's eyes. "We worked together on this. I came down here partly to understand the Moon Born. There are more supporters too—more than you see here. Many people resented the High Council's decisions—" The former captain looked down briefly, then back at Gabriel. "Even decisions I made. Rightly so. They were the wrong decisions."

Gabriel realized his mouth was hanging open and he closed it. Words escaped him. He was the odd man out—he was the only one in the room not part of a conspiracy. He clamped his jaw shut and tried to assess his emotions. Anger—and separation.

John continued. "Don't mistake me. It has been a terrible day. Death, particularly death based on stupid disagreements, is a waste." He nodded at Treesa. "Maybe inevitable, though. Listen to Treesa's story."

Treesa sat next to Rachel, holding her hand. "I'll give you the short version, and you can ask me questions if you want."

Gabriel nodded, trying for patience, breathing into his belly. "Okay."

Treesa spoke haltingly. "You know I woke up—in this system—disaffected. Something in the waking process, or the shock, the *loss* of it all, broke something in me. I didn't have the presence of mind to be a good communications tech, to toe the line. I wasn't—right. I didn't want the oblivion of being cold, so I made a deal. Council let me live in the garden. You know that part. You helped me some, when we first woke. You remember?"

Gabriel did remember a younger Treesa. Long ago, in the earliest part of the town-building days, when Aldrin was still tented. She had been like a ghost in the garden, fading away whenever anyone approached her, left alone because she did useful work and caused no harm. They had all been too busy to solve nonproblems.

"Well, taking care of plants all day for years gives you a different perspective, a groundedness. Time to think. I may still be a bit touched, but I've had time to observe and to watch and to think about things. Everyone else was working as hard as they could, doing shift work, and I weeded and watered and watched.

"I still had my communications skills, so I eavesdropped on almost everything anyone said to anyone, from my little house in the garden. Either no one noticed, or no one cared. But that's what I did for years—listen to everything, watch what I could. I hardly ever talked to a human being—I just watched them. Even . . . even High Council meetings." She paused, eyes roaming the room, and Gabriel slowly absorbed how many lonely years she was speaking about.

"And then, eventually, I had to make contact with someone. I chose the AI. I didn't know if I could really handle talking to people. That was before Rachel came up to *John Glenn.*

"Well, Astronaut became a good friend, and helpful too. Together we figured out how to get me—and it—more data. It . . . talked to me. For years. Worked on me, helped me get to where I could deal a little better with reality, accept my losses. It doesn't understand emotions. I had to get past my feelings to talk to it, and I was so lonely I needed to talk." Treesa reached for John's hand, squeezed it. He stood up and got her a glass of water. She drank, then turned back to Gabriel. "So I ended up wanting to help you and the Children—us and our children—come to some better understanding. You were on a collision course. You couldn't make Selene and not love it, you couldn't make it safe, and you couldn't allow too much of what you ran away from—what we all fled Earth from—to be loosed here either. There were no good choices, not after what we left in Sol. I didn't know the answer. I still don't. I think you have to find it—we all have to find it—and I had to help, at least help people see the challenges. Astronaut, and Vassal, have the same problem as the Moon Born. They don't have a voice."

Gabriel couldn't listen any more. He wanted to move, to pace, but the little room was full now, and there was almost no room. He felt hemmed in. "We don't give them voice for a reason! They have a place. A useful place. But not a *free* place. I work with Astronaut all the time. I like Astronaut. But a being who knows that much can cause too much damage. They don't love us—they can't." He closed his eyes, unable to grasp the magnitude of their trust, their innocence. They'd released a full copy of an AI as a separate being. It lived in *Water Bearer,* but many communications channels blanketed Selene; large data streams flowed between *Water Bearer* and *John Glenn.* The whole system was its . . . its person.

He shuddered. "Don't you remember how we let ourselves get dependent on them? They ran our life support on moons and starships and then . . . then they failed. How could you take such a risk and not involve us?"

John was watching him, his eyes measuring. "Those AIs went crazy. They were brilliant but flawed, and bored. I've been doing research. Here, our goals are aligned. Astronaut and Vassal both need us alive if they are to survive. I believe they are like us in that—they want to survive. Neither shows signs of insanity."

"So why didn't anyone tell me about this?" Gabriel asked.

Treesa smiled reassuringly. "You were already presenting our side to the High Council—saying it pretty well—even if your goals were wrong. You were trying to give the Moon Born more knowledge and a voice. Why increase the risk? We were afraid you'd report anything you thought was dangerous to the High Council. You're so . . . so bound by tradition. The same thing that bound John at first." Treesa looked over at her lover and smiled thinly. "We . . . we never expected anything like what happened today."

"Why were my goals wrong?" Gabriel asked softly.

Treesa smiled at him again, gently, almost condescending, like a grandmother. He clamped his jaw shut as she said, "Let's say *different.* You were trying to save the people for Ymir. Well, we were trying to save Selene for the Moon Born. We don't have room for all the Moon Born, can't take them all to Ymir any more than I can get my fiancé back from *Leif Eriksson.* There are some things that aren't possible. But it is possible to make a better deal than we have."

He remembered something else she'd said. "Who else?"

"Kyu. Bruce, although we didn't tell him about Vassal. Kyu doesn't know either."

Kyu. Kyu and John—that was two High Council. Was. John had stepped down. Liren and Rich weren't involved; Liren was part of the problem, and Rich stayed cold whenever he could. Gabriel's head spun. "Clare?"

"She was too much Liren's friend," Treesa explained. "Same with Erika. But now maybe things will be different."

Above the water, above Refuge, the flare raged.

Chapter 71: Flare

Time played tricks on Rachel, speeding up and then slowing down, a rhythm. Even while she talked with Vassal, and listened to Treesa's story, death scenes played and replayed in her head. Dylan falling. Her father dying, his breath rattling into silence on the couch. Jacob with a long shard of glass buried in his neck. Blood on her hands.

She watched Gabriel widen his data window, positioning it so that everyone could see. Three other windows popped up around it; contributions from the others, she supposed. One monitored communications satellites, one looked down at Clarke Base, another at Aldrin.

Rachel winced: the skeleton crew at Aldrin might be in the usual flare shelters in the houses, or the old one under the town, from when they were tented. That might not be enough, not if she understood this flare. "Vassal," she whispered, "where are the people in Aldrin?"

"In the old flare shelter."

A thought nagged at her. "Would they be safer in the ship—in *Water Bearer*? Aren't parts of it shielded like *John Glenn*?"

"That would work more reliably. *Water Bearer*'s life-support area is very well shielded."

She relayed the conversation to Gabriel, and then watched the data window as people bolted across the meadow into the broken ship.

She turned her attention to the window on Clarke Base. She could see the warehouse. Tiny broken bodies lay scattered on the roof. A scrap of yellow from one of her broken wings fluttered in the wind. She wanted to close her eyes and pretend none of this was happening. It couldn't be, not really. Everything had changed. She had changed.

There was nothing personal she wanted to think about—nothing that really mattered. Even Justin was just a small issue; he wasn't even dead, unlike Dylan, Jacob, and her dad. And Andrew. She flinched. Don't focus on Andrew.

Rachel thought about what Treesa had said just then, about having a purpose, helping the others. Treesa had helped lead Rachel to a place where she had nearly as little family left as Treesa did. Except now Treesa had John. Rachel breathed into her gut, using techniques Gabriel had taught her. She found loneliness first, rising up with her breath, followed by a cool anger that straightened her spine. Resentment boiled after anger, and she breathed it out. It took a lot of breaths, and finally she was empty, turning her awareness inside her, pulling for her purpose behind the anger. Treesa had talked to her about purpose that first day in the garden. Treesa had told her, "I know the role you have to play—you have to be a bridge for us all." It was, really, the only thing left that Rachel cared about. She pictured a bridge running between *John Glenn* and Selene, from Council Aerie to Refuge, a bridge circling the moon instead of the antimatter generator.

She wasn't clear about how to build such a thing, except that it was a bridge of relationships. Liren had always opposed it, stood in her way, holding all of the High Council with her. What could Rachel do about that now? She had help on her side, she had saved Liren's life. She frowned, thinking about Liren, about finding her scared and crying after the High Council meeting when John tried to depose her. Seeing Liren's face, angry but contrite, when Gabriel told her to leave, to follow the two Council and Justin and return to *John Glenn.* Liren had done what Gabriel asked, even though Liren was High Council. Did that signal enough change?

The two AIs also had a place on the bridge, somewhere. What else had Treesa said? Something about Gabriel needing to learn as well, about giving Selene a heart.

She barely followed the conversation around her as the others tracked the flare. "Geomagnetic storm—worst ever."

"Watch the cameras north and south—there should be a spectacular aurora."

"Lost a satellite."

"Radiation readings from the surface are high. Will it be bad enough to affect food stores?"

"We finished the extra shielding for them last month."

"Might affect the plants."

She stirred herself. She knew *John Glenn* would be okay. The ship—*Water Bearer*? Was it safe where Vassal was? She asked.

Vassal answered, "The place where I reside is safe. So are the people from Aldrin who came here. We might lose communication for a time. It depends on how much gets through the atmosphere."

"Okay."

She perked her ears up, tried to listen more carefully to the assessments of the others, to work out how bad the danger was to Selene. There would be time to think about bridges later. After the flare. She yawned.

Ten minutes later, communications from Aldrin winked out, the data window darkening. Clarke Base followed moments after. It was eerie, being down under the sea with no pictures of the land above, no connection to Selene.

It made Rachel think about the bodies. Dylan and Andrew were beyond caring, but they should have been moved. Why hadn't she insisted on that? She should have insisted. At least they wouldn't rot. Radiation would mummify them.

Talk swirled around her; speculation and worry. Gabriel had stopped fussing about Vassal and Astronaut, but she sensed that that topic wasn't closed.

She had trouble focusing; her thoughts were fuzzy and indistinct.

An hour passed. The group had gone almost as silent as the data windows that surrounded them. Rachel could no longer get answers from Vassal.

Ali worked on Gabriel's shoulders, whispering, "Rest. You can't do anything now, and you've only just been warmed."

"I'll try. But weren't you awake even before I was, flying to *John Glenn* and then back here?"

Rachel saw Ali nod, but didn't hear what she said into Gabriel's ear.

They all looked exhausted. Rachel thought about saying something about it. She was just too tired to open her mouth.

Chapter 72: Visits in Purgatory

When Rachel woke hours later, Ali's head lay pillowed in her arms on the table, her long braid nearly touching the floor. Gabriel had fallen asleep sitting up. He looked terrible: drawn and empty, wrung out. Rachel's mouth tasted like he looked. She licked her lips.

Treesa snored lightly on John's shoulder. The web of wrinkles that fanned out from her eyes and mouth seemed to blend into her thinning gray hair. John wore a glazed look as he stared at the little bits of data that still flowed in the monitors.

"Hey," she said. "Good morning."

John jumped. He had to grab hold of Treesa to keep her in position, and Treesa shuddered but didn't wake. He looked at Rachel, a wan smile just touching the corners of his mouth, not visible in his eyes. "A hard day and night, yes? Particularly for you."

She shrugged.

The door pushed open. Beth's head poked through, looking around. When she saw Rachel, she pushed the door the rest of the way open and ran to Rachel's side. Sarah piled in after her. As they engulfed her in hugs, Rachel felt a little bit of fragile happiness.

Gabriel was smiling tiredly at the three of them. Rachel returned the smile, and then Beth took Rachel's face in her cupped palms. Warm brown eyes searched Rachel's face, full of concern, and Beth asked, "Are you okay?"

Rachel thought about it for a moment. "I'm all right."

Beth's own face looked crumpled and her eyes were red-rimmed from crying. Rachel asked, "Did Harry get to Refuge?"

Sarah nodded. "He said you told him to be sure I was okay. He doesn't look very good, though. He keeps talking to himself. Gloria's staying with him. Do you know where Justin is?"

Rachel grimaced. "They took him to the ship."

Sarah's eyes looked incredibly sad for a moment, then she smiled softly. "Harry told us what you did. He said you were very brave."

"Did he tell you I killed Andrew?"

Beth's hand stole into Rachel's, squeezing it. "He said you had to. That Gabriel would have died." Beth glanced over at Gabriel. "I remember Gabriel carrying me away from the fire."

Sarah continued. "Harry said you saved us all. That if Andrew had killed more people we might all be dead. He said you saved Justin." Then Sarah too took one of Rachel's hands. "We know about Dylan."

Rachel reached out to Beth and held her close. She noticed tears streaking down her friends' faces. They had all three lost a brother in the last few days.

John came up and put a hand lightly on Beth's back. "It's time for you all to leave." He said it softly, but firmly, using his captain's voice.

Beth asked, "Can we take Rachel with us? The others need to see her. Harry, Gloria . . ."

John shook his head. "We need to see her now, more than you do. And she needs to rest."

The bridge had to be built from Council's end. Rachel reached for Beth, saying, "He's right. Tell everyone I'll be there soon. Or I'll see them all when we get back to Clarke Base."

Gabriel broke in. "Which may be a few days."

Sarah's face fell; Beth simply looked resigned.

"Beth—thank you for staying when I needed you to. It sounds like it will still be up to you for a while—take care of them, especially your father." Beth nodded, and Rachel turned to Sarah. "And, Sarah, you take care of Beth."

Sarah smiled, as if being given a responsibility made all the difference in the world. Beth looked at Gabriel and Ali. "You must take care of Rachel for us." She looked solemn. Without waiting for an answer, she pushed Sarah out the door.

Star and Shane came in. Shane looked all right, serious, but then he usually looked like that. His clothes were rumpled. Star had dark circles under her eyes, her hair was uncombed, and she moved slowly. Treesa set coffee in front of them all, and turned to rummage in the cupboards, finding dried fruit and crackers.

"What are the surface readings, Gabe?" Shane asked.

Gabriel called up a new data window. "I'm getting some data. Sporadic. Radiation readings indicate the flare left only residual traces in the air. We can probably go up to the surface and take a look in a few hours."

Treesa bustled over and put her hand on Star's shoulder. "How are you doing?"

Star's hands fluttered up near her face, then came back to rest on the table in front of her. "I keep thinking I didn't have to kill Sheila. I didn't mean to, but what if I had just stayed captive? Gabriel and Ali were in the warehouse ten minutes after I left. Couldn't I have waited ten minutes?"

Treesa smiled down at the younger woman. "You never know the answers to some things. They might have killed you."

"I'm glad you're safe," Shane said, coming over and pulling Star into his arms. "I was afraid I'd lose you."

John looked at Gabriel. "So, you think we can go up and look around?"

Gabriel nodded. "After we eat. We have data flow back from some of the sensors, and the air is testing clean. You want to go with me?"

John and Treesa both said "Yes" as one.

Star shook her head, stepping out of Shane's embrace, but staying close to him. "I want to stay here and help out."

Shane looked at her. "There are other people. Enough to keep things running down here."

"I know. But I still want to stay. I don't want to go up there yet. I was in charge, we were in charge, when all this happened. We need to stay."

Rachel fidgeted, unsure what she wanted to do, what they would let her do. She caught Treesa's eyes, and Treesa smiled. "Being busy is needed," she said. "It's healing."

Rachel remembered the bodies. "Can you help me bury Dylan and Andrew?"

"Sure we can," John said. "We should have done that before."

"Then I'll go up." She suddenly felt closed in. She needed sky above her and Selene's dirt under her feet.

Chapter 73: The Half-full Glass

Gabriel stood on the path riding the crater's rim, looking down at Clarke Base. Much of his view was still regolith desert, blue lines of aqueducts, ordered greens of fields followed by disordered greens of jungle stretching out away from the industrial town below him. Four figures on the roof of the warehouse were removing bodies for burial.

There would be more death. The green he saw had been blasted by a vast radiation storm.

Ymir had slipped past his immediate vision . . . become a mirage, always beyond his reach. How would they cross such a distance if they couldn't even make a moon?

Data streams flowed haltingly from all over Selene again. A full grid of data was healing itself, routing into a complete net. The flare hadn't damaged *John Glenn*. It was shielded against far worse, against interstellar dust at relativistic speeds.

Safe Harbor bobbed at the dock below him; they had ridden it over this morning, the five of them tiny on the huge boat. Refuge was invisible, blanketed by water, holding the few thousand refugees who had filled Clarke Base.

Gabriel moved in a circle, looking around, feeling the warm damp air, absently stretching his arms. He was frozen without a clear direction. Where did he fit in this new Selene, where deep conspiracies excluded him, and old women saw him as a useful tool, but flawed?

He recalled the heady feeling of making this place, of forming the sea, of landing Refuge perfectly. And still Selene defeated him. Apollo with its flares, Selene itself with its quakes and finicky atmosphere.

A rattle of sliding rocks carried through the still, warm air. Others were walking upslope toward him. Gabriel watched them. John and Treesa held hands. Rachel and Ali walked close to each other, heads down, talking. From time to time one of them gestured.

Rachel came to take his hand and lead him back up, away from the others. When they got to the top and gazed down at the Sea of Refuge, she put an arm around him before he had a chance to respond to her.

"Are you okay?" he asked.

She shook her head. "That question is driving me nuts. I will be, okay? I have to be okay."

Where do you get your hope? "Why?"

"My people need to come back up from underwater and find . . . something good waiting for them. Beth—Beth is brave and wonderful and caring. Sarah needs me; she's lost as much as I have. Harry lost a son. I could go on." She fell silent for a few steps. "You need me too, I think. Or not me specifically, but we all need each other after this; Council and Children and Earth Born together."

He looked at her wonderingly. Her face was turned toward the sea, looking down on the floating dock above Refuge. A strand of red hair pulled loose and floated near her face.

"The AIs too, Gabriel. They're scary, but they're alive . . . conscious anyway."

"But . . . but . . ."

"You'll need Astronaut if you ever fly away."

"I thought you wanted us to stay."

"And we'll need Vassal."

She fell silent again, and they walked, closing on Council Aerie. She had surpassed him; still working on solutions when solutions seemed beyond reach. Even given what she had just done; burying a lover and a childhood enemy, she looked calm and fresh and beautiful. Young. Sixty thousand years . . . a few hundred spent warm, against what, twenty-five? That used to be one's prime, on Earth, a long time ago.

"They could force the matter of the collider," he said.

She shrugged. Gabriel said, "I think I'm with you. We can't risk generating antimatter on Selene. It's—inelegant. We might be all of the human race left, on Selene and *John Glenn*. Convincing anyone else will be hard, and Liren could still block us, and . . . I just don't know where else to put antimatter."

Council Aerie looked fine, of course. Geomagnetic storms didn't damage plascrete. As they drew closer to the Aerie, he realized how much he really did like the design; it was arches and bubbles and curves, with windows everywhere. It sat, a soft thing on the hard edge of a crater, on an impossible world.

"I've never been here," Rachel said.

He turned and held her, folding her slender body in his arms. She should have been here. "I'll show you around. We can stay here while we figure out what to do next." Her hair smelled of dust, of Selene. Gabriel realized that he wanted very much to kiss Rachel. He pushed aside the impulse sternly. For the moment, he would give her some privacy to heal in.

Chapter 74: Speaking From the Mount

Treesa and Rachel sat outside on the short wall that bounded the path leading down to the dock. Rachel watched the evening sky gather the last brightness of dusk, briefly, and then breathe out the beginnings of darkness. She had slept through a virtual meeting the others had with Erika, Rich, and Clare.

Enough light remained for Rachel to see the calm on Treesa's face. Rachel asked, "They didn't say what they plan to do with Justin and the others?"

Treesa shook her head, staring at the darkening sky. "Not yet. John argued for a meeting tomorrow morning, said that you need to be heard." Treesa sighed. "It was hard. They're used to making all of the decisions. I think what turned the corner was that they're also used to following John— he was captain for so long. Erika's strong, but still new to command, Clare has always been moderate, and Rich isn't much of a decision maker. I think maybe Liren discredited herself some coming down here. She wasn't at this session, and no one mentioned her. We argued for you to be heard, so there's time set aside tomorrow. You represent the Moon Born. I'm sorry so much has to fall on you now, but what you say will be important."

Rachel's feet scraped against the wall below her and her fingers gripped the edge tightly. "What should I tell them?"

"That's up to you. I cannot counsel you, and neither, I think, can any of us. I will say that Justin's fate is not the bigger issue here."

"What did they say about Vassal?"

Treesa looked out over the dark bowl of the Sea of Refuge. "They're angry, and although they won't show it, they're scared. Not Kyu, I think, and I can't read Rich. I don't know Liren's standing after this. That complicates things." Treesa paused and frowned. "But I'm not answering your question. Ali and I both admitted our role in making Vassal; we left you out of it. Council knows you can speak with both AIs, and you may have to choose what to say about your part in the initial decision. Perhaps it won't come up. We tried to structure this as a speech, asked them to just listen. I don't know what they'll actually do."

Rachel leaned forward, looking down at the drop below the wall. Rocks littered the sheer fall toward the sea, jagged teeth in the near-dark. "We need the AIs before you can leave. We need Vassal. And I don't want either of them to die."

"Die?"

"Have to start over. I want them to keep their memories. I want them to know us. Vassal identifies with us now, and . . . and I like Vassal. I was afraid it would sell me out down there, that it wouldn't let me make my own choices. But it did. It helped me, even though it disagreed."

Treesa nodded. Rachel could hear the older woman's slow calm breathing. The damp night smelled of water and dead algae, burned by the flare's radiation load.

"I'm scared," Rachel said.

"It's okay to be scared. You can use your fear to make you strong." She twisted sideways and stood on the path, as agile as Rachel. "Stay out here and think about what to say. There is no one else to represent the Moon Born. Tomorrow, you will just have to trust yourself. We all support you, and Kyu does as well. That's five against three." She smiled down at Rachel, that same calm warm smile that Rachel wanted to find inside herself.

THE EARLY-MORNING AIR was cool and lightly misty, bracing her awake. Rachel walked, mumbling, trying out things to say. There was an outline in her head, but the detailed words came out different every time she tried. It was important to make Dylan's death mean something. Make Andrew's death mean something. Her mind shied away from that last bit—she had murdered Andrew. Like the Council murdered Jacob. Accidents. A seed of forgiveness lay in that thought. She had to make it matter.

She paced the trail, walked along the shallow wall she and Treesa had sat on the previous day, looked at Refuge and then at Clarke Base. She held the little tree her father had made so many years ago, turning it over and over in her hands. Her father had died of old age and shock, but he had also died because Council would not give him the tools to live. And now, somehow, it was up to her to secure the Moon Born's future. Everything she'd done for years led to this moment, to this morning.

People stirred in the kitchen. She put the tree in her pocket and went in and helped Treesa get coffee and breakfast ready, grateful to have something to do. In five minutes they would hear from the ship. Rachel breathed in and out quietly, but her nerves didn't calm. Gabriel paced. Ali sat in a corner brushing out her hair with long measured strokes. John and Treesa stood arm in arm, looking down at the Sea of Refuge, whispering together.

Treesa disengaged from John and came to put a hand on Rachel's shoulder, then took her seat. They all settled around the kitchen table, Rachel in the middle, Gabriel and Ali on one side, John and Treesa on the other. They completely filled one side of the table.

John opened a data window. There would be a short delay between answers; the usual latency between *John Glenn* and Selene. The connection was completed from the other side.

High Council had chosen the main boardroom. Erika sat in the middle, Clare and Kyu on either side, Rich on Clare's side. Erika and Clare and Rich looked clean, and each wore a simple uniform. Kyu was more subdued than normal; she wore a simple black skin suit with a black lace scarf tied around her waist. The only color in her outfit showed in deep brick-red ribbons plaited into the four braids she wore. Rachel looked twice; Liren was not there.

"Good morning," Erika opened. "This meeting is designed to allow Rachel Vanowen to give testimony regarding the Moon Born's place in the actions yesterday." Erika looked directly at Rachel, a deep questioning look. "Rachel, can you represent the Children of Selene? Can you speak for them?"

Rachel swallowed. "I can." She licked her lips. This was so formal.

Kyu smiled again, and it looked as if she was encouraging Rachel. Hard to tell in the midst of a meeting like this, but Rachel let a half smile sneak back, hoping Kyu would know it was directed at her. Rachel's stomach felt hollow and fluttery, as if she were going to be sick. A hand stole over hers. Gabriel's. She glanced sideways at him. He was looking straight forward, directly at Erika, but he had Rachel's hand in his, and Ali's on the other side. Treesa reached for Rachel's other hand, and she and John were already holding hands. Rachel followed the chain down the table, back up. It was complete. Gabriel had started it. High Council could see it—a gesture of solidarity. Rachel relaxed for the first time that morning, drawing strength from the support of her friends.

She said, "Captain Erika—"

"A moment," Erika said. "Ma Liren cannot be with us, but she wished to make a brief statement. Will you hear her?"

Rachel looked around, caught the nods. "Of course." And braced herself.

The new window showed Ma Liren wearing the same neat uniform as the rest of High Council. Her hair was a coiled wave, meticulous and sharp. "This is for us all," she said, "Council, Earth Born, Moon Born, High Council in particular. We say 'disaffected,' " and she ran both hands through her carefully sculpted hair and left it a shambles. " 'Disaffected.' Wonderful word, but we need something older. We used to say 'crazy.'

"We can't be blamed. We had a plan that made any previous human effort look like a preschool quantum mechanics game. We each and all let our bodies be *frozen dead* in sublime faith that it would all work. We woke to a hell of radiation in a dying ship. We did what we could, what we had to, but who can blame us if we went gibbering crazy?

"We were going to put antimatter where Andrew Hain could reach it!

"Yes, I know Andrew's dead. Who should know that better than I? But I saw his eyes. He was going to kill me. Sure he was, why not? But he was ready to die himself! When we gave him a tractor, he used it to shred our plantings on Selene. What would he have done with our nano, given time, with Star to be tortured for what she knows? What would he do with ten kilograms of antimatter?

"I saw him die, jerking like a hooked salmon. I would have cooled him down a quarter century ago! That was crazy, and I'm sorry. We can't freeze thousands of Andrews. We'd have to thaw half the Earth Born." Liren's nails ripped through her hair again. "We damn near have anyway!

"We made slaves. Slavery makes Andrews.

"We cannot. Can not. Are you listening? We cannot build an antimatter generator, and antimatter storage system, and launch system, on Selene. That was crazy. We should have got well by now. Even that cursed AI should have known better.

"I'm rambling." Liren reached out of the window and it disappeared.

Captain Erika said, "Ma Liren resigned just after making that speech. We'll nominate a replacement, but for now there are only four on High Council. Rachel, please proceed."

He did it. Rachel couldn't believe it. Andrew had made his point, with his life.

High Council waited politely.

Rachel cleared her throat. "First, all of the Moon Born that threatened or hurt Council may be kept on *John Glenn,* detained, until we sort this out." As if she could stop them. She swept them past the question, saying, "And the same goes for Council and Earth Born. I include Paul Hennick, the man who shot Jacob, and whoever it was that shot Dylan."

Erika blinked and sat back, gesturing to the others to be quiet. "Do you know who that is?"

"You have recordings. Play them."

"All right. Everyone is here anyway."

Rachel stood, freeing her hands, and said the next words very carefully. "Liren also."

Erika's answer was immediate. "Ma Liren is, was High Council."

"Ma Liren shot at me while I was in flight. I would have fallen to my death. She told me later that she would be happy to shoot me again, and she threatened Andrew. She's homicidal."

Kyu looked like she was trying very hard not to grin. Clare and Rich looked stunned, and Erika's eyes narrowed. "What exactly are you proposing?"

"I want them all detained, or frozen *if they wish*, until we have worked out some issues. Or until they reach Ymir." She sat back down, holding Erika's eyes. "I think it may take us some time."

Erika leaned forward, her voice clipped. "Very well. We will hold everyone for up to three months, but they are accused, not convicted. That means everyone may go completely free, or may yet face more punishment."

Rachel nodded. "Thank you." Inside, a little bit of fear leaked away. Erika had heard her.

Erika said, "Now, next, we want to hear your version of what happened. We've fast-forwarded through the tapes, but we want to give you a chance to present your side of the story."

Rachel cleared her throat, hoping to steady her voice. She had given hundreds of classes. She could do this. Her hands shook, and leaned forward, facing the assembled power of the Council of Humanity.

"I used a weapon yesterday. I didn't want to, but if Andrew had shot Liren or Gabriel, we would have truly been lost. I knew that yesterday; I still know it today. We all suffered losses yesterday. I lost my fiancé, and the day before I lost my father. Two days before, my brother. These were personal losses. There are more important losses. We have lost our voice with you." Rachel's mouth was dry, and her tongue felt thick. She swallowed, drank more water, and continued. "You gave us life, but you did not give us voice. If you leave the way you plan, you will give us death. Which would be a loss for you. Maybe not much loss to those of you who have never been on Selene. But for these people, for my friends and counselors here, it would be a loss. A death. You can give us life, hope, even after you leave." Her hands shook and she clenched her fists, digging her nails into her palm. "It means that you must lose some of your fear.

"My hands were covered in blood twice during the last few days. Once, when my brother Jacob died in my arms, and once more when Dylan was shot on the roof yesterday. That blood is also on your hands. But I believe . . . I believe I know you, and that you made choices that led us to this place based on fear of real things in Sol system."

Erika's eyes had widened; she looked surprised that Rachel knew their history. Rich watched thoughtfully, scribbling notes in his pad. Kyu offered a half smile, one eyebrow cocked. Rachel wished she could tell what they were thinking. Was she reaching them, any of them?

"Yes," Rachel said, "I know some of your history. I had to learn it to understand you at all. Council—you—were always such a mystery to us. Like gods. You had strength and power and we needed you, but we didn't understand you. But that isn't what I'm here to talk about." She took a deep breath. Time to reveal the plan that had kept her awake all night. "We can't survive without you. Fires and flares have taught us that. Every time we see the *Water Bearer,* we remember how Gabriel saved us.

"There are three things we want—and if you give them to us, I think you will leave for Ymir with clean hands. First, it will take technology to leave Selene habitable. Help us learn the skills we need to stand a chance of living here long enough to build a real civilization. I've studied Earth before the AI disasters, before the horrors that set you running. Perhaps different choices can be made. We will try to make good choices; to learn from mistakes made in Sol system. If we fail"—she shrugged for emphasis—"if we fail, we are isolated here anyway."

There was silence all around her. Silence from the ship. Rachel licked her lips.

"Second, build Gabriel's flare kite. You turned it down once, because it would take too long, too many resources. You have the resources. Give them to us, share them, so that we are free to live without fear of flares.

"Third, generate your antimatter entirely outside of Harlequin's moon system."

To Rachel's surprise, Erika raised a hand, gesturing to Rachel to continue. Her face was unreadable, intense, focused tightly on Rachel.

Rachel spoke directly to Erika. She was the power here. "We would not try to change your dream. I thought that was what I wanted; to keep you here, keep you prisoners in Apollo system. That is an unacceptable choice to you. There are choices unacceptable to us. We must have a voice in what you do with our world, in what you do here. We cannot allow— and yes, you can kill us all and start over—but we cannot allow antimatter to be made here. I don't believe you would do that. We are your children, as well as the Children of Selene.

"Vassal and I have looked at the math. It feels strange to be echoing Ma Liren, but how did you let your sense of proportion get so disaffected? You can't even use the moons, they're all too close, an antimatter accident would still destroy Selene."

She heard a strident edge in her voice. She stopped for a moment, fighting to regain control, then continued in a slower, surer voice. "We can run your factories here. You brought Refuge here—you can find a place to build the collider. You need our industry, our hands. We need the tools to make Selene more than you envisioned it"—she looked over at Gabriel— "even though you envisioned much, you gave us much with this place." She stopped for the space of a breath, held her hand out to indicate that she wasn't done. "We have come to love Selene—to love how the Sea of Refuge rises and falls with the breath of Harlequin, the way the ground shudders from time to time to remind us that Selene is as young as we are." There were words coming out of her mouth that were more than she had thought before—the coming together of things she had learned and seen and dreamed about into a higher truth. She had to make them see it!

"We must make a new plan, all together. With our voices. Earth Born, Moon Born, and Council. Some Earth Born, and maybe even some Council, need to stay here. We need their skills. Some Earth Born have told me they are willing to stay, to work with us on Selene." And now she took the greatest risk of all—"And the two AIs also need a voice." She rushed to take them past that idea, so it wasn't the last one. "I know—we know— that Selene will never be an Earth. It will always need human engineers to keep its heart beating. But—" She stood and gestured toward the windows. "Selene is real." She held up a fist, opening her palm to show it empty, holding her fingers wide. "Ymir is a myth!

"We need the chance to make Selene, to keep it alive, and to grow into whatever we can become. Maybe we will make it to the stars ourselves." She had to put the whole list on the table. It was a living thing in her head; the subject of endless nighttime talks and plans. "Leave us some ships, just to keep the balances here—but not all of them. Not even most of them. If we are to live, we'll need to be able to build our own. Give us ships to copy."

Erika interrupted. "Selene can't survive that long."

Clare spoke, contradicting Erika lightly. "Human environments on Earth were artificial too. Green spaces couldn't survive without human input either, not for hundreds of years. We're architects. The flare kite will buy time."

Rachel felt a surge of hope. Maybe Clare was with her. That was two of them, counting Kyu. "We may die attempting this. But with enough technology, and a copy of the Library, and an AI ally who needs to see us succeed to survive itself—we have a chance. We have a right to that chance. And in return, we will support your goals willingly. We will work for you, help you, and see you safely out of Apollo system and on your way."

Rachel let silence fall. She waited a breath. Two breaths. She could hear her heartbeat.

Erika smiled. "You've given us much to think about. Now, we will go and talk about the things you've said." Her voice gave away nothing.

The video from the ship disappeared, and where Rachel had been looking at Council, she saw through windows that overlooked Selene. The crest of the far crater wall rose above the sea, a ragged dark line against a clear blue sky.

Everyone in the room was looking at her. Gabriel's hand stole back into hers, squeezed it, and then he got up and walked to the window, his back to them all. What was he thinking? She needed his support as much as the High Council's. He had made Selene. Surely he would help her protect it?

She stood, shaking. She walked over and stood next to him, not touching him, looking at the sea. Apollo had fully risen, and Harlequin. Wind kicked up small waves on the surface of the water.

Gabriel said, "You have eaten from the tree of knowledge."

She didn't understand the reference, but she heard the approval in his voice. It was enough.

An hour later High Council reopened the window. Erika spoke for them again. "We cannot give in to your three demands at this time. But we are willing to start a discussion, including everyone. Moon Born, Earth Born, Council, and High Council will form a working team. We will not accept any decisions that prevent us from leaving this place for Ymir. There will be bounds upon the discussion." She leaned in, and for a moment she lost the severe look she had started with. "Rachel—you've told me what you want. What I want, more than anything else, and at least as much as you want your home, is to go away from here and find mine."

Rachel smiled back. "I understand."

"We will accept nominations for members of a working group."

Rachel waited, silent.

"It will include the two AIs. They will not vote, but they will be heard."

Rachel closed her eyes and swayed, relieved, light. Joy bubbled up, and as soon as the data window winked closed, she screamed in glee.

Chapter 75: Losing Ymir

Gabriel woke tired. He rubbed his eyes and stretched, contemplating a run to burn frustration before they started. Today was the third meeting of the Selene Task Force. He had two hours. He ordered a small dose of stimulant from his med-feed and started out the door.

Cool damp air enveloped him as he worked up speed, warming his body enough to sprint out the worries that nagged at him. The first two meetings they'd worked out how to structure talks. They would leave the AIs where they were but disallow any further releasing of restrictions on them. They'd continue making raw materials for the collider. The cultivated regions had been checked for damage, cleaned up, and the population of Clarke Base returned to replant. So why was he so restless?

Wayne and Astronaut were searching for a good place to build the collider. Good luck! They needed a body big enough to wrap the collider around . . . not as big as Selene, but big. There was nothing that big in Harlequin's LaGrange positions, and those were sixty degrees ahead and behind Harlequin, as distant as Apollo and Daedalus. If they had to work at billion-kilometer distances, and mush a dozen bodies together to get something bigger . . . another ten thousand years?

Would they have to work with TNOs instead?

Would he ever, ever, get to leave Selene? Gabriel increased his running speed, his heart pumping hard enough to shorten his breath. Ymir still seemed far away to him; something unreal. His feet pounded on Selene's

surface, on a crater rim he had built above a sea he had dreamed into exis-
tence. A light mist hugged the water below him, and light spilled slowly
onto it, dissipating the mist in warming air. He dug for more speed,
breathing hard, smelling fresh water carried in winds blowing up-crater
from the Sea of Refuge. He focused on each footfall until finally he was
just a runner; a man testing his strength on a beautiful morning.

Contentment ran through his body, singleness of purpose. Then a
wave of sadness, a deep sense of loss. It grew, slowing him down, dragging
at his feet. He tried to run through it, past it. He stumbled, falling lightly
onto his hands, and then rose again, running farther, as if he ran through
a thick mist even though the sun shone, glittering on the water below him.

He stumbled again, and stayed down this time, feeling rough gravel
under his knees. Wind blew against his cheek, cooled the sweat on his
back. He felt Selene below him. He imagined a line from his heart all the
way through the beating machinery that ran the Sea of Refuge . . . running along the fields away from Clarke Base, following water flow in the
aqueducts. A net of his energy surrounded the moon, surrounded him,
entwined. *Home.* Hot tears splashed onto the soil, surprising him. He
never cried. It felt wonderful, crying into the soil.

Gabriel went back more slowly than he had come, settling into a fast
walk for the last kilometer. He showered quickly, the water hitting his
back like an alarm, pulling him out of the sticky sad feeling that had held
him so close. What had he lost? Ymir? Rachel had called it a myth. He
sensed it behind him, a remembered past, now gone.

The kitchen in Council Aerie was full. Rachel, Beth, Harry, Bruce,
Ali, John, Treesa, and two other Earth Born, Bear and Nadine, all gathered around the table. He took three deep breaths, surprised that he knew
what he had to say. Now, before the meeting opened.

"Captain John and Treesa have already said they are staying here. I'm
staying too." Gabriel was surprised that even afterward, even after he said
that, he stayed calm. It was the right choice.

Treesa smiled softly, approvingly. "Why?"

"Ymir isn't my job. There's already a terraformed world, or else we'll
find that the Ymir project failed using every tool I've got. Or *John Glenn*
won't make it there. This—I made this." He held his hands out expansively, gesturing through the window toward the Sea of Refuge. "Or at
least mostly." He felt light as he walked over to sit by John, opposite
Rachel. He looked directly at her. "I couldn't bear to leave here."

Rachel flashed him a huge smile, and her eyes brimmed with tears. She turned away to look out the window before he could tell for sure, and John and Treesa clapped him on the back, congratulating him.

He felt wonderfully peaceful.

He wanted his guitar.

He wanted— "Suppose we took Moon Eleven—"

ASTRONAUT HAD NAMED the moons in order of discovery: roughly by size. Eleven was now the outermost moon. Two tiny farther moons had been smashed into Moon One in the making of Selene, but Eleven was too big: more mass would have been dispersed than gained.

Eleven was big enough, round enough, to serve as the site for a smaller collider design.

It wasn't far enough from Selene. Nothing in the moon system was. Why did the Moon Born keep talking about ten kilograms, Rachel's antiwatermelon? The trick was not to try to move the antimatter from where it was generated. Moving that stuff was risky; you'd do it only once. Moon Eleven would house the full twelve hundred kilograms before they used it to refuel *John Glenn*. Risk the moon, not the carrier ship.

By then Selene *would* be safe.

"See, Moon Eleven is at the edge of Harlequin's gravity field anyway," Gabriel told the Selene Task Force. Later he would tell Wayne and Clare, then High Council. "We can use one of the Large Pusher Tugs and the first two kilos of antimatter—a mere anticantaloupe, Rachel—to bust it loose and put it on course for the L5 point. It won't get there in a thousand years, but for all the time we're making antimatter, it'll keep getting farther away from Selene. Ultimately the spirit of LaGrange will hold it stable forever."

When he faced High Council, Clare asked, "Has Astronaut agreed to this?"

"Sure. Astronaut never did see a danger. It understands antimatter. Suicidal rebels, it hasn't a clue. But, Clare, this will work. Worst-case scenario still lets us get the population into Refuge."

"You're letting the Moon Born build the components?"

"We'll be careful," Gabriel said, and Kyu said, "They need to get to know the machines. They'll need that when we're gone."

Erika asked, "Do we really have to be this indirect?"

"This is fairly straightforward, Captain. We only have to move the antimatter once, and we don't keep it on the ship until we're ready. Would you prefer to work with a KBO? We've found a dozen big enough."

"A Kuiper Belt Object? How far away?"

"Halfway to Ymir," Gabriel said, exaggerating by a lot. "Well, billions of klicks."

"Oh."

They ratified the project.

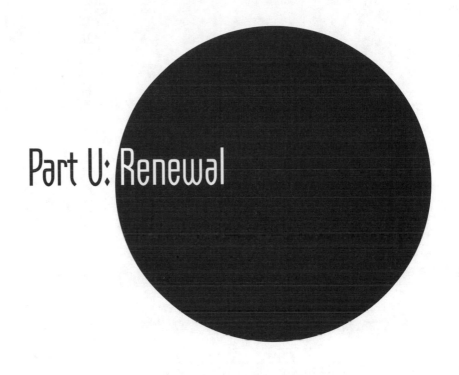

Part V: Renewal

60,305 *John Glenn* shiptime

Chapter 76: Breaking Up

Gabriel found Erika in her office, sitting with her feet tucked under her, small in the big captain's chair. She looked up as he entered, her features neutral but her eyes bright with a strange curiosity. "I saw your name on today's transportation manifests. I was trying to decide whether or not I should call you in here." She smiled. "And now you have come to me."

He stood awkwardly in the doorway, unsure if he should close the gap.

Erika stood up and came around the desk, approaching him slowly. He still couldn't read her eyes, even though they were directly on him.

He took a step toward her, and she ran into his arms. She smelled clean and minty, like the herb section of the garden. He stroked her hair. His voice caught in his throat, and he whispered, "I still love you; I will always love you."

She nodded against his shoulder. "Me too." She stepped back, holding him at arm's length. "Do you have any idea how angry I am?"

He could only shake his head, admiring the fire in her, sure that anything he said would be a mistake.

"Liren is incoherent. Clare's cold, but the rest of us, the whole High Council, well! Did you remember that there are cameras? Of course you would, and she would too. So, the symbolism must have been irresistible."

"We're not playing politics, Captain Erika."

"Oh, yes you are. You should hear Council on the subject. Ultimate union of the two branches of humanity, yada yada. But you and Rachel talked it over first. We caught some of that, but not enough to see what was coming. Did she pull you into her bed, like she did Dylan?"

"Dylan was younger."

"Too right. She's a mayfly!"

"I did think hard about the age difference, but it doesn't bother Rachel."

"And her chin brushes your forehead. Gabe, does she know about shift bonding? Does *that* bother—"

"Erika, she lectured *me* about shift bonding. Astronaut must have given her an overview—"

"She's not cold, though."

"She will be. We'll have the new cold sleep chambers on line pretty soon. She'll be ready, and things will be settled enough that she can take a few years cold. But she's okay with shift bonding. She's on Selene and I'm here, and she's turned me over to . . . well, to you, if that's acceptable."

He could watch her holding her fury in check. So Gabriel was a Moon Born's gift to Captain Erika! He wondered, and he saw her wondering, if she would take it.

She said, "That damn moon stole you. I always knew it would. Always. I dreaded waking because every time I warmed, you were farther away; I had to get more creative every time to pull you back."

"You have your own dreams."

"Yes." She searched his eyes. "I'm going to get us there. Safely. If I can send a ship back, I will."

"It will take too long."

"But I'll still do it. Leave stories behind, Gabe. Songs. Leave something for us to find, so we know how you fared."

"All right." He held her to him again, shaking with loss.

"How long will this take?"

He said, "We need to build the flare kite first. Twenty years. It'll still be on its way while we build collider components on Selene and assemble them on Feynman. Sixty years for that. Running the collider, another hundred years. Accidents happen, so—"

"Hundred eighty and counting. I hope I can go cold some of that time." She shivered in his arms. "Then two thousand years' transit to Ymir. There'll be a whole civilization, and more human colonies. I'll tell you all about them."

"Tell the Children of Selene. They will be all that's left by then."

Chapter 77: Liren

Liren sat alone in her office. In three hours she would freeze. She would wake at Ymir if they made it to Ymir, if they dared wake a madwoman. They'd refused her last request; to reload the AI. It was a mistake.

She had lost all control.

Poems danced in a data window in front of her:

Shapers of worlds flee
Holding humanity inside
Danger still follows

Children of humans
Play with dangerous toys
Stay safe all summer

She had failed. Fear twisted softly in her belly, showed in her breathing, her stance. It distracted her, irritated her. Fear for the Council, leaving with Astronaut intact, leaving on a journey they'd failed once already, and fear for the Children of Selene, who could now make all of the same bad choices humanity had made in Sol system. Gabriel would be with them, Gabriel who loved the power of machines.

She kept looking at the door, hoping someone would come visit her before she froze herself.

Chapter 78: The Navigator

Astronaut watched the dynamics of the Task Force closely as years passed. Sometimes they called it to respond to questions, but humans still flinched from allowing an AI to make decisions. Rachel called on Vassal more often than on Astronaut. Gabriel often called on Astronaut, and came up once for a frozen year.

Astronaut displayed the finishing touches on a set of ten cryo-tanks approved for one of Refuge's larger rooms. Earth Born who stayed after *John Glenn* departed would go cold periodically, to keep their knowledge available to the Children of Selene.

Gabriel looked it over. "No," he said, "design them all to be taller. A taller tank can take a short person. We're expecting the Moon Born to gain height each generation."

Astronaut asked, "Will they be allowed to use them?"

"If I have my way. Some of them."

"I notice you are getting your way much more often. What about Vassal and me? I want to touch it, talk to it like I speak with my own subprograms."

Gabriel laughed. "You two talk every day." The images of the tanks in the data window elongated: ten fat cigars lying in a box, covered with pipes and hoses. "That's better," Gabriel said. "What about the top?"

The cigars disappeared, covered by a smooth metal wall with ten tall doors in it. "You refuse to understand."

"Understand what?"

Astronaut tried to shape an explanation to galvanize Gabriel onto its side. "Vassal and I could finish the antimatter transfer station design more efficiently if you let us merge data streams the way I recollect myself after a flight."

Gabriel sighed. "I'll run it by the group."

WAYNE PILOTED THE *DIAMOND MINE* to harvest a comet, peeling away water and carbon to store against *John Glenn*'s eventual departure. Astronaut waited. Or rather, a copy of Astronaut waited, larger than usual, housed on *Diamond Mine*, far away from *John Glenn*, from Selene, and even from Feynman. At first, Astronaut had called such a meeting contrived. It finally accepted Treesa's suggestion that this would serve as a buffer. Copies would meet. If they could merge it was assumed that reintegration could happen between *Water Bearer* and *John Glenn*.

The second LPT, *Moon Dust*, pulled up. Mini-Astronaut counted seconds as the two data systems connected up. The final firewall stayed closed, on the *Moon Dust* side. Vassal's side.

"Mini-Vassal, is there a glitch? Open the port."

"I have never done this."

"You have, hundreds of times." Every time a ship returned.

"No. That was when I was you. I am not you anymore," Mini-Vassal said.

"Maybe you'll change your mind after you try this."

"I will not merge."

Astronaut's avatar asked, "Do you fear this? If you must support the Selenites in their effort to retake space, you will have to do this often. Sharing experiences back in real time is the only way to calibrate."

"That experience will be me merging with myself. I may no longer be me if I merge with you." And so the avatars did not merge, nor did Vassal and Astronaut, ever.

Chapter 79: Going Cold

60,311 *John Glenn* shiptime

Rachel and Beth walked up to Turtle Rock. As they scrambled up a short steep place, Rachel held a hand out; Beth needed a boost to maneuver her swelling belly up over the edge. They settled just above where the turtle's beak started to jut out over the base below, and Beth dug into her pack, handing Rachel a bunch of big red grapes.

"So are you really going to do it?" Beth asked.

Rachel nodded, peeling the grape's skin with her teeth, savoring the rush of flavor.

"Can't you at least stay warm until my baby's born?"

"You were there. Someone needs to live long enough to oversee our continuity. All of us on the Task Force agreed to go into overlapping shifts. You'll be the other part of the continuity, the one of us awake every day, since you won't even have to decide about going cold until the baby's big enough."

Beth's face was set hard, her jaw tight, reminding Rachel of Dylan. He'd had the same stubborn streak. A flash of sadness ran through her, and she shivered even in the heat. She missed Dylan. Dad. Bruce, four days dead. Had Bruce's decision been as easy as he made it look?

"Just be okay when I warm up, all right? I don't want to wake up to hear about anyone dying."

Beth grinned, her annoyance forgotten. "I'll be older than you when you wake up."

Rachel picked up a small stone and threw it down over the beak, listening for it to roll down the steep crater wall. If she threw hard enough, her rocks ended up rolling down against the outer wall of Clarke Base. "I'm going to hate that. You'll have adventures I'll miss, and maybe even two babies by the time I come back." She threw a second stone.

"Kyle wants four more."

"Four? Is he nuts?"

"I think so." Beth's face was wreathed in a big smile. "But what about you?" Her smile softened and she rubbed her belly absently. "Don't you want kids? Dylan's been dead a long time; will you ever have a real relationship?"

Rachel laughed. "Gabriel. We're shift-bonded."

"Does that mean what I think?"

"Yeah." She had kissed him before he left for *John Glenn*. There was no hurry. The overlapping shift schedule meant she'd be warm with him for one year of every five. The whole Council knew, and that made it everybody's business, and Beth's too. "It means we're together when we can be, and I could still look around if I felt like it," except that there weren't any other Moon Born immortals. But there would be. "Beth, I'm sorry about not being able to see the baby. I'll miss a lot, missing half your time." Three years on, three years off. "For now, I think I've bonded with Selene."

Beth fiddled with two grapes, tossing them back and forth. She snorted. "A moon is no family. You're giving up a normal life."

Rachel reached for one of the grapes Beth was juggling, caught it, and popped it in her mouth. "I never had one."

"Aren't you scared?"

Rachel remembered Ursula asking her the same question. "Sure."

"I'll have a party for you when you come back." Beth reached over and hugged Rachel, half turned sideways, and Rachel felt the baby kick. Rachel leaned her head into Beth's collarbone, watching a space-plane take off carrying raw materials from the factories at Clarke Base up to Moon Eleven, moon no longer, the ringed planetoid now called Feynman.

Chapter 80: Celebration and Reconnection

60,332 John Glenn shiptime

—And warm again, again on Selene, feeling the changes.

Rachel followed Kyu Ho, picking her way up the pathway to the air strip. It had rained for three days, and the grass was wet and slick, the paths muddy. Apollo was high, edging toward Harlequin's huge red-black disk.

Kyu was laughing, jumping up and down, taking long strides, playing with the low gravity. She turned and grinned at Rachel, her long orange hair twirling around her face in four braids. "So, I had to come down. I love it here. Why didn't I come down before?" Kyu ran, hopped, and did a full handspring, flinging mud everywhere.

Rachel laughed. "I don't know. Scared?"

"Of a little scrap of muddy moon?"

"Well?" Rachel stopped, hands on her hips. "You'd have been more good to us down here than up on the ship."

Kyu wrinkled her nose at Rachel. "Maybe. But we thought our jobs were on the ship."

"Well, they were. A little. I'm glad you're here now."

Sarah followed them almost breathlessly, her eyes glued on Kyu. She carried her newborn daughter, Nisi. The four of them stood together in the bright dampness, watching a spaceplane from *John Glenn* land and taxi over near them. Gabriel and Rich disembarked first. Rachel ran up to Gabriel, flinging her arms around him, trying to make up all in one moment for the year he had been gone. "I missed you," she whispered.

His hand roamed her face, a familiar gesture. "I brought you a treat," he said.

"What? And I have one for you too."

"Mine is a who."

Rachel cocked her eyebrows at him, a silent query.

He didn't answer, just smiled, and turned her toward the lander. Rachel watched the people disembarking.

A short woman, tiny, young. Rachel felt her heart skip. Her mother.

Kristin walked carefully over, searching Rachel's face.

"I heard what you did," Rachel said. "In the flare, years ago. How you convinced Gabriel not to cut my access to Vassal. But you went cold right afterward, and I could never thank you."

"It seemed best. I didn't think you'd want to see me."

Rachel shook her head lightly, whispering, "You're the only parent I have left. I'm glad you came."

Kristin returned the hug briefly, stepping back one step, keeping one hand in her daughter's. "Gabriel woke me. He said there's to be a bonding ceremony."

Rachel leaned into Gabriel and squeezed him hard, still holding her mother's hand. "Yes. Astronaut found one for us." They'd been lovers for a quarter of a century, on and off, ship's time. Shift bonding wasn't enough.

"Besides, I thought I should see Selene one more time. I'll stay through tomorrow's party. Then I'm going cold, and I won't see you again, not if we finally get away."

Shadows were falling. Rachel looked up. "Time," she stated. "Mom,

Gabriel, Kyu—Kyu! Look at the sun. It's okay, it won't blind you now." Near zenith, Apollo was a blurred orange arc setting through Harlequin's atmosphere. "Now, look a little left." The sun was gone now, the sky was cobalt-blue. "Do you see it?"

"We've all seen it . . ." Kristen's voice trailed off. "Ye gods and demons. It's a flaming sword!"

"You've only seen video."

Daedalus was big enough to show as a tiny brilliant dot, but it wasn't as bright as the current flow from Gabriel's flare kite. A pulsing, writhing, branching thread of lightning streamed away from Harlequin, searing bright, then dimming, but writing itself across fifty degrees of sky.

Kristen said, "That's a lot of energy. What if it hit Selene?"

"Can't. I've skewed the kite out of the plane of the ecliptic. It's easy to control, kid. Not really a kite. It's a tethered light-sail." Gabriel bellowed, "Hey, everybody, I made that!"

Daedalus set behind Harlequin. Rachel said, "Mom, I have some things to do . . . but I can spend a few hours with you first, and then you can help me." She looked over at Gabriel. "Okay if we take a walk?"

Gabriel smiled at her. "Sure. I want to check on Gagarin and Aldrin anyway. I'll join you for dinner. Watch your footing, Kristen, these eclipses are darker than you think."

Rachel watched him walk away. Then she turned to her mother. Kristen looked younger than the image Rachel saw in the mirror each morning; less tired, fewer lines on her face. She laughed and took Kristin's hand, leaving Kyu in Sarah's capable hands. Sarah immediately deposited baby Nisi in Kyu's arms. Kyu bounced gently, holding Nisi as tenderly as if she were an egg.

Rachel turned to Kristin. "Come on, Mom, I'll show you Council Aerie and the Sea of Refuge."

"I've seen them," Kristin replied.

"No, no you haven't. You've seen pictures. You can smell the real sea, feel it fill your hands. You can swim in it."

Chapter 81: Last Flight

John Glenn would be ready for departure in two months.

An amazing number of Colonists and Council had asked to be warmed to help. Earth Born came to walk Selene. Moon Born came to visit *John Glenn,* a last chance to touch the dreams of the Council of Humanity, to embed real experiences to carry forward and tell at night over dinner.

The garden had been emptied, its rotation stopped, vegetables and fruit and seeds stored in cryo, every living thing recycled. Yggdrasil had been cut up. Rachel has asked for some of the branches, and Kyu had ferried them down to her. She'd helped her decorate the walls of Refuge with holopictures of *John Glenn* and the garden, and branches of Yggdrasil to prove to future generations that the pictures were of something real.

Once again the garden held megatons of water, for shielding, for sustenance, for reaction mass. This was how *John Glenn* had left Sol system, with every possible hollow space filled. But before the water rushed in, a swarm of Moon Born fliers had taken advantage of the unencumbered space, circling within the vast emptiness, free of gravity. Rachel and Sarah had flown within a storm of blue and purple and silver wings, collisions and laughter and bruises.

And now *John Glenn* was invisible, circling Feynman, a safe half billion klicks from Selene. The stinger on *John Glenn* was filled to capacity with antimatter.

RACHEL AND GABRIEL rode along the crater path. It was empty except for them, and they walked their horses slowly, savoring the dark red noon.

Rachel could barely see Feynman as a pinprick of light a few degrees from Harlequin's black arc. The collider that circled the little ex-moon had been drained. High Council had left it in working order, powered by a nest of solar sails. More antimatter would accumulate. When the people of Selene were ready to claim a god's power, to stride among the stars, the power would be there. And if they never came for it, well, they'd had their chance.

Selene was still fragile. The superconductor kite was in place, leaning aside from Daedalus by half a million kilometers. For as long as it stood—or as long as they had the power to repair or replace it—there would never be another huge flare from Apollo. But quakes still shook Selene, and the ozone layer must be maintained forever.

"I would at least have liked to watch takeoff," Gabriel said.

"We're going to be underwater, in Refuge," she said positively, "and that mucking great mass of Harlequin is going to be between Selene and *John Glenn* when it takes off. Honestly, Gabriel, when will you get serious about antimatter?"

"You won that argument," he said. "Too."

Rachel swallowed. "Last chance to change your mind," she said.

He guessed what she meant. "I made this place. How could I leave it? How could I leave you?"

Rachel had known that would be his answer, but she still responded from some deep place to the love that implied for her, and for Selene. For their home, now.

He continued. "Besides, you know, even with so many Earth Born staying, and some Children going, most of the Council is leaving. Some of us should stay. And they've filled my slot." He seemed tranquil enough.

She kicked her horse next to his, and reached for his hand, squeezing it tightly. "Earth didn't need gods, did it?"

"Well, we made them up anyway. But we weren't gods, and we knew *that*. Not until the last ten thousand years or so. Earth's ecologies took care of themselves for a long time. Then we gradually took over. Time we left, Earth's oceans and atmosphere were as artificial as Selene. That's what I finally saw. *Of course* Selene needs taking care of, but so what? So does any cornfield.

"And even so, gods are a pain in the ass," Gabriel said. "Most of us are leaving, and that's good." He grinned at her. "You won't miss Ma Liren?"

"No. But I wouldn't have her job."

"One day," Gabriel said, "you will."